F ee

Fiona Woodifield

For my mother with love and thanks
and for those who appreciate the small things in life
such as the perfect cup of coffee

Skylark Press 2023

For the Love of Coffee

Chapter 1

'What have I done?'

I stumble precariously along the uneven pavement, desperately trying in vain to drag my unyielding lump of a heavy bag behind me. I don't think pull along holdalls are designed for cobblestone pathways. This one certainly isn't. It buffets and bounces, catching on everything it can, rather like an unwieldy tortoise on wheels. My slow progress is closely followed by Elise and Summer, both the picture of unhappiness. Elise appears on fleek as always, her long brown hair thrown carelessly into a haphazard bun, fine tendrils hanging down to frame her face, which in contrast is sporting a sulky scowl. On a scale of nought to ten, we are registering an eleven and a half in grumpiness. Summer, on the other hand, is tired and at the point of nothing's going to be right until she gets food and bed, in that order.

'You're going too slow,' moans Elise, treading dangerously close to the back of Summer's heels.

'I can't go any faster,' Summer snaps, slowing her pace to nearly a standstill.

'Come on, girls. We can do this, it's not much further,' I say in a faux cheery sort of tone destined to inspire Girl Guides to trek to the top of mountains, but which I can tell isn't fooling anyone.

'Yes, but where to?' Elise stands glaring, her hand on her hip. 'Why aren't you telling us where we're going?'

Because I don't know, I think silently. Oh God, this was such a bad idea. What on earth was I thinking?

'Good afternoon!' an old lady waves in a friendly manner as she passes, miraculously avoiding our out of control baggage.

'Who was that?' asks Summer in an embarrassingly loud voice.

'I don't know,' I reply.

'Well, you must know her or why would she say hello?' remarks Elise, sulkily.

'I can assure you I don't. I haven't been here since I was a child. I think she was just being friendly.'

'Huh! Total weirdo more like,' huffs Elise.

'I don't think so, Elise, she looked perfectly nice. This is a village; people probably do say hello to each other. It's kind of normal.'

Elise remains unimpressed, convinced we're in alien territory surrounded by savage and hostile forces. She continues to pick her way over the cobbles, mincing along daintily in her mules, her distaste for this whole experience blatantly evident.

'I like it,' pipes up Summer. 'It's nice when people say hello. No one does that at home, they all walk past with their heads down.'

She's right actually, everyone does. If a stranger in our town said hello, I'd probably pull the girls closer to me and quickly move on, at most giving a conciliatory sort of smile in a courteous nod to our English necessity for politeness. Our distrust is patently audible. Sad, but true.

We drag to a halt outside the information centre. 'Here we are!' I remark.

'Yeah, but where are we?' Elise rolls her eyes.

The building is slightly unprepossessing I must admit, rather like a temporary structure but more promisingly, outside there's a shelf of second hand books; a treasure trove of classics, mixed with dodgy old copies of *The Joy of Sex* and outdated Delia Smith recipe books from the '60s. I love collections like this. We used to have a second-hand bookshop near my childhood home. It was an ancient church building which housed three floors of equally ancient books crammed into every nook and cranny, and was absolute heaven. There were mezzanine floors simply piled with dusty tomes, spilling over onto the floor. I can remember to this day the handwritten labels scribbled on brown card, separating the different genres and sections. How I long for another sanctuary like that, but it was swept away years ago, along with small pet shops with baby rabbits in, long hot summers off school without a care in the world, and the dulcet tones of Spandau Ballet and a-ha. Things were so much simpler then.

'Mum!'

I'm jolted out of my reverie by Elise's bored tones – 'Are we going in or what?'

I turn my attention back to the task in hand, simultaneously steering Summer away from an impressively intact looking copy of *The Subtle Art of Not Giving a F**k* (in fact I might come back and grab that later. I've been itching to read it and never got round to getting a copy) and push my way through the door into the information centre.

'Good afternoon,' a well-bred aristocratic voice greets our entry.

We all peer vaguely round the room, which is like a visitor centre, full of picturesque postcards, nick nackadee noodles and bits and bobs for the budding tourist, but none of us can tell where the voice is coming from. Then we spot her, a formidable looking woman guarding a corner desk. She has steely grey curls, and a rather impressive crop of long whiskery hairs sprouting from her chin. I try to focus on her eyes as a distraction. I always find that when someone has a large wart, it's so difficult to talk to them without focusing on it. It's as if an invisible force draws your eyes straight to it like a magnet and you find yourself trying to stare over the person's shoulder in a desperate attempt not to look at their face. You're desperately avoiding eye contact, but then, just as you think you've got away with it, you glance without meaning to and it's too late – they've noticed you peering.

Barbara Asquith, that's her name according to the badge on her cardi, has got to be in her '70s, perhaps a little younger, though to be honest age is such a difficult thing to judge. She's one of those women who you feel can see right through you. Her voice is brusque, no nonsense, manly even.

'Can I help you?' she barks. It really is a bark. I swear she has two wire haired terriers at home called Dennis and Bunty.

'Erm yes, good afternoon.' Oh no, posh voice on. My girls always laugh that I've got a telephone voice reserved for older people, teachers and my mother-in-law. Right now it's out in full force.

'We're looking for somewhere to stay please?' I annunciate.

'For a holiday?' Barbara opens a large A4 book and starts flicking through the pages in an authoritative manner.

'No, not really. More somewhere to stay for a while.'

Barbara gives us all a quizzical look. 'Oh dear, not on the run, are we?'

'No,' cue mock hysterical laughter from me and a scornful look from eldest daughter. 'No, definitely not, just thinking of relocating so...'

'Just my little joke, haw haw,' chortles Barbara. 'When do you require accommodation for? May and June are rather busy, but we might have something in April.'

'No, I meant something for now. We're looking for somewhere to stay tonight.'

'Oh dear me, you really are on the run then? Hmm, this is most irregular. You do know Melstock is an extremely popular holiday destination? Gets booked up very early in the year.'

'Yes, I thought that might be the case.' God, what was I thinking? I can't go home now, not after all this. I glance anxiously across at Summer and feel an additional pang of guilt. Having plonked herself down on a bean bag in the corner, she looks exhausted, her little head drooping with tiredness.

Barbara gives us a surmising look, rapidly assessing the situation. 'Would you be happy in one room?' she asks, flicking back through her book.

'Anything would be fine,' I reply. I sound desperate, but then we are.

'Everything is totally booked but...' she scans further through the pages as she talks. 'I could try Martin at The Skylark. They might just have something.'

She picks up the phone and has a rapid conversation with someone on the other end, most of which I can't make out as I'm too busy trying to persuade an even more sulky Elise in a furious undertone that we have no choice but to sleep in the same room, and we'll be lucky to even find that.

Barbara puts the phone back in its holder with a resounding bang. 'Well, that's it then. Not exactly The Ritz I'm afraid, but it will do you for a night or so until you've sorted yourselves out.'

I approach the desk gratefully babbling. 'Thank you very much, it's getting so late.'

'Yes, yes,' remarks Barbara. 'Now let's give you the details and get these poor little dears somewhere to eat and rest.'

'Of course.' I nod and fidget, thoroughly chastened like a naughty and careless schoolgirl. What on earth's wrong with me? I'm past 40 for God's sake and yet I still act like a little kid around authoritarian women. Though to be fair she reminds me of my old secondary school maths teacher, Miss Spokes.

'Romilly,' she would say, in her shrill voice, which was just like a cheese grater. 'Romilly, you will never be able to do maths, you simply do not have a mathematical brain.'

To be fair I suppose she was right to a certain extent and the angrier she became, the more I would spout random numbers in a desperate attempt to give her the right answer.

'Mum?' whined Summer, tugging my trousers. 'Are we going now? I'm sooo hungry.'

'Yes, sweetheart, we're just finding somewhere.' I hold my hand out to Barbara for the details, which she has just been busily scribbling on a piece of paper.

I thank her as surprisingly she has actually been quite kind, and we traipse out of the centre and up the steep hill in the direction she had described.

'I'm so not walking up this hill,' declares Elise going along at the pace of a snail. 'You know I don't do hills.'

'I know, but we're nearly there. It's just a short way up the lane Barbara said.'

We trudge up the steep and narrow road, ducking in doorways when cars come down fast.

'What's that smell?' asks Summer. 'It stinks.'

'Burning brakes. The hill's so steep, the cars have to break extra hard,' I explain.

'Yeah and you're making us walk up it,' moans Elise. 'Knowing our luck, one will fly off the road and that'll be the end of us.'

I try to ignore her depressing prediction. 'Look, there it is,' I cry, my voice loud with relief. The Skylark is an attractive whitewashed building with an ancient, thatched roof. It appears to be built into the hill with quaint little windows all invitingly lit as evening is now setting in.

We troop gratefully through the half open stable door into hustle and bustle, the smell of peat fire and beer mixed with chips. I push through into the bar area and silence takes hold of the room. We're definitely strangers in town. There is a group of guys lounging propped against the bar, gawping unashamedly at us. They are all attired in tweed, wellies and caps; it's rather like a scene from *Last of the Summer Wine.* A middle-aged couple in the corner sit eating something which smells totally delicious.

I can't get near the bar and hover awkwardly, hoping to get someone's attention. Nope, it's just not working, the barman is totally ignoring me. I long for the old uni days where I had soon forgotten my gawky shyness and found my inner diva, learning to push my way to the front of the swarming students flocked round the bar with confidence, fluttering my eyelashes and youthful vivacity at the barman. I was usually served pretty darn quickly. Where has that sassy girl gone? Right now, I'm not too sure but I think she might have had all the vivacity crushed out of her by the scary combination of married life and motherhood.

Anyway, why is it that as a middle-aged woman I always feel kind of invisible? Is it just me? Not that I was exactly body confident before, but I remember at least getting some sort of reaction. Though to be fair, in my '20s I used to rock a pretty mean sashay in my short skirts and stilt like heels, but back then I didn't have varicose veins or a couple of stone of extra weight either for that matter. Sadly, I would probably be quite flattered these days if builders even looked at me. Not that I enjoyed their attention. I guess there's no pleasing some people. For goodness' sake, Elise would be horrified if she heard this. I'm a feminist. Honestly, I guess it would just be nice to still feel attractive sometimes or at least as though I exist. Though Elise is 13 years old, she bloody knows it all and a bit of her sass might just help me get through this awkward situation.

After what seems like three years later, but was probably only ten minutes or so, the barman seems to notice us. 'Alright?' he asks, not appearing to require an answer. I try to brush aside my nerves but I don't remember the last time I went into a pub without Dan.

'Hi, yes. We're booked in for a room tonight?' I reply in a weirdly squeaky voice. Where on earth did that come from? Anyone would think I'm aged about ten the way I'm acting. Why can't I get it together? I clear my throat authoritatively; I'm a strong middle-aged woman and I know what I'm doing but... it's not working. I mean, I've never done anything like this before, not without Dan. I knew I should have got out more.

'Must've been a late one, I thought we were full tonight,' mutters the barman. 'Jan! Family here looking for a room.'

A sharp faced, busty blonde woman appears from nowhere and peers at us speculatively. I choose to think maybe she's short sighted rather than rude and stary. 'First I've heard of it,' she remarks.

'We were sent by Barbara Asquith, the lady in the information centre,' I say somewhat defensively.

'Oh, bloomin' Barbara,' she responds glaring sideways at the barman. 'Thinks she owns the village, that woman. Should blimmin' well stick to breeding dogs and hunting.' She flicks idly at the computer,

'Right family room – here's the key. Do you need something to eat? You've left it pretty late, haven't you? Serving stops at 7pm.' She peers at the girls who are both pretty much wilting by this point.

'If it's not too much trouble,' I say politely, inwardly seething. So much for a warm country welcome. Fortunately, our room when we find it isn't too bad, it's up a small windy staircase and is small to put it mildly, but it will do.

Dinner is hot and filling, delicious locally cooked pub grub and we are all grateful for it. Better still, Jan seems to have disappeared and the guy who serves our food is quite friendly. I quite enjoy eating in the corner of the bar at a small table where we are fairly unobserved apart from occasional curious looks from the locals.

I'm even brave enough to pop up to the bar to order Elise another Coke when a tweedy old guy leerily lurches slap bang into me. 'Hows about a drink then, darlin,' he chortles. I'm literally knocked backwards by the physical combination of him and his alcohol infused breath, it must be 70% proof. It makes me want to laugh actually if he weren't slightly sinister and pretty pungent on the nostrils.

'Oh, I'm fine thanks,' I reply, politely resisting the urge to dust myself off.

'What's the matter with you? Don't you drink nuffing?' he puts his fragrantly unwashed arm round me, pushing his craggy, unshaven face far too close to mine. He's obviously been drinking for some time. I don't look at the girls because I'm pretty sure they're both in fits of giggles at my predicament.

I attempt to edge away ridiculously polite as ever, but before I can do anything else to rescue myself, I'm stopped mid- track as a tall, dark floppy haired man in riding jodhs and jacket strides across from nowhere, pulls the rambunctious old chap up by his collar and returns him firmly to a stool at the other end of the bar. Most impressive! I heave a sigh of relief as dealing with drunken old men was definitely not on my wish list this evening. My rescuer, however, who puts out a well-groomed hand and introduces himself as Mark – Mark Whittaker to be more precise – is worth getting to know a whole lot better.

'Oh, thanks, erm, Mark.' I simultaneously spill my drink and try to shake his hand, which suddenly seems an impossible task.

'Not a problem,' he replies in a plummy, well-bred aristocratic voice. I feel flustered and at a disadvantage. A large wet patch is spreading down my shirt. Most embarrassing! I try to dab it with a tissue from my bag but can't seem to hold this, my drink and the bag. Of course something's got to give. It does and I drop the bag and it ricochets spectacularly across the floor, falling wide open and spilling its contents far and wide across the pub floor. Unsurprisingly, Elise, over in the corner, is pretending she doesn't know me.

At this point, you need to be aware that my bag and its contents are a phenomenon all to itself. It contains everything and anything, and weighs like half a ton. I always figure that if I get mugged I could hit my would-be attacker with it, though the girls insist I'd be had up for GBH. Returning to the current situation, which is a complete and utter disaster, I scrabble about on the floor, giving up on any last vestige of trying to be cool while attempting to grab lipstick, rescue remedy pastilles and sweet wrappers. My trusty pot of rescue remedy (invaluable by the way for off days, impromptu visits from mother-in- laws, stressed out kids, etc) has hit the floor hard, exploded its lid – which ironically is pretty bloody impossible to undo normally – and discarded its little round pastilles far and wide on the floor boards of the pub. Worse still, Mark, my knight in jodhs and shiny riding boots, is helping, passing tissues, receipts and oh God, why me, a large blue ST, clean and still wrapped of course but nonetheless mortifyingly embarrassing.

'Thanks, so much. Yes that's fine.' I shove everything haphazardly back in my bag.

'It was nothing, really. Anyone would have done the same,' Mark smiles, and I'm ashamed to say I find myself babbling and blushing like a teenager, though I can only add in my defence, he is like a model from *Horse and Hound* and I'm not used to seeing guys who look like this in my sheltered little life. He straightens up, 'Now I must wish you good evening, I'm late for my dinner.'

And with that he's gone and that it seems is that. I pull myself up short. What's wrong with me? As if I'm in any state to even look at a guy ever again. In any case, I expect he went off home to his beautiful blonde wife. I can picture her now in her cream jodhs, polo shirt and immaculate ponytail serving up dinner. Or maybe he'll meet her at a posh local restaurant where they'll dine over candlelight and discuss the finer points of the cross country course. My dream life basically, sigh...

We finish our meal and troop off to bed. The girls both fall asleep immediately; even Elise who is usually a night owl, is exhausted by the events of the day. I check my phone. Nothing. Today I've left my husband of 15 years, just walked out with the girls and a couple of suitcases and yet there's not a word, not a reaction from anyone. But then what else did I expect?

Chapter 2

The next morning I awake with a start, my pulse pounding, feeling stressed without quite knowing why. In fact, at first I don't even remember where I am. The ceiling looks unfamiliar, as do the faded rose covered curtains hanging at the window.

It soon comes flooding back however, a little sooner than the feeling in my left leg, which has gone numb due to the heavy weight of Summer slumbering on it.

It's quiet, too quiet. Normally at home there's at least a couple of sirens blasting through the peace at this time in the morning.

It's nice actually. A snatch of birdsong drifts through the window, then a large vehicle lumbers past, disturbing Summer. Elise is still completely out for the count in her little bed in the corner, the only evidence of her presence betrayed by the small lump curled under the duvet.

I feel a pang of guilt as I survey our higgledy piggledy scene – stuff thrown everywhere as we were too tired to do anything last night. We are like self-created refugees. Well, created by me anyway. Surely a mum is supposed to keep her family together?

I do miss Dan. I missed his comforting presence in the bed last night. Maybe we should just pack up, grab all our belongings, go home and pretend all of this never happened. Then I remember Charlotte's words. 'If his cuddles are all you're going to miss, get yourself a dog!'

In any case, lately he's never been there, and when he was he'd taken to sulking way over the other side of the bed, the gap between us silent, gaping and ever widening.

Summer stirs again. 'What are we doing today, Mum?' she asks sleepily.

'Well,' I say, jumping out of bed more enthusiastically than I feel, which is a mistake as I have to put my head down again quickly as I feel dizzy. Dan always said I was over keen in the morning, 'I think we should go exploring and find some delicious breakfast.'

'Yay!' shouts Summer.

'For God's sake,' grumbles Elise from the lump in the corner. 'Why do you have to wake me up at the flippin' crack of dawn?'

Nope, it's better to be on our own. I've spent too long hoping things are going to get better, pretending there's nothing wrong, waiting like an eager little puppy for the occasional pat on the head which was becoming less and less frequent.

This is it. I, Romilly, am a new and independent woman. No more meek and mild, apologising for my own shadow. I'm strong and resilient, and we're going to be an invincible team. Though to be honest, right now I feel like running home crying to my mum.

We scramble through breakfast as Summer is desperate to escape outside and explore the village, and I have to admit I am pretty excited about it too. I've had a word with Dean, the barman – who turns out to be quite nice without the scary Jan, and apparently we can stay a few nights 'til we've sorted something more permanent.

The village is beautiful and pretty much unchanged since my childhood holidays. We admire it as we wander lazily through the pub car park and along the lane to the road. Everywhere birds are singing and we spot swallows darting to and fro from tiny mud crammed nests under the neighbouring rooftops.

Summer is ecstatic and drags us closer to peer up and notice the tiny hungry beaks bobbing up and down to be fed.

'For God's sake! Do we have to look at every bloody animal along the way?' snaps Elise.

'They're beautiful,' I glare at her.

We walk on down the lane, past romantically large old-fashioned roses, their heads drooping under the weight of multi-layered blooms. Sparrows cheep contentedly from the bushes and all feels surprisingly well with the world in spite of my numbness squashed deep within.

And overriding everything is an all pervading, amazing scent of coffee; freshly ground, earthy, heady. I wonder absentmindedly if it is coming from one of the cottages at the top of the lane, but then I realise.

'Oh, of course!' I exclaim.

'Of course, what?' asks Elise still grumpy. She is so not a morning person. If we were at home she'd still be lounging in the pit she calls her bedroom.

'The Coffee Factory – it's along here. That's what the amazing smell is.' I trot off happily picking up pace along the road, til round the corner the familiar chimney stands impressively high up ahead of me; the warm brick walls of the factory comfortingly the same. And the aroma! The aroma's amazing, all pervading – it's hypnotic. Freshly ground coffee.

Summer has run enthusiastically after me 'What is it – is it like Charlie and the Chocolate Factory?' she asks breathlessly.

'Er, no not quite,' I respond. 'Sadly they don't make chocolate, though that would be pretty cool. The factory produces coffee, that's what the incredible smell is.'

'Oh,' Summer's face falls. 'I don't like coffee, it's yuk!'

'Well, it's exactly what Elise could do with right now!' I smile as Elise rounds the corner and stomps up to us.

'What are we doing and when are we going home?'

'It's coffee – beautiful, freshly ground coffee. You'll love it,' I exclaim, jumping around like an overenthusiastic Oompa Loompa.

'I don't want coffee. I want to go home. I want to see Dad.' Elise is on a roll now, her lip is quivering and I can see her eyes are filling with tears.

'Come on, sweetheart.' I go and put my arms around her, but she pulls away. She never was one for cuddles; liking her own personal space, but right now all I can feel is her simmering anger.

'Why did you leave him, Mum? Why aren't we going home?' she demands.

'We're going to stay here for a while,' I reply gently in an undertone. Summer is momentarily distracted, happily peering up at the nesting swallows under a nearby roof. 'Just while we sort things out.'

'But things aren't going to be sorted out with you here and Dad back at home, are they? You've left him, haven't you?'

'Well, yes, but I needed a break, to get away for a while to think,' I stumble to justify my actions.

'Why couldn't you just go out for the day on your own or go out to coffee with your friends like any normal person?' snarls Elise.

'I don't have any friends. Your dad doesn't like having people round the house, does he?'

'No, but you can go out the house and meet for coffee, can't you?'

'Yes, but it's not the same. Honestly, Elise, your dad and I have got serious problems and I need some space.'

'I don't understand why. I don't want things to change – most of the kids at school are from broken homes and it's crap. Weekends backwards and forwards, never in the same place as a family.'

'I know. That's why I wouldn't have taken this step unless I felt it was absolutely necessary.'

'Necessary for who? I'm happy as we were.'

'Not really. You spend your whole life in your room and you've always said you wanted to live in the country.'

'Yeah, with Dad. I didn't mean on our flipping own.'

'Well, none of us want that to happen, but sometimes things don't turn out the way you want them to.'

'They never bloody work out at all, not for us.' Elise

stomps off past a nearby cottage and out of sight. I let her go.

'What's up with Elise?' asks Summer.

'She just needs some space,' I reply.

'Is it her hormones?' asks Summer. 'Stacey at school has hormones and it makes her really moody.'

'No, I don't think so,' I say, suppressing a smile and absently wiping away my own tear. There's a healthy dose of those too to be fair, my own included. As a woman hormones seem to be the bane of your life. When I was a teenager the doctor always blamed everything and anything on my hormones and it doesn't seem to have got much better as I've got older. While I was pregnant it was my hormones, then when I'd had the kids, it was my hormones, now I'm in my '40s, it's my hormones. Bloody men, they don't know they're born – if they had hormones like ours they'd simply never survive.

Summer skips ahead, still transfixed by swallows swooping overhead. I'm grateful for the reprieve, knowing it is only a matter of time before she too asks when we will go home.

Suddenly my phone blasts out, the energising tones of Sam Ryder incongruously invading the Devon air, informing everyone that he's a space man. 'Hello?' I answer, simultaneously dropping my bag.

'Romilly, where the heck are you?' My sister Jess is unamused. I'm not surprised, I always tell her everything.

'Erm, Devon?' I reply.

'You didn't tell me you were going on holiday,' rebukes Jess. To be fair, I do tell her most things.

There's just one issue with her...

'I phoned your house this morning and Dan said you've left, just shoved off without telling him where you are and you've taken the girls out of school.' Jess' voice is reproachful. 'I've told him you must be having some kind of mid-life crisis.'

'Thanks! For God's sake, Jess.' Why does everyone think any time you do anything slightly out of the usual in your '40s, it's a mid-life crisis? Though I guess things do look a bit that way.

'Rom, Dan's really worried and it's so unsettling for the girls.' She breaks off abruptly. 'Bradley, will you stop doing that, it's going to break. Can you hang on a minute, Rom?'

I smile to myself as I hear muffled disagreement in the background, culminating in a smashing noise rather like broken glass. An irritated Jess returns to the phone, 'Bloody kids, should come with a health warning. I think he's just broken Uncle Clarence's photo frame.'

'Not at nursery today?' I ask innocently.

'No, he's off sick with a tummy upset, and Uncle Clarence has turned up out of the blue with a photo of his dog.'

'Nice, but he doesn't have a dog?' That explains her cranky mood then, but I'm confused about the relevance of the dog.

'He thought Brad would like to see the picture of the dog he used to have, so he lent it to us.'

'Random,' I comment, 'and now it's broken.'

'I know, it's a complete nightmare, it was in a really old ornate frame. I'll have to buy him another one, and

I've had to spend half the morning hearing about his bagpipes.'

'Oh God, not the bagpipes again.' For years now my Uncle Clarence (who is my mother's brother and is aged about 97) has been complaining about his neighbour's penchant for playing bagpipes in the middle of the night. Bearing in mind the fact that 1) my Uncle Clarence lives in a block of sheltered living flats for the elderly, 2) he's had the council out with noise detecting machines only to find nothing and 3) no one else in the neighbouring flats has ever heard it, we all think the most likely diagnosis is that Uncle Clarence has tinnitus.

The GP even diagnosed tinnitus to be met with complaints and outrage from Uncle Clarence who felt he was trying to accuse him of being mad. I think the GP has probably long since gone off with stress. This neighbour is Scottish and Uncle Clarence believes he plays his bagpipes every night when he comes in from the pub. He's even gone and had a go at him about it.

It puts my own life in perspective actually. When I'm feeling sorry for myself, I think of poor old Uncle Clarence's neighbour who's minding his own business each morning when he's accosted by an irate elderly gentleman accusing him of playing bagpipes deliberately loudly every evening. Although it's quite sad really. I even offered for my uncle to come and stay elsewhere for a night because then if he still hears the bagpipes, we'd know it was tinnitus. But, funnily enough, he won't hear of it.

Sometimes though in my weaker moments, having read *Three Things About Elsie*, which I loved, I wonder if it is a double bluff and every evening this neighbour, Jock, deliberately puts on a tape recording of a bagpipe playing, whilst rubbing his hands together, hoping it will make Uncle Clarence move out of his flat for good.

'Rom?' Oops, I've been daydreaming and haven't been listening to a word of Jess' conversation, though I think most of it involved more breaking glass and shouting at Bradley. 'Are you coming home?'

'Look, Jess, it's complicated. I've had enough,' I reply.

'We've all had enough, love. I've frequently had enough before 8am but we don't actually do anything about it.' Quite honestly I can believe it with Bradley. I love him dearly, but he's pretty hyper when he gets going.

'You know what I mean, Jess. I'm sick of Dan's controlling ways.'

'It's probably his way of showing he cares. Come on, Rom, he loves you all.'

'Does he though?' I ask. 'Enough to let me be myself? Allow me to go out? And he barely knows the girls, he's hardly ever bloody well there.'

I hear crashing in the background, which sounds suspiciously like breaking china. 'Bradley, there's going to be no treat for you this morning. I'll ring you later Rom, but if you take my advice – have a couple of days holiday, get it out your system and go home. You're out of your depth.'

With that Jess has gone and I'm left to contemplate Summer and the swallows flitting in the warm balmy air. They seem so free and uncomplicated and right now to be honest, I envy them.

We meander our way along the lane to the village. The first shop is the little grocers. It's like a treasure trove, packets of everything from Bisto to baking soda granules. In the corner is a cheese counter with olives and every type of cheese you can imagine from French brie to Cornish yarg wrapped in seaweed. Wicker baskets spill over with gorgeous smelling vine ripened local tomatoes and juicy Victoria plums. Little brown paper bags sit ready to be filled with delicious produce. So much better than plastic – why can't supermarkets be this exciting?

We are greedy with our purchases, but I figure we will soon eat everything, it all looks so delicious. I pass the basket over to the nice young guy at the counter, he seems a little older than Elise and polite enough, if a little shy. A woman appears from a nearby doorway and stands at the counter.

'You're not from round here, are you?'

'No, just arrived yesterday.'

'On holiday?' she asks.

'Perhaps, although we're thinking of staying a little longer,' I reply glancing nervously to see Summer is investigating some sweets.

'How nice! We could do with some more young families in the village.'

'Well, it will depend on whether I can get some kind of work. I've just separated from my husband, you see.'

'Oh, I'm sorry.'

I feel rather odd in the face of this kind stranger's sympathy. Sort of numb, yet saying it out loud makes it seem more real. I don't know why it hasn't really sunk in yet, but then I guess it's only been a day since I left. Already my old life feels miles away.

'Don't be,' I smile. 'I feel better for it, although I do need to find my feet.'

'Of course, dearie, best keep an eye on our window here – all our ads go up there, and you'll be after a school for this little one.' She smiles in a friendly way at Summer who looks totally confused.

'And you'll be wanting to join our Zumba class,' a petite woman of about my age with a curly blonde ponytail appears behind the counter, mostly hidden behind a pile of boxes. I wonder if she is the mother of the lad working in the shop.

'I don't know about that! I've never done Zumba before,' I say apologetically. I don't want to seem unfriendly.

'You'll soon get the hang of it. It's at the Village Hall on Tuesdays and Thursdays.'

'But I don't have a babysitter, I'm afraid.'

'That's no problem, you can bring them along. Loads of people do.' She gives me a friendly wink.

'I haven't danced since I've had the girls,' I laugh.

'Don't worry. Come along on Tuesday – it's a real giggle! None of us care what we look like, it's just good fun. I'll be there – it's run by Tania, she's nice too. My name's Debs by the way, and this is Molly.'

I introduce myself and Summer and leave the shop twenty pounds poorer but emotionally richer than I have been for years. Debs and Molly feel like friends already and perhaps I may pluck up the courage to give Zumba a go. I could do with the exercise to be honest as I always have eyes bigger than my stomach and nothing really fits anymore. Food's a full-time hobby for me, especially since the issues with Dan. Food is reliable, comforting. Even on a diet I'm always thinking of my next bowl of rice or lettuce leaf.

We spend a happy hour or so milling around the village centre. At the Post Office, Phil is jovial and balding, hiding behind shiny specs like Where's Wally and full of fun. He even gives Summer a little notebook she's found and a bouncy ball for free. I buy a copy of the Melstock Messenger, hoping to find out what's on and whether there's any work going.

Unlike many villages these days, Melstock is very much alive and kicking. There's a butcher, resplendent in straw hat and striped apron; a steady stream of customers in and out. The pet shop is quaint and prosperous looking, rather worryingly adorned with a mismatch of deer antlers, walking boots and dog collars. 'Good morning, good morning!' calls a buff guy in army combats lurking in the doorway. 'Need any pet food?'

'Morning! No thanks!' I reply, cheerily.

'Look at the sparkly pink dog collars, Mum,' Summer says excitedly. 'Can't we have a dog?'

I was about to say 'no' followed by my stock answer, 'because your dad says so' but then I realise with a rush of adrenaline that it doesn't matter what Dan says as he's no longer part of the equation.

'Maybe,' I reply. 'We'll have to see what happens when we're settled.'

'Yes!' she yells, but then a shadow comes across her face. 'But we'll be going home soon, won't we?'

'Well,' I say carefully, 'we can go back to visit, but

this may become our home now.'

I can see her computing the facts. 'Will there be horse riding?' she asks.

'Maybe,' I realise I need to push home my advantage.

'Yay!' she skips along happily holding my hand and I wish for the hundredth time that life could remain as simple as it appears when you are a nine-year old child.

We hear the clopping of hooves coming along the high street.

'Horses!' exclaims Summer.

We stand to one side on the pavement to admire the approaching hunters, long limbed and graceful, sidestepping along the road.

'Morning!' I reply automatically as the riders nod their heads in greeting.

'Hello!' I recognise the deep voice as belonging to Mark, my valiant rescuer from the other evening. I didn't recognise him initially under his riding hat. He reins in his horse and comes alongside.

'Can I stroke him?' Summer asks.

'Of course! Give him a pat on his neck,' replies Mark. He looks at me and grins, his devastatingly blue eyes crinkling up at the corner, 'Sorry to dash off the other evening. I forgot to ask your name?'

'Romilly,' I reply, shyly.

'Very unusual,' he replies, neatly pulling on the reins to expertly contain his horse's antics. The hunter is obviously restless and highly-strung, but Mark controls him effortlessly.

'What's his name?' asks Summer.

'Sultan,' Mark replies, turning in the saddle to

speak to his companion. 'John, this is Romilly.'

John nods curtly, both he and his horse are obviously keen to get on.

'Are you staying long?' Mark continues, undeterred.

'I don't know. Probably. I'm thinking we might get a small property here.'

'If you're looking for a place to rent, I might have something available just off the high street.'

'Really? Though it depends on the price,' I add hastily. I haven't had a chance to start looking at my finances, but I know they'll be pretty unhealthy. Dan always used to deal with all that. He had control over the banking passwords and the account numbers. I used to joke that he reminded me of a James Bond villain sat hunched over the computer, moving money from one account to another. Stupidly, I left him to it, naïve fool that I was.

'I'm sure we could sort something out,' he meets my eyes and I feel a flutter somewhere. I'm not quite sure where because it's so long since I've felt like it. I mean, he's pretty fit but I'm rubbish at these things. I don't know how to answer. I'm still married after all, and I can't remember how to do this. How do you flirt? Then again, I don't think I was ever very good at it – I always looked like I had something in my eye when I tried to flutter my eyelashes. Yet my friend at school had known exactly what to do, one flash of her beautiful doe eyes, a flick of her hair and any guy was hers. Except Dan. She had been there when I met him and I thought my chances were over, but he had picked me. I wonder why.

For goodness' sake, I must stop this. I give myself a mental shake. Dan is past history, and I'm here with two daughters who are vulnerable and upset. This is not the time to act like a lovesick teenager falling for some fancy local horse-riding guy, even though he is really hot. I'm first and foremost a mother, and I mustn't lose sight of that. Past it, that's what I am. Though the signals my body is giving out are definitely not in agreement.

'Why don't you come and look at it?' he suggests, looking at me expectantly.

'Look at what?' Did I really just ask that? How embarrassing!

Mark seems unperturbed. 'Come and have a look at this place.' He pulls out the latest iPhone from his Burberry jacket.

'What's your number?' he asks.

I give it to him, pleased to have memorised it correctly. I found it pretty difficult to learn, but then you don't phone yourself, do you? Mark nods and goes on his way. 'I'll be in touch,' he calls back over his shoulder as he and his unfriendly friend trot off down the road. Cars and people alike move aside for him. As I gaze after him, I realise he's probably used to that happening. Perhaps a real life Rupert Campbell-Black has trotted into my life and is reawakening thoughts in my head I figured had disappeared a long, long time ago.

'Did you see that?' asks Summer, tugging at my arm as we continue our wander.

'What?' I ask, distractedly.

'He had an iPhone 14 Pro Max.'

I wish I was nine again. Life was so much more straightforward!

We trek past the medieval church with its unusual dome and village green. 'Where do you think Elise might have gone?' She's been a while and I'm beginning to worry. Not that she could come to any harm in this idyllic village surely.

'What about the park?' Summer suggests and we take a right turn down a quaint little lane. There's a tiny stream flowing underneath a bridge, which we cross, and arrive at a lovely park with swings and even a moving horse with lots of seats. The panoramic view spreads across playing fields, past tennis courts up into the tree- lined valley beyond, which reaches up and up into the surrounding hills. Overhead, a couple of buzzards soar effortlessly in the unblemished blue sky. It's breathtaking and I feel at peace from all the arguing, the endless restrictions and the suffocating control. I take great soothing gulps of the air, which is both fresh and reviving.

In the far corner of the park is a large round swing seat with Elise stretched out in it, swinging backwards and forwards, gazing blankly at the view. As I approach, she wipes away a couple of tears.

'I'm sorry, sweetheart.' I stretch out my hand and pull her out of the swing. To my surprise, she launches into my arms and I hold her awkwardly for a second before she pulls away.

'We saw some horses,' chants Summer.

'Flipping typical. Why do you get to see horses without me when you don't even like them that much!'

I smile and we walk together back through the

village wending our way home to the welcoming Skylark.

'Excuse me! Hey?' I turn abruptly at a woman's voice.

It's Debs, waving from the cheese counter as she comes running out the grocer's shop. 'Did you say you're looking for work?' she asks.

'Yes. Yes, I am,' I reply.

'Well, you might like to take a look at this.' She pushes a piece of card into my hand and then runs back inside before I barely have a chance to thank her.

I glance at the note.

It reads:-

The Coffee Factory, Melstock is looking for an enthusiastic, front of house part time sales assistant. Must be bubbly, personable and crazy about coffee. To apply please phone 014598 77543 or call in at The Roastery for an application form.

'What is it?' asks Elise.

'An opportunity,' I reply excitedly, and for once I really think it is.

Chapter 3

This is a complete and utter disaster. What on earth am I going to do? I stand open mouthed in front of the cash machine. I must look bizarre standing here like a gawping goldfish.

The machine spits my card back at me with a resounding and reproachful beep. The message on the screen is loud and clear. I have no funds, no money, nada, nothing. Now what am I going to do?

It's been three days since I left Dan, and actually it's been a bit like a holiday. The girls are getting on really well for once, the stress and agitation has vanished. We've paddled in streams, walked for miles, eaten like horses and slept like logs, tired out with physical exertion and fresh air. I haven't heard anything from Dan and have managed to avoid Jess' repeated messages. I've sent her texts to say that we're all okay and that's about it.

But now without any money, I'm stuffed. Totally stuffed. My little bubble of safety has burst.

'You alright, love? You look like you've lost a pound and found a penny?' It's Debs hurrying along the road, her arms full of shopping bags.

'Yeah, I mean, no not really, I'm a bit stuck.' My voice breaks with tears, which I've done such a good job of keeping in until now and I must look a complete mess because I don't really do quiet and tidy crying.

'It's okay, love. Best to let it all out.' Debs dumps her bags, passes me a tissue and I dab my tears, sniff furiously and try to get a grip.

'It's just for the first time I've managed to break free and be an adult, but it's all a ridiculous dream. I'll have to go back to him. He's won.'

'You don't have to do anything, love. You're a free and independent person. No-one can make you do anything you don't want to do.' Debs is outraged.

'When I have no money, I have no choice,' I sob.

'Yes, you do, especially if he's violent.' Debs is adamant.

'But he's not violent,' I reply quietly.

How can I describe Dan to this jolly young woman, and explain that there are other ways to make life hideous for someone; slowly gradually suffocating their positivity, personality, everything unique about them. The cold cruelty of withdrawal, the icy draught of long sulks when I didn't do what he wanted me to, the punishment of social isolation. The clever duplicity of his behaviour to the girls, the change of warmth from one moment to another. I used to wonder if it was me or whether he was tired or unwell. Perhaps I wasn't trying hard enough. He would be in an awful mood with me, but the next minute on the phone to someone else he would be charming. Had I imagined it? Perhaps I was being clingy, nervy he used to say, or difficult? If the girls were naughty it was my job to deal with it, otherwise he was going to walk out and leave us. Then I would beg and plead him to stay, afraid to be left to cope on my own as a single parent. I would pull my socks up, prepare his favourite meals, and try to get the girls to behave better. Until one day years later, Charlotte helped me realise that it wasn't me at all. I'm a nervous wreck because of the erratic nature of his behaviour, the way he was treating me, his changeability. It always reminded me of that Katie Perry song 'You change your mind like a girl changes clothes. You're hot, then you're cold.'

The meeting with Charlotte a few weeks ago was arranged by an acquaintance – stupidly, I had been nervous initially meeting with a psychologist. Dan only came once. People had previously suggested counselling, but he wouldn't even admit it was necessary. He didn't need to talk to anyone, *if* the girls behaved, *if* the house was tidy, *if* I hadn't wound him up there wouldn't be a problem. I was drowning in a sea of 'ifs'. But I went along and he came too under the pretext of talking about the girls. He had been charming as always, but Charlotte had seen through him. 'A swan gliding on the top of the water but underneath his feet are paddling like crazy,' she had said.

It is thanks to her advice I've escaped. All those threats of his leaving if I didn't do the right thing hung over my head for too long, piling up like crazy until finally they overbalanced and crashed about my ears and as soon as I could, I ran the heck away. I've found a sanctuary here in Melstock and I'm not giving it up.

'He's not violent,' I repeat carefully, 'but he is controlling. He would go through my receipts, check my spending, knock my confidence, I was suffocating...' The tears begin to roll again.

'Look, love, I do understand. I had an ex like that once and it saps the bloomin' life out of you and your kids. My son, Josh, and I were better off without him. We'll find a way out of this for you and those lovely girls. So has he blocked your bank account?'

'No, it just says there's nothing in it. It's a joint account, but I reckon he's cleared the funds,' I say.

'Have you anything left?'

'About a hundred,' I reply. 'I managed to tuck some away over the last couple of weeks in case he tried a stunt like this, but I didn't think he could control our joint account.'

'Well, he shouldn't, but then he's obviously a complete asshole.' Debs doesn't mince her words, making me smile a little. 'Cheer up. There'll be something we can do. What about that job I showed you?'

'I've got an interview this afternoon. That's why the girls are up at the park. I'm meant to be buying myself a new lippy and going on to the meeting. Then again, I'm going to have to go back to The Skylark and redo my entire face now. Talk about bubbly, my first impression is going to be more like depressed and drippy today.'

'Nonsense! We'll soon get you sorted. Your first stop is Marina at the Pharmacy and then Phil at the Post Office.'

Debs is a woman on a mission. She takes my arm as though I'm a child, which is nice actually and together we visit the quaint little pharmacy with its bottles of old-fashioned lavender water, furry hot water bottles and racks of homeopathic meds. I love it in there. We manage to pick out a bright cherry coloured lipstick that I hope makes me look a little less tired and jaded, and more executive coffee seller.

Next Debs marches me to the Post Office where we are greeted once again by the ever-cheery Phil. 'Lost your children?' he jokes as we enter.

'Only for a minute,' I smile weakly in return.

'Phil, we need your help,' states Debs authoritatively. 'We'll need your back room.'

'Oh, dear. No-one's died, have they?' quips Phil.

'No, but they will do if we don't get this sorted.' Debs takes his arm and ushers us both into the back room of the Post Office before I can even gather my thoughts together. She sure is a force to be reckoned with when she gets going.

'Can you take over the shop, Alexandrine?' Phil calls to a formidable looking lady who I assume is his wife. She raises her eyebrows comically to the ceiling, but gives me a conspiratorial smirk. 'I'll be alright, don't you worry. Just leave me here all on my own.'

Half an hour later I leave the room feeling as though I have another ally, with a small amount to tide me over, and a completed claim for benefits. It feels like a lifeline yet...

'I feel bad,' I had said to Phil and Debs.

'Nonsense, child!' Phil had said. 'You're in a spot of bother and need help. What's there to feel bad about? It's not your fault apart from the fact it sounds as though you have rubbish taste in men!'

I had smiled at him then, a larger than life ex-Londoner, and larger than life in more ways than one. I'm fond of him already.

'Do you know what? Life doesn't always work out the way we want it to, but there's no point in suffering in silence. Plenty of less deserving people than you come in here and spend their cash down the bookies before it ever gets back to their little 'uns, so don't let me hear you feeling guilty.'

So I had accepted help, something which has always been difficult for me as I'm always too proud and too used to trying to sort things out myself. Instead, I sat and sipped my tea whilst Phil and Debs argued and offered advice on the pile of forms in front of me.

Then I wave my thanks to Phil and Alexandrine, and follow Debs back out into the sunshine.

'I can't believe how lovely he was,' I exclaim.

'The best,' replies Debs.

'I defy anyone to feel miserable with him around, he's so full of fun. Is he always like that?'

'Always.'

'Life would be a lot more fun if everyone were like him,' I remark as we round the bend towards The Coffee Factory.

'Well, he's a special guy, but he hasn't had an easy ride. His wife has cancer, you know? They have to drive to Exeter twice a week for chemo.'

'How awful! And it's over an hour away,' I reply.

'Yep, but you never hear a moan from either of them. His wife, whose bark is worse than her bite, Alexandrine – she's lovely too.'

I'm not sure how to reply. It's humbling really. I've rarely met such kind, warm people and although they have troubles of their own, they're so happy to help others. Makes you think really.

'Right, break a leg.' Debs gives me a hug. 'Do you know what? I feel like I've known you forever! You'll have to stay now.'

'Thanks – the last time I had a job interview was over 15 years ago, I'm ridiculously nervous.'

'You'll be fine. Just be yourself,' Debs says as she disappears off down the high street.

With a pang I realise her advice is exactly what my sister, Jess, would have said. Perhaps I'll ring her later. I really miss her and Bradley... but then when I think of her perfect life with her husband John, and how much she has always loved Dan, I have second thoughts.

I take a deep breath and walk into the warm aroma of coffee.

Chapter 4

'Romilly Greene?' A slightly rotund immaculately dressed young man springs forward to greet me. He has a very neat moustache and goatee and brings a whole new meaning to well-groomed.

'Yes, that's me.' I leap to my feet, then wish I hadn't as I bump my head rather noisily on the beam above me.

'Oops a daisy! Are you alright?' asks the man.

'Yes. Sorry, I'm afraid I'm a bit of a clumsy...' I start to blither, then stop myself. Get a grip, Rom, cool, calm and collected, slow it down. I put my hand out in a business-like manner and smile pleasantly. Mind you, I want to laugh out loud. Does anyone say things like oops a daisy anymore?

'Ciaran Hardcastle. Lovely to meet you.' Ciaran shakes my hand. He smells divine with his really amazing aftershave. 'It's my job to give you a little tour of the factory, so follow me if you please.'

In spite of my nerves, I'm super excited as I've wanted to explore this coffee factory since I was a little girl. It's always fascinated me with its gorgeous aroma and landmark tall chimney – which can be seen for miles from the neighbouring Devonshire hills.

'This is the factory shop. Have you visited it before?' asks Ciaran, sweeping his hand dramatically in the air.

'Yes, many times. I used to come in on family holidays as a child, although I don't think it had a shop when I first used to visit.'

We pause a moment in the cosy little space with its tiny gift packets of fresh ground coffee, cafetieres of all sizes, novelty teapots and beautifully crafted pottery coffee mugs. 'Well, this is where you would be based if you came to work here. You'd be keeping on top of stock, arranging shelves, etc, but mainly meeting and greeting visitors, serving at the counter and in the café, redirecting visitors to the factory on open days.'

'Do you offer samples of coffee?' I ask interestedly. 'I know it's delicious as we always bought some when we used to visit. Coffee doesn't taste the same anywhere else.'

'No, not currently,' replies Ciaran, 'although I've told the boss it would be a good idea. It would certainly boost sales.' He lowers his voice to a whisper. 'I used to work as a buyer for John Lewis, you know.'

'Oooh really? I bet that was fun. I'd love to have a job like that. Start trends and be in the know.'

'Oh yes,' he taps his nose mysteriously. 'I still keep abreast of what's hot and what's not.'

'Wow – so what's going to be the next big thing? My daughter Summer is really into unicorns, but I guess it'll be something new by Christmas.'

'Most definitely. Unicorns are so last year. Since then it's been llamas, but it's all about hedgehogs now.'

'Hedgehogs?' I'm a bit taken aback about that actually. I didn't know hedgehogs could be cool, but I guess you never know. I make a mental note to keep an eye out for any hedgehog designs when I'm out and about.

'Absolutely the next biggest thing, you mark my words.' And with that Ciaran sweeps off, leaving me to follow bemusedly in his wake.

The factory is a delight with its higgledy piggledy staircases leading to further floors, a bit like a relativity painting but fortunately none of them are upside down. Tardis-like, the building reveals new surprises at every turn, a small window here with a beautiful view out to where the rolling moors meet the sea, a cubby hole there filled with pipes and levers moving on into other rooms, flowing seamlessly between them.

Ciaran opens a door with a flourish. 'This is where the magic happens!' he announces triumphantly and I wander on in open mouthed. The room is the entire length of the factory building, long and narrow and is not unlike a scene from *Charlie and the Chocolate Factory*. I wish Summer was with me, she would love it. In the centre are several large vats with steam rising in great clouds spiralling right up to the high ceiling, which seems an infinity away as it is covered with a roof of misty vagueness. The pipes drop down from a great height and the noise and tumult of production is mesmerising. Downstairs in the quiet simplicity of the shop, you would never know this hive of activity was here.

'So,' twirls Ciaran, almost spinning an entire turn. (He really ought to be on *The Greatest Showman* or something, he's totally wasted here.) 'These,' he puts out his hand, makes a fist, then slowly reveals its contents as though performing a wonderful magic trick, 'are the raw material, little nuggets of gold or rather to be more precise, green.' I want to chuckle actually, as it reminds me of Lord Percy on Blackadder producing the most amazing, valuable green, thinking it will make him rich.

I peer vaguely at the contents of Ciaran's hand. In his beautifully manicured palm are several small green beans, which look rather like green peanuts.

'Wow?' I say tentatively, as I feel this is the response he's looking for.

'I know! Aren't they amazing?' he adds wonderingly.

'Well yes, quite,' I reply, gazing at them again. Maybe I've missed the point.

'They're not just any coffee beans. These are from Indonesia,' he announces triumphantly.

'But...' I pluck up the courage to venture. I mean, I'm by no means an expert, but in my geography lessons we didn't learn where things were made or where countries were located. We learnt about litter, deforestation and tropical diseases commonly caught in Ghana. I've found this most useful I can tell you when I haven't travelled further than Northern France, but I guess you never know. 'I thought coffee came from Columbia or South America?'

'Ahh, that's the beauty of it. Of course most of it does, but here in Melstock we produce the finest Indonesian coffee. Did you know that it grows best in the shade as it increases the flavour?'

'No, I didn't. No wonder it tastes better than any other coffee I've ever tasted.' And it does actually; I'm honestly not just sucking up to the guy to get the job!

Well, perhaps I am a tiny bit, but you can't blame me. I need this work and the flavour really is incredible, a luxurious burst of caffeine mixed with sumptuous sweetness in a hint of fruit, followed by a slight bitter zing adding an unexpected wildness.

'That's right,' agrees Ciaran. 'It certainly has a unique flavour, which was spotted by Mr Montmorency back in the day. If you'd like to follow me?'

I hide a smile at Ciaran's wonderful old-fashioned civility – it makes such a refreshing change – and follow him down the corridor and up yet another flight of stairs to the third floor. The fragrant aroma is incredible, just so pungent and evokes such happy childhood memories.

'And here we have the roasting room, which is my personal favourite because it simply smells so damn good!'

It does too. If I thought the smell was strong downstairs, this is far more intense. It is pure unadulterated coffee, and I feel wired just inhaling it, high on caffeine. The room is full of large vats with trays of coffee beans all drying at high temperature, sealing in their treasure ready to be unlocked in the grinding machine.

All too soon the tour is over and I find myself back downstairs in the shop, sipping a delicious cup of coffee kindly brought to me by a woman in a pinny. I'm so grateful for this as my coffee craving was so ridiculously strong whilst on the factory floor, I thought I might have to rush up, grab some beans and cram them straight into my mouth – which would have been a big mistake as they probably taste pretty disgusting uncooked.

'So what makes you want to work with us?' asks Ciaran, directly.

I know I should have thought about this during my interview preparation, but any pre-rehearsed speech goes out the window and I find myself babbling. 'As I mentioned, I remember this factory from my childhood visits to Melstock. It's always been a huge presence in the village and I love this place and want to be a part of it. I mean, it would be wonderful to live and work here and I am a total coffee buff, well at least I drink a lot of it. I am completely fuelled by good strong caffeine.' I finish pretty lamely, but by the look of Ciaran's face he seems to understand what I'm trying to say.

'Have you ever worked anywhere like this before?'

'Not really, but I used to work in a café serving teas, coffees, cakes etc and I worked in a clothes shop during my student days.'

'Not recently though? What was your last job?'

'I helped out at my younger daughter's previous school on a voluntary basis, hearing pupils read, doing craft, walking the children to church, some light administrative duties, that sort of thing,' I reply.

I wanted to add that I had desperately wished to find myself a niche, but my husband wouldn't allow it. He didn't forbid it exactly, that would have been far too obvious. Oh no, he's far cleverer than that. He just made it pretty darn impossible for me to hold down a job. He said he never knew where he was going to be or when, so I was unable to organise childcare arrangements. Then my mum had been ill and I needed to be around, so to be fair it wasn't just him. But it wasn't only work, but going out in general. I cast my mind back to the time I found a dance class I loved on a Tuesday at 7.30. I only managed to attend twice when strangely he always seemed to have a meeting on Tuesday evenings or he had to be away. Once, maybe twice, it might have been a coincidence but then it kept happening. For a while Jess offered to babysit and this seemed to stop him, but unfortunately she had her own issues with Bradley and it all fizzled out and Groundhog Day like, he was back to being out exactly that evening. Eventually I gave up and dance classes were no more.

'Well, I don't think that has to matter – do you have references we can contact?' Ciaran scratches his immaculate goatee thoughtfully.

'Yes, of course, no problem.' I'm sure Jean and Mel from the school office would give me a good reference if I asked them. I scribble down their contact details.

'Well then,' awkwardly I scrape the chair back as Ciaran, gentlemanly as ever, stands at the same time. 'We'll be in touch,' he says, and I so hope he is. I really want this job. It's perfect for me.

I say goodbye and reluctantly leave the wonderful aroma of the shop. Just as I walk across the car park, a large dark navy Bentley swooshes around the side of the factory. I happen to glance back, and as I do so, I notice a familiar figure get out of the car, walk round and go in the side door at the other side of the building. I can't be sure because he's wearing a suit, definitely designer by the look of it, and to be fair I've only seen him in jodhs before, but I could swear it's Mark Whittaker. I don't stop to find out as the guy's going to think I'm stalking him, so I leave rapidly to find my girls and the relaxing bliss of the park.

Chapter 5

'I don't bloody well want to go to the local school. It's totally crap.'

Oh dear. This is not going well at all. Today Elise is due to start at Stamforth Secondary and she's not a happy bunny. To be fair, I can understand it. Her previous school, Riversmeet Senior, had a good reputation and she did have a group of friends there. More guilt for me; as if I didn't have enough already, but Riversmeet Senior is now several hundred miles away. Yet another reason why Elise hates me at the moment and sometimes I hate myself. But in spite of the fact we've been in Melstock for more than a week, I still haven't heard from Dan. Nada, nothing at all, so I can't help but feel this has been the best decision.

Unfortunately though, I have heard from Mum, and let's just say I'm not the flavour of the month right now. The phone call was something of a disaster to be fair, and it went something like:

'Romilly, what's all this I hear about you leaving Dan and disappearing off to the middle of nowhere?'

She didn't even give me time to reply, just carried straight on:- 'You realise you're throwing everything away? He's been good to you. Think of your lovely house, the appliances, the furnishings, everything top notch and now look at you; you'll be left with absolutely nothing. Where on earth are you living? Jess says you're in Melstock. I know it's pretty, but you'll never find a decent hairdresser.'

'Yes, we're in Melstock. It's as lovely as ever, the girls....'

'And think of those poor girls, left without a father. I know what you're going to say. I know Dan isn't always the best husband, but how do you think you've managed to have all those lovely things if he wasn't at work a lot of the time?'

'It wasn't just that, Mum. You know how he could be.'

'Well, I'm sure he could be difficult, but think how stressful his job is. Quite honestly, you haven't had to put up with half the things I've had from your father, remember that time....'

I had gazed at the view over the park whilst Mum continued to tell me in infinite detail about the time my dad had forgotten their anniversary and by the time he had remembered it, he had already invited his horrible mother out with them for the day. I've heard this story so many times I could accurately recount it myself word for word.

I don't want to have this conversation here. In fact, I don't want to have this conversation at all. The park is my happy place.

'Find a happy place,' Charlotte had said at the end of the therapy session. 'When everything's going wrong and all those problems are whirling around in your head, pull them up short and inwardly shout STOP! Then go to your happy place. It can be anywhere; anywhere you want it to be.'

The trouble is people keep stomping on my happy place from a great height. Initially I chose the memory of being high up on a mountainside as a child. I had run on ahead from my parents, up and up along a clear tumbling stream. White topped mountains loomed above in the distance and all around was green, with beautiful orchids and wild flowers. Vivid blue butterflies fluttered around me and I felt a sense of such peace. It was just how I imagined Paradise to be. So when Charlotte had told me about finding a happy place, I reconjured it in my mind. To be frank, at first it wasn't easy. The image had flickered and glimmered slightly out of reach. It was too difficult to bring back. But in time, with practice, I could see it clearly; I remembered that feeling of sheer joy of living in that moment. Charlotte was right. I felt better for this escape into a happier time and place, away from the never-ending worry.

Unfortunately, it all went horribly wrong when I told Dad about my happy place. 'But it was full of bloody mosquitos, Rom. Terrible they were, I got bitten all over!' he had insisted.

So that was the end of that, and I had to think of another happy place, which was pretty impossible so I gave up. But now I've found it, right here, right now in the present. Somewhere to come and escape, and Mum is ruining it with her negativity.

Instinctively I had started to walk quickly, so I could move somewhere else. No-one is pooping on this idyllic spot, full stop. Mum continued undeterred, 'We went wrong with you. You're spoilt, that's your problem. We sheltered you too much from reality, you really have no idea...'

Finally I had managed to break into her tirade. 'Mum, I've made the right decision for me, and that's what counts.'

'And how selfish is that, may I ask? You have two beautiful girls to think about. What about their happiness? Sometimes we have to make sacrifices. Think of England, that's the trouble with this snowflake generation, no idea of how to cope with anything.'

'Mum, that's a bit unfair,' I interjected.

'Is it? Is it though? At your age I had two kids, a full time job and a difficult mother-in-law to look after.'

'Yes, yes I know,' I interrupted hurriedly before she started again in yet another tirade. 'And that's why I put up with it all, but then I realised...'

'Realised what?' Good grief, was Mum actually listening for once?

'What sort of example am I setting for my girls if I let a man continue to sap all my energy, friends, and take away my identity and my freedom?' Desperately, I hoped my mum might finally understand where I was coming from but obviously I was totally wasting my time.

'My God, child! You're not turning into one of those raving feminists are you? Next thing you'll be shaving your hair and growing a beard.'

This made me laugh, which fortunately broke the tension a little. 'Mum, I've always been a feminist. It just means I believe in equal rights for men and women, nothing sinister.'

'Hmmph! That's what they all say to start with. Next thing you'll be burning your bra and getting rid of men altogether.'

'Hardly, Mum,' I had laughed, but she had continued to rant for another half an hour or more until I managed to get away. The end result was the usual one, me feeling full of doubt and pretty rubbish about myself again.

The decision is made, however, and by all accounts I've been lucky to get Elise into Stamforth Secondary so we basically just have to get on with it. The drive only takes a short while but I feel pretty sick when we enter the drop off point outside the huge line of fencing which surrounds the school. It just needs a couple of snipers and some barbed wire to complete the unwelcoming effect. For ages now we've passed teenagers in hideous dark green jumpers, all walking or biking in their droves. They're like a swarm of ants. I'd forgotten what the school run was like as Elise used to get the little bus to Riversmeet Senior. She had loved the journey, sitting quietly with her headphones in. Another thing to feel guilty about, but I shake away the thought like an irritating gnat.

'Right, here we are,' I say far more cheerfully than I feel. 'Lila's going to be meeting you at the gate.' Lila is the daughter of Tania, the lady from the Zumba class. We've met her a couple of times and she seems a nice girl. She's in a different year, but has been at Stamforth Secondary since Year 7 so she knows the ropes. 'It's not brilliant,' Tania had admitted. 'I've had to go in several times about this and that, but there's nowhere else really.' And there isn't, so it looks like we are stuck with it.

'I can't see her,' states Elise firmly.

‘Neither can I, but I’m sure she’ll be there.’ I peer anxiously towards the gate but there is no sign of Lila at all. ‘We’re a bit early. I’m sure she’ll be here in a moment.’

There’s a queue of cars nose to tail behind me and I’m painfully aware that we’re causing a hold up. Not a good start at a new school.

‘Hop out, and just wait at the gate. I’m sure she’ll be along in a mo,’ I say, passing Elise her bag. ‘Have a good day, love, and text if you need me.’

‘Yeh right.’ Elise hops out the car, slams the door with meaning and strides into the sea of green uniforms.

I drive like a snail, peering so hard behind me that I nearly mount the pavement and I can still see the impatient and slightly threatening face of the father in the car behind. I decide to drive round the block just to make sure Lila has met Elise. When am I ever going to stop helicopter parenting? Probably never, as these girls are my everything.

I whizz round the block. ‘Mum, I feel sick,’ moans Summer, dramatically clutching her stomach.

‘Sorry, love. I just thought I’d go round the block twenty times or so.’

We queue back round the drop off trying not to look suspicious as I now have no child to be dropping off, and I’m not really sure what I’m supposed to be doing. As I get to the gate there’s no sign of either Elise or Lila. Does that mean they’ve both gone in or that Elise is wandering round lonely and not sure where to go? I drive off, feeling horribly guilty, then a horn toots and I see Tania waving madly and sending a thumbs up signal. Lila isn't in the car so I assume she's dropped her off and Elise is alright.

I breathe a sigh of relief and instantly feel better. It's just Summer to take to the junior school now. I whizz the car back in the pub car park and we jump out into a flood of little ones filing down the alley from the park towards the school gate. I smile as much as I can at the other mums but no one really notices. I wonder if I'm invisible to be honest. They continue their chats, jostling their children along, their heads full of their own schedule, indifferent to anyone around them. Others are so deep in conversation they barely notice us as we stand politely to one side. Is it just me or do you find that the politer you are, the more you get side lined? I've always found this to be true as I was brought up to be polite and stand aside or wait my turn patiently in a queue, yet these days it's survival of the fittest. Stand to one side holding a door open and you'll be there all night! Wait politely at the back of a queue and you'll be queueing forever as all the other kids will push in front of you. My girls are too considerate and diffident when it comes to other people and always end up last, unnoticed and pretty much squashed. Perhaps I should stop trying to bring them up to be so polite and instil a bit more grit and determination.

Summer clutches my hand anxiously but we manage to wend our way to the school gate. It's a picturesque scene, situated next to the church and a quaint old Victorian building.

'Look, Mum! There's a train in the playground,' says Summer excitedly, 'and skipping ropes and hoops.'

'It looks lovely,' I reply, and it does. Somehow I feel

safer, happier dropping Summer here. It's a typical traditional little village primary school not unlike the one I went to a hundred years ago!

We walk past the crowds of mums, all standing in their little cliques, to the office. It's funny how I always find there are two or three types of mothers at the school gate. First there's the 'Yummy Mummys' in their high boots, tight jeans and immaculate hair, towing little Cressida and Johnny behind them. Glancing round the playground here in the country, I mentally add Hunter boots, jodhs or chaps and riding jackets to this group. Then there's the young and hip mums – cool and on trend in the latest label tracksuits, highlighted hair in a messy bun, foreheads suspiciously immobile whenever they try to pull any kind of facial expression. More elusive, but occasionally spotted are the smartly dressed working mums who fly in and out of the playground driven by their tight schedule, but more often than not the children are dropped to breakfast club or delivered by grandparents. The rest of the mothers turn up in leggings and baggy T-shirts or whatever they happen to be wearing, just glad that they made it to school. Some mornings I'm ashamed to confess that I've forgotten to brush my hair or remove my eye make-up from the night before. I must look a right sight.

This morning I've made a slight effort I must admit, if nothing else for the simple reason that it might make me feel a little better about things.

The lady at the office is a bulldog of a woman guarding the front desk from unwary parents, late children and anyone who has not met the current attendance figures. I make a mental note to come up against her as little as possible.

Fortunately we are rescued by a young looking guy with glasses and floppy brown hair, who I smile at vaguely thinking he must be here on work experience.

'Hi,' I say blithely. 'Are you here to take Summer to her teacher?'

'I am her teacher, Mr Barton,' he replies, raising his eyebrows into his thick ruffled thatch of hair. I squash away the desire to tell him he should have brushed his fringe before coming to school and that he must have missed out a few years at training college as he's far too young to be a teacher. Instead, I shake hands politely.

'Sorry, I mean I wasn't sure who you were,' I finish lamely.

'It's fine.' He turns his back to me abruptly. It's obviously anything but fine. 'Hello, Summer, looking forward to your first day at a new school?'

'Yes,' says Summer solemnly, 'but I'm a bit nervous.'

'Of course you are,' says Mr Barton. 'We all get a bit worried when we start anything new.' He pauses and waves to a girl of similar age with a high blonde ponytail. 'Samira – this is Summer. I'd like you to be her buddy today, show her round, that sort of thing.'

I thank Mr Barton, who nods curtly in reply, kiss Summer goodbye and escape out into the playground. His manner was slightly odd. I mean, it's a complement he looks young, so perhaps I'm just being a bit sensitive. I guess it's not surprising I'm a bit down at the mo, but he was lovely with Summer and that's the main thing.

I wander through the school gate and out into the lane. It's such a gorgeous morning and I enjoy meandering up the hill around the side of the park. The babbling little brook tumbles down the hill on the right-hand side of the lane and I walk up past cosy little cottages, each individually thatched, some with little birds carefully crafted from straw on the roofs.

My phone rings out loudly, rudely disturbing the peace of the beautiful April day. I really must change the ring tone. Fortunately, no one seems to be about to be annoyed and having checked the number I don't recognise it. Could it be Dan phoning from another number? Not that I know the area code.

'Hello?' I answer politely.

'Good morning. Is that Romilly?' asks a slightly familiar Irish voice.

'Oh hi. Yes, good morning, it is. I mean, I am her or should that be she?' I reply awkwardly.

'It's Ciaran, from The Coffee Factory.'

'Hi, sorry about that,' I stutter.

'That's fine.' God, once again I feel such a fool. I'm never going to get this job now.

'I was just phoning to let you know....' Oh please let me have this job, please, I need it. '...we have decided...' Please spit it out... 'We would love you to come and work with us,' Ciaran finishes.

'Yes!' I fist punch the air, then realise I have deafened the poor man. 'Sorry about that,' I apologise.

'That's okay. It was your enthusiasm that got you the job,' remarks Ciaran drily, 'but there is just one thing,'

'Yes?' I reply, prepared to agree to anything, within

reason. Anything at all.

'You must stop apologising for everything.' I can tell he's smiling on the other end of the line.

Oh, I'm not sure that's humanly possible. I mean I'm British, I'm used to apologising for my very existence.

'I'll try,' I say, and I mean it. I really do.

Chapter 6

I'm actually amazed. Amazed at how suddenly life can take a different turn. One minute you can be trundling along doing the same old, same old, and then a tiny decision can change the whole course of your life. Well, some of it anyway, and mine certainly feels pretty different right now. Both girls are miraculously in local schools, the days are beginning to have a bit of a routine to them and I'm about to start a new job for the first time in years. Not that things are easy incidentally. Elise hates her school and is refusing to talk about it, she's so supremely angry with everyone and everything. Summer, on the other hand, has made friends and is mostly excited about an up and coming school trip to a farm.

More to the point, our accommodation issue will hopefully soon be resolved. I'm about to meet Mark at Larkin Cottage (love the name incidentally) and to be honest, I can't help but feel a teensy bit excited about seeing him again. I mean, not from a relationship point of view, definitely not, but a girl can look, can't she? After all, it's okay to admire how fit someone is without taking it further. Not that he'd be interested in someone like me anyway. Besides I'm not convinced I'm over Dan yet.

I pull myself together out of my Jilly Cooper-esque

daydreams and steel myself to knock on the door of Larkin Cottage. It's in a very convenient position just off the high street and is suitably covered in wisteria in the best tradition of all quaint old cottages.

There's a long enough delay to make me wonder whether I've got the right time and day, but to my relief Mark opens the door and rather incongruously climbs out of the doorway, ducking heavily to try to avoid banging his head.

'Hi,' he says coolly, bending to kiss me on the cheek. Wow! That was unexpected, he smells amazing, like Versace or something. It's a funny thing with aftershave. It really works on the pheromones or whatever they're called. I remember once nearly falling off the pavement because some guy who walked past smelt so amazing, only to be disappointed to discover he was rather unattractive and garbed in a scruffy old tracksuit – a bit of a let-down, to be fair.

'Hello, this is very sweet,' I say, as I follow Mark into the cottage. We step straight into the lounge, which is small and cosy with plain original walls, and to my delight a log burner in the centre. 'I love a real fire. We can toast marshmallows and I know I'll be fighting with Elise over the window seat. I can see myself sitting there lost in a book.'

''Right,' smiles Mark. Not really a book enthusiast then, he's probably more outdoorsy than that. Mentally I give him a cross. Dan didn't like reading either. Mark, oblivious to my racing thoughts, continues his guided tour, 'Through here is the kitchen, small but perfectly formed.'

It's lovely actually. 'I've always wanted one of those

old ranges,' I exclaim.

'Yes you'll be able to cook your landlord a scrumptious roast,' says Mark, unexpectedly smiling and revealing his whiter than white perfect teeth.

'Oh yes. We do usually have a roast on Sundays. You'd be more than welcome to come with your ...' I flounder slightly. It's always awkward asking if someone has a girlfriend or not. 'Partner,' I finish cautiously.

'Partner?' he replies with a laugh. 'Nope, it's just me right now. Well, and the dogs and horses.'

'Oh,' I reply trying to sound disinterested. I mean, I've only been apart from Dan for a few weeks and my life is complicated enough.

'So I don't often get a nice home cooked roast unless I go home to Mother's.'

'Oh,' I reply again, unsure what to say next. 'Well, I'm sure your mum's roasts are always the best.'

'I think you're right. I used to dream about her roast dinners whilst at Bryanston. Nearly as much as I missed our dog!'

'Wow – did you board?' I ask. I never can understand why anyone would send their child to boarding school.

'Yes,' he says cheerfully, leading the way up the narrow staircase. 'I got used to it in the end. Terribly homesick at first though.' He stops at the top and looks so little boy lost that I have to fight the urge to touch his face with my hand.

'How old were you when you were sent to school?'

'Nine,' he said, abruptly clearing his throat. 'Well, this is the upstairs. Compact and bijoux, but it does the job.'

I'm still reeling from his disclosure. He was sent away to school when he was only Summer's age. It makes me feel sad actually, as I love our time together. I remember shedding a tear or two when she turned four and went to school for the day. I missed our walks, the way she shouted 'train' when one went by, her habit of picking up leaves and guessing which tree they came from. It was several months before I could go near the leisure centre without feeling sad as that was where she had gone to toddler groups, where we used to sit and watch the swimmers whilst snacking on yoghurt covered raisins. I still can't eat them to this day without feeling a little emotional, hankering for those times when it was just the two of us. Perhaps it's my hormones again. Maybe the doctor was right, for goodness' sake!

I follow Mark up the stairs trying not to be distracted by his tight white jodhs.

The bedroom is cosy, overlooking the cobbled pavements and twisty high street as it rounds the corner and up the steep hill towards The Skylark. There are two other small bedrooms just big enough for a single bed each. I breathe a sigh of relief as I really couldn't face Summer and Elise sharing a room. We tried that years ago at our last house and they fought like cat and dog.

However, one major issue bothers me. This cottage is not going to be cheap. It's in a prime tourist location for a start. 'I love it but how much are you thinking of charging for rent?'

'Oh, I'm sure we can come to an arrangement.'

Mark wanders to the window and stares out at the beautiful view. The rest of the cottages in the village are scattered in a picturesque fashion all the way towards the sea. Then to the right, the moors reach down to a grassy hill, which stretches into craggy cliff edge and finally the blue streak of sea. I stare at his broad shoulders and try not to look at his tight jodhs and the gleaming leather of his riding boots. I am honestly not that shallow really. He turns and smiles endearingly at me and I feel a definite quickening of pulse. I take a deep breath and try to focus on the mess I've got myself in.

'Look, I don't wish to be rude, Mark, but this is business and I need to pay my way,' I say firmly but with a smile to soften the blow.

'Of course.' He is dismissive, adding, 'We'll sort all that later, but do you like it?'

Like it? I love it and it would be even better with him in the bed. I shrug the thought away like an irritating fly. He smiles at me and to be honest I can't help smiling back. He has an aquiline nose which lends him stature and I find his habit of flicking his mop of hair back with his hand totally fascinating. I don't know what I'm thinking – I'm a middle-aged woman who has just left her husband, with two girls, one of whom is a difficult teenager.

'Yes,' I reply cautiously, 'but I'll pay full rent and I need to know how much it is so I can work out what I can afford.'

'Has anyone ever told you that you're a very determined young lady?' he asks. 'Come on. Let's go out into the sunshine.' He places his hand on the small of my back as he motions for me to go down the stairs in front of him. I walk down carefully, simultaneously enjoying the pressure of his hand and hoping my bum doesn't look too large in my tight jeans.

We pause out in the cottage garden outside the kitchen. 'Enjoy gardening?' he quips.

'Yes actually. House plants I'm not so good with, I'm afraid. They usually only last a couple of days as I either dry them out or flood them.'

'I'm sure you'll be quite capable of looking after this little patch,' Mark points at the foxgloves and hollyhocks. 'If not, I'll have to come and give you a hand.'

Now, is it me, or is this guy definitely flirting? It's been so long, I just can't tell.

'That would be nice,' I say lightly, 'but you would have to put up with one overenthusiastic helper and a sulky uncooperative teenager.'

'I might just cope,' he says with that smile again. 'Do you ride?'

A bit random. What kind of riding does he mean? I presume the kind with horses.

'Not properly for years,' I reply – that should work for both options.

'You'll soon remember how when you get back in the saddle. I have a nice little grey mare who would suit you.'

'That would be amazing, but are you sure?'

'Of course! We've several in our stables. How about Saturday?'

Okay, Rom. Don't be too available. You need to think about it, play hard to get.

‘That would be lovely,’ I say happily. My life really is turning into *Riders*. Oh darn. Never mind, sod it, I never was any good at this game anyway.

Chapter 7

I'm so organised this morning, I've even surprised myself. Summer and Elise are at school on time and there was only one row before we left the building we still call home. It's definitely an improvement on yesterday anyway. Today's my first day at The Coffee Factory and I'm as nervous as a child about to start a new school.

I've opted for a plain black pair of trousers, a colourful cream shirt with large poppies on it and a reasonably high pair of heels. At least no one will be able to miss me. I am so not going to mess this up. I'm outside The Coffee Factory at 8.50, plenty of time before opening. Ironically I haven't had time for a coffee yet, but that's fine. I'll just have to inhale some for now; the air is already pungent with the delicious aroma and I'm sure that will work nearly as well.

Ciaran greets me at the door, dapper as ever, 'Good morning and how are we?'

'Fine thanks,' I smile back. 'Raring to go, but a bit nervous.'

'I'm not surprised,' he replies, his face deadpan. 'This place can be a little scary. There's no escape once you start, but you'll soon get used to us, won't she, Mrs Miggins?'

The lady with the apron I remember meeting the

other day laughed. 'That you will, my love. Now come on in and hang up your jacket. Then we'll make a coffee and I'll show you where the magic happens.'

'Thanks,' I smile. My nerves are beginning to settle; everyone here is so welcoming. I follow her through the shop into a large kitchen area with butler sinks, mugs hanging up on a beautiful old dresser and vast pots of coffee. This is my kind of work.

In no time Mrs Miggins is showing me the ropes. (Rather amusingly, I can't think of her name without picturing Mrs Miggins' pie shop in Blackadder.) She's a bit like her in manner, but not looks, and fortunately Baldrick doesn't seem to be in residence. I learn how to make coffee, whilst sampling various blends throughout the morning. I'm buzzing actually, partly with excitement at actually doing some work again and partly because I'm not used to drinking so much caffeine. I discover which flavours work with which milks, and how coffee is roasted. I find out that the computer system is extremely dated and has probably been around for the entire fifteen years that Mrs Miggins has been working here. Yet I find it strangely comforting as I haven't been at work for so long and am perfectly happy with antiquated machines and systems. All the orders still seem to be on paper, which is a bit old fashioned, but the system appears to work so who am I to meddle with it?

By the afternoon I'm serving in the café with some guidance from Mrs Miggins and some amusing comments from Ciaran, who has previously witnessed my inherent clumsiness. I've handed out several cups of coffee without spilling any over anyone, so as far as

I'm concerned if I can get through the rest of the day with this record intact, it will be an achievement in itself. I'm just sitting down momentarily catching up on some orders, tapping info into the computer, when an elderly gentleman appears in front of me.

'Good afternoon,' he says, politely removing his cap. 'Any chance of one of your delicious cups of coffee?'

'Of course,' I smile and jump up. 'Come this way. You can sit in the window if you like and enjoy the view.'

'Thank you, my dear.' He follows me, sprightly in spite of his advanced years, sits himself down at a little round table, starts to rummage in his pocket and eventually produces a pair of glasses. He puts them on. 'Oh, you must be the new lady,' he pronounces.

'Yes, that's me. News travels fast round here,' I laugh, and put my hand out. He has a nice firm handshake.

'Lovely to meet you, m'dear, I'm Walter.' He holds my hand a second too long, but somehow I don't mind.

'Now what can I get you?' I ask.

'Well, I can't say my usual, can I, as you wouldn't know what that is?' he chuckles.

'No, but I'll soon learn it, I'm sure.'

'I should hope so. I come in every day and have done for the last fifty years.'

'Fifty years? Crikey! You must have won the best customer award,' I joke.

'Best customer and best worker too,' he replies. 'I worked here for more than forty years. Gave the best years of my life, I did.'

'Gosh,' I reply impressed, 'and you still drink the coffee every day.'

'I do! I'm ninety-one, you know, and look at me! I don't look a day over ninety!'

I laugh. Walter looks really good for his age. He's even wearing a tie and a neatly pressed shirt. Quite remarkable really. I bustle out to the rear of the shop where Mrs Miggins is washing up. 'Everything all right, dearie?' she asks.

'Yes fine, thanks. Walter's in the coffee shop.'

'Oh, Walter! Bless him. You'll have to do his usual.' She dries her hands briskly on a miraculously pristine wiping up cloth. Everything here is clean and tidy, ship shape and Bristol fashion. I could do with her running my house. In fact, my entire life actually. I tried to be tidy with Dan around but in spite of the fact he always said I was messy, he would leave his stuff everywhere. I tried buying shoe racks and putting his smelly old trainers away for him but to no avail. I even attempted asking him politely, doing it myself, getting angry but nothing worked and he would always leave his belongings, his car keys, his clothes all around the place. His mother's house is immaculate, not a thing out of place. I wonder how she coped with him as a teenager? She's not the shouting kind. More deadly than that somehow. Silent but deadly.

Mrs Miggins opens up the coffee machine. I'm still quite scared to touch it to be honest, as apparently it's worth a fortune and I do have a habit of unwittingly jamming computers, gadgets and other machines. I think they sense my uncertainty and go wrong deliberately. She reaches up to the top cupboard. 'Now, these are something really unique,' she remarks, proudly. I peer at the tin, which is quite attractive with a decorative elephant on it; it is beautifully ornate. 'This is our special blend and it's Walter's favourite. In fact, he was working here when old Mr Montmorency first brought the beans back from Indonesia many years ago.'

'That's incredible! I bet he's got the most amazing stories to tell. Does he take milk?'

'Definitely not. He always takes it black so he can savour the flavour.' Mrs Miggins carefully measures the freshly ground coffee into a beautiful blue cup. 'Walter likes a toasted teacake as well with plenty of butter.'

I fetch the teacakes and pop them under the old grill. 'Does he really come in every day?' I ask.

'Ooh yes, part of the furniture is old Walter. Been coming as long as I can remember, come rain or shine.'

Finally I take the finished work of art to Walter who has a crossword book out in front of him. 'Thanks, m'dear. Got to keep the mind active, you know.' He pats the book next to him.

'Of course, though I'm not very good at them,' I confess.

'Well, sit yourself down and we'll have a go,' he replies, adding some sugar lumps to his coffee and patting the chair behind him.

'I'm not sure... I mean, I'm meant to be working,' I say awkwardly.

'Nonsense, Romilly. It is Romilly, isn't it?' I nod. 'Mrs Miggins always sits a moment with me to do the daily crossword if it's quiet in here. It's tradition.'

'Oh well, I wouldn't like to break with tradition.' I

sit down and soon we are both poring over the clues. It's a funny thing, I'm normally useless at crosswords but working together I begin to see a bit of a pattern and even manage to make some tentative suggestions of my own.

'You're not bad, you know,' says Walter as he finishes the final clue with a flourish. 'Reckon we'll have to get you in our team for the Melstock quiz night. Right,' he drains his cup. 'I'm off then, thank you for the delicious coffee. It was nearly as good as usual.'

'But,' I say to his retreating back, 'Mrs Miggins made it.'

'I know,' he chortles. 'I was just messing with you. It was perfect. Same time tomorrow?'

'Yes, definitely,' I say, and I must admit I'm looking forward to it.

I make it through to the end of the day, having met the rest of the team; several lively young lads and some middle-aged like myself, who mostly work up on the factory floor, practising their alchemy with precision. I rush home like a woman on a mission, grab a snack and try to no avail to persuade Elise to accompany me this evening. She's plugged into her iPad and is watching a slightly unsettling series on aliens taking over the world. Summer, however, agrees to come along in spite of the fact she's tired. I decide to bring an iPad because at least it will give her something to do if she gets fed up. Tonight I'm trying Zumba for the first time.

I rush along to the village hall at 6.25 because typically Summer had some totally unintelligible homework and she had no clue how to do it. It took all my imagination to try to work out how to do it myself.

To be fair, we didn't learn about homophones in my day. It was just the three Rs: reading, writing and arithmetic (does that count as an 'R' even though it's not at the beginning?) Anyway the system worked. We knew our tables and seemed to have far less homework.

I've managed to stick on a pair of leggings and a nice baggy T-shirt I can hide in. My trainers are a bit embarrassing as I bought them some time ago when Summer was young, and bizarrely though my feet were bigger then, they seem to have shrunk a bit now so they look a bit like flat boats. But anyway, as I explained to Summer, it isn't meant to be a fashion show. I walk into the foyer at the Village Hall and am met by a tall, impressively fit looking woman with a scrunched up messy bun standing behind a desk with a signing in book and a money tin. She is wearing a tight pair of three quarter length leggings, a sassy pink sports bra and a black vest over the top emblazoned with 'Zumba!' in big pink letters. I feel huge and frumpy in my oversized shirt and hope no one notices my tatty old trainers.

My approach to exercise even at school was a bit lackadaisical. In fact, I had a variety of bandages, which I would put on various parts of my body saying I had sprained something. For swimming I had a pretty much permanent time of the month, which nobody seemed to see through. Of course, in the end my cunning got me into trouble as once I pretended I had sprained my ankle and my friends took me to matron. She had given me an icepack to hold on the 'injured' limb. Now if you have ever (and you probably haven't) held an icepack on any part of your body for no reason at all, you will know that it actually hurts like heck. My friends were all crying with laughter when as soon as Matron went out of the room to get something, I immediately removed the icepack with relief and was banging my foot on the ground, trying to get the feeling back in it! The only time I enjoyed PE was when we had a dance class. It was the only sport I was good at, having done ballet for ten years as a child. There's something about the music and rhythm of dance that I love.

'Hi!' smiles Tania, as bouncy as she looks. She has perfect white teeth, which she reveals in a friendly smile.

I pass her a note to pay for Summer and myself. 'Oh no, you don't need to pay for the little one,' she passes me back some change.

'Thank you. I don't know if she's going to join in for all of it,' I say.

'She can dip in and out, that's fine. Are you fit and well?' asks Tania.

'Yes, generally, as long as you don't look too close,' I quip.

'Ooh, Tania will soon sort you out,' laughs Debs who has just appeared behind me with Molly and Skye from the craft shop, and a couple of other ladies who I've seen in the village.

'I don't know about that,' smiles Tania. 'Any joint problems or anything else I need to be aware of?'

'Well, my back can be a bit grumpy since having the girls and I haven't done much exercise lately apart from walking,' I admit.

'Just take it steady then and make sure you're

warm before you start jumping. Right, I think we're all here.' Tania grabs her box of money and the book in which we all have signed our names.

We all trundle into the hall where there are chairs round the edge of the room and a stage. Women stand chatting round the edges. To my relief they're all different ages, shapes and sizes. I'd been worried they would all be tiny sticks but they're generally quite normal looking. I heave a sigh of relief.

Tania climbs on the stage, plugs in the sound system and strides to the front. 'Come on then, girls, let's do this!' God, she's fit! If I look anything like her by the end of this, I'll be happy.

Everyone meanders into vague rows lined all the way to the back of the hall. They talk and laugh, and the air is buzzing with lightness and energy. I take my place in the back row totally in the corner (old school habits die hard) next to Debs.

'Here goes,' I say nervously.

'You'll love it,' she grins back. She makes me smile, she's wearing tight lycra all over with a baggy jumper and Nike trainers. Her water bottle, which she has left on the chair emblazoned with 'Dance it, don't gym it,' is absolutely huge. If I drank all that I'd be in the toilet for the rest of the day.

The music starts, the disco ball in the ceiling which I hadn't noticed until now begins spinning, and Tania leaps into a rousing warm up involving lots of grape vines, clapping and stretches. When it ends, we all remove our jumpers because we're warm already and gulp water from our bottles. The music is from the recent charts. Elise keeps me fairly updated with the latest music trends and I must admit I love jiving along when no one is looking. We dance to track after track, with me getting half the moves wrong and no one seeming to mind. At times Debs and I are doubled up with laughter as I go the wrong way round as we do some turns, but somehow we're all laughing at ourselves rather than at each other. I find myself picking up some of the moves easily, other songs I just haven't got a clue about but it doesn't matter because I realise I have a huge grin on my face and for the first time in ages I feel happy. In some songs Tania whoops along for the first bit of the move and we all join in loudly – it's so much fun!

Summer comes and joins in some of the easier moves but soon tires and goes back to curling up in her chair with a book. I have to join her at one point as I'm just too unfit to finish the dance. Some of the moves are so funny. In 'Applause' we have to squat, stretch our arms out from side to side and then clap in the middle. 'Well done me!' laughs Debs and we giggle away like a couple of children whilst messing up the rest of the moves.

I'm incredibly sweaty by the end of the session. In fact, I didn't think I was able to sweat very much. Even when I've been to the gym I've tended to stop before getting too hot and sticky. I really don't think it's good for your health. The gym is so boring that I always feel as though I've been there for hours when it's only been ten minutes.

Yet Zumba is the complete opposite. I've been so busy concentrating on the moves that I haven't even thought about Dan, the children or how I've screwed everything up. All I could think about was moving to the music. I'm not going to say I feel amazing, but I certainly feel a heck of a lot better.

'Coming back on Thursday then?' asks Debs.

'You bet!' I reply, and we wander home companionably along the cobbled village street of the place, which within a couple of weeks feels more like home than anywhere ever has before.

Chapter 8

'You're going riding without me?' demands Elise, incredulously.

This is not going well. I wasn't going to tell her about my impending outing with Mark. I knew she would be mad; riding is so much more her thing. Then again this is the irony of life. When I was a child I would have done anything to be given the opportunity to go hacking with a friend on a proper horse rather than on a stubborn riding school pony. Yet the offers never came. Now I'm older, haven't ridden for years and I'm a tad nervous about the whole idea, here is the most wonderful chance to ride on an amazing show horse. My thirteen-year-old self would be wild with envy; I definitely need to rewind the clock.

'Yes, but it's just a one off. I'll probably make a complete fool of myself and that will be that,' I say cheerily.

'You probably will and that will be karma.' Oh well, that's me told! 'Have you still not heard from Dad?'

'No, I told you, absolutely nothing.' I haven't actually, not that I've contacted him either. But then why should I?

'Don't you think you should have called him? I mean you're the one who walked out.' It's all so simple in Elise's world.

Not really. I told him so many times that there was a problem and he walked away, slammed the door, said I was nagging him. I'm not going to be the one who picks up the phone. I'm done.

'I'm sorry, love, but you can call him. There's nothing to stop you talking to him.'

'I already have!' remarks Elise. We've arrived at the school gates and she steps out and slams the door before I can ask her about it. I wave and she walks away. I guess she considers herself too cool to wave back.

There's no time to brood over Dan or anything else for that matter as I need to get ready for my ride with Mark. Sadly, I haven't brought my jodhs which I last wore aged about thirteen when I was tiny, so not a hope of fitting in those again. I remember even Elise, who is pretty slim, peering at the offending garment and asking how on earth I ever fitted in them.

So having rummaged through my sparse wardrobe, I settle for a pair of black leggings, a blue jumper and my Hunter wellies, which at least have a small heel. My old riding hat would be deemed unsafe for anyone to wear these days so I hope Mark might lend me one. The address he has given me is Melstock Manor, but when I arrive, having pootled down spring laden country lanes bursting with buds and wild primroses, I'm totally unprepared for the size of his estate. Impressive would be putting it mildly. I drive through imposing gates with stone eagles, or they might be buzzards, perched either side. The manor house is built from warm pink Devon stone and looms slightly intimidating ahead of me. I follow the drive, past the house and through to a large sweeping circular forecourt the other side. There's a daunting line of jeeps and expensive looking 4x4s parked in the crescent outside the house so I pull up my old Volvo and park as inconspicuously as possible by a large bush.

I climb out and faff with my coat in the hope that someone will come out to meet me, preferably Mark. Unfortunately, no one appears to rescue me so I've no choice but to amble round by myself under an archway into an old-fashioned stable yard.

My heart sinks as I notice Mark, impeccably attired and chiselled as always in his white jodhs and impossibly shiny boots. He is already mounted on the fidgety dark bay he was riding the other day and he is not alone. Next to him is a tall blonde, majestically astride her horse, her long limbs flow into his body, it's as though they are one. Her mount is of course a stunning palomino stallion with a long flowing mane; to be frank they look as though they are about to go on a photo shoot in Country Life Magazine. She's wearing a cream polo neck with matching britches and I wonder how she can keep them that clean when doing anything with animals. Mind you, I get stuff down my front all the time even when I'm nowhere near a horse. Usually chocolate! A couple of spaniels dash and frolic at the horse's hooves, one of them coming up to jump with its hideously muddy paws all over my inadequate Primark leggings. He's a friendly fellow and I pat him gratefully to buy myself some time as at least he is giving me a warm welcome.

'Hello,' I venture.

'Morning!' replies Mark. 'Penny, this is Romilly.

She's the new kid on the block.'

'Good morning?' articulates the blonde goddess speculatively as though a) she's questioning whether it is morning, b) whether it is a good one or not, and more to the point c) whether it is a good morning or not now I have arrived. Personally, although I have only just met her I think c) is the most likely scenario. I advance shyly and shake her proffered gloved hand. There's a bustle as we are joined by a couple of other riders; all well turned out, all obviously used to this as a daily routine. Unlike me.

'Who's she riding?' Penny asks Mark. I'm already summarily dismissed from the conversation.

'Tess,' replied Mark, carefully inserting his leather glove onto his right hand. 'Nina, have you got Tess?'

An attractive young girl who had been surreptitiously sweeping the yard, jumps to attention and rushes off to a nearby stable. 'She's all ready, Mark,' she says returning with a beautiful dapple-grey mare. I like the look of her, elegant and knowing looking. For a fleeting moment however, I panic. I'm not sure I can remember how to get on a horse and I still haven't got a hat. Nina leads the mare to the mounting block which I climb onto in what I hope is a confident manner. I take the reins in my hand, place my foot in the stirrup and lower myself gently into the saddle. So far so good.

'Let's go then,' Mark is obviously keen to be off.

'Erm, I haven't got a hat?' I say anxiously.

'Nina, get Romilly a hat, will you?' Ever keen to please the handsome Mark, Nina lopes effortlessly on her endless long legs back into a nearby tack room and returns with an old battered blue show jumping hat.

'Thanks,' I mutter sheepishly, aware I'm keeping everyone waiting yet again and feeling a complete nuisance. Thank goodness the hat seems to fit, although the strap under the neck is far too loose. I take it off and start to fiddle causing Mark to let out a snort of laughter. 'For God's sake, Nina, give the woman a hand otherwise we'll still be here at Christmas!'

Between us we manage to get the hat fitting reasonably and finally we're off.

Mark leads the way, his horse champing down on the bit, the spaniels giving little yelps of joy as they run through the gate and onto the ornate driveway of the manor. Penny goes after him at an effortless sitting trot as the other men and a lady follow on behind. I give Tess a tentative squeeze with my legs and she moves forward readily, her breath snorting in the cool morning air.

We step out alongside an older gentleman riding a rather stocky horse, and for the first time I look about me. Perhaps it's going to be okay after all. Much like riding a bike, it's all coming back to me and I'm beginning to enjoy this. The feel of the horse under me, her willing step out, her ears are pricked forward; the day begins to feel like an adventure. I wonder if I might just ask her to go forward just a tiny bit, but......oh my God, before I know what's happened, we are off galloping at full tilt, rocket like, towards an outbuilding, past cars, surprised looking grooms and an outraged old gentleman who is fiddling about on the front lawn, 'Watch out!' I cry, as we thunder past, leaving a clear imprint of hoof marks across the immaculate grass.

'What the bloody hell do you think you're doing?' he shouts raucously after me, rather comically waving his fist. Bit cheeky for a gardener, I remember thinking randomly but then I'm unable to think at all. I'm far too busy trying to hold on to the horse. Tess is galloping flat out amongst trees and flower borders; I can do nothing but crouch low over her shoulders desperately hanging on. 'Stop her,' shouts Mark a way off. I can hear him distantly, but the wind catches his voice and snatches it away. I remember vaguely that if a horse bolts, you should sit up, lean back, take a deep breath to slow it down, and increase the weight in the saddle. To be honest, after the roast dinner I ate yesterday evening I would have thought my weight would be more than enough to weigh the mare down. Yet any thought of leaning back vanishes from my mind as Tess bolts under low lying ornamental tree branches. There's simply no question of doing anything but try to hang on and hope for the best.

I'm aware that I'm causing complete chaos and leaving carnage in our wake, kicking up turf, upending flowers and crushing hedges. Gardeners stand back helplessly horrified and I find myself praying we don't come across any obstacles over which Tess feels she may have the need to jump. Finally her pace seems to slacken somewhat as we reach an ornamental pond, or it could have been a lake, my muddled mind can't seem to compute. 'Please, Tess stop,' I call. 'Don't dump me in the lake, it would just be too embarrassing.' Either Tess or a higher entity seems to hear me and as we near the water's edge, she draws to a shaky standstill, her sides heaving and steam rising from her lathered back.

I slump over her shoulders trying to regain my breath and lost nerve. In the distance Mark appears at a fine collected trot proceeding rather incongruously down the garden path. He's followed closely by a disgusted looking Penny, even her horse looks outraged, rather like a Thelwell cartoon. Behind them lopes what looks like a swarm of rebellious yokels with pitch forks, but turns out to be a few seriously unhappy looking gardeners.

'Are you okay?' calls Mark unconcerned.

'Never mind is she okay. It's the poor bloody horse I feel sorry for. I thought you said you'd ridden before?' annunciates Penny superciliously.

'Well, I have many times,' I say, 'but to be fair they were mostly riding school ponies.'

'Bloody amateur!' rebukes Penny. 'You can't get on a top thoroughbred and ride like a thug.' Her words cut and I feel extremely small. I always had light hands, I guess it's because I haven't ridden for so long.

'Actually you did pretty well to sit that gallop and I must say it livened the gardeners up somewhat,' remarks Mark, matter of factly. 'Right, shall we get on with the ride?'

We return through the garden although I'm a shaken bag of nerves. Whatever misplaced confidence I had felt has been replaced by a feeling of anxiety as to what the mare is going to do next. In spite of her flight, she still feels bunched up, muscly like a coiled spring. I wish I could just sneak back to the stables and give the horse back to Nina or whoever is around and run home to the safety of the village and The Coffee Factory. There's no chance however, and beyond the trees and out in the open country we rejoin the other riders who seem to think it best to ignore my earlier antics, for which I am grateful. Yet they don't really speak to me either and I feel terribly out of place. Penny maintains an icy silence, riding daintily with her nose high as though she has a horrible smell under it.

I pat Tess gently on the neck. 'Good girl,' I whisper, in the hope that somehow it might make her behave herself and not take advantage of my nerves. Her skin flinches – it's so thin that you can feel the veins through it, and I long for the thick neck of the reassuringly furry snail-like plodders that I used to complain about at the riding stables for being stubborn and slow. I know from past experience, albeit long ago, that horses can smell fear a mile off. The mare however seems to hear my prayer for the moment and we amble along happily enough through the attractive green countryside. As we climb up the hill, the track becomes narrower and we are soon above the trees and onto open moor. It is picturesque and I gaze in pleasure at the view over heather clad grassland stretching ahead of us for miles. The valleys tumble into deep green folds as though they truly are the land of counterpane, sparkling twisty turning lines which must be streams, run joyfully through the folds. In the distance I can see the tiny toy town of Melstock and beyond it moor clad hills lead down to the cliff and the tumbling sea – the same view I enjoy from The Coffee Factory each day at work but from a different perspective.

'How's about a good gallop then, Mark?' shouts the lumbersome guy I had met at the beginning of the ride, and before I can think or barely shorten my reins we are off. And by off, I mean off! Tess is galloping at full tilt, hooves beating out a sinister rhythm along the sandy moorland path. I hope fervently she is sure footed, as I know even walking along these little lanes it's all too easy to catch your foot. I try not to think about who would look after the girls if I fall off and hurt myself badly. Dust kicks up under our hooves. I've given up trying to pull on the reins. This horse seems to have one speed and one speed only, and no braking system at all.

The other riders up ahead canter on like well-schooled rocking horses, but we speedily gain on them and outpace them instantly. Tess is like a racehorse and we leave them behind as riders and their surprised faces flash past. My heart is in my mouth and I pray fervently we don't come to any more trees. A rider comes alongside. I'm aware of the extra beats of his horse's hooves but I can't look sideways. It's taking all my concentration to stay on the horse, but I recognise his handsome chiselled face and I can feel Mark's presence on the dark bay galloping alongside. He leans across from his horse and grabs Tess's bridle. 'Whoa, Tess, that's a girl,' he says authoritatively. He must be strong or maybe she's just used to his commands as she slows into a canter and gradually we come to a trot.

'Thanks,' I pant heavily at him. Oh God, I must look a sight! My hair has come unstuck under my hat and I bet sweat patches are visible on my jumper after all that hanging on.

'Anytime,' he grins boyishly, and in spite of my recent terror and not for the first time I wonder what it would be like to feel his arms around me. 'But a word of advice...'

'Yes? I think I need some,' I say embarrassed. 'Don't ever get on a horse again?'

'No,' he replies. 'Just go steady with your legs. Event horses aren't used to anyone giving them much encouragement to go forward. They don't need it.'

'Oh,' I reply, about to explain that I've never had a chance to ride a horse like this. You don't when you ride at a stables. Even for that I had to save birthday money and do odd jobs for weeks to pay for a lesson, which might end up being a disappointment because the pony was stubborn and didn't like trotting, or in the group ride there was hardly any room left in the ring to canter. I realise I am wasting my time. These people have practically grown up in the saddle. Riding a horse every day is as natural to them as my going for a walk or making a cup of tea.

Before I can think about replying, the rest of the gang catch us up and we amble steadily towards the stables. I just hope there won't be any more open stretches, but despite a couple of short trots we arrive home without mishap and I remember Mark's advice to keep my legs off Tess' sides. As we cross down from the fields to the stable yard, I notice rather guiltily the flurry of activity across the formal gardens. Men are carefully removing squares of turf and replacing them with new sections, or desperately trying to pat down tufts of torn grass. Other gardeners are attempting to prop up torn and broken climbers from the trellis. It looks a bit like the aftermath of a tornado. I keep my head low and vow to dismount, make my excuses and rush away as fast as I can.

As we approach the stable yard my plan is working. I keep Tess at the back of the riders, meaning to get off, give her to the groom and slink away. I make good my escape, free my feet from the stirrups, and with more luck than judgement manage to swing myself off the horse and to the ground. My feet tremble, as though they are going to give way. I turn to give the reins to a nearby chap who I assume is a groom, when I realise it's the angry gardener from earlier. He snatches the reins from my trembling hand.

'I don't know who taught you to ride, but they should be bloody well horsewhipped!' he ejaculates. I'm too astonished to reply. 'Have you seen the damage you've created in these gardens? Forty years we've worked on that formal parterre, cultivating generations of seed and plants, and in one ill-judged rampage you've trampled the lot. Not to mention the damage you could have caused the poor bugger you were riding.'

'I'm so sorry,' I apologise. 'I haven't ridden for years so I guess I'm a bit rusty...' I falter as I'm not sure where I am going with this.

'Young lady, I suggest you take yourself off my estate and refrain from riding any more poor animals.'

I'm so ridiculously embarrassed. On closer inspection, the old chap's tweedy clothes scream wealth, and his face resembles his son. For this is no gardener, this is Mark's father.

'I'm just so sorry.' I almost bob a curtsey, run to my car, climb in and drive for the gates as fast as I safely can.

'Mind my bloody lawn!' shouts the old tyrant.

For crying out loud! I think I might have put tyre tracks across the corner of the formal grass. I round the corner of the drive and leave in a puff of diesel smoke.

Chapter 9

'Oh my God!' Debs is incapacitated by laughter at my earlier escapade. 'I can't believe it.'

I laugh too, as apart from anything else Debs' rich chuckle is contagious. Even I have to see the funny side now although I can hardly move in spite of the hot bath. All those muscles that are not used to working, ones I didn't even know I had, are all checking in and reminding me vociferously of their presence. I take a sip of the hot sweet tea Debs has kindly made.

'Are you serious? You trounced the lawn of Melstock Manor on your horse and then drove over it with your car for good measure!' Debs is clearly enjoying my embarrassment.

'Erm yes,' I confess, my hysterical laughter releasing all the built up tension from the horrible experience.

'I'd have given good money to see old Pa Whittaker's face. He's a real old duffer.'

'Well, I'll tell you next time I'm going riding and we can sell tickets to the village,' I say sarcastically. 'Tho' I don't think I'll ever be invited round again after that performance.'

Debs dries her eyes, which have been streaming with laughter. 'Have you heard from Mark since?'

'No, funnily enough, though I sent him a text

apologising and offering to pay for the damage. Perhaps I'll have to find another house to rent although we're due to move in at the weekend.'

'I don't think he'll hold it against you,' says Debs, now more serious. 'As you've probably realised, Mark and his family are the local Lords of the Manor. Well, it was a manor until you trashed it!' She starts to laugh again.

'Thanks, Debs. Make me feel worse,' I say sheepishly.

'Yes, but although his Ma and Pa are a bit starchy, Mark has always seemed decent. He opens local charity events and stuff. He's a bit 'la di da,' I guess, but I've always put that down to his upbringing, and his boarding school sounded pretty stuffy. I think he's got a sense of humour in there somewhere.'

'He'll need to have if he hangs out with me for very long,' I laugh.

'He also owns The Coffee Factory, or at least his family do,' Debs says, getting up to pour more water in the pot.

'Oh my God, you're not serious!' I choke on my tea. 'I'm going to be out of a job now too.'

'Yes, you'll be back on the streets!' Debs laughs, then realises I'm actually seriously worried. 'Only joking, kid. He wouldn't do that, and besides I don't think he has much to do with the day to day running of the place.'

I've been pondering whilst scoffing a chocolate biscuit. 'So that *was* him who I saw at the factory getting out of his Bentley on the day of my interview.'

'Probably. He's a bit of a catch actually,' says Debs,

digging me in the ribs with her elbow. 'I should imagine he knows how to give a girl a good time and you could do with some proper wining and dining. Build your confidence up again after a bad experience.'

'Do you mean with Dan, or the horse this morning?' I jest. 'Anyway I'm not sure I'm in his league although, yes, he's pretty cute…'

Debs snorts. 'He's majorly hot, love.'

'True, but reality check, he's not going to be interested in me and especially not after this morning's riding. We haven't got anything in common.'

'Oh, come on. Who needs to have anything in common when he's that cute? What about sheer animal attraction?' Debs asks.

'I'm too old for all that,' I protest. 'Also, I have the girls to consider. They're too stressed out for me to get involved with another guy.'

'Maybe,' but Debs doesn't sound convinced. 'I actually think they could do with a positive male role model after Dan, and you do deserve a life, you know. As well as being a mother, you have the right to get out a bit and have some fun with people your own age.' She catches my eye. 'Or a bit younger.'

'Yes, he's got to be in his thirties. Besides, I'm not sure Elise would approve, not after what I've done to her father. I'm still very much the bad guy,' I say sorrowfully.

'That's because she's hurting. In time she'll understand. Sometimes we only really realise how difficult it is being a parent when we become one ourselves.'

I ponder these wise words of Debs as I meander

back towards the church to pick Summer up at the end of the school day. I stand awkwardly amongst the parents all chit chatting away, waiting at the gate like a stranger in town. I get out my phone and peer at it; at least it makes me look as though I have something to do. Strangely it pings the arrival of a text whilst I am looking at it. I don't recognise the number.

Stop apologising! To be honest, I haven't been so amused for years and it gave us all something to talk about at The Dog and Duck. How about I drop over tomorrow with the key to the cottage and you can move in when you're ready? Also have a van if you need it. Mark. x

That's a relief! I save Mark's name to contacts, thinking that if he can forgive me for what happened yesterday, he must surely be one of the good guys.

'Mum!' Summer comes running towards me; she's the first out. I smile inanely at Mr Barton who nods curtly and I recoil, puzzled. What is this guy's issue? I notice he talks and laughs and is friendly enough with other parents. Bizarre. Maybe he doesn't take well to new people.

I muse over this as Summer skips along next to me chatting happily about the events of the day. 'Summer,' I interrupt casually. 'Do you like Mr Barton? Is he a nice teacher?'

'Oh yes,' she replies. 'He's the best teacher ever. He makes us all laugh.'

'Bit of a joker, hey?' I smile inwardly, not that this is particularly evident I smirk to myself.

'Yes, he's good fun but he does make sure we learn our lessons. Milo Dunstable was being annoying in class the other day and Mr Barton got really angry with him. Milo's been quite well behaved ever since.'

'Oh, I guess that's good,' I say positively. 'Okay, so maybe it's just me he doesn't seem to like.'

'Afternoon,' comes a voice. We're walking down the hill by the stream trickling under arched bridges which leads to the picturesque cottages the other side. Summer runs to peer down into the stream. 'Hello!' she calls politely.

I wander across, and like Summer I lean over the bridge. To my surprise it's Walter, who is immersed up to his knees in the tumbling water.

'Hello, Walter. What on earth are you doing?'

'Just shifting some rocks, m'dear.' Walter bends and hauls a great large rock from one side of the stream to the other.

'Rocks? They're more like boulders!' exclaims Summer, impressed.

'I should be helping you,' I comment, 'but my back hasn't been the best since having the girls.' Then I realise this guy is ninety something and my excuse sounds pretty useless.

'Nonsense. I do this every year, otherwise the stream gets silted up. They're on about this being a flood risk. There's even an evacuation plan so we can all congregate at The Coffee Factory if everything else gets washed away. Blimmin' council. I told them that it won't flood. It hasn't flooded for all the years I've lived here and that's been pretty much a lifetime.' Walter shoves a few smaller rocks to one side for emphasis. 'Anyway, enough of that rubbish. That's me all done now. Who's for a cuppa?'

‘Oh, we couldn’t possibly. Summer has homework and....’

Summer tugs my sleeve. ‘Please, Mum. Is this your cottage, Walter? I’ve always wanted to see inside.’ She hops about from one leg to the other.

Summer’s right. We’ve passed this picturesque cottage many times and discussed wanting to go in. Even Elise loves the look of it. As a child I had a *Dean’s Book of Prayers for Children* with stunning illustrations. My mum used to give it to me to read during the rather long communion services at church. I particularly loved the pictures, although the poems were lovely too. In one, there was an old lady picking flowers in a cottage garden. The cottage was just like Walter’s, with a long low thatched roof, whitewashed stone walls, quaint little barred windows and a cottage garden filled with hollyhocks, rudbeckia and old-fashioned roses. The only thing missing is the tortoiseshell cat.

‘I guess I could text Elise to tell her to come and find us from the bus stop,’ I relent.

‘Of course you can! The wonders of modern technology!’ Walter’s soon up and out of the bed of the stream. He really is incredibly spry for a man of his age. We follow him to the door, which he opens and ushers us in warmly. ‘Just give me a minute. You two sit yourselves down.’

He immediately bustles off, having removed his waders with the help of a bristly hedgehog brush sensibly placed by the door. We are left to admire the spruce and snug little sitting room, a neatly swept fireplace, the newspaper, logs and coal all placed ready for the fire I'm sure Walter will be lighting later. All around the room are little nick nacks but it doesn't feel cluttered. On the sideboard are pictures of a smiley lady with brown curls and lovely laughing eyes. There are other pictures of a young woman with a couple of beautiful children.

I feel conscious I'm intruding, so I sit down on the comfy sofa. It has small white lacey squares where you rest your head and big puffy cushions. Walter rather comically appears from behind a doorway and pokes his head round it. 'I won't be a minute,' he says. Through the open door prowls a tabby cat, fluffy and contented looking.

'Can I stroke him?' asks Summer, immediately getting on the floor.

'I expect so, he seems friendly,' I reply, as the cat obligingly rubs himself along our legs.

Walter returns with a tray of fine bone china cups beautifully laid out with a plate of crumpets. 'I thought we could toast these on the fire,' he announces to Summer's delight.

'But the fire isn't lit,' replies Summer.

'Aha, you noticed! We're going to learn how to make a fire and light it,' says Walter, steadily placing the tray on a low table. 'You be Mother,' he says to me with a smile, 'and pour the tea.'

I duly pour the milk from a dainty little jug into the cups and add the tea. Summer has a frothy cup of milk. Walter, meanwhile, gets Summer to place small sticks in a criss cross pattern across the grate. She then puts scrunched up newspaper and scatters coal over the top. 'Now we light the paper,' Walter says, passing her a box of matches. She gingerly takes one, strikes it and lights a paper, which immediately takes up the flame soon spreading quickly across under the twigs.

'They're not going to light,' says Summer.

'Yes they will,' replies Walter. 'You have to have patience with a fire. It's one of those things that takes time, but it's so worth it.'

Sure enough, the fire soon takes hold and the twigs start to crackle and leap under the hot flames. Once the coal starts to glow, Walter passes Summer a long toasting fork with which she duly prongs a crumpet and places over the flame. We're soon munching away on delicious hot crumpets, dripping with butter until we're interrupted by a knock at the door. 'More visitors,' exclaims Walter, hurrying to answer it. He's totally in his element.

It's Elise. 'Come in, come in,' says Walter, oblivious to her teenage awkwardness and hesitation on the doorstep. Within minutes however, Elise is miraculously happily ensconced toasting a crumpet on the fire with one hand and stroking the cat with the other. A comfortable silence takes over the room; the only sound is the soothing crackling of the fire.

'I love this cottage,' I say to Walter. 'It's absolutely beautiful and a haven of peace and tranquillity.'

'You should be here when the grandkids are down,' laughs Walter. 'It's jolly well total mayhem then.'

'Just as it should be with children around,' I remark. 'How many do you have?'

'Two.' Walter goes and picks up the photos on the dresser – 'This little tyke is Ben and the princess is Nikita.' I look at the smiley little faces in the pictures.

‘They love coming down to stay, especially paddling in the stream,’ remarks Walter. ‘Unfortunately, their mother, my daughter Beth, lives quite a long way away in Cumbria and has a farm to run, so their visits are not as frequent as I’d like.’

‘That’s a shame,’ I empathise, ‘but I guess that makes you all look forward to it even more.’

‘True,’ Walter agrees, ‘and I couldn’t have them here all the time spoiling the tranquillity!’ His eyes become a little misty. ‘When my wife was alive we would drive up to their farm and stay, but since Vera went, I don’t feel like driving quite so far.’

‘I’m sorry,’ I say and I really am. It strikes me for the hundredth time how ironic life is. There are so many elderly ladies sitting around growing old and lonely in nursing homes for want of male company, and yet here’s this vibrant guy who’s now alone.

‘This is her picture.’ Walter passes the image of a smiling lady for me to admire.

‘She looks full of fun,’ I remark.

‘Oh she was,’ replies Walter with a smile. ‘I met her at The Coffee Factory, you know.’

‘Did you? Wow! So you not only worked there, but it was where you met your wife. It must be your lucky place.’

‘It is. There’s a certain magic about it. I can see you look dubious, young lady.’ Walter addresses this to Elise.

‘No,’ she says, surprisingly, ‘In this place I can believe anything. This is the first time I feel like maybe, just maybe, things might just work out. So that must be magic, mustn’t it?’ She blushes after this long speech and retreats back into her task of toasting more crumpets.

'You're quite right, young lady,' Walter nods his head mysteriously. 'Some people don't believe in magic, or in anything else for that matter, and their lives are much the worse for their lack of belief.'

'You mean like believing in Father Christmas and the Tooth Fairy?' asks Summer.

'Well, yes, but not just those two very important characters,' replies Walter, 'but the power of Mother Nature, providence, kindness and God himself.'

'Katie says her dad doesn't believe in any of those,' says Summer sadly.

'Well, I feel sorry for him,' replies Walter. 'Those with no belief in anything make life so much more difficult for themselves.'

I ponder his words as we make our way home, having thanked Walter for his kind hospitality. For once we are united, Elise has even asked to go round again and learn how to weave with willow sticks and Summer wants to take some fish for the cat. As I listen to their happy and unusually harmonious chat as we walk along the lane smelling the coffee and looking out over the beautiful view from the Devon moors tumbling down towards the sea, I can believe in Walter's magic myself.

Chapter 10

I stare dumbly at the piece of paper in front of me. It's all handwritten in black biro, the writing long and sprawling over several pages. It's a letter from Dan, mailed with a stamp. Somehow it reached me via the Melstock Post Office, thanks to good old Phil, or perhaps Jess must have told him where I was living.

'What's that?' asks Summer. This child notices everything!

'Oh, just a letter from my old aunt,' I reply, folding it abruptly.

'I thought she died,' retorts Elise sharply. She doesn't miss a trick either.

'This is my other one, Auntie...erm...Norma,' I reply casually.

'Hmph,' remarks Elise and retreats back into her book.

I need to get out of here to read the letter pronto. I've never been so desperate to read anything in my life.

'I'm just going upstairs to check something,' I say and leg it out of the room with the missive tucked under my jumper. It's been a couple of weeks since we moved into Larkin Cottage and I have to say it's lovely to have some space and privacy in my own room. The floral curtains are a bit disturbing though. I must make a mental note to change them when I can, but I guess they go with the cottagey theme.

I shut the door quietly and curl up on my bed. I don't remember the last time anyone wrote me a letter. It was probably my aunt when I was at uni. I tear open the envelope and take out two large pages of A4. Crikey! He's got more to say than he had for the most part of our marriage.

Dear Rom,

I'm writing this sitting on my own in our kitchen just wondering where it all went wrong. The house feels empty without you all and I know maybe I took you for granted because you were always there, but coming home to a cold dark house has made me realise how warm and cosy you always made it.

(I should think so – I hardly ever went out. I was like a shabby old homely piece of furniture, making sure tea was on the table ready for him when he got in from work. The girls were always doing their homework and I was wrestling with that, cooking at the same time, longing for some adult conversation but none would be forthcoming as Dan would come in tired and grumpy. 'I've been talking to people all day,' he would say tetchily and disappear off upstairs.)

I know I wasn't always grateful, but I guess we all take people for granted when they're easy going. My work, as you know, takes a lot of my time, but I was trying to earn for us to give us all a better life.

(I understand that, but it was a little strange that he always had to be working the occasional time when I needed to be out or whenever the kids were ill, or things were difficult. Then he'd be in the office working every hour he could. But funnily enough, he could take time out to go and visit his parents in the middle of the day or go out to lunch with his mates for several hours at a time.)

And I know I was too tired to go out much but if you come home, we could change all that, it's not too late.

(Yeah right! He wouldn't even agree to a babysitter, so we never got a break and when his mum came round to sit with the girls, I discovered she had been rifling through my wardrobe.)

We have it all, Rom. There's everything here you might need, but I guess you must have been feeling fairly unhappy to just leave like that. Perhaps I didn't pay you enough attention?

(You don't say! I've only been telling him for months and he's been refusing to listen.)

Maybe I was too busy to listen and I'm sorry for that now. But you've made your point, can't you and the girls come back so we could talk it over?

(No, because he didn't want to hear it. Funny how he's happy to talk it over now when I've been saying we need to talk about things for weeks. He kept saying there was nothing wrong.)

I miss them, you know; I know they can be irritating sometimes but perhaps if you'd just been a bit stricter with them when they were little, things might not have got so bad.

(So bad! They're just normal children and are actually a lot better behaved than most. Dan's problem is they don't come with an instruction manual and an on / off button.)

I miss you, Rom. Mum does too. She keeps asking where you are and I've had to tell her now you've been gone so long. I know you feel she doesn't like you but she's very fond of you really. She's just like that with everyone. I told you that before.

(No, that's because I know she doesn't like me. No one with any respect would treat their daughter-in-law the way she does. I know for a fact she doesn't treat Dan's brother Mike's wife like it, so it's bloody well not her way.)

I know you don't like me saying it, but you're a very sensitive person and I do think it makes things difficult for you. But it's one of the many points I like about you. Please come back and talk about things. I promise I can try to change and we can think of a new plan. Perhaps we'll even go and start a new life somewhere new altogether. If nothing else, think of the girls. This is so unsettling for them, their mum having some sort of breakdown and flitting off elsewhere. You've made your point, now please come back. I do love you really, as you know. Dan xxxx

I think about this letter as I drop the girls off at school, as I make coffee and finish the typing at work, and as I get ready for my Zumba class. I don't know how to feel about it at all. I'm just so confused. Maybe he's changed, perhaps I've made my point and now I need to just go home. Yet there are some points in the letter which make me question whether he really has changed. The truth is, I'm not sure he has.

Also, if I am honest with myself I love my life here in Melstock. I know it's early days but I don't know if I want to walk away from it now. To go back...to go back to what? Being at home all day waiting for a pat on the head from a shiny new Dan. He might start off with good intentions and try to appreciate me more, but in time will things just slip back as they were before? More to the point, is it fair to Dan to expect him to be my everything? My entertainment, my solace and conversation? Is it fair to expect that of anyone?

I love my work; I spend the day busy and fulfilled at The Coffee Factory. Ciaran's hilarious, and I have some new ideas I'm just working on, suggestions for marketing which I thought might grow the business further. Walter is a regular visitor and I've grown really fond of him. On Tuesdays the toddler group meets and I love setting up a play area in the corner for the little ones. I'm beginning to know all the mums and I adore watching the babies start to babble and the toddlers begin to toddle. In any unexpected lulls I catch up on paperwork and think of promotional ideas which may just work, such as sample tasting and tours of the factory floor. Thursdays are knit and natter mornings, which Walter likes to refer to as tit and tattle mornings. That's probably true, but I am fond of the group of ladies, even though one or two of them are slightly scary and I did have an incident the other day where one of them tried to attack me with her walking stick. There was a reasonable explanation though. I had noticed her stagger slightly as she was trying to get out of the chair. I had immediately jumped to grab her before she fell over and she had angrily waved her stick at me and accused me of trying to attack her.

'What do you think you're doing, girl?' she had harangued. Miss Melchett was her name.

'Erm, sorry.' I fortunately managed to duck out of the way of her lethal stick. I of course apologised in spite of the fact I hadn't done anything wrong. 'I was worried you were falling.'

'Falling? I've never fallen in my life. Do you realise I'm eighty-seven, girl, and I have no intention of starting to fall now?'

'No, of course not, quite right.' I passed Miss Melchett her bag and gloves, which she snatched away as though I were trying to steal them. I noticed she was still glaring at me as she tottered precariously off down the path outside the factory.

'Don't worry, dearie,' a nice old lady called Doris said, warmly patting me on the shoulder. 'You're doing a fine job. Take no notice of old grumpygrots. She's cantankerous with everyone; we just invite her along in the hope that knitting will help her to become a nicer person.'

I was grateful to Doris and I now look out for her, always passing her an extra cake or muffin. This is a community, they all matter, and besides I feel like we belong here now. More to the point, after Zumba tonight I have something which will certainly take my mind off Dan for a minute. I am finally, after much persuasion from Debs, going to Mark's house for dinner. To be honest, I would far rather have been going to The Pines, the posh hotel and restaurant along the coast but I guess dinner at a manor house will be pretty special. I just hope Penny isn't there, as I don't feel like facing her again after the fiasco on horseback the other day.

Debs had popped round earlier to give me some

extremely necessary wardrobe advice as I was upstairs surrounded by the meagre contents of my cupboard thrown all over the bed.

'Hellooo?' she shouted from the front door.

'Hi, Debs, come on up,' I called down.

'Oh dear, is this what you call organised chaos?' she laughed.

'Erm, yeah maybe,' I laughed back, throwing a pair of trousers at her head. 'I don't know whether I'm coming or going today.'

'Nothing new there then,' replied Debs glibly.

'Thanks. Take a look at this,' I said passing her Dan's letter.

'Oh,' said Debs and sank down on the bed to read.

I fidgeted nervously with bits and rearranged my wardrobe without actually doing anything whilst she read.

'Whew,' Debs exhaled loudly. 'This is heavy.'

'I know, it is a bit.'

'What are you going to do?' she asked.

'I don't know. Maybe nothing.'

'Nothing?'

'Yes, my dad always says if in doubt do nothing and the answer will often come to you,' I said sagely.

'Mmm. I can see his point, although doesn't that also qualify as burying your head in the sand?' asked Debs.

'Probably,' I said, 'but in all seriousness, I don't know what to think.'

'Well it's quite simple,' she replied. 'Do you still love him?'

I stop what I am doing abruptly to ponder. 'No,

though I don't know. Maybe a little?'

'You don't sound very sure.'

'No, because I'm not sure anyone who loves someone should treat them the way Dan did, however sorry he is now,' I said slowly.

'Wow, that's the first sensible thing you've spoken about Dan since I've met you. I think this place might be curing you.'

'Also,' I smiled at her, 'maybe I am improving as I love it here. There's you and The Coffee Factory, Tania and the girls at Zumba, Molly, Phil and Alexandrine, Walter...'

'Don't! You're going to make me all emotional,' Debs wiped her eye dramatically, but I think it did look a little teary actually. I love these people; they've been here for me during one of the biggest crises of my life.

'Do you think he's changed?' I asked, moving on quickly before I started blubbing.

'Do you want the honest answer, or the one you'd like to hear?'

'The honest answer,' I replied after a slight pause.

'No,' she said simply, and I think she's right even though my stupid stomach betrayed me by lurching slightly with a disappointment it had no right to feel.

We then moved on from a subject I didn't want to even think about any more, and I tucked the letter away at the bottom of the cupboard. If only it would be so easy for me to stop thinking about it.

After some consideration and throwing more clothes about, I decide on a simple little dress which I bought from Monsoon years ago. It's dark blue with tiny flowers and teams very nicely with high heeled ankle boots and though it sits above the knee, I don't think it's too short.

'You'll do very nicely,' Debs says admiringly. 'Now off you go and don't forget to come home before midnight otherwise you might turn into a pumpkin.'

'Huh!' I reply and stalk out into the night to the smooth elegance of Mark's Bentley and a world I'm not sure how to inhabit.

Chapter 11

I must admit Melstock Manor is an impressive building. I try to dismiss any remembrance of the antics of the other day regarding the dreaded lawn and notice with relief that there are no longer signs of any damage to its manicured brilliance. I smile across at Mark nervously, partly because to be frank, his driving is fast and has made me feel a bit anxious. This has been further agitated by the announcement of the fact we'll be dining with his parents this evening.

'But your father will still be angry after the lawn incident,' I protest.

'Nonsense. He'll have forgotten about that by now,' laughs Mark.

I'm not so convinced. The memory of his angry florid face glaring up at me whilst on the back of a stampeding horse makes me feel hot and cold all over. I try to focus on being someone else. That's the advice my mother always gave me. 'Imagine being an actress. You're simply playing a part,' she'd always say. It's surprisingly good advice actually because whilst pretending to be anyone other than yourself, you forget your own silly thoughts and worries. Well, that's the idea anyway.

I bear this in mind as I alight on the driveway. Mark saunters round and opens my door for me. Nice.

A butler comes to the large oak door.

'Good evening, Madam,' he intones solemnly.

'Good evening,' I reply, breezing in effortlessly as though I have butlers opening doors for me all the time. The effect is slightly marred by the fact I trip on the doorstep. Flipping old buildings! Why do they always have uneven flagstones?

'Are you alright?' asks Mark, concerned.

'Yes, yes,' I brush his politeness aside as this is ruining my gracious acting.

I follow him into a spacious lounge with ancient, battered sofas and a fat smelly old Labrador who mooches towards me. To be honest, sometimes Labradors are my nemesis because they always seem to sniff your crotch somewhat embarrassingly, and this one is no exception. What is it with them? It's always Labradors, never any other breed of dog. Some are lovely and never do it, but this one is particularly persistent. I try to stroke him and look suitably dog lover-ish whilst surreptitiously pushing him away. This is definitely a test of my performance skills. I bet Emma Thompson never had to cope with these sorts of situations.

'Evening, Mummy!' I look up abruptly from my machinations to try to keep the dog away from my skirt, and notice an older lady reclining on a chair by the fire. Mark goes across and kisses her leathery cheek. She is certainly one of those women who ride hard to hounds, weather beaten, tanned skin, vivid auburn hair snatched back angrily into a severe ponytail. She's wearing jodhs, the old-fashioned baggy variety which would have looked at home in a

Josephine Pullein-Thompson book and a tweed jacket. I feel horribly overdressed and wish I'd gone for a Kate Middleton country casual look. Not that I have anything vaguely like this in my wardrobe, I couldn't afford it and besides, I'm several dress sizes bigger than Kate. I step forward to receive a hearty handshake.

'This is Romilly, Mother!' Mark introduces me casually.

'Oh!' replies Ma Whittaker. I'm not quite sure how to take this, but I do have a pretty good idea.

I remind myself firmly I'm playing a part, so I smile and act as though she has given me the greatest compliment. 'Good evening, Lady Whittaker.' Darn it, this acting thing isn't working. I feel like the poor heroine of Rebecca meeting Mrs Danvers.

Lady Whittaker's smile doesn't quite manage to reach her eyes. 'Call me Mary,' she replies, but I wish I didn't have to. Lady Whittaker keeps her at a safer distance.

'Monty! Monty! Give over boy.' Mark seems to have finally noticed I'm struggling with the Labrador's over enthusiastic attention which has now developed into full blown leg mounting and is wreaking havoc with my tights.

'Monty, come here!' bawls Mary, and the dog slinks instantly like a black shadow back to the basket in the corner of the room. The volume of her hearty shout makes me jump about twenty feet into the air, betraying the state of my nerves. I guess she's used to hollering for miles over good ground. Mark seems oblivious to any of this of course.

'Where's Daddy?' he asks, which seems a bit

incongruous at his age. I mean, he's not a five year old boy. Obviously it's a class thing I've read in novels but never heard it used in real life until now.

'He's just coming down, darling. Had a problem with the pheasant.' Mary pats the sofa next to her. 'Come and sit down, Mark and you too, Bromwyn, was it?'

'Romilly,' I say patiently.

'Oh, unusual name,' the tone in which Mary says this implies that she hates it. 'Do you hunt, Romilly?' She rolls the 'r' at the beginning of my name in an emphatic manner.

'Erm no, I have ridden, but I'm a bit rusty this days.' I meet Mark's satirical eye and stop abruptly.

My answer is obviously not even worthy of a reply, so Mary opens a copy of *Horse and Hound* and proceeds to discuss the local hounds page in detail with Mark. I half-heartedly pick up a copy and start to flick through it. It doesn't really appeal to be honest. There's plenty of pictures of hounds and some horses, but I prefer *Your Horse* or *Rider Magazine* with their interesting images of beautiful horses and fabulous jodhs and shoes, which I imagine buying if I had loads of money and a valuable horse. Oh, and an amazing figure like the models in the magazine. I'm beginning to feel a bit bored and restless actually and am almost relieved when an interruption occurs in the form of an older gentleman pootling in, until I realise with misgiving it's Mark's dad.

'What's this, guests?' he mumbles, throwing down the paper in his hand to peer at me short-sightedly through his glasses. At least I hope he is short sighted because it suspiciously looks like he is peering at my legs like an old lech.

I get up politely to shake hands and wish I hadn't, as his is slightly sweaty and unpleasant. 'You a local gal?' he asks, his breath reeking of whisky. He is wearing moleskin breeches and rather comical yellow stockings in the style of Malvolio in *Twelfth Night*.

'No, I've just moved into the area,' I say.

'You know that, Daddy,' remarks Mark impatiently. 'Romilly's renting Larkin Cottage.'

'What? Oh, yes,' replies Pa Whittaker, throwing himself down in the chair with a grunt.

'You a riding to hounds kind of gal?' he mutters at me, swigging from a glass. He's obviously partial to a wee dram or several.

'No, not really. More of an amateur, a dabbler.' A dabbler, what am I on about? I sound like a moorhen.

I smile anxiously at Mark, willing him not to give me away.

'Romilly was riding here last week, Daddy,' Mark says.

Oops, that's blown it; telepathy with Mark obviously doesn't work then.

'Good God!' blusters Pa Whittaker, heaving himself upright in his chair in outrage. 'Bloody nightmare that was, bally lawns only just recovered.' I'm momentarily fascinated by a tiny bit of saliva hanging delicately on his chin.

I shift awkwardly in my seat. 'I'm most terribly sorry, Mr... Erm, Lord Whittaker, it's just the horse...'

'Only the worst riders blame the horse,' blusters Pa Whittaker.

'Quite right,' chips in his wife who until now was totally engrossed in *Horse and Hound*. 'Terrible fault that, blaming a poor innocent creature for one's own ineptitude. Bloody bad horsemanship.'

Thank God, at that moment the door opens and the butler shimmies in, 'Dinner is served.'

Mark offers his arm to his mother and escorts her out through the door, grinning at me over his shoulder. I begin to wonder if this is some kind of initiation ceremony. It's an endurance test, that's for sure.

I stand awkwardly, wondering if I'm supposed to follow or not when the butler kindly points me in the right direction. 'If you'd like to follow me, Madam?' I mooch after him, still feeling incredibly out of place in my high street dress and boots, followed by a still muttering Pa Whittaker who appears to be addressing his whisky glass with expletives about rubbish riding and spilling most of it on the carpet on his travels.

The dining room is formally laid with a long dark oak table; the walls and ceiling are panelled, giving the room a rather dark and heavy feel. At intermittent spaces are the heads of some poor unfortunate creatures who obviously ended up at the wrong end of a hunter or some hounds. I try not to look at them and fortunately am placed with my back to a stuffed fox who has a particularly malevolent sneer, perhaps unsurprising considering the indignity of what happened to him.

I take my place, which turns out to my dismay to be next to Pa Whittaker, with Mark the other side of me and Ma Whittaker opposite.

'What a shame Penny had to return to London, eh?'

remarks Ma Whittaker. My hackles rise instantly. Blimmin' Penny. I'd taken an instant dislike to this particularly sneery paragon of country pursuits.

Mark, however, appears unperturbed. 'Yes, but she's back at the weekend. We thought we might ride out over Spenmoor.'

'Nice idea. You could take Nero with you. He's due a good run and I think that slight lameness has cleared up,' Ma Whittaker continues. I'm lost in thought. So I'm not here as Mark's date. Penny's the family favourite. Why am I invited then? His parents obviously don't like me. What on earth am I doing here? I suppose he feels sorry for me, the new woman in town left without a man. How embarrassing, now I feel like a spare part that everyone feels sorry for, but no one really wants to go out with.

The butler returns with steaming plates of something which looks rather like a small bird, a mound of reassuringly tasty looking mashed potato and some veggies. I don't like to ask what it is, but pick up my knife and fork ready for battle. Think actress, Romilly. I tackle the mash first because it seems safest, and indeed on closer inspection the tiny bird is pretty much inedible. I pick at it delicately, but only miniscule bits come off and I can't help feeling it would be more satisfying and less pretentious to eat chicken.

'Romilly's working at The Coffee Factory,' announces Mark munching loudly.

'Oh?' piped up Pa Whittaker. 'Serve the teas, do you, eh?'

'Erm yes, amongst other things. I also help out with marketing and paperwork,' I reply.

Mark smiles at me, flashing a glimpse of his perfect white teeth. 'Romilly is a very enthusiastic kind of person, just what we need at the factory.'

'Huh. Well, as long as she doesn't keep all the customers chatting. Some of the old people don't seem to have a home to go to, and it's no good if they spend half the day over one cup of coffee,' states Ma Whittaker.

'They're very sweet actually,' I say, 'and many of them have been coming for years. They're part of the furniture.'

Ma Whittaker looks doubtful and her husband slurps noisily at his red wine, muttering something noncommittal which sounds suspiciously like, 'sentimental rot' but I could be mistaken.

'More to the point, Romilly is suggesting ways to increase profit. You have a background in marketing, don't you?' Mark asks.

'Yes, absolutely! I've lots of ideas on how to spread the word about Melstock's famous coffee factory,' I add, glad to be able to talk about anything I know vaguely something about.

Pa Whittaker stares at me blearily, then drains his glass of wine. 'Everyone who's anyone already knows about Melstock's finest coffee. I don't know where you come from, m'dear, but we do things differently round here. None of this highfalutin, new-fangled market what not. It's who you know, not what you know in this life.' He taps his substantial nose with a hoary finger, 'Now that Penny, she knows...'

'Some more wine for my father,' interrupts Mark. 'Daddy, you were going to tell me about the plans you have for the training ring outside.'

Pa Whittaker is distracted by his son's interruption and I feel momentarily grateful to him. Not for inviting me this evening, however. I just don't seem to be able to manage one topic of conversation that actually works. Both the Whittakers are onto me, recognising a stranger in town and hate me for it. I try to engage Ma Whittaker in a discussion about her horse training. Apparently she breeds eventers so this is a subject in which she excels.

'Melstock Manor produces some of the finest horses you will find in the western world,' she boasts. 'We often export throughout Europe and even as far as Dubai.'

'That's amazing,' I bluster, desperately hoping that dinner will soon come to an end. Unfortunately it just gets worse. The butler clears the plates and serves the port as we have by now finished dessert. I sip mine in a ladylike manner but it's quite nice actually and I'm tempted to slug it down in an attempt to block out the hideous company, when to my horror I feel a hot and sweaty hand on my left thigh. It must belong to Pa Whittaker who appears to still be deep in conversation with Mark about the new arena but is obviously feeling up my leg. Who said men can't multitask? Dirty old man. I shift uncomfortably in my seat. I mean, what do you do when in polite company and some moron is surreptitiously acting like a pervert? In fact, I do what any self-respecting lady does. I bring my solid boot heel down firmly on Pa Whittaker's toe.

'Ow,' he exclaims loudly, his already florid face turning puce.

‘Are you alright, Daddy?’ asks Mark, concerned. Ma Whittaker breaks off mid-sentence from her rant about the only way to corner a pregnant filly with a randy stallion and glares at me suspiciously. This is all too much for me. I jump up abruptly. ‘I must go and powder my nose,’ I say breathlessly and leave the room.

‘Powder her nose?’ I hear the dulcet tones of Ma Whittaker float into the hallway. ‘Who does she think she is, the Duchess of Sussex?’

I don’t hang around to reply, but blunder about looking for a toilet. There’s a billiard room which I discount immediately, a sort of study, all in dark leather. I don’t like to ascend the large sweeping staircase as it feels like bad manners to go upstairs in someone else’s house without permission. So I wander on round the corner into what seems to be a flagstone kitchen with a couple of elderly members of staff bustling around on food prep, washing up and cleaning the floor.

‘I’m so sorry,’ I apologise to their surprised faces. Okay, so I’m going to have to go upstairs after all.

At the top of the steps I find a large, panelled bathroom and gratefully lock the door and sink onto a nearby chair. Yes, it’s big enough to have a chair, a washstand, a bidet and a table with some dusty flowers on it. I mean who has a toilet that big? This would do as a bedroom in our house.

A few minutes later I return to the dining room slightly refreshed, to find that no one seems to have batted an eyelid and the conversation remains pretty much the same, except now they’re discussing the next hunt meeting.

'I presume Percy will be there. I'm relying on catching up with him this month,' mutters Pa Whittaker, who for the moment at least, thank goodness, appears to be keeping his hands to himself.

I feel like interrupting with 'Who's Percy?' because we all know there's nothing more boring than whole evenings of inane chat about people you don't know or care about.

Fortunately Mark comes to my rescue. 'Percy is Penny's father. He's Master of Hounds.'

'Oh, that's nice,' I reply inanely. How jolly dee and comfortable it is for these people who all know each other. 'Have you known them long?'

'What? Ginny and Percy? Known them for years, old hunting stock, don't you know?' Mary is faintly scornful.

Thank goodness the evening drags to an uneasy conclusion and I am so grateful I find myself genuinely thanking the Whittakers for a pleasant evening. I would win an Oscar for my acting. Well perhaps not; they don't look particularly convinced, to be fair.

'Quick walk through the stables before we go?' asks Mark, 'I always do the rounds at this time of night.'

'That would be nice,' I reply. I could do with some air after that ordeal.

Mark lends me his old leather jacket and I snuggle in it, appreciating the smell of his aftershave and its solidity over my flimsy dress. As we walk, to my surprise he takes my hand and I enjoy the feel of its warmth as the evening is fresh. We wander amongst the stables and Mark pats and talks to each horse in a low undertone. He obviously loves his animals; that's for sure. In fact, he seems far more tender to them than his fellow humans. We wander companionably back down the path along the meadow.

'Did you enjoy your evening?' he asks.

'Yes, it was lovely, thank you,' I lie admirably.

'You're adorable,' he smiles, and taking my chin in his hand he draws me to him and places his lips on mine. He has a delicate grazing of stubble, which brushes my skin and I snuggle into his height enjoying the feeling of his hard tight muscles. Hmm! Surprising, but pleasant, and whether it means anything or not it is a wonderful end to a pretty hideous day.

Chapter 12

'Oh my God!' I duck quickly into the doorway of a nearby boutique.

'Are you alright, dear?' asks a concerned voice. I peer at her vaguely. It's Doris, the lovely old lady from Knit and Natter.

'Yes. No, I mean I'm not sure,' I stammer.

'You don't look alright,' she says worriedly. 'Do you want to take my arm? You're a little pale.'

I brush aside any amusement at the irony of an eighty something year old woman offering to help me along the road.

'Thanks, Doris.' I recollect myself. 'I'll be fine, just feeling a little fuzzy, must be my hormones.'

'Ooh, I know what you mean, dearie. I had a terrible time at your age, but don't worry, it'll only last a few years and then you'll be right as rain. I found taking black cohosh worked quite well. Full of good things, you know.'

'Oh, right.' I still feel a little odd. Doris continues to chat about her various hideous sounding menopausal sufferings as we wander down the road. I think I might be a bit young for all this yet, but don't bother arguing as she means well.

Thank goodness she spots another acquaintance outside the Post Office and I manage to dash inside, making polite excuses all the while. I sit numbly on a little chair meant for customers trying on walking boots, carefully hidden behind some coats. I still feel quite shaky because I thought I saw – Well, I mean, I'm sure it was, even though it couldn't have been. You see, I thought I saw Dan's mother walking down the high street. The natty Yves St Laurent fitted coat; the immaculate hair, the 'v' shaped outline. It sure had looked like her, but I must have been mistaken. It's all probably been a bit much.

'Hello, love.' Phil peers at me amusedly from behind a pile of 'North Face' anoraks.

'Hi, Phil. Just resting my legs a moment,' I say casually, instantly leaping to my feet as though they have suddenly miraculously recovered. 'I popped in to thank you for redirecting my letter.'

'Oh, no probs at all. Hope it brought you some luck,' he smiles wryly.

'Mmm not really,' I say briskly, 'but you can't win 'em all.'

'You can't win anything these days.' Alexandrine appears wielding a pile of bank statements and a calculator.

'Hi, Alexandrine. That looks like a fun job,' I remark glibly, feeling much better now I'm with my friends. Vanessa, my mother-in-law, must have been a figment of my imagination. 'A touch of indigestion' as Scrooge said to the ghost in *A Christmas Carol*.

'Not really, but it has to be done.' She returns to the desk where Tania from Zumba is waiting to cash some cheques. She looks amazing as always, her blonde hair shiny and immaculate in its high ponytail. Her daughter, Lila, smiles at me shyly.

'Coming on Tuesday?' Tania asks me enthusiastically.

'Can't wait,' I reply. 'It's my weekly de-stress. In fact, Elise begs me to go as she says I'm foul if I don't!'

'Teenagers!' laughs Tania. 'Don't we just love them?' Lila gives her a look.

'Most of the time,' I smile wryly.

After a few moments more small talk, I say my goodbyes and meander back along the road towards the cottage. I have just enough time for a quick tidy round before going to pick Summer up from school. Until the suspected imaginary sighting of my dreaded mother-in-law I had been feeling quite good after my stolen moonlight kiss. I have to say it awakened emotions I thought had long disappeared and feeling Mark's strong arms around me, whilst being surrounded by the comforting sounds of horses contentedly munching and pulling on their hay racks, was total bliss. I wonder when I'll see him again.

As I meander along, lost in *Riders'* style fantasies of frolicking in the hay, I am suddenly struck with horror at the sight of my mother-in-law in my front garden picking the heads off a couple of recalcitrant daffodils. She witnesses my approach with a slightly surprised smile, which is laughable considering she must know this is where I'm living. Even I can't have eaten enough food to cause this kind of indigestion.

'Ah, Romilly!' she comments in her understated manner. 'There you are.' Her tone makes it sound as though we've been playing some kind of impromptu game of hide and seek, which I guess we have rather, but one in which I didn't know I was taking part.

'Yes, hello, Vanessa!' I bluster heartily as though it's every day you bump into your mother-in-law in the garden of the cottage you're renting after having left her son and taken her two grandchildren with you. There's a silence. God, this is awkward. She casually passes me the two dead daffodil heads. 'Have you got somewhere to put these?' she breezes. I stare at the crushed petals in my hand; of course I had automatically taken them. Somehow their sorry appearance reflects the reality of the situation.

'Would you like to come in?' I ask between gritted teeth, meaning the exact opposite as I turn the key in the lock, hurriedly splitting the stable style front door to let extra air in. Goodness only knows what state I left the house in this morning.

'Rather!' she doesn't need asking twice and is straight into the front room before I can even put down the key. 'What a darling little room, must be awfully small for you all though.'

'Yes, it's compact.' I busy myself by sweeping drying washing from the radiators, now as stiff as cardboard. I really miss the luxury of the tumble drier from the days of Dan, and shove the laundry down the back of the sofa whilst Vanessa is distracted trying to sideways read a couple of cards on the mantelpiece. I'm sure I can grab the washing out again later. I try to distract myself by flicking on the kettle. 'Cup of tea, Vanessa?'

'No thanks.' Vanessa delicately wrinkles her nose, managing to give the impression she wouldn't dream of drinking anything in this house. 'I've just had one.'

'Are you staying nearby then?' I ask tentatively. Please God, don't let her want to stay here. I really can't face it, but am bound to enquire by my annoyingly courteous upbringing and constant people-pleasing need to be courteous.

'Oh no,' she replies too quickly for politeness. I heave a sigh of relief. 'I'm staying at the Mannerton-Smythes'. Do you remember them?' Vanessa always knows everyone who is anyone as long as they are someone important, and I never have any clue who on earth she is talking about because I just don't mix in those kinds of circles. In fact, thinking about it, I don't mix in any circles at all.

'No,' I reply. 'Are they local?'

'Oh yes, they live at Smitherton Manor at Bramstock. You must know the Mannerton-Smythes; they've lived here for years. Beautiful estate, twenty acres; self-contained golf course; twelve bedrooms, terribly grand, used to be in power boats, you know. Anthony's out playing golf with Richard Mannerton-Smythe.'

'How nice,' I say, more enthusiastically than I feel. 'Are you staying with them for long?'

'Oh, probably a few days this time,' Vanessa replies vaguely while disappearing up the stairs. This is one of my pet hates about Vanessa. She has no manners. 'Just off to use your loo,' she calls glibly in her horribly tootling tones.

Huh! And going to have a good sneak round upstairs, I think. I'll never forget the time she came to visit when Dan and I were together and I happened to pop upstairs for something, opened the door to our en suite and out she walked as cool as a cucumber (I never did understand that saying, are cucumbers particularly cool?) To be fair, she did have the grace to appear slightly embarrassed, but the way she had trilled, 'Oh hello?' in a questioning tone, as though it was the last place she expected to see me, was most comical. In any case, as I had said to Dan, 'What the heck was she doing in there?'

'Using the loo,' Dan had replied, unconcerned. He always was bloody unconcerned or disinterested when it came to his mother's motives.

'But we have an upstairs family bathroom. She could have gone in there,' I had protested.

'I expect one of the girls was in it,' he had said simply.

'But they weren't,' I had continued. I checked.

But Dan wouldn't have it. I always thought she was like a female dog. No, I don't mean in the way you're thinking, although maybe that too, but I mean from the point of view of marking her territory even when it is someone else's.

I nip upstairs to check the girl's bedrooms quickly in case Vanessa decides to have a look in. On the way, I pass the loo door and as I glance, 'Oh Sorry!' God, how embarrassing! I look away instantly horrified at the sight and scurry into the refuge that is my bedroom.

My mother-in-law is sitting on the loo with the door wide open. Why on earth didn't she shut the door? We have a lock, for goodness' sake. She really does get weirder by the minute. I take a moment to brush my ruffled hair, but it's no use. I still look as though I've been rummaging about in the bushes. I wish I had been. Thinking back to Mark, it would be a very pleasant way to spend the afternoon. Much more fun than hanging out with Vanessa, but this seems to be the story of my life. There really is no escape.

I troop back down the stairs, having listened carefully to make sure Vanessa has safely vacated the toilet. Typically of her, there is no reaction or comment about what just happened at all, nada, nothing. Mind you, at least this sticking to type is reassuring; it saves me the emotional stress of thinking she might be a normal person after all.

'Right. Well, if you'll excuse me, I'm just off to pick up Summer from school,' I say in a rather fake upbeat manner, hoping Vanessa will just pop off back to the Smetherton Pikes or whatever their name was.

'Oh, she's in school then?' asks Vanessa, surprised, her thickly pencilled eyebrows rising incredulously into her hair, vehemently reinforcing her disbelief. 'Does she like it?' She makes it sound most unlikely that she does.

'Oh yes,' I reply glibly. 'She's made some good friends and it's a lovely little school.'

'How nice,' she replies unconvincingly, and to my horror adds, 'I'll come along. Anthony won't have finished playing golf yet and I'll still be back to join them for a G and T afterwards.'

'How nice,' I say meaning the exact opposite, but there's absolutely nothing I can do about it, so I grab my jacket and lead the way out of the door. Vanessa follows me silent, but deadly. The air between us crackles with unspoken resentment. I feel rather like an amateur surfer waiting for a huge wave to crash over my head. I know it's coming and I'm dreading it. In fact, I hate atmospheres. I guess that's what finally finished it with Dan; his constant sulking, his avoidance of the nub of the matter, I just couldn't stand the waiting. Give me a good old row any day, clear the air and then move on. Dark brooding storm clouds and tense atmospheres make me feel downright anxious.

We meander along the lane, every pore of my being resenting Vanessa's presence in this, my place of safety. It feels as though she's polluting it with everything that was wrong in my life and it's seeping back in.

'Nice little church,' she comments, 'but the prices in the shops are ridiculous. I suppose you drive into Billinghurst or Stamforth to the supermarket.'

'Not if I can help it,' I remark. 'I try to support the local shops as they need our custom. I also prefer individual products.'

'Yes, you always did have expensive taste.' Vanessa says the words as always pleasantly enough with a smile on her face, but they sting like lemon in a paper cut. All the old wounds remain red raw.

Vanessa wears darling little outfits, which are obviously designer but has convinced Dan she's extremely economical with her clothes.

'My mother's very thrifty,' he always said proudly.

When I first met him I had been naïvely puzzled, as Vanessa's clothes were so obviously better quality than anything anyone I knew had ever worn. She had been a debutante back in her day, for goodness' sake. Later, on closer inspection, I realised that they were designer. Yes, I did try to look at the label on a jacket she left on the hook in our hall, but she had cut it out. I mean who does something like that? Why would you bother? And who cares in any case? Many of us like clothes, so why pretend we don't?

‘Another new outfit?’ she would remark when I went round for dinner with Dan. ‘She does like her clothes, doesn't she?’ she would prod at Dan. To be fair, I love clothes but they’re from Primani as we love to call it, or New Look and cost about a quarter of one of her shirts from whichever designer she uses. Dan would never believe me though.

‘My mother never spends much on clothes. She’s far too frugal for that,’ he would insist. ‘You must be mistaken.’

If I pushed it, in my fury providing evidence (I mean how petty is that arguing over someone’s mother’s clothes?) he would say blithely, ‘Well, all you women are so manipulative and cunning.’

‘But I’m not,’ I would insist. ‘I’m really not,’ but he would simply smile inanely and wander off. Once the three of us went shopping in London. Vanessa and Dan both bought designer shoes, and I bought ... precisely nothing, but it didn't dispel the myth that I was extravagant and Vanessa wasn't. She’d spent so many years pretending she never spent anything on clothes and telling everyone how economical she was, that she had pretty much brainwashed everyone into believing it was true.

It’s a funny phenomenon this. I remember working as a temp in a company where I sat opposite a young woman who would constantly sigh over her work, ‘Oh dear, I’ve a terrible amount to do today. Right,’ she would sigh heavily, ‘where shall I start?’ She would rustle bits of paper busily and huff and fuss. And another time, 'Right, this bit's done. I'm not sure I'm going to manage to get through this pile till late. Dear me.'

I presumed, even though we were both secretaries, that she must have a higher profile job with heavier responsibilities than mine. That was until I was asked to cover her annual leave for a couple of weeks. I was amazed to find the role was no different from my own. I whizzed through the work which was all perfectly manageable, but from the way she had always huffed and puffed and moaned and groaned, I thought it must be a difficult and heavy position to manage. It just goes to show, we all believe what we're told half the time. Perhaps I should try it. Life for some people is just one big PR stunt. Trouble is I'm so busy trying to cope with firefighting, I don't think I've enough time to try to pretend to be something I'm not.

Right now however, I'm too caught up with trying to think how I'm going to ditch Vanessa.

We arrive in the school playground and I notice the other parents looking at her curiously. Perhaps Vanessa's helped me move a few notches higher in the smart mother's brigade. She does at least look as though she gives some kind of damn about what she looks like. As soon as the posh mothers notice she's with me however, they look away again, disinterested. I long for the support of Debs' friendly face and sense of humour, but she doesn't seem to be picking up tonight. Nor does Tania. Stupidly, in front of Vanessa I want to look like the most popular kid in the playground, but unfortunately I'm looking more like Norman no mates.

After what seems like forever, the school door opens and the children start streaming out. The little ones always appear first, waddling along, looking cute but exhausted in their overly large uniforms.

'Oh, is that Summer?' remarks Vanessa. 'I really wouldn't recognise her now. I haven't seen the girls for *such* a long time.' She spits out the 'such' with venomous emphasis.

I squash down my usual feeling of guilt mixed with anger as I'm a nice person really and I never wanted to keep the kids from her. I mean, she did see them a couple of weeks ago, and I did try to let her have them, but she always did the opposite of what I asked, had absolutely no qualms about leaving a child unattended in a large store even if they were only little, and spoilt and fussed them until they came home sick and ill. Later, when they were older she would make unpleasant remarks which they repeated to me, as you can imagine.

The kid she is rather embarrassingly pointing at looks nothing like Summer as she has short dark hair. Vanessa is oblivious however and starts walking towards her. Good grief, at this rate she'll be had up for trying to snatch someone's child.

'Vanessa,' I call. 'That's not Summer.'

'Goodness me,' she says, abruptly stopping in her tracks. 'Well, it has been too long. Oh, here she is,' she coos, her voice changing immediately from the terse note it had contained. 'Hello, darling.'

Summer comes stumbling towards us and I can tell immediately that something's up. She has that stoical look that she sometimes cultivates when she's trying not to cry in front of others. She had that expression when the vet said her gerbil had to be put down. I had been sitting there with tears streaming down my face and Summer said with that exact look on her face, ‘Can’t you keep it in, Mummy? You can cry when you get to the car?’ I know, totally embarrassing. My only excuse is that since having children my emotions seem to be all over the place.

‘Hello, sweetheart,’ I say brightly, hoping she’s able to keep the act up.

She doesn't. She just manages to blurt, ‘Mum, Mr Barton wants to speak to you,’ before starting to cry.

‘Oh dear. Are you not very happy at this school, darling? It must be so difficult.’ Vanessa puts her arm round Summer and starts to steer her towards the gate, leaving me stumbling behind them. I try to talk to her, but she interrupts, waving her arm at me dismissively. ‘Off you go, Mummy, and talk to the teacher. I’ll look after Summer.’

I’m left looking after them dumbly and then realise that several parents are staring. Oh great, and Mr Barton is such a fan of mine too – not. I meander reluctantly back to the school reception area, and brave the harridan sitting there. This reminds me of how my own mum had to cope with parents’ evenings, when I probably hadn’t been doing what I should, and that’s putting it mildly. Whoever invented the expression ‘What comes around, goes around,’ really had a point.

‘I need to speak to Mr Barton, please?’ I tell Mrs Klebb at the desk.

‘Is he expecting you?’ asks Mrs Klebb. I don't know why, but sometimes school secretaries and doctor’s receptionists can be veritable Rottweilers. The power of holding the diary just seems to go to their heads and that's it. They probably start off as really nice, sweet natured people but end up power crazed and officious. Mrs Klebb is no exception to this rule. 'I really don't think it will be possible without an appointment,' she adds. I wonder idly if she has a flick blade in her shoe, true to her namesake in the Bond movie and I resist the temptation to peer over the desk to check out her footwear.

'Well, apparently, he's asked to see me,' I say as politely as possible. No point in annoying this woman. We're in enough trouble as it is. Also I'm secretly a little scared of her. James Bond has a great deal to answer for.

'Oh,' snaps Mrs Klebb, looking absolutely disgusted. She might as well say, 'It's like that, is it?'

Fortunately, at that moment I'm rescued by Mr Barton appearing round the corner from the school hall.

'Oh, here he is!' I exclaim in a falsely bright tone, accidentally smiling far more than the occasion demands.

Mr Barton glances across and does not seem to be in a good mood. 'Mrs Greene?' It's a statement of fact and not a welcoming one. I follow him silently, picking up on and further flattened by his tone.

He leads the way into a classroom with bright light shining in from the windows, the walls scattered with rainbow fish; one of my favourite stories incidentally. He motions me to sit down at a table and I do so, belatedly realising I'm squatting on a small child's chair, one of those plastic ones I haven't sat on since I was little. 'I hope I can get out of this again afterwards,' I quip before I can stop myself.

'Sorry?' snaps Mr Barton.

'Erm, nothing,' I say politely, but feeling like a rebuked child. Stop it Romilly, act your age.

'Right. Well, I expect you've realised I've asked you in to talk about Summer.' Mr Barton does not beat about the bush.

I am momentarily distracted by his long brown hair which falls floppily over his forehead. He looks ridiculously young and almost vulnerable but yet...

'Yes, I hope everything's okay,' I say hesitantly.

'No, not really,' he says. Well, that told me then. 'I'm very worried about Summer.'

'Oh, why?' I ask, confused. 'She seems fine. I thought she was settling in well. She's always talking about her friends and stuff.'

'It's not that. I'm afraid I've had to give her a demerit today.'

'Oh dear, why? What did she do? She's normally well behaved.'

'That's as maybe, but Mrs Jenks caught her throwing wet tissue down the stairwell this morning.'

'That's not like her,' I reply. 'Did she tell you why she did it?'

'Apparently she wanted to see what happened,' Mr Barton replies.

'Oh.' I'm tempted to smile. I mean it doesn't sound like such a big crime. 'Well, I'm sure she was sorry.'

'Yes, she was but that isn't the point. Mrs Jenks was very annoyed. To be fair, however there were another couple of girls involved.'

'Well, I guess there's no more to be said, although at least it wasn't an unkind thing to do.'

'That all depends on how you view it, doesn't it?'

I squirm uncomfortably under his gaze and wonder idly if he has a problem with too much testosterone or something. He's just so moody, 'Look, Mr Barton, of course I view it seriously, but at least she wasn't saying another pupil looks like Donald Trump's sister just because they have a fake tan.'

Mr Barton glares at me through penetrating brown eyes. He really would be quite attractive if he weren't so bloody stern and annoying. 'The situation you're alluding to is totally different and the child in question was reprimanded.'

'Yes, but she wasn't given a demerit,' I retaliate.

'No, because this is a question of safety.' Mr Barton sighs heavily. 'You're an intelligent woman, Mrs Greene. I'm sure you're aware that throwing objects down a stairwell is dangerous.'

Patronising git; he's really annoying me now. 'Yes, I'm aware it would be dangerous if it were a hard object, but a tissue?' I know deep down he's right. It could start with a tissue and move on to harder objects or she could have fallen down the stairs. I know Summer deserves to be punished but there's something about this guy that just really annoys me. He's so flipping, I don't know what... Pompous and self-satisfied?

'It was a dangerous situation. She could have overbalanced whilst throwing anything – no matter what it was – down that stairwell as it's high. She's a nice kid and I feel sorry for her, but she's obviously struggling right now and we don't need to look too far to find out why.'

I stare at him, speechless for probably one of the very few moments in my life.

'You obviously had your own reasons for coming here and leaving your previous life, but you can't expect it not to affect those around you, especially your children.' He spits the words out angrily and I'm amazed by his vehemence, even considering the fact he obviously hates everything about me.

'Right. Thank you for your feedback, Mr Barton. I'll talk to Summer and obviously I'll make sure nothing like this happens again.' I rise to my feet, the dignified effort of making a graceful exit ruined by the fact the tiny school chair has momentarily stuck to my not so small behind and then suddenly released, drops with a noisy bang to the floor like a gun shot. Mrs Klebb comes running to the door. 'Everything okay in here?'

'Everything's just fine,' I reply, and leg it out of the room.

Chapter 13

Except of course, nothing is fine, nothing at all. I stumble down the path from the school after my uncomfortable meeting with Mr Barton, furious and seething. Who the hell does he think he is, speaking to me like that? He has no idea, no clue what it cost me to come here, to run away from it all. It was not a whim, by any means. It was a sensible, adult decision. Well, maybe not very sensible or adult, but it was about time I did something for me.

My phone pings with the arrival of a text. *Hi Mum, Vanessa has come to collect me from school and Summer is with us. We're going into town. Hope that's okay? Vanessa said she would buy us McDonalds, Love Elise xx*

I stare at it momentarily, feeling bereft. It's just been the three of us up until now, like the Three Musketeers and Vanessa has come and spoilt it. I'm never going to get away from her. It's not going to happen, I'm totally trapped.

I blunder along the road trying to think about what I need to get from Melstock Stores on the way home. I should be grateful the girls are out to tea so I can just have a plate of pasta but now my temporary freedom has come, I'm not sure what to do with it. At least I have Zumba to look forward to this evening; that always makes me feel better. I just can't get rid of the nagging feeling that Vanessa will be up to her usual tricks with the girls, turning them against me. A sickening thought suddenly occurs to me. She wouldn't take them home with her, would she? What if she just went off with them? I take some deep breaths, trying to calm myself down; I need to look at the evidence. Would my mother-in-law do such a thing? Has she gone behind my back before? Oh God, this isn't helping. She's deceived me more times than I've had hot dinners. I don't trust her as far as I can physically throw her.

I feel hot and cold all over. I shouldn't have left Summer with Vanessa, but bloody Mr Barton distracting me meant I let my guard down. I'm so lost in thought I fail to notice a familiar dark blue Bentley swoosh past.

'Romilly!' Mark has pulled the elegant car into the corner of the road outside the church. 'How are you, darling?'

'Erm okay,' I say as convincingly as possible in the circumstances.

'Doing anything important?' he asks casually. 'I'm just on my way to the saddlers and then we could have a spot of dinner...' He peers at my doubtful face. 'Come on! You can't make me spend a whole evening on my lonesome!'

I hesitate a moment too long, but I really am tempted. I just want to run away from everything right now, responsibilities, kids, ex-husbands, ex mother-in-laws, the lot of them. 'Do I have time to pop home quickly and change?' I ask.

Twenty minutes later (thank goodness I am a master – or should I say the mistress of quick-change transformations), I find myself sitting in Mark's comfy cream leather clad car. It glides along like a luxury aircraft swooshing through the country lanes.

'This is very kind of you,' I say nervously.

'Not at all,' Mark smiles. 'I'm at a loose end and I hate that.'

Oh, that wasn't really the required response. I mean, Mr Darcy never told Elizabeth he was at a loose end. It's not really that romantic to be honest. Still, I must learn to relax. This is just a nice interlude, not real life. I have to face facts; I'm a forty year old woman with two daughters and baggage. A vision of Vanessa sitting on my toilet flits unwelcomely back into my mind. Yep, a whole lot of baggage.

At least I've managed to squeeze into a decent pair of skinny jeans and a nice little top with a pink cardi so I feel fresh. However, I can't stop worrying about Elise and Summer.

'So everything okay?' asks Mark casually.

'Not brilliant,' I reply. 'My youngest daughter's in trouble at school and I got called in to speak to the teacher.'

'What a terrible mother you must be!' Mark says mockingly. 'What did she do?'

'An awful case of vicious soggy tissue throwing down the school stairs.'

'Naughty girl. No doubt her mother put her up to it?'

'No, I don't think so,' I reply, sombrely.

'I'll have to have a word with her,' says Mark.

'Teach her some decent tricks to play at school. I can't believe they'd even bother to tell you about something so jolly trivial.'

'Apparently it could have been *very* dangerous,' I say sulkily emphasising the 'very' with venom.

'How terrible, your reprobate child could have had someone's eye out.' Mark adopts a stern persona, which makes me laugh. Mr Barton and his crap attitude seem to drift further away.

We arrive at the saddlers – a traditional shop full of gorgeous smelling leather and frighteningly expensive designer riding wear. I wander about tentatively fingering Ariat Jackets and £300 black shiny riding boots, which I think would look quite nice. I mentally put together a pretty cool outfit, a little trick I have often used to make myself feel better about the fact I can't afford any of it. I peer across to see where Mark is, but he seems to be flirting with the stunningly attractive girl who's in charge of fittings. They obviously know each other and she really is gorgeous, long dark, shiny hair, spray on jodhs and just the right amount of curve to look attractive. No saggy boobs or signs of childbirth there. I try not to feel depressed and to cheer myself up I try on a headband. Oh no, I look terrible, how come Katie Price and all the other teen something's at Mark's stables look so fab in them and I look like someone who has escaped from somewhere?

Okay, perhaps I should go for something a little more country set and fitting to my age. I pick up a trilby style hat with a jaunty feather sticking out the side. I glance at my reflection in the mirror. I look more Camilla Parker Bowles than Kate Middleton.

‘Jolly fetching, you look like my mother!’ Unbeknown to me, Mark has sauntered over and caught me in the act. How embarrassing! That’s me out of the running for the girlfriend stakes. Not that I was thinking I need that kind of hassle in my life but we all like to feel attractive and desirable, don't we? Either way, being described as looking like someone’s mother is never a good start in the romance stakes and quite honestly the thought of appearing anything like Ma Whittaker is downright horrendous!

I dust off any remaining dignity I can cling hold of, replace the hat on its stand and attempt in vain to fluff my hair up so it doesn't look completely squashed. Mark is oblivious to my useless attempts to restore any sang froid I may have had and flirts outrageously with the giggling girl on the checkout.

‘Keep the change,’ he smiles, his fingers touching her hand a moment too long and we leave the shop. To be honest, this guy’s a bit of a woman magnet. I know he’s stunningly attractive, so I guess it’s just one of those things but actually it’s kind of annoying.

During dinner Mark is charming and chatty, and I find myself drinking several glasses of fizz because it’s one of those fancy restaurants where the waiter just materialises from nowhere and tops up your glass without you even noticing. Things miraculously all seem so much better than I thought, everything has a rosy coloured glow, which didn't seem to exist before. And yes, I know I sound really fake and shallow, but it’s just so nice to be treated to champagne and delicious food you haven’t had to prepare yourself, and to be honest, I’m loving it. My phone pings during the second course and I peer at it in my bag, momentarily distracting me from the tasty steak but decide to leave it where it is. I'm always telling Elise that checking your phone at meal times is the height of bad manners. In between courses Mark disappears to the gentlemen's loos, so I quickly grab my mobile and scan the screen.

Hi Mum. It's okay, we're fine, but Vanessa has asked us to stay the night at her fancy friend's house coz she's had a drink, Gramps has had some whisky and we can't get home. I don't really want to stay, but Summer is happy as they have a really sweet spaniel and we'll be fine til morning, as long as you're okay? Love you, E xx

Okay, take a deep breath. I knew she would try something like this. (Not Summer, I mean my monster-in-law.) There should be a new law which says that we can divorce our mother-in-laws. Can you imagine the stress this would save? You could even stay married to your husband if you liked him, but if the mother-in-law – or let's not be sexist – your father-in-law – were a pain, you could file for divorce. At least then there would be terms and conditions, such as visiting rights once every three weeks, no more. Then you could prepare for the more exacting mother-in-law's routine inspection and have a good tidy up, or better still hire forensically impressive professional cleaners just to be on the safe side. Some top mediators and diplomatic professionals would come in handy too, although I feel I qualify quite well for those roles with all the experience I've had.

I've often been tempted to Ebay my in-laws. I'm sure someone would like them. Someone with a cleaner, tidier house would be more than happy. Or someone who enjoyed being stick thin and discussing which diet is most effective. Then I could bid for some in-laws that I would like, a cosy, comfortable non-judgemental couple who really care and give you hugs and stuff. Oh God, perhaps I've had more wine than I thought.

'Everything okay?' asks Mark, sitting himself down and adroitly refilling both our glasses with sparkling fizz.

'Not really,' I say doing that ridiculous thing where you try to smile but actually you're crying uncontrollably inside. 'My horrible mother-in-law has run off with my children for the night.'

'Sounds perfect to me, you should be thanking her.' Mark raises his glass in a toast, whilst grinning wickedly. 'You can stay with me.'

'No thanks,' I reply a little too quickly for politeness. This is just getting far too complicated. 'Apart from anything else, my mother-in-law is a complete controlling cow.'

'Perhaps she is,' Mark smiles lazily, 'but she's hardly going to let any harm come to the kiddywinks overnight, is she? And, my darling, the additional bonus is that you get some well-earned time off. Come on, put a smile back on that gorgeous face and let's have a toast.'

I'm so busy reeling from his compliment (I don't remember the last time anyone said I was gorgeous) that I absentmindedly clink glasses and take a large slug of champagne. I cheer myself up throughout the sweet course with a huge bombe surprise, which I proceed to try to bludgeon with a dessert spoon to get to the chocolate inside.

'Darling! You use the hot sauce to melt the bombe.' Mark is choking with laughter as he lifts the delicate little jug of white chocolate sauce and pours it over the round brown ball. The sides magically melt away to reveal the delicious filling.

'Oh!' I feel a complete idiot now.

'You are adorable!' says Mark, and holds my hand across the table. He feels warm and I gaze at his strong hands with a touch of longing. And adorable rather than needy and complaining – I'll take that! In any case, it's been many weeks since I slept with Dan and I do still miss him in spite of his controlling ways, I miss waking up in a warm cocoon in bed. Not that the sex had been that great. To be fair, it was more like eating McDonalds; nice but quick, squeezed into a few minutes and snatched between being too tired to stay awake, or before I had to get up for the school run. In any case I'm a morning person and Dan is a night kind of guy so he would be up for it when I was just going to sleep, exhausted at the end of a stressful day and then in the morning when I'd be hoping for a bit of affection, he'd be snoring away. They never warn you about these kinds of things when you're getting married, do they? You should always check if you are compatible with your sleep arrangements – if he's an owl and you're a lark, you need to book appointments for sex in the middle of the day or something.

I definitely think I've drunk too much as I feel slightly woozy, but at least it numbs things nicely. I feel rebellious; I don't think I've felt this way since I was seventeen.

'Shall we?' Mark takes my arm and we wander to the car.

'Wait!' I say unsteadily. 'Surely you've had too much to drive?' I may be drunk but not that drunk.

'No, not at all. Just a couple of small one's, Officer,' Mark smiles at me with his charming boyish grin.

'No, I really mean it. You've had a bottle of champagne and a large French coffee,' I stutter, hating my shrill voice.

'The caffeine will sort it out,' he says opening the door. 'Come on, old girl. Let's go home and you can warm my bed.'

To be frank, I don't feel so keen, I mean no one likes being called an old girl. I fold my arms and turn my back, leaning against the paintwork. Dan would have gone mad if I had done this to his car.

Mark just laughs. 'My God, I have a filly as spirited as you, and I've a good mind to use the same technique to sort you out.'

I turn my back completely. This guy is the limit. 'Rom – I'm joking, I meant more exercise. We'll walk home.'

Okay, so that's not so bad then. I allow him to loop his arm in mine and we meander down the country lane. Too late I realise that I should have brought some more practical footwear for walking, my feet are killing already. Mark thinks it's funny. 'Come on. I could probably try carrying you, darling,' he quips.

Huh, blimmin' men! It's always so easy for them, although I notice with satisfaction he has a tiny smudge of leaf mould, or it could be manure, on his expensive suede brogues. It seems like forever, but we finally arrive at the long winding driveway to Melstock Manor – I never thought I'd feel pleased to see it after the last couple of visits. It looks feudally cosy, the lights glimmering out over the sweeping drive and the neighbouring countryside.

'Back at the gaff,' comments Mark drily. 'Hope you're not too tired for a nightcap?'

'Lovely,' I say, as I'm now thoroughly cold in spite of the warming brandy in my coffee at the restaurant.

'Evening, Smithers,' drawls Mark as the butler shimmies in our direction, having opened the great oak door.

How fabulous I think to myself. I could really get used to this, although I can't stop myself from peering around anxiously for the indomitable Ma and Pa Whittaker or the overkeen Labrador.

Mark throws Smithers his long coat and mine. 'Go fetch us both a ginger mac and then shove off to bed, will you?'

Smithers gives Mark a baleful glance, tho' he's obviously used to this kind of abrupt treatment.

'Come on then, my cross-country walker. Take off those shoes, you won't be needing them anyway.'

I follow Mark rather shyly into the vast living room where a gorgeous log fire is crackling away in the enormous hearth. I throw myself on the sofa, which seems quite comfortable actually.

'What about your parents?' I ask, feeling like a teenager again.

'Out, darling, til the small hours, so you needn't worry your pretty head about them.'

I relax a little and by the time Smithers has brought in a tray of whisky and shortbread biscuits I'm beginning to thaw out a little. I take a sip of the liquid, which burns down my throat and makes me cough, and my eyes water in a most unglamorous fashion. I probably look horrendous now.

'Smithers knows how to pour a good strong 'un,' laughs Mark, downing his in one. 'He must have an oesophagus made of asbestos as he doesn't even bat an eyelid. 'Come here.'

He takes me in his arms in a far too expert manner for my overstressed mind, but it feels so good and I melt into his warm embrace. He leans over me, takes a sip of whisky from my glass, then pours it into my mouth from his own, kissing me deeply at the same time. I am literally on fire, everything is burning, all my senses are totally in flame and I think I like it, although to be honest I'm still trying not to cough. Might ruin the moment somewhat. Mark expertly removes my top and puts his hand in my bra. For a moment I worry, he's probably used to perkier young boobs than mine, but then I give up worrying. He seems to be enjoying himself anyway and in confirmation takes off his trousers in one swift movement and I try not to look at the Yves St Laurent jockey shorts which are in a rather disturbing bright shade of blue. I attempt to concentrate but am slightly concerned the horrible doggy occupant might return. I can still smell him to be honest and I wonder in what century this sofa was last cleaned. Stop it, Rom. Enjoy the moment, and I am, really I am. It's just, well it's been a long time since I ever was with any man other than Dan. I try to stop myself thinking about him, but it's proving difficult. Is it gin that makes you maudlin? Mother's ruin my mum always calls it. But I haven't had any gin so I don't think I can be ruined just yet.

As if sensing my unease, Dan moves his hands and starts to massage my back. He's just so good looking and he really knows how to kiss. I begin to lose myself in the feeling, my skirt is off and I've forgotten everything when suddenly and most bizarrely I'm transported up into the air and unceremoniously dumped behind the sofa.

'What the heck?' I'm totally winded and stuck on my back like a grounded beetle, waving my legs in the air.

Mark's face appears over the top of the sofa. 'Just stay there a moment, I need to check something.'

In spite of the drink, I'm outraged. What does he bloody well need to check? Here I am with hardly anything on, grounded behind a smelly sofa, I'm not even too sure what the carpet smells of, damp I think, and I'm covered in dog hairs. My mind runs through what he thinks he is checking. Has he suddenly remembered he has a girlfriend or that he forgot to turn the gas off? I mean, really?

The minutes tick by and Mark doesn't return, I finally manage to right myself although the room is spinning slightly. Surreptitiously I crawl carefully round the side of the sofa, retrieve various bits of my clothes and clumsily start to put on my tights. This in itself proves impossible; I must have drunk far more than I thought. The sound of footsteps along the corridor makes me scurry back behind the sofa like a scalded cat, one long thin tights leg trails behind me.

'I thought you were going out, darling?' It's Ma Whittaker, I'd recognise her foghorn voice anywhere.

'No, no, just been up at the stables,' Mark replies. He sounds totally sober and completely unruffled, the bastard.

'Not with that dreadful Courtney, I hope.' Pa Whittaker is there too. Bloody great!

'No, you sacked her last month remember?' Mark's voice is dangerously smooth.

'Best to be strict with staff,' comes another hearty voice I don't recognise. Just wonderful, there's obviously a whole flipping party coming along.

'Yeth, abstholutely I always sthay to Harry, sthaff should do asth they are told.' I have to stuff my top in my mouth to stop myself laughing out loud, what on earth sort of voice is this? More to the point how many people are coming along, it's like a bloody party out there. Please don't let them come in here, I pray, but I think my mum's right and my ruin is complete as the large oak door squeaks open and the guests meander on in.

Mr Deep Voice has the old-fashioned kind of sensible lace up boots my grandfather would have worn and Mrs Squeaky Lisp totters in a pair of unsuitable looking court shoes. That's all I can spot from my hiding place.

'Right then, everyone take a seat and I'll get some drinks,' says Mark authoritatively.

'Nonsense, darling, I'll call Smithers,' says Ma Whittaker.

'No, no, it's no trouble.' Mark busies himself taking

orders, seemingly oblivious of my half naked, irate presence behind the sofa.

'Sucth a nice boy,' clucks Mrs Squeaky Lisp. I think she is called Shirley.

'Bone bloody idle,' snorts Pa Whittaker. 'When I was his age, I worked twenty-five hours a day.'

'You pwoor thing,' twitters Shirley, 'that's twerrible.'

'Youth of today have no idea – no bloody backbone. Wouldn't know a day's work if it hit them,' blasts Shirley's other half – I think he's called Harold but if he weren't, that's the sort of name I would give him.

'He's a lamb, just hasn't found his feet yet, and a damn good rider to boot,' chunters Ma Whittaker.

'Yes, if he would only stop riding every damned woman in Somerset,' shouts Pa Whittaker.

I literally want to curl up and die. I had a suspicion Mark was like that, but I guess I was along for the ride too, though I've never been that kind of girl. And I didn't get one of those anyway. I just got thrown off over the sofa. The assembled party are making a fair bit of noise and I feel far too vulnerable sat behind the sofa half naked. Very, very, oh so quietly I put on my top, I could almost smile to myself, I am actually quite good at this. Half bending, half kneeling I manage to slide my skirt on and slowly, gently I pull on the other leg of my tights, which has annoyingly caught behind the other side of the sofa. It won't give; it's completely stuck. For goodness' sake, this is ridiculous. I'm getting impatient. Perhaps I'm not so good at this espionage thing after all. I give it a good tug and ping! It lands on my nose.

This would have been a triumph and I'd have totally got away with it but for the bloody dog who has obviously unbeknown to me just wandered in and started barking furiously at me from the front of the sofa. He is obviously either cleverer than he looks or used to his horrible master's wooing strategies. I will him to shut up but he doesn't at all.

'Monty that's enough!' blasts Pa Whittaker. 'That's no way to treat our guests.'

Monty continues to bark belligerently in my general direction.

'Most unlike him, jolly clever dog he is,' says Ma Whittaker.

'Oh, I don't really like barky dogs, they're so sthcary.' Shirley jumps up on the sofa in a panic, I can see the roots of her bleach blonde hair as I crouch myself further into the back of the sofa hoping to make myself invisible.

'Nonsense, not a bad bone in his body,' booms Ma Whittaker. I can hear footsteps coming nearer. 'Never known him be wrong either, perhaps there's a rat or something behind the sofa.'

Unable to bear it any longer, I crawl out from the end of my refuge, grabbing my bag and scrambling desperately to my feet, manage to run from the room, barging slap bang into Mark who is returning with a tray of drinks. They fly up in the air, spilling their contents all over him and a bloody good thing too. In another situation, I would laugh out loud as I had run past a roomful of simply aghast faces, fortunately managing to dodge Ma Whittaker's horse head metal tipped walking stick, which she had been stabbing randomly behind the sofa at a fictitious rodent.

As I leg it down the corridor I hear Harold's booming tones, 'Bloody large rat!' I don't stop to hear anyone's response; I just want to get out of here and fast. This is becoming far too much of a bad habit; for the second time in all too short a space, I run from the presence of the Whittakers and back into reality, whatever that is.

Chapter 14

'Morning, Sunshine,' Ciaran's cheery voice strangely seems twenty decibels too loud. I'm definitely feeling a little fragile although I've miraculously managed to crawl into work. The Ibuprofen and porridge are proving uncomfortable bedfellows, slopping round in my stomach but I'm here and on time. Reality has hit hard, crowding in with a crushing headache and a sense of total cringeworthy embarrassment. Last night was a total, unmitigated disaster. It had got worse after the hiding behind the sofa incident. I had to lurk in a barn and call a taxi, for goodness' sake. The driver was totally grumpy about coming all that way in the dark and I had to surreptitiously creep down the long dark scary drive without anyone noticing me, or being attacked by Monty, the stinky Labrador.

What on earth was I thinking hanging out with Mark in the first place? He didn't even message me to check I'd got home safely. The guy is a total and utter creep, and what if I lose my job? I peer at Ciaran anxiously, wondering if I might be given my notice.

'The shelves could do with restocking when you get a moment but more importantly.' Oh no, here goes... 'When you've grabbed yourself a coffee, I thought we could have a meeting about those marketing ideas you passed me the other day.'

‘Oh, yeah, great. That would be great.’ I must sound a little odd as Ciaran gives me a strange look.

‘Are you okay, Romilly? You don't seem your usual self?’

‘I was just going to say the same thing myself,’ says Mrs Miggins bustling in and flicking switches and pouring coffee with her usual efficacy. ‘You look a little peaky. You need to sit down and have a nice cuppa. It’s hard work being a single parent. When my first husband left, I was slaving day and night just to feed and clothe the little ones.’

‘I must get to work,’ I protest in vain as they both insist I sit down for a moment, and I admit I’m grateful for the coffee. ‘But yes, it’s difficult, although the girls are being quite good on the whole but my mother-in-law has turned up.’

‘Oh, the drama, I just love the drama.’ Ciaran draws up a chair and a coffee from Mrs Miggins. ‘Come on, girl, spill.’

I tell all after an initial hesitation, apart from mentioning Mark because that would be really embarrassing and as he’s the boss here it could be awkward for everyone.

‘I just love my partner Mick’s mum, she’s a darlin – bakes me cake and sends me food parcels as though I don't have enough to eat,’ Ciaran pats his tummy appreciatively. ‘I always thought I was quite lucky but now I realise I’ve hit the jackpot.’

‘You sure have.’ I have serious mother-in-law envy, if that’s a thing. This is not for the first time either. My sister Jess’ mother-in-law is just lovely. She gives her a really big hug hello and goodbye and seems genuinely fond of her, as well as being supportive. I just don't know how I ended up with one like this, but to be fair I guess her son wasn't that great either.

'There's still time,' reassures the kindly Mrs Miggins. 'Second time lucky. That's what I reckon you'll be. I can feel it in my waters!'

Their conversation cheers me, and the coffee seems to have worked its magic on my pounding headache. I've had a reassuring text from Elise to say that she and Summer have been dropped to school by Vanessa and they would both see me later. I was worried she might have run off with them permanently, but apparently they had a trip planned with the Smitherton Smythes or whatever ludicrous name they're called. So that was more important, thank goodness!

My meeting with Ciaran goes well and we discuss all my plans for potential marketing strategies.

'I think the idea of samples for different blends is fabulous,' enthuses Ciaran.

'Well, I just thought people often stick to what they're used to, but it might get customers trying different flavours such as the jasmine, and Walter's favourite Deckchair Dreaming tea!'

'Yes that's true. Visitors often are loath to buy an entire pot or gift box of tea they haven't tried. Your sample cup ideas are great.'

'We could use the cute little cups you have in the shop and it might encourage shoppers to buy.'

'Your suggestion of special interest days and courses will take a little more planning, but I'm going to take your folder to the management team and we'll go from there. Thank goodness you came to us,

Romilly. You're the breath of fresh air this coffee business needs.' I am embarrassed by Ciaran's warm words but touched too.

I leave for the school run totally buzzing and am even strong enough to cope with Summer's recounting of the size of the Smitherton Smythes' estate and their cute spaniel. Mr Barton catches my eye as I collect Summer from the gate and we both nod in a formal but hugely cold manner. I can't stand this man. What on earth is his issue?

'I hope Summer had a better day today,' I can't resist asking Miss Timmins, the Teaching Assistant, who's standing in the doorway.

'Oh yes, she did some beautiful work on the Titanic. She's bringing some of it home to show you, she's such a good little worker.'

I smile and thank Miss Timmins who is actually so sweet. Not that I'm biased or anything because she said something nice about my daughter, although that does help of course! I can't resist smiling triumphantly at Mr Barton but he merely glares and walks off. I can't stand that man or any men at the moment; they're simply a totally different species. I've had about twenty missed calls and messages from Dan, which I haven't mentioned previously because I'm in complete denial. When I needed him, he rarely messaged even to let me know he had got somewhere safely, and now I don't want him he plagues me with sentimental stuff, which a few months ago I would have done anything for. In the last one he even admits his mother is a pain and his father was rude but it's too late, the damage is done. I'm off men and have forsworn them forever. I'm going to concentrate on being a good mum and then I might become an eccentric old spinster like Barbara Woodhouse, training dogs or horses or something. Maybe just not Labradors.

We meet Elise at the bus stop, but she's not in a good mood. I thought she might be pleased to see me after her texts, but instead she storms straight off to her room and slams the door. 'Do you know what's wrong with Elise?' I ask Summer.

'No, she was fine yesterday,' Summer replies, whilst colouring a large picture of the Titanic. 'Did you know there were 1700 passengers on board and only 700 survived?'

'That's really sad,' I reply absently, thinking simultaneously, a) why do they have to study something so miserable and b) what is wrong with Elise? Was it something I said? Was it something the horrible monster-in-law said? Is it just hormones or is it just life in general? I really think teenagers need to come with a guidebook.

I give Summer her snack, then creep upstairs with a steaming plate of Elise's favourite cheesy pasta, tomatoes and spinach. 'Can I come in?' I ask politely, although to be fair I usually just barge in regardless.

'Yeah.' Elise is lying on her bed peering intently at her phone as though it has all the answers to the mysteries of the universe. I guess to most teenagers it probably seems as though it has. I notice she quickly turns it over the other way when I sit down on the bed.

'Oh, Mum, you're on my bed,' she moans.

'Well, yes,' I reply, 'I need to sit somewhere.'

'I hope your trousers are clean.' Elise has been

rather obsessive about cleanliness lately. I’ve been ignoring it as much as possible as I figure it’s just her way of dealing with things.

‘So?’ I ask cheerily.

‘So what?’ This is going well then.

‘You know what I mean. How are things?’

‘Fine.’

‘Obviously they’re not fine at all,’ I reply gently.

‘Okay, so it’s not fine. Everything is totally crap.’

‘I thought you had a nice time and school’s maybe not brilliant but you’re getting through it.’

‘No, it’s all crap. Yesterday was rubbish. Vanessa’s a complete bitch and school is total bollocks.’

‘Elise, I don't expect language like that in my house,’ I rebuke.

‘Oh, come on, Mum. Everyone swears at school.’

‘Not here they don't.’

‘Dad swore all the time!’

‘One of the reasons I left him,’ I say blithely.

‘You do too!’

‘Very rarely, only when totally provoked.’

Elise gives me a baleful glare. ‘Last night was awful; I’m never talking to Vanessa again.’

‘Oh, I thought you got on quite well with her,’ I say surprised.

‘Well, she’s always been okay to me before...’

‘You mean bought you clothes, taken you out and stuff. Yes, I know.’

‘Okay, so maybe I’ve been a bit shallow because she’s actually a total cow. She just buys people.’

I refrain from saying I told you so as no one likes to hear that, but I’ve tried to gently explain in the past that perhaps Vanessa is not quite what she may seem.

Elise continues angrily, 'She has an opinion on everything and everyone. Sebastian's doing 12 GCSEs, so why am I only doing 10? Anthony's done his D of E Gold Award. I've just done my Bronze, have I? Oh really?'

Sebastian's the only son of Dan's sister, who is of course brilliant at everything.

'But it doesn't make sense anyway because Sebastian's older than you. You don't take your Gold Award until Year 11 at least.'

'I know, and I tried telling Vanessa that, but she wasn't listening.'

'No, she never does!' I reply, laughing.

'You wouldn't be laughing if you heard what she said about you,' says Elise.

'Well, no, I expect it was quite rude, but I don't really expect anything else,' I say cheerfully.

'She said you're a manipulative scheming woman, your house is always a mess and you have no sense of duty or responsibility.'

'She did, did she? How dare she speak of me like that! Just because she's obsessed with tidiness, no one's allowed to bloody move in her house. And at least I shut the toilet door when I go for a wee!' I am warming to my task now.

'What?' gasps Elise, momentarily distracted.

'Oh, never mind. Did she say all that to you?' I ask, totally incensed that Vanessa would be so mean as to say such horrible things in front of my daughter.

'No, she wouldn't dare. She's far more manipulative and scheming than that. I overheard her bitching about you to Gramps as the wall between their bedroom and mine was really thin.' Elise is outraged.

'I guess she's bound to be angry with me after leaving her darling son, and to be quite honest she didn't like me much before,' I say.

'I'm sorry I didn't believe you, Mum.' Elise has tears running down her face and I give her a big hug. After the stress and upset of the last few days I feel as though I've won a million pounds. Thank God the highs of parenting outweigh the lows.

'Come on, chicken. I'll go get some chips for supper,' I say, and we walk downstairs companionably together, much more so than we have been in months.

I'm feeling happier as I walk round to the local fish and chip shop. Elise has stayed behind to lay up, she's even picked some willow buds from the garden and put them in a tiny vase. They look so pretty. For once Summer has been helping, tidying up and finishing her homework so we can watch a movie later. Maybe things aren't so bad after all. The birds are singing at the end of another sunny day and I smile and nod happily at fellow villagers, at peace with the whole world. It's funny how one minute your life can feel as though everything's terrible and nothing will ever be right again, and the next, some tiny thing can make the sun shine and you just feel like dancing. Parenting is definitely a rollercoaster. The trouble is, I was never very keen on them. I just need to get better at sitting back and enjoying the ride.

On my way back to the cottage with the fish and chips, I pass the Post Office as Phil's shutting the doors. 'Okay, Phil?' I smile at him.

'No, not really, love.' He is definitely not his usual smiley self.

'Is Alexandrine okay?' I ask immediately worried.

'Yes, but...'

'But what?' I am really dismayed now.

'You'd better come in for a second.' I follow Phil into the tiny Post Office, now flooded with fading sunlight. The rows of crocs and wellies, walking boots and sticks are all incongruously but neatly lined up next to each other. I sit beside Phil on a rather tatty little sofa used for trying on wellies.

'Come on, Phil, you're making me nervous,' I say. 'It can't be that bad.'

'I'm afraid it is,' he says sadly. 'The Coffee Factory's closing down.'

Chapter 15

I sit in stunned silence, as I'm just not sure what to say. Very unusual for me, I know! In fact, I'm almost sorry no-one who knows me well is here to witness it, as I'm never quiet. It simply doesn't happen.

'But it can't. I mean, why would The Coffee Factory close? It's been here forever,' I manage to blurt.

'I don't know any details I'm afraid, but Alexandrine and I are always the first to hear any local gossip. Word on the ground is that there aren't enough funds to keep it going,' Phil replies.

'But I was having a marketing meeting with Ciaran only this morning and it was really positive. I've got loads of ideas of things we can do to really increase profits,' I blabber.

'That's as maybe but I think perhaps it's too late.' Phil seems unusually resigned and seeing this usually cheerful man crumble is making me really anxious.

'But I thought it was owned by the Whittakers and they're rolling in it?' I ask.

'Well, that's what we all believed, but I suppose they might rely on investment. Perhaps they don't want to keep it anymore?' He muses a little, 'though it's a total disaster for the village. Our life revolves around it. The community centre, the tourism, the whole being of this place centres around The Coffee Factory.'

'It's the very heart of this village. It always has been, ever since I came here as a little girl.'

'Since long before that, kid. You're not that old, you know!'

'Oh my God! What about Walter? Does he know?' I ask breathlessly.

'He will do soon, I'm afraid. Don't think it'll be long before it's common knowledge,' says Phil sadly.

I think of Walter and his memories of The Coffee Factory, of his beloved wife and his days working there, his favourite coffee, the tea we were going to name after him and something inside me snaps. 'No!' I exclaim loudly, bringing my hand down on a nearby shoe rack. In fact it makes poor Phil jump.

'Are you okay?' he asks. I think he's worried I'm having a funny five minutes or something.

'I'm fine, just fine; in fact I've never been better. Well, maybe I have but never mind, that's irrelevant.' Okay, so maybe I am having a funny five minutes. 'We're totally going to fight this.'

'How can we?' asks Phil. 'You've no idea how much rank these local gentry can pull. In fact I think Mr Whittaker is a member of the House of Lords.'

'I don't care if he's the Lord Mayor of London himself,' I declare, jumping to my feet. 'I'm sick of taking things lying down and for once I'm not going to.'

'It's great to see you so enthusiastic, but to be honest I'm struggling to get Alexandrine through her latest treatment and I'm not sure we've got any fight left.' Phil looks vulnerable and bereft standing there surrounded by his jackets and walking gear.

I take Phil's hand. 'I know. It's okay, Phil. I mean

I'm going fight it. Well, not just me, everyone, Debs, Mrs Miggins, Ciaran, the girls at Zumba, Knit and Natter, the schools, we're all going to get involved. The future of Melstock as well as its past (an image of Walter springs to mind again and I have to fight back tears – probably those blimmin' hormones again, they're on fire right now) is relying on us. This village has saved me in more ways than one and I for one am not giving up on it.

In any case, I spent more than one evening working on those ideas for the future of The Coffee Factory and they're not going to waste. In fact, I'm quite proud of them if I may say so myself.

I rush home to Elise and Summer who have disappeared into the mystical parallel universe of social media so don't seem to have noticed how long I've been gone. Maybe there are advantages to the wretched invention after all. I refrain from telling them the news as I don't want to spoil the evening, but tomorrow I've got some serious work to get started on.

Just as I'm finally rolling myself into bed, the phone rings. It's Mark. I'm instantly all of a dither as I haven't heard from him since the incident at his house, and quite honestly I don't really want to speak to him after that. Yet somehow I manage to press the green button. 'Hello?'

'It's Mark. Are you okay?' For goodness' sake, it's a bit late to be asking and he sounds four sheets to the wind. Bloody man, he's just too good looking for his own good.

'Yes, I'm fine,' I reply cagily.

'You don't sound fine,' he slurs. 'Look, darling, I'm

so sorry about the other night, a complete bloody disaster.' He sounds like a recalcitrant little boy. I hesitate a moment. To be honest, I'm still trying to get used to being called darling. Maybe the guy at the market stall in the Branksome Road called me it once, but that wasn't quite the same. Dan never called me darling. We just weren't that kind of couple. His mum and dad always refer to each other as darling, which always strikes me as quite pretentious in their case. I mean they'd be having a disagreement but keep the darling in, so it would go something like, 'But darling, I asked you to put the plates out ready for the MacPhersons.'

'I know, darling, but then I forgot and you know how busy I am at the moment, darling.' The 'darling' would be spat out with emphasis and not meant in a pleasant way at all! Yet strangely from Mark's lips it's quite nice. Oh dear, stop it, Romilly. No melting, just because he's young and cute. I force myself to sound disinterested. 'Well, it wasn't quite what I'm used to.'

'How did you get home?' he asks.

'I had to hide in the barn and then call a taxi,' I say obdurately.

'My poor darling.' I can hear the amusement in his voice. I should be furious, I mean for goodness' sake, what's wrong with the man? 'Why did you come out from behind the sofa?' he continues.

'Your bloody dog gave me away,' I retort crossly.

'What a bounder! Good old Monty. He has a great nose, named after Montgomery, you know. Great fighting general,' snorts Mark.

'With a penchant for sniffing crotches and giving

away innocent women concealing themselves behind furniture,' I remark, but I can't help myself as we both start laughing hysterically down the phone because after all you've got to see the funny side really.

'Let me make it up to you?' Mark suggests. He does sound sorry and I could do with his help right now.

'Not sure I've got time,' I reply. 'Got bigger fish to fry right now.'

'What?' asks Mark. 'You're going into the fish and chip business?'

'No, but I'm worried about The Coffee Factory.' I figure I might as well come out with it; he must know what's going on.

'What about it? Was alright last time I looked.' Mark is annoyingly flippant. I wonder idly how much he has had to drink.

'Of course it's okay at the moment, but I understand it's closing down, in trouble, finished.' I'm tired now and feeling frustrated.

'First I've heard about it,' he says, and to be fair he sounds pretty genuine.

'Don't your mum and dad own it? How can you not know?' I ask incredulously.

'They do, but they own loads of stuff as well as the old family shack. We don't spend every minute wittering on about it or we'd never bloody do anything.'

I suppose he has a point about that. I mean, it's such a different world for rich people. Then again I think of Walter and anger surges up in me again. 'This matters to an awful lot of people,' I say crossly. 'So you could do with bringing it up on the agenda at the next family dinner.'

‘Oooh, that’s me told then!’ Mark has definitely consumed too much alcohol. ‘Come over to the stables tomorrow and we’ll have a chat about it. Come riding.’

‘I don’t think that’s wise, do you?’

‘Maybe you’re right. We’ll go for a walk instead, but I need to see you. I’ve missed you, Rom.’

I ring off unsure what to think, but I need to find out what’s going on with The Coffee Factory ASAP. I totally trust Phil. If he says something’s up, it must be. On the other hand, Mark sounded genuine so perhaps he’ll be able to help shed some light on the matter.

Of course by the next morning, the news is all over Melstock. ‘This is a total disaster,’ moans Debs as she plonks my croissants in a paper bag. ‘Apparently the factory is bankrupt.’

‘But I just don't understand how this can happen so suddenly,’ I comment, ripping a piece of delicious croissant off and stuffing it in my mouth. I always comfort eat, it has to be done. Well, it’s either that or something stronger.

‘I understand it’s been in trouble for some time,’ says Debs, helping herself to a pain au chocolat and munching emphatically.

‘Why did they take me on then?’ I muse. ‘I mean you’d think they’d be cutting back on staff rather than hiring more. Tho’ of course I’m glad they did.’

‘Yes, it’s all a bit strange.’ Debs has finished her pain au chocolat in record time and proceeds to unpeel a bar of Galaxy – ‘have a piece.’

I take it and munch gratefully; chocolate always has all the answers.

‘Perhaps you’ll find out a bit more from the

gorgeous Mark later,' Debs remarks. 'That is if you have time for talking.' She gives me a cheeky wink.

'Huh! After the other night I don't think I'll be able to get anywhere near him.' I'm still smarting from being thrown behind the sofa. 'And I'm not sure I want to.'

'Oh, come on! Mums are allowed some fun, you know, and you're still quite young.'

'Thanks,' I smile. 'I don't feel that young after being thrown over the top of the sofa.'

Debs grins. 'Yeah, not very romantic I guess, and the dog – I mean that was just hilarious!' She dissolves into laughter. I join in too, because sometimes you have to laugh before you cry.

'Anyway, back to the factory.' I feel as though I've had enough laughing at myself for one day. 'We need to get a committee together. We're not going down without a fight.'

'Too right. I'm right behind you and so's everyone else. This community's tougher than this.'

I find her words comforting; this community can survive anything, can't it?

My mood is not improved by a new text from Mark postponing my visit. *Sorry Rom, darling, but something's come up at work so please can we reschedule our walk for another day? I'm free later this week x*

Maybe I'm slightly relieved as I wasn't really in the mood for Mark today. I do feel more proactive though, as I need to get things started. I've already phoned Ciaran who doesn't seem to know any more about the situation than the rest of us.

‘No one’s told us anything,’ he’d said, unusually ruffled. He’s normally so calm and collected. ‘Mind you, nothing new there. The management are always pretty hands off. I rarely even see Mark to discuss matters and the big decisions happen well away from the shop floor. The actual workers will be the last to know what’s going on.’

‘But what about my ideas?’ I asked. ‘Surely if we could just convince them that things are going to improve?’

‘I don't know,’ Ciaran had said doubtfully. ‘It depends on what the deficit is. Your ideas are fab but it’s going to take time to implement them as well as possibly some further investment. It’s a question of how much in debt the factory is.’

It’s very dispiriting and I’m not sure what to do next. It’s very hard to fight a situation when you don't know what that situation is. On the plus side, Summer is in a happy mood when I pick her up from school. ‘I’ve been given the Pupil of the Week award,’ she sings enthusiastically, waving a piece of paper.

‘Wow, what’s that for?’ I ask, hoping the other parents might be looking. I know it sounds a bit petty, but I’m still a little sore after the fiasco of the Titanic project. I mean this was supposed to be the children’s own work. Summer had worked hard on hers for days and I couldn't believe it when one Monday morning several jubilant fathers had appeared at the school proudly clutching anatomically correct, professional looking models of the majestic ship with working lights and everything. Are we really supposed to believe that a nine-year-old produced this sort of project by themselves? It made me chuckle actually because as Debs and Tania had pointed out, their kids had done theirs with minimal supervision and at least it had been their own work rather than an entry for the world's greatest parenting award. But still...

'It was for helping other children,' skips Summer happily, 'with their work and when they find something difficult.'

'That's lovely,' I say, squashing down an irrational wish that it was for academic prowess. My mother has a lot to answer for. 'After all, being kind is the most important thing.' And it is, it really is and I'm super proud.

Elise's expression at the bus stop brings everyone's mood right down to basement level in one second. 'Good day?' I ask brightly.

'Ugh,' she replies.

'Look, I won an award,' says Summer shoving her certificate under Elise's nose.

'What for? The most bloody annoying child?' Elise snaps.

'Elise, you are to apologise to your sister, or your phone will be confiscated for the rest of the day,' I say firmly.

'So what? I don't care,' Elise mutters.

'The rest of the week then,' I retort angrily.

We've reached the cottage by now and I unlock the door, illogically hoping that my mother-in-law isn't lurking in there somewhere. It's a bit like having a bogeyman as a grown up. I really need to get a grip.

'Elise!' I call after her retreating hunched shoulders.

'Take it then!' She throws the phone down on the sofa. 'I don't bloody well want it; you can keep it.' She storms off upstairs and slams her bedroom door.

'Oh dear,' I sigh, picking up the phone and popping it in my pocket. 'I wonder what's upset her today.'

'Probably boys or something,' remarks Summer. 'My friend Alice's big sister, Casey, has a boyfriend and Alice says she's always upset coz of something he's done.'

I give her a hug, grateful to still have one little person who likes cuddles and wish illogically that they could stay little for ever. I am still trying to work out what might be wrong with Elise, cook tea and think of a plan to save The Coffee Factory when my mobile rings.

'Hello, long time no speak,' comes a cheery voice.

'Oh my gosh! Jess, it's great to hear from you.' And it is. I've really missed our chats, although to be honest I've stayed out the way so I didn't get a lecture.

'I know. I've missed you so much, Rom.' Jess sounds genuinely pleased. There's an awkward silence. 'So how are things?'

'Great,' I reply as enthusiastically as I can, considering the day I've had.

'You don't sound too sure.' Oh great, here she goes making me doubt myself again.

'Yes, it's lovely here, just having the usual teenage problems. Elise has come in from school in a stroppy mood. You know what it's like.' Here I go blathering again when I should just be calm and collected, in control, everything here's just fine sort of thing. I wait for the usual 'Well, if Dan were there, things might be more settled.' But it doesn't come.

Jess is unusually accommodating. 'I know! Bradley's bad enough and he's way off being a teenager.'

'You'll be okay with him; boys always just go quiet and Kevin the teenager-ish.'

'True. I can't imagine him being quiet for five minutes to be honest,' Jess laughs, and quite frankly neither can I from my last visit to their house.

'So how are Mum and Dad?' I ask nervously. I haven't heard from either for some time. I think I'm under the 'she who shall not be mentioned list'. Either that or they probably whisper about me in social circles with hushed tones since they come from the generation where divorce was not an option. 'A total stigma, divorce in those days. Many times I wanted to divorce your father but it would have been an absolute disgrace for a bank manager.' Such comforting words on the subject of marriage and relationships, No wonder my love life's a mess.

'Yeah, they're okay.' I can tell by the pause before Jess replies that all is not okay at all, but I don't feel like pursuing it. At the moment I'm still obviously persona non gratis.

'What about Bradley?' I ask, happy to change the subject.

'Bradley's fine. Just as lively as ever, but loves his nursery. They've started doing forest school and he adores it, clambering on log trails and climbing trees.'

'Sounds great,' I reply, 'and perfect for Bradley.'

'Yes, the other day he was so tired he fell asleep over his petit filous!'

'Job done then,' I laugh.

‘I know, John and I got a whole evening off. It was just wonderful.’

‘That’s exactly what you need.’ I can clearly remember the lack of quiet evenings together due to wakeful children, although more recently it’s because they’re old enough to stay up. They don't warn you that when children get older they often stay up later than you do, and lovely though their company is, sometimes you just want a bit of time off without prying ears, to be yourselves, to have an impromptu snuggle or whatever. Not that this happened any more with Dan – I think we’d both given up.

‘How about it then?’ he used to say, wriggling over to my side of the bed.

‘Er no, I’m a bit tired,’ I’d reply.

‘Oh!’ he’d mutter in a disappointed tone, and return to his side of the bed.

‘You could try asking me why?’ I’d say hopefully.

‘Not really,’ he’d just reply.

‘It’s just it might help if you tried a bit of romance first. You can’t just expect me to switch on like a light bulb,’ I’d say.

He would grunt something about if only I had been designed with an on off switch and go off to sleep. It’s not surprising we’re no longer together, to be fair. I give myself a mental shake. It’s the past, it’s done, move on, Romilly.

‘Speaking of which,’ Jess is continuing to talk and I haven’t heard a word she’s been saying. For God’s sake, concentrate, girl. ‘We have an opportunity to get away for a bit.’

‘Wow that’s lovely, Jess, just what you need,’ I say

enthusiastically and more hopefully, 'without Bradley?'

'Yes, he'll be staying with Marjory, thank goodness.' Marjory is Jess' mother-in-law.

'That's a result. Has he stayed with her before?' I ask.

'No, so we need to make the most of this break as she might never have him again!' Jess is deadly serious, but I want to laugh as she is so right. Bradley is the most hyperactive toddler I've ever met.

'So where are you going?' I ask, trying to change the subject.

'We're coming to stay in Melstock. John has a conference in Bristol, so I thought it would be nice to visit you whilst he's working.'

'Oh, yes, that would be lovely!' I exclaim, hoping that I sound sincere after a stunned pause. 'When is it?'

'This weekend,' says Jess enthusiastically. 'It's going to be so much fun coming to visit and check out your new life.'

'Yes, definitely,' I say trying to be upbeat but failing miserably. Of all the timings, we have The Coffee Factory to save and I was kind of looking forward to catching up with Mark. Also I don't want to hear about Dan. It's bad enough having his mum to visit, although thank goodness I haven't seen hide nor hair of her for a day or so. It's typical of Jess to never think I might have something else on, or it might not be convenient; she always does exactly what suits her.

After a short chat about timings and this and that Jess rings off. I slump on the sofa and stare aimlessly at the wall. This running away from it all business seems to have backfired, what with determinedly toilet dwelling mother-in-laws, sisters who have a thing for my husband, with one thing and another my old life and baggage seems to be catching up with me. For goodness' sake! There really is no escape.

Chapter 16

As always I have a plan. Well, sort of a plan. First, we need to get a campaign together for The Coffee Factory and I'll just have to deal with my complicated personal life later. My first visit is to Walter, as at ninety-one years of age, I figure there isn't much in life he doesn't know about.

'Romilly!' he exclaims, happy to see me. 'Come in, come in, this is a treat.'

I follow him into his kitchen, which is flooded with sunlight. Everything is as spick and span as always, not a thing out of place to disturb his organised life. There's even a small jar of flowers fresh from the garden on the circular Ercol table. Walter's house is like a time capsule of seventies life, blended with old cottage and simplicity, but I love it.

Winston, the cat, meanders out from by the Aga, yawns and stretches in an unhurried fashion and rubs his head along my legs. Not for the first time I envy this cat – he is definitely living his best life.

'Coffee?' asks Walter, flicking the switch on the kettle.

'Yes please,' I reply, 'as long as it's proper coffee.'

'Of course!' Walter starts to fill his coffee mill with delicious, scented beans, 'but for how much longer?'

'You've heard then?' I ask, although I'm not

surprised as most people in Melstock know what happens before it even occurs.

'Yes, terrible business.' I'm distressed to notice Walter's hand shake slightly as he grinds the beans. 'Melstock won't be the same without The Coffee Factory, it's the end of an era.'

'We can't let it happen,' I say resolutely.

'Not sure we'll have much say in the matter,' says Walter. 'Biscuit?' He passes me a plateful and I nosh thoughtfully on a hobnob. 'You know what these rich toffs are like,' he continues. 'Us workers are just their playthings.'

'But I thought the Whittakers had loads of money,' I say.

'They certainly have, but perhaps they've decided to spend it on something else. Mr Whittaker Senior might want to buy another property in the City, or it may be that The Coffee Factory is simply not profitable enough.'

I peer angrily into my coffee. 'They can't just play with people's lives like that.'

'They can, my dear, and they do. It's been like that since the beginning of time and it always will be. We just have to accept it was a good thing while it lasted. Things change.'

'They do,' I say slowly, 'but there are things we can do something about and I reckon this is one of them.'

Walter smiles tolerantly at my enthusiasm. 'You young things! I wish I had half your energy.'

'You have,' I smile and we'll be needing it with what I've got in mind. 'Are you in?'

'Of course I am,' says Walter. 'Where else would I

be when I am sitting here?'

'No, I mean are you in with us on this campaign to save The Coffee Factory?' I ask resolutely.

'Well, yes, I suppose, depending on what's involved. I'm not sure I'm much good to you at my age.'

'Walter, you're invaluable and we're going to need you every step of the way,' I reply. After some more chat and clutching a tiny pot containing some forget-me-nots for my cottage garden, I wander back down the lane to our cottage. I'm worried about Walter as he suddenly looks frailer and more vulnerable, and I'm not so sure about this campaign as I was at first. How are we, a group of ordinary village people going to afford to do anything about The Coffee Factory?

I drop in to see Debs at Melstock Stores. She's already mocking up posters on her laptop at the counter. 'We're trying to get a meeting arranged,' she says, 'for a committee to save the factory.'

'Brilliant,' I reply relieved. If Debs is organising this campaign, it could work as there's nothing she doesn't know about this place. 'When are we doing it?'

'Saturday night,' she answers. 'I'm putting up notices around the village so we can get as many people there as possible. Okay, Josh, I'm nearly done.' I smile and nod at Josh who has just wheeled his bike out from the back room. 'Josh is delivering flyers to businesses and houses so no one's left out.'

'That's wonderful,' I say enthusiastically. 'I was wondering if I should have a chat with Mark,' I add in an undertone after Josh has gone out the front of the shop. 'Just in case he can shed some light on what's going on.'

'Good idea. He must know something; you can't tell me he's ignorant of at least some of the facts here. I'm afraid you're going to have to take one for the team, Rom.' She glances at my face. 'Not that I think that's going to be too difficult for you considering how much you like him.'

'Well I do,' though I don't feel too sure actually. 'Not as much as I did before he shoved me behind a sofa and left me to find my own way home.'

Debs laughs. 'Well, we all know romance is pretty much dead, and anyway he's pretty hot. Just flutter your eyelashes at him and find out what you can.'

'Alright, I'm already on it, but my sister's coming to stay at the weekend which will definitely cramp my style.'

'Oh that's bad timing. Do you get along?' Debs applies the finishing touches to the screen and presses send.

'In the main, yes, but she's a huge fan of my ex, Dan.'

'Awkward!' I love Debs, she's so understanding.

'Yes, I often wondered if she'd have liked to have married him herself,' I grumble. 'She'd have been welcome to him. I'm sick of men, they really are from another planet.'

Too late I realise Mr Barton has wandered into the shop and is waiting silently behind me to be served. What is it with this guy? Why can't he be normal and make some noise?

'Hello, Mr Barton.' Debs is her usually friendly self.

'Oh sorry,' I jump aside in my usual overpolite manner to let him past to be served.

He ignores me and smiles at Debs. 'Hello, Mrs Finchley. Lovely day!'

'It certainly is. Just a pound of your usual?' Debs adeptly serves out some slices of Cornish Yarg. I must admit I love that cheese, and I try not to glare at him shouting, 'Hands off the Yarg, it's mine!' After all, that would be a little strange.

'Yes please. You know it's my favourite. How's Josh? I heard from Mr Bridges that he's doing really well in Science?'

'Top of the class apparently. I think it might have been something to do with his Junior School Science teacher though!'

'Not at all! He's really bright when it comes to Maths and Science. I reckon he'll be a great engineer or something equally clever,' replies Mr Barton.

I'm listening to the conversation open mouthed, as I've never heard Mr Barton be so pleasant and supportive. Not that I've spoken to him much but then he's always so flipping abrupt.

'That's what he wants,' says Debs. 'I guess he won't be choosing to stay around here to run the shop for me. By the way, are you free on Saturday night? We're having a committee meeting to save The Coffee Factory.'

'Oh right. Yes, of course. I'll be there as soon as I've finished tennis coaching.' Mr Barton gives a cheery wave to Debs, nods coldly and formally to me and disappears out of the shop.

'Such a nice guy,' sighs Deb as she watches him leave. 'Coaches the juniors at tennis at weekends. Brilliant teacher too.'

‘Yes,’ I try to sound convincing. ‘He’s Summer’s class teacher this year.’ I peer at Debs whilst she prints off the flyers. ‘Erm, Debs, have you ever noticed Mr Barton is a bit...’

‘Bit what...?’ Debs sticks her tongue out as she thumbs through the sheets but still manages to peer up at me in a puzzled way.

‘Well, a bit unfriendly to me?’ I ask, awkwardly.

‘Not really,’ she answers. ‘I mean, he doesn’t really know you, I expect. She stacks all the sheets together. ‘Come on, Josh, here’s a load for you to start with.’ Josh reappears and grabs the flyers, shoves them in his backpack and whizzes off on his bike.

‘Now then, you.’ Debs looks me straight in the eye. ‘You need to run along and do some probing with a certain Mark Whittaker.’

In theory this should be easy, but the reality is proving a more difficult task than it seems. First of all, I get home to the cottage to find my mother-in-law has turned up again and is sitting in my lounge with Summer. ‘Ah, there you are, Romilly.’ She gets up on the pretext of air kissing either side of my cheeks. ‘She’s a bit young to be left alone, isn’t she?’ Vanessa mutters under her breath but loud enough for Summer to hear.

‘Yes, but Elise is upstairs so she’s not on her own,’ I reply calmly.

‘Is she? She hasn't come down. Most insular behaviour. Doesn't take after her father, does she? He’s always so sociable, but it’s rather difficult for them at the moment, isn’t it?’

‘She’s probably doing her homework or listening to her music. I don't expect she even knows you’re here,’ I reply, taking off my jacket and jogging up the stairs as fast as I can to try and get away from the bloody horrible woman. She used to constantly turn up unannounced at our last house. 'Cooee,' she'd call up the stairs, having walked in without ringing the doorbell. This woman takes 'mi casa es su casa' to a whole new level.

'Okay, Elise?'

'Yeah, but I'm not coming out my room until that woman goes away.'

'Elise, being rude is hardly going to solve anything.'

'I'm not being rude. I'm just avoiding her; that's a totally different thing.'

'Not in my house it isn't,' I reply sternly.

'Oh, come on, Mum. You can't stand her either and after what she said about you.'

I sigh. 'It's called being and acting like an adult. Boring, but it has to be done.'

'You always said you were never going to grow up.'

'Yes, I know, but I guess we all have to conform to society's rules at some point.'

'She doesn't,' humphs Elise.

And to be fair I can't really argue with that.

'Elise will be down in a bit. She has a bit of a headache,' I fib glibly. I mean, what else am I supposed to say? She can't stand you and doesn't want to see you, Vanessa? I guess it might sort things out for once and for all, but I just can't fight against all those years of being polite.

'Poor girl, such a trying age, especially in such terrible circumstances.' Vanessa gives me a condemning look which she manages to switch off immediately as soon as Summer glances up at her from her book. She transforms her face instantly into a smile, tucking a note into Summer's hand. 'I thought you might like to buy some things with this, especially as things must be so difficult living with your mum.' She says the last few words in a tone which implies such a fate is worse than any other possible outcome.

'So,' she turns to me abruptly, 'the reason for my visit other than to keep in touch with my two lovely granddaughters, is this...' She produces an expensive looking embossed card and hands it to me. 'As you are no doubt aware, this year is the Golden Wedding Anniversary of my husband and I (I have to bite back a snigger as she sounds as though she's addressing the room as the Queen) and we felt it should not be allowed to pass without a significant celebration.'

'Of course not,' I say numbly. Whatever's coming next I really don't want to know.

'So we're having a sumptuous Summer Golden Wedding Party at the Mannerton-Smythes' and Elise and Summer are invited,' Vanessa smiles sardonically. 'It is imperative that my granddaughters are there.' That's a statement of fact instead of a request, a right, which as everything else Vanessa does is a demand. As always no checking in advance whether the date is convenient or anything else. I know we're not important enough to consult with on such matters. We're just expected to drop everything and turn up regardless of any prior commitments. Furthermore, in spite of being their mother, the royal brood mare although less and less royal I feel as time goes by, I as always have no say in the matter at all.

‘Oh, I love a party,’ skips Summer jumping up from the sofa. ‘Can I wear my new best dress?’

‘I hope you will, darling,’ says Vanessa, smiling.

‘And will Mum come?’ Summer presses.

I am about to demur, all ready with a pressing excuse of a prior engagement such as washing my hair or something equally as important, even though I don't even know when it is, when Vanessa answers for me.

‘Of course Mummy’s coming. We can’t possibly have a party without the whole family there; it will be a perfect reunion.’ She casts me a steely look from the corner of her eye. ‘Won’t it, Mummy?’

Chapter 17

'But that's lovely! I'm sure you'll really enjoy it.'

I peer at Jess with a mixture of dismay and disbelief. 'Yeah right, you know what Vanessa and Anthony are like. Any event involving them is obliged by the law of probability to be a complete nightmare.' I reply. That was the only bit of maths I was good at, probability.

'I guess, but to be fair you're lucky they've invited you at all, having run off with their grandchildren. And at least you'll get a chance to see Dan and maybe talk things through.' Jess sips thoughtfully at her glass of wine. We are sitting in the sun-kissed garden of Larkin Cottage, looking out at the beautiful prospect over the vivid purple heather clad moor dipping down into the sparkling sea. 'This really is a beautiful view; I can see why you like it here.'

'Yep, it's perfect. It's a vista I never tire of.' Yet somehow I still feel sick if I even think of having to talk to Dan, let alone see him. The thought of it makes me top up my wine.

'Don't you think maybe you just had enough of the way things were? You needed to get back into work and have a change of scene. Now you've got that out of your system you could have Dan back. He could even move here and you could live this fab new life together.' Jess is serious now.

I hesitate. 'I love it here, and yes I needed to get out, but it wasn't just my old life I was trying to run from. It was Dan and his controlling ways.'

Jess is already frowning at my words. 'But I think he's so caring. So many wives would be glad to have a guy who wants to know where they are, what they're doing. At least he wasn't off seeing other girls or screwing around. He really wasn't that bad.'

I take a deep breath and try to keep calm as this is such an age-old argument for us. 'Look, Jess, we just don't agree on this. Dan is subtle; he might appear caring and loving, always giving me a kiss when you and John were there. He was affectionate in public but when we were alone he'd sulk for ages if I went out with friends. He'd give me the cold shoulder for weeks...' I break off as the tears are dangerously near. I feel as though my shiny new life is crumbling and Jess questioning it makes me doubt myself. What if Melstock is just a holiday and not a reality? If The Coffee Factory goes, will there be anything left for me?

'But he's a nice guy really. He's always smart and clean, he works hard and he's charming.' Jess blushes as she meets my eyes. 'John can be so grumpy and yet Dan's always in a good mood.'

'But that's just it,' I protest. 'He might appear to be in a good mood all the time but it's all a front. You don't see what he's like in between times. When he's had too much to drink, a bad day,' I break off as it's all too much.

'I've never really seen him drink,' protests Jess.

'That's because you don't exactly see him that

much.' I look at her face, which currently has a definitively guilty expression, 'do you?'

'Just a couple of times,' Jess has gone bright red, 'just to talk. About you of course, he's a broken man, totally lost without you and he misses the girls.'

'I'm sure he does,' I say forcing myself to be hard, 'but he can still see them from time to time. We're setting up access rights, and Vanessa took them out the other day.' I refrain from pointing out how much she upset Elise with her unkind comments about me.

'Elise and Summer need both their parents together,' continues Jess, 'and whatever you say, you two always made such a good team.'

'You're sounding like Mum now,' I groan.

'Don't ever say that, Rom. We're nothing like each other.' Mum and Jess don't ever really agree on anything at all. 'Speaking of Mum though, she did mention that she might be coming to visit you soon.'

'Oh no, when?'

'Soon, she said. She thinks you've had some kind of hormonal mid-life crisis and should see her latest quack therapist, Dr Quango or something, so I thought I'd warn you she's on the warpath, armed with a tank full of arnica and lashings of rescue remedy.'

I laugh in spite of the terrible impending threat. 'Too late, I've already taken some rescue remedy, but I think it's going to take something stronger than that to make me even vaguely think about going back to Dan or my old life.'

I contemplate all of this as I make my way through the crowded throng at the back of The Coffee Factory community hall. It makes me feel so anxious that I push it to the back of my mind and put on my best actress smile.

‘Hi, Romilly.’ I’m so pleased to see Debs, I give her a huge hug. ‘Everything alright? You look pretty darned stressed.’

‘My sister’s here with the chief aim of trying to persuade me to get back with Dan,’ I lament.

‘Oh dear, just what you need when you’re trying to get over him. Never mind. In the words of Jane Austen, she’s not going to be able to persuade you to feel something for him you don't!’

‘That’s true, it’s just...’

‘Just what?’

‘I doubt myself, and for the girls’ sake I wonder if I’m doing the right thing.’

‘All you can do is go by your gut feel and stick with it. Time will make it clearer,’ advises Debs. ‘Come on, we’re about to begin. Stuff Dan, we’ve got a factory to save!’

I follow Debs through the crowded room, feeling a bit better. She’s right as she often is. There’s a really good turn out; the hall is packed, chattering people spill out on the street, everyone who’s anyone from the village is here and some from the neighbouring area too. Walter is sitting at the back of the hall chatting to Doris from Knit and Natter. I smile at his oak apple lined face, which is animated and lively and he gives me a little wave which I return, feeling more cheerful.

Debs strides up to the front of the room, clambers onto an upturned box and addresses the room, ‘Well, hello everyone! Thank you so much for coming along. What a fantastic turn out!’

The room buzzes with hellos and murmurs of welcome.

'We've got everyone together as you all know, to discuss the very serious issue of the possible closure of our beloved Coffee Factory.'

The room echoes to a chorus of boos and hissing. It's rather entertaining actually, a bit like TV scenes of politicians at The House of Lords although there are rather more people here and they're all awake.

'Of course we're not going to let this happen, so we're meeting to discuss how we're going to campaign and ultimately prevent the loss of this wonderful community facility and local tourist attraction.'

'Hear hear!' cries Walter from the back.

'So initially we believe the factory is struggling from a lack of funds, so there's no one better than Mr Mark Whittaker to tell us a little more about the problem.' Debs stands to one side and Mark takes his place on the box. I'm surprised to see him here. Debs is a dark horse for keeping that one under her hat, but I guess I've been too busy worrying about Dan for her to be able to mention it.

'Good evening, Ladies and Gentlemen.' Mark smiles charmingly at the assembly. 'Now, of course, as the owners of The Coffee Factory, the Whittakers as a family wish to preserve its existence as part of the very lifeblood of Melstock. Yet we are a business, not a charity (he pauses as there is some muttering and murmurs of dissent amongst the floor) but this does not mean we do not care about the future of the factory.'

'Huh! Could have fooled me,' shouts someone at

the rear of the hall. It might have been Walter, but I can't be sure.

Debs intervenes. 'Come on, everyone, let's hear what Mark has to say.'

Mark continues, 'Thank you, Deborah. Now currently there is not only a shortfall in the profit of this enterprise as sales have been dwindling, but we have also lost the support of a large sponsor who has recently withdrawn their funding.'

'Shame,' shouts Barbara Asquith. She is seated at the front with a large Jack Russell on her lap who seems to have taken a dislike to the feather in the adjacent lady's hat, and is barking shrilly and vociferously.

'If you could control your dog,' Mark interjects at her, his voice icily cold.

Barbara taps the dog on his nose and shouts 'Quiet Barnaby,' in a loud voice, at which the dog sensibly resides into semi-silence, contenting himself with a low grumble at the offending hat.

'Can I just say something?' comes a familiar voice. It's Ciaran, who I had failed to notice, dapperly dressed as always, propped in the doorway.

'Of course, Ciaran. Speak away, old fellow,' drawls Mark.

'The staff at The Coffee Factory are well aware that sales could do better, but since the appointment of Romilly as our new sales advisor, they're picking up. She's introduced several new ideas which if implemented will substantially improve the figures.'

To my great embarrassment, the entire assembly peer round at me interestedly and burst into a round of applause.

Mark holds his hand in the air for silence. 'Yes, we are all aware of Romilly's great talents.' He manages to give me a sexy look, which makes me feel as though my attractions are nothing to do with my clever ideas. 'But obviously these things take time and we do not have much of that as a commodity.' I feel a bit dismissed actually.

'How long are we talking?' asks Barbara.

'A matter of months, I'm afraid,' replies Mark. 'Financial support is being withdrawn immediately and without such a significant injection of funding we'll only be able to cope for a short period of time.'

'Right then,' says Debs matter of factly, taking back the centre stage. 'We need ideas and fast.'

'What about fund raising events?' asks Jim, the butcher. 'We've had country fairs before on the playing fields by the park. They attract plenty of tourists and I can sell my local meat.'

'Great,' says Debs making a note in her pad. 'Anyone else?'

'I think the country fair's a super idea,' remarks Barbara. 'We could have terrier races, country sports etc, which will attract more people in.'

'Absolutely,' says Debs. 'I think we are agreed that fund raising is key.'

'I'd like to get the school involved,' chips in Mr Barton. I hadn't noticed him sitting a couple of rows back; he appears so different, even more young and boyish in a shirt and jeans. I'm really not surprised I thought he was a teaching assistant as he looks fresh out of college.

‘Lovely. What are your thoughts on that?’ asks Debs.

‘Sponsored events, readathons, sports, music events. Let me get my thinking cap on and I’ll get back to you, but of course I’ll need to check with Mr Briggs.’ Mr Briggs is the school headmaster.

‘I was thinking of organising some polo matches,’ remarks Mark casually. ‘Ma and Pa are always happy to host them at Melstock Manor and any proceeds we can give to the cause.’

‘Jolly decent,’ mutters Clive, the pet shop chap.

After some more chat and various suggestions of sponsored events and donations from possible charitable causes, Debs thanks everyone for their support and we disband for the evening.

Absentmindedly, I smile at Mr Barton as he goes out the door just before me. I then wish I hadn’t as he looks blankly back at me and goes on to talk to someone else. Stupid man.

‘Romilly, darling?’ Mark trots after me, ‘time for a nightcap?’

‘No sorry, I need an early night as I’m entertaining my sister tomorrow,’ I reply, glad of an excuse to be honest.

‘Darling, since when have you become such a party poop?’ moans Mark putting his arm round my shoulders.

Mr Barton looks back and I swear he overheard; I can feel the disapproval radiating from his retreating shoulder blades.

‘Since half my family seem to have decided to descend on me, but,’ smiling in a manner which I hope is seductive, ‘I’m free later this week.’ I try a flutter of the eyelashes for extra appeal.

‘Do you have something in your eye?’ Mark peers at me. Okay so maybe I am still rubbish at the whole seduction thing. I never could flirt, it always went wrong, yet other women do it effortlessly, flicking their luscious manes and trapping men with their fine eyes. Sickening!

‘No.’ I’m totally embarrassed now and surreptitiously pretend to wipe my eye from any imaginary dust as if to give substance to the story. Perhaps I’ll just stick to being myself.

‘On Saturday my family’s having a point-to-point meeting at the old ancestral shack. Come along. There’ll be some good sport.’

Oh great! The last thing I want to do is hang round with Mark’s hideous family again. In fact, I can’t face his parents at all. Maybe I could alter my appearance and pretend to be someone else. It would however be a fantastic opportunity to snoop about and find out what’s going on with The Coffee Factory.

‘Absolutely! Looking forward to it already,’ I say in a fake cheery manner. I am so not cut out for this espionage thing, but if it’s the only way to save The Coffee Factory, I’m going to give it a darn good try.

Chapter 18

'This is absolutely stunning!' exclaims Jess, happily.

'I know, isn't it perfick?' We always laugh about Pop Larkin and his perfick outlook on life but since I've been in Devon, I can see why he said it so much in *The Darling Buds of May*.

We're strolling along in the nearby Davenham Valley, our favourite family walk since coming to Melstock. The footpath winds alongside a tumbling, chattering clear stream with great moor-clad hills rising magnificently either side. Before the moor line, sheep graze contentedly in the farmer's sloping fields and we walk a little lower down, our feet traipsing through long lush grass. Further along the valley from the tiny, picturesque church, the bells ring out and above us the sky shines blue and endless.

'I defy anyone not to feel all is well with the world here,' I say watching Summer paddle upstream, a dipper oblivious to her presence diving in and out from the rock pools. Even Elise who, at her age you'd think would be too cool for such things, is happily striding along near the sheep looking out for newborn lambs.

'It's idyllic this escape of yours,' smiles Jess. 'You've been different too, since you've been here. More relaxed and sort of independent. I kind of admire it.'

'Oh, thanks.' I reply, as to be honest I've been

worried everyone thinks the opposite.

'You are! Look at you, you're tanned and healthy looking, I reckon you've lost a fair bit of weight and you just seem much more together somehow.'

I laugh. 'Yes, but you've always been more together in the first place.'

'Not really,' replies Jess, nonchalantly brushing her carefully highlighted and beautifully cut hair out of her face.

I smile to myself. Jess is super organised; her idea of a crisis is if she hasn't put her outfit out the night before. 'Come on – you're super woman!'

'You don't see me all the time, and to be fair Bradley does his best to cause as much chaos as possible.' Jess pulls a wry face.

'How's he getting on with John's mum?' I ask.

'Apparently quite well. I haven't heard any complaints yet, just a phone call yesterday from him to say goodnight and that he'd been to the farm park all day, so I reckon he was pretty happy.'

'Wow – that's great! You might even get another break where you and John can spend some quality time together,' I remark.

'Yes, that would be nice,' sighs Jess. 'We had a nice dinner last night and it was so lovely to be in a luxury hotel, but John had to rush off early this morning to the meeting room and that's pretty much how it always is.'

'I know, but that's part of the deal with high paid sales, isn't it?' I reply. 'Not that I don't understand, I really do – look at Dan and I. Hardly ever saw each other in the end. I used to hang around like a needy puppy waiting for a pat on the head.'

‘Is that why you left him?’ asks Jess, gazing absentmindedly at a nearby grazing sheep.

‘Not really. The problem was more how he was when he was there,’ I say slowly and then stop in my tracks. ‘This waterfall here, was where local hero Joshua Bell climbed into the lair of the local bandits to rescue his love.’

‘How romantic,’ sighs Jess. We wander up the steep slope to the side of the tumbling water. ‘It’s not that dangerous is it, though? I mean, I think even I could climb up this in a good pair of Hunters!’

I laugh. ‘The water level’s higher in the winter and far more hazardous, I’m sure. The floods absolutely torrent down it then, but I see what you mean, it doesn't look quite as spectacular as legend has it!’

Jess sighs. ‘Is anything quite as the books describe it? Such heroes are few and far between.’

‘Is everything all right with you and John?’ I ask.

‘Yes I guess, it’s just...’

‘Just what?’ I reply.

‘Nothing really. Sometimes I just wish he were different, that’s all. More like Dan for example.’

‘Dan!’ I exclaim. ‘No, John’s worth twenty of Dan.’

‘But he’s always so charming, John can be quite crabby when he comes in from work. Well, a lot of the time actually.’

‘Believe me, you’re much better off with him. He’s a good man with a normal family and healthy coping strategies,’ I say firmly.

‘I guess.’ Jess plucks at a leaf overhanging the path. ‘Are you really going to be happy here on your own? I mean, what if it’s just holiday euphoria which eventually wears off, so you don't belong anywhere? We all miss you, Rom. John, Mum, Dad, Dan, Bradley too – I mean who else is there to plot and giggle with? Besides, running away isn't always the solution, you know.'

'I know, Jess.' I stop and give her a big hug, 'I think the world of you all, but I love it here and we can still meet up. This is something I have to do for me.' Oh no, the hormones have set me off sniffing. Her words have got me thinking and I don't know if it's my imagination, but the sky seems a little less blue and the sun a little less glowing on the route back to the village.

Back at The Coffee Factory on Monday morning things still seem difficult. Mind you, I always dislike Monday mornings. I think they should be banned; a three day week would be much more civilised. Starting on a Tuesday wouldn't seem half so bad. Bizarrely, I used to hate Mondays even when I didn't work. There was always that slightly depressing, just going back to school feeling about Sunday evening and then on Mondays I would be left to feel sad on my own. I always tried to keep extra busy on a Monday to alleviate the situation. Now, at The Coffee Factory, we always have a little moan about it over a wonderful cup of motivating steaming freshly ground coffee beans, and I never know whether it's the beans or the company that makes me feel better. Probably both, I think. This morning however, the atmosphere is rather less positive.

'Barely two months we've got, I understand,' remarks Mrs Miggins, deftly placing out the baking trays ready for chocolate brownies.

'I know. It doesn't give us very long to act,' I reply.

'We need to get going on your ideas, Romilly,' says Ciaran.

'I'm game if you are,' I reply, trying to appear more motivated than I actually feel right now.

'Trouble is, our friend Mr Whittaker doesn't seem very able to help us.' Ciaran's tone is slightly sardonic.

'I'm sure he's a very busy man,' Mrs Miggins replies matter of factly, placing mixing bowls in order.

'I guess, although surely this should be his priority,' continues Ciaran, 'but he's not willing to put any money towards our marketing campaign.'

'What on earth is his excuse?' I ask puzzled. 'That's very odd.'

'That's what I think,' comments Ciaran, downing his coffee and pouring himself another cup.

'Have you tried saying how urgent it is?' I ask.

'Well, yeah,' remarks Ciaran sarcastically.

Okay, so I asked for that. 'I guess there's no point moaning about it. We'll just have to get on without him.'

'Mark Whittaker is a lovely man. His family have run Melstock Manor for centuries. I'm sure he won't let this factory go to wrack and ruin,' insists Mrs Miggins.

Ciaran looks unconvinced and I must admit there seems little point in sitting around hoping for a miracle without helping one along a little. My fairy godmother got up and left a long time ago, so I figure waiting for her to show up now is a little pointless.

'Yes, of course, Mrs Miggins, but there's no harm in getting things started as he's so busy at the moment,' I say.

Mrs Miggins humphs and disappears into the

pantry for more ingredients.

'I suggest we get going with the plans for now. If necessary I'll pay for the printing out of my wages and I'll get Phil at the Post Office to help me with advertising the taster sessions,' I whisper so Mrs Miggins doesn't hear.

'Good idea and I'll organise some volunteers for the talks on speciality coffees and a couple of the boys upstairs will advise me on the itinerary for the factory tours.' Ciaran whips out a notebook and starts scribbling away.

'I'll go and speak to Walter, who I know will be only too pleased to help out with a talk or two. It would be great for people to know how the factory was way back when. There must even be some photos hanging about somewhere, or Walter's bound to have some. If not, I could try the Devon Record Office.' I'm warming to my task in spite of the possibility of the closure of the factory. Failure is not an option; this means too much to too many people.

At lunch time I leg it across the road to the Post Office and look over some flyer designs with Phil.

'We need to include all the information about the programme of talks on the poster. Perhaps the one on May 9th could be Walter giving 'A Personal History of The Coffee Factory' then Ben's 'Tales From the Factory Floor' will follow on May 15th.'

'Okay,' Phil deftly moves the dates and figures around on the screen. 'Are these going to be weekly talks, or is this just a trial to see how they get on?'

'Very much a trial run,' I comment, flicking through my notes. 'We need to add Mrs Miggins' talk on 'Baking with Pure Coffee' and Ciaran's lectures on 'Coffees from Indonesia' and 'The Little Beans Initiative'.'

Phil soon adds everything I need. He really is a whizz on the computer.

'Are you okay to finish those?' I ask, 'I've got parents' evening for Elise tonight up at the school and I could do with popping in on Walter before I go?'

'Of course,' says Phil, still peering at the screen. 'They'll be ready by close of play tomorrow.'

'You're a star!' I shove all my stuff in my bag. 'Oh, and let me know what I owe and I'll settle up then.'

'Nonsense,' replies Phil. 'I refuse to charge you for something which is for all of us.'

'I can't let you pay,' I protest. 'That's hardly fair.'

'Well, maybe you could contribute a little to the cost of ink, but nothing much.' Phil pats me on the back.

'You're a gem,' I reply, and rush out of the shop before my emotions threaten to get the better of me. I bump into Alexandrine coming in with bags of shopping. 'I've left the designs with your lovely husband, I tell her.'

'Ha! which one's that?' she laughs.

'You're both fab,' I smile. 'Project 'Save The Coffee Factory' is officially underway.'

My visit to Walter is of course a success although I'm genuinely sorry not to be able to sit and have one of his delicious coffees and a teacake. In true Walter style, he's absolutely thrilled to be asked to do a talk on his time at the factory. He even grabs a couple of photos from a battered old album with sepia images of a young optimistic looking Walter and his pretty young wife laughing over a small puppy kneeling on the lawn in front of this cottage. There were before and after pictures of the garden, 'dug the stream out ourselves we did, it was full of mosquitos and weeds' and also of his wife in her pristine apron in the coffee factory, grinding beans smiling enthusiastically.

I surreptitiously wipe a tear from my eye as I look at these images from so long ago. Walter and his wife's eager young faces radiate optimism, but I realise I needn't have worried as I notice Walter does the same. 'Wonderful memories,' he reminisces. 'We were very happy together.'

'Ah, the secret of a happy marriage,' I say brightly, hoping to cover my own sadness.

'We were very lucky,' he continues. 'I loved her from the very first moment I saw her, but over time it was the little things, the small touches, the hidden kindnesses she always did, the manner in which she flicked her hair, her smile, the scent of her perfume, the way she set the table.'

I gaze at him, finding myself smiling in a ridiculous fashion at this genuine love story. I am envious. It's as though romance existed a long time ago; something which is no longer possible, no longer exists. I can't imagine anyone spending long enough not looking at their phone or their iPad to notice such small caring things.

Walter looks up at me, his eyes shining. 'There was no doubt she was the love of my life and I was hers.'

'You make me envious,' I say shyly.

'Your time will come,' he says patting my hand.

'You just have to believe in the magic.' I think he must have noticed my doubting expression because he jokes, 'Well, that, and stop picking complete and utter cads.'

I laugh. Walter becomes serious again for a moment. 'Can I just add a little something? It's not my business to interfere, but as an old man of ninety-one I've learnt a thing or two along the way.'

'Of course,' I'm intrigued now and lean in a little closer.

'Be wary of that Mark Whittaker,' he says soberly.

'Oh, okay.' I wasn't expecting that.

'I gather you've been walking out together,' he continues.

'Well, in a manner of speaking, but it's nothing serious... I mean, I'm not sure he's really my type,' I reply, not knowing what else to say.

'Just be careful, m'dear. I'm not sure he's a gentleman and quite frankly, you could do so much better.'

'Believe me, I've done much worse,' I laugh, embarrassed.

'I'm sure you have but that's simply because you don't believe in yourself,' he takes my arm, 'but you must. You're a wonderful person and there's someone out there who's right just for you, who cares about you, looks out for you, helps you win your battles, is fighting your side.'

'Sounds like Mr Perfect,' I laugh. 'Do you think he really exists?'

'I know he does,' replies Walter. 'He won't be perfect. Goodness only knows I wasn't, but when I lost Vera it was like losing my right arm.'

I think on his words as I drive to Elise's school. Relationships are a funny thing. How come some people meet the right person first off and remain happily married to them for a lifetime and yet others marry several times and it ends in tears every time? I read somewhere that there's no point getting divorced because you'll only end up marrying the same type – in fact that's exactly what Dad cheerfully says to Mum every time she feels fed up, and although they both laugh I can feel the tension under the humour.

For now, I have no more time to reflect on marriage – happy or otherwise – because I have the joy of Elise's parents' evening to face. To be fair, Dan never came to them anyway so going alone is not exactly a new experience, but it would be nice to have someone to come along and share the burden and discussion of choosing GCSEs. Dan was always too tired, or too busy or too tired *and* too busy. 'I can't think about the kids and my job,' he would remark, so that was the end of that. Neatly compartmentalised, the kids and me out of the way, in a box clearly marked, 'not my problem'. Are all men like this, I wonder? I did read *Men are from Mars, Women are from Venus*, once. I learnt all about the man cave and how they need time in it. I dutifully made sure Dan had his own space when he got in from work, when the girls were younger. They were always in bed anyway. I made sure he had his dinner on the table and there was no stressful chat as soon as he came in from work. No stressful chat during dinner. No stressful chat after dinner as he wanted to watch TV. No stressful chat just before bed because he was trying to go to sleep. No stressful chat first thing in the morning because he was going to work.

'When *can* I talk to you?' I would ask, exasperated.

'I don't know,' he would always reply angrily, 'but not now.'

Yep, I'm definitely better off without him. And he didn't ever read *Men are from Mars, Women are from Venus* anyway. It's all very well us women spending hours reading self-help books, but it's not much good when men don't think they need to. That's kind of the whole problem.

I pull into the school car park, climb out the car and wait for Elise to come out. Bizarrely, she isn't in the front seat, but she isn't outside the car either. I peer round randomly. 'For goodness' sake, Elise, we're late,' I say, looking in the back of the car. She's on the floor in front of the back seats. 'What on earth are you doing?'

'It's Courtney,' she whispers. 'Don't talk to me, I don't want her to see me.'

I look about completely confused. There's no-one about at all, just a couple of harried looking parents running in from outside the school gate, which is what we should be doing. Then I spot her. Yes, she looks just like the well off, but super cool bullies who made my life miserable at school. Long blonde hair, that perma tan look that seems to just be effortless, even the way she wears her uniform, the length of her tie, all of it is unmitigatingly nonchalant and chic. She saunters off round the corner. 'It's alright, she's gone.'

'Are you sure?' Elise pokes her head up like a recalcitrant meerkat.

'Yes, I'm totally sure.' I open the car door next to

her and she climbs out sheepishly. 'I presume you don't like this girl, Courtney, whoever she is?'

'Shhh, someone might hear you,' Elise stalks into the front door of the school like a cat on hot bricks.

'Good evening, I'm Miss Minchin, Head of Year 9.' A rather rotund, kind looking lady shakes my hand. 'If you'd like to sign the list and make your way through to the hall for the talk.'

I scribble my name and make my way into the vast school hall, Elise skulking along behind me. Old habits die hard, so I sit at the back so I can make fast my exit at the end of the evening. The talk consists of three members of staff lecturing on the GCSE subject choices, how to choose them and how the system works. It makes sense I think, although I am amused mostly by how much the school witters on about how brilliant their results are and how their green jumpers (which I still think are hideous) make them better than anyone else. I'm not really sure how that works. I'm also distracted by the constant whispering of two people behind me who I thought were students as their behaviour's so rude, but they in actual fact turn out to be two parents. Why they can't have their mother's meeting outside I do not understand at all.

Finally the talking drags to an end and the Vice Principal is just reiterating her final points on choosing the right courses, when the bell rings and all the parents get up in one swooping movement and start walking out of the hall. The Vice Principal starts spieling faster as if to try to get her last few words out before everyone leaves. 'This is a serious decision for your child's future. Please ensure you fill in the form correctly and support them with their choices.' She raises her voice desperately to the retreating hordes. 'And thank you for coming.'

Unbelievable. This would never have happened at Riversmeet Senior in a million years. I remember the parents' evening there; the atmosphere was very different. Instead of everyone milling in looking dishevelled and disinterested, they were all queuing determinedly over half an hour before the talk was due to begin. Then when the doors opened, they charged on in, elbowing each other out of the way, ambitious mother's clutching notebooks or iPads so they could note down the best way to get their little Freda the advancement she deserved. They would do anything to get ahead of the game and sit at the front, poised, hanging on every word. It used to make me laugh when the head teacher would say, 'Don't worry about getting tuition to get into the school. Just a little practice each day is all you need.'

As if he didn't know what a serious business this was. For some mums it was a full time job. Not get any coaching? He must have been joking. Surely he was aware the parents started coaching their little darlings from the age of four. Leaving it until they were six was surely too late and it couldn't just be any tutor, it had to be the very best.

I smile to myself and wait for the charging parents to leave the room. 'Bit different from your old school, isn't it?' I grin. Talk about the sublime to the ridiculous.

Elise glares at me so I get myself back under control and try not to be embarrassing, although it is quite tempting to be honest. Personally, I think it's part of our jobs as mums to be embarrassing; it's in the job description. In any case it's payback for all those times our children were unreasonable tantruming toddlers. 'Where now?' I ask.

'Up to the classrooms to meet the teachers,' Elise replies, looking uneasily around her. I follow her up the stairs to what appears to be the language block. I wander around the classrooms talking to teachers who don't really seem to know who she is. I guess she's new and this isn't a small school. She's one of fifteen hundred, so I guess she's bound to blend in a bit.

We meander down the corridor and I follow Elise into the Science room, then she stops suddenly. 'We can't go in there!' she says abruptly and backs up against me.

'What are you doing?' I ask, puzzled, but I follow her retreating back down the stairway.

'We can't go in there,' she repeats tearfully.

'Why on earth not?' I ask. 'Has there been a chemical explosion?'

'Mum, that's not funny.' I thought it was actually.

'We'll go to English,' she says and I follow her into another class. I'm idly flicking through a textbook when she grabs my arm. 'Mum,' she says desperately and disappears out the room leaving me gawping after her. I look a bit stupid now standing there on my own, so I hurriedly replace the book and follow her.

'What on earth's going on, Elise?' I ask. 'This is really strange behaviour.'

'Jenna Evans and Courtney Weaver are in there,' she says as though this explains everything.

'Well, is that all the classrooms we're able to go in?'

I ask.

‘Yes it is,’ she says matter of factly.

‘Okay. Then we might as well go home, I suppose.’ We walk out to the car and start the short drive back to the cottage.

‘Elise, there seems to be a problem here,’ I say gently as I mechanically follow the last few bends between the fields to the village.

She has her back to me as much as possible; all I can see is part of her profile and her ponytail, staring blankly out of the window.

‘No, there’s nothing wrong,’ she mutters.

Great – the usual response then. But there obviously is a flipping huge problem. That’s another one to add to all the others, which all seem to be piling up one on top of the other into a huge mountain of problems. My gran always used to say that she felt as though she were pushing a large boulder up a hill for most of her life. Every time she stopped to rest, it would roll back towards her and she would have to carry right on pushing. This feels exactly like my life right now except currently a whole load of boulders are rolling down the hill towards me and I don't seem to be able to get out of the way.

Chapter 19

'Where's Elise?' I ask Summer, whilst hurriedly slurping the rest of my cereal and spilling some down my front in the process. Darn! That top was clean on and ready for work. I run upstairs to rummage frantically around in my drawers to find another one.

'Dunno, she was here a moment ago,' replies Summer, tipping out the entire contents of her schoolbag on the floor. 'Have you seen my project book?'

I return down the stairs to find Summer surrounded by pencils, a mouldy apple and several squashed exercise books. 'Come on, we're going to be late!' I notice Elise in the kitchen. 'Oh, there you are. Let's go.'

'I'm not going!' retorts Elise. On closer inspection she's not even properly dressed.

'Where's your tie? We can't afford to be late today. I'm working and you don't want any more late marks.'

'That's fine, because I'm not going in.' Elise storms out of the kitchen and towards the stairs.

'You have exactly five minutes to finish getting yourself dressed and back down here ready to go,' I declare in my *you've pushed it too far now my girl*, authoritative tone. My only reward is the sound of a slammed bedroom door. 'Make sure you're absolutely ready for school,' I inform an open-mouthed Summer. I run round the house turning things off, brushing my hair and pass Summer her packed lunch. It's 8.05 and there's no sign of Elise. I storm up the stairs, shove open the door and survey the room. She doesn't appear to be in there. I look in all the usual hidey holes, behind the door, the wardrobe, although to be fair it's so full of rubbish that she wouldn't be able to get in there anyway. She seems to have vanished. I peer out of the window. Of course there's a bit of flat roof, then an overhanging cherry tree. She must have climbed out.

'Mum, I'm going to be late,' shouts Summer.

'Okay, I'm coming.' I rush down the stairs, grab my bag and we leave the house. We march to the Junior School, peering behind walls and bushes just in case Elise is hiding. This is such a bizarre situation and I feel well out of my depth. She's been challenging at times before but is usually so law abiding. She hates being late for school, let alone refusing to go.

'Morning, morning!' blasts Jim from the butchers.

'Morning, Jim. Haven't seen Elise, have you?' I ask pathetically.

'Nope – not seen anyone much except Mrs Miggins on her way to the factory. You lost a child?'

'Temporarily yes,' I admit with a rueful smile. 'A bad case of not wanting to go to school.'

'Don't blame her,' retorts Jim. 'By her age I'd left and was working in the shop. No point sitting looking at books all day when there's proper work to be done.'

I don't stop to explain that she usually quite likes studying, it's more a case of the other kids by the sound of it. Summer and I arrive at the school gates. I've given up looking around for Elise as she certainly wouldn't try and hide here, although I did scan the park on the way round.

'You alright?' asks Molly. 'You look a bit stressed.'

'No, I've lost Elise. She doesn't want to go to school and has done a bunk,' I say, anxiously looking up to spot Mr Barton lurking alongside.

'Morning, Summer,' he comments brightly, although I notice he's looking intently at me. Why is that man always where I don't want him to be? He makes me feel so judged.

'Don't worry,' Molly replies. 'I'm sure she'll have a little sulk and then turn up. You know what teenagers are like, although I must admit mine always liked school.'

I smile weakly and hurry back towards home. At this rate I'm going to be late for work, but there's no way I can go without having a last check around for Elise. I rush in like a tornado, casting off my shoes and turn the cottage upside down from top to bottom, which doesn't take long as it's pretty small really. I go to grab my jacket for work. It's no good, I'll have to give up. I think I must have left it in the car so open the door to root about for that and my lippy when I see something move in the back. It's Elise curled up in the foot well of the rear passenger seat. She's obviously been crying as her face is all red and blotchy. She looks terrible.

'Elise, what on earth are you doing?' I ask, I mean, it's totally obvious that she's hiding, but in my defence it has been a rather trying morning.

'Hiding from you,' she sniffs.

‘I think I probably worked that out for myself. This is ridiculous, come out and at least talk to me.’

‘Not if you’re going to make me go to that school,’ she says defiantly with all traces of tears gone and a note of steel in her voice. It always amazes me how teenagers – and girls in general – can go from calamitous weeping and distress, yet turn it off in an instant into determined defiance. Or maybe it’s just my two; drama queens the pair of them.

‘Okay,’ I sigh. ‘I won’t make you go today, but please let’s go and talk about this like civilised people.’

‘You won’t make me go tomorrow?’ she bargains.

‘I’m not promising anything,’ I say quietly, giving her my hand as she tries to climb out of the cramped space.

‘I’m not going in tomorrow,’ Elise reiterates, as she retreats into the house.

Oh great, this is going really well. I follow her in and flick the kettle on. ‘I’ll get you a nice cup of camomile tea,’ I suggest. ‘Very calming.’

‘I hate that,’ she remarks huddled on the sofa. ‘It tastes like cat wee.’

‘Yes, I see your point,’ I sigh again, ‘not that I’ve ever tasted cat wee – admittedly it does smell a bit like it, but it’s more likely to make you feel calmer.’

‘I’m totally calm. I just don't want to go to school.’

‘Rescue remedy?’ I produce some and place some drops in a glass, which at least she takes. I put some in a glass for myself because goodness only knows I need it.

‘Right, what’s all this about?’ I ask sitting next to her in what I hope is an understanding mum/non-threatening best friend manner.

'I just hate the school and I don't want to go there anymore.'

'But you have to go to school. It's the law,' I remark.

'I could be home schooled,' she replies.

'Not really, I mean who would teach you?'

'You could,' she says hopefully.

'But I have to go out to work and I'm rubbish at Science anyway.'

'If you were still with Dad you could have stayed home and taught me.'

'Hardly, I'm not a teacher.'

'I can teach myself. I've got books.'

'Oh, Elise, that's not really the answer, is it? So what's so terrible about this school?'

'I could write you a list,' remarks Elise. At least her sense of humour seems to be returning.

'That would be helpful,' I say. 'It's all very well studying at home, even if you could get by without the teaching, but you need friends.'

'I don't have any friends,' she says sadly. This seems odd as she was so popular at her last school.

'What about Lila?'

'She's nice, but she's in another year so I don't really see much of her.'

'Well, there must be someone else?'

'Not really. They're all so immature and silly, messing around in class and stuff. No one seems to want to do any work.'

Oh dear, it does sounds pretty rubbish to be honest. 'But some kids must want to work as some of them come out with good results. I've seen the league tables.'

'I haven't seen any of them,' hurrumphs Elise.

I take a quick look at my watch. I'm now super late for work. 'I'm going to have to go, Elise. I'll be back late morning and we can have some lunch together. Will you be okay?'

Elise nods.

'And make that list of things about the school you're struggling with.' I leg it out of the door.

'It'll be half a mile long,' her voice retorts after me as I run down the path.

'I'm so sorry,' I pant at Ciaran who is wrestling with spreadsheets on the computer.

'Trouble in paradise?' he asks smiling, no doubt at my dishevelled and dramatic appearance.

'Total disaster,' I remark, 'but I'm here now and ready to rumble.'

'Great. Walter's in the café and asking for you to bring him his coffee.'

Walter is just what I need this morning with his calming wisdom and gentle routine. I feel soothed by his very presence. 'I'm struggling with nine down,' he says, 'I'm sure you can help me with it. Cat got your tongue. Seven letters.'

'Let me get your usual, Walter, and I'll think on it. Any clues?'

'Starts with the letter a.' Oh, that doesn't really help much; I disappear back into the kitchen to prepare the coffee beans.

'Kids giving you trouble?' asks Mrs Miggins.

'Don't they always?' I smile.

'It's probably just a phase, you know,' she says

philosophically. 'My mother always said that about mine and I thought she was making it up as she went along, but she was quite right, you know. All of the phases passed eventually.'

'Yes,' I remark with feeling, 'but just as you think you've got to grips with one phase, they start another one you know absolutely nothing about.' I leave Mrs Miggins open mouthed, coffee spoon in her hand.

'There you are,' I pass Walter his coffee. 'Have you worked it out yet?'

'No, I was relying on you.'

'Oh dear, that's probably not a good idea,' I say awkwardly.

'Come on, sit down and drink in this beautiful view,' says Walter, moving his crossword book out of my way. 'You're not your usual bubbly happy self this morning. What's up?'

'Just teenagers,' I say ominously.

Walter laughs. 'Been there, done that,' he says, 'but seriously Vera always used to say keep talking to them. That's what she did and it seemed to work. Of course there were rows. My daughter was so strong-minded at that age and I was hopeless at the whole talking about it thing. Vera was simply brilliant.'

'Thanks. I'll certainly try it. Vera sounds a wonderful person,' I say and put my hand on Walter's.

'She sure was,' he replies. 'Now, I'm here to talk about the future, not the past.' He bends down and rummages with a slightly shaky hand in a holdall hung on the arm of the chair.

'I've brought you this.' He brings out a tattered old envelope, which I stare at, puzzled. 'Now this isn't much so don't get too excited, but I reckon it will give the factory a start.'

Walter passes the envelope and its contents into my hand. 'Open it,' he says excitedly.

I open the envelope and pull out a huge wad of notes. 'Oh, my gosh! Walter, what on earth is this? Have you robbed a bank?'

'Wish I had done, but I don't fancy prison at my age. Apparently the food's terrible.'

I don't like to openly count the money in front of him as that seems somewhat vulgar, but as they're £50 notes I can tell there's over a thousand pounds here.

'But seriously, Walter, where did you get all this? Don't you need it to keep yourself in the manner to which you'd like to become accustomed?' I'm joking because I just feel so awkward.

'I sold a couple of things, that's all.' Walter busies himself with his crossword book. 'Now what about nine across? I thought of 'dumbfounded' but it doesn't start with 'a' and it's too many letters.'

'Walter,' I protest. 'What did you sell? Nothing of sentimental value, I hope?'

'Not really,' he pauses and looks a little sheepish. 'It was just my old medals.'

I stop and stare at him, completely shocked. 'Not your war medals?'

'Yes, m'dear. They didn't hand them out for working in the factory and to be honest, they were only sitting in a drawer catching dust.'

'But you loved those medals.' I remember Walter showing them to us one day when we were having tea and cake. I can picture the pride in his face when he was handing them round, the memories they brought back of comrades from long ago. Momentarily I have a job to control myself as my eyes fill with tears.

‘You’re a very special person, Walter,’ I say simply.

‘I know,’ he says. ‘I’ve solved the crossword. The missing word is aphonic.’

‘What on earth?’ I stutter, ‘I didn't even know that was a word.’

‘Well, there you go,’ he says. ‘Not just a pretty face, me. Have you any more coffee where that one came from? You’re getting quite good at making it, you know.’

Chapter 20

'Mrs Greene?'

'Yes,' I jump up and shake hands with the approaching lady who is, according to her badge, Mrs Hardick. I bet that name causes more than a few sniggers in class. I'm amazed I've still got a sense of humour as I've just spent the last ten minutes staring blankly at a screen blazoned with news headlines. I think the school believe it's a good idea for the students to be aware of world affairs, but to my mind it just depresses them. It certainly has me, and I've only been here a short while.

I follow Mrs Hardick down the corridor and into a meeting room, which on first inspection already contains another three people. This was not what I was expecting and I feel like running back out of the door again. It's times like this when I would have liked a supportive husband with me, but right now it's me, myself and I, so I'll have to muddle through somehow. I give a vaguely pleasant smile at the assembled company and sit down.

'Right, Mrs Greene,' Mrs Hardick sits down next to me and shuffles her officious looking pile of papers. 'We are here to discuss your daughter, Elise.'

'Yes,' I say simply, because quite honestly what else are we here to discuss?

‘This is Mr Huxtable, Head of Year,’ she gestures towards a thin, gawky man who looks a little like Wally from ‘Where’s Wally?’ I smile and shake hands. ‘This is Miss Mandy, the School Welfare Officer, and this is Miss Luke who is Assistant Head of Year, she also teaches PE in some years. I shake hands with everyone wondering why we need so many people here; I mean I just wanted a quick chat with someone about Elise.

‘Is Elise’s form tutor here?’ I ask hesitantly, wondering if I’ve missed something.

‘No, she’s teaching, but that’s fine, we can tell her the upshot of the meeting,’ Mrs Hardick briefly dismisses any such request.

‘It’s only I thought it would be useful to speak to someone who teaches Elise,’ I mumble, feeling seriously outnumbered.

Mr Huxtable gives a little laugh, which is quite comical really. I’ve never heard anyone laugh so much like Father Christmas, it was so ‘ho ho ho’ like. It makes me peer at him rather strangely. ‘No, no, the form tutor doesn't teach any of our students,’ he guffaws.

‘Oh,’ I say. ‘I thought that was the whole point.’

‘No, no, no. They just meet them for form lesson in the morning for ten minutes and then the students go off to other lessons.’ His ‘no, noing’ makes me think of the funny old chap on *The Vicar of Dibley* who was always ‘no no noing’ about everything.

‘Oh right.’ I’m still confused, as at Riversmeet Senior the form tutor looked out for the youngsters in their form and were first port of call if there had been any issues, not that there ever were actually. They did fun activities in form time and they also met early afternoon to take the register and give out notices. 'I haven't quite learnt how it all works yet.'

'Quite,' Mrs Hardick says in a patronising tone. 'So what seems to be the problem with Elise?' She emphasises the word 'seems' to add impetus to the suggestion that it might only appear to be a problem, rather than actually be one.

'I think Elise might be having difficulties with some of the other girls,' I say, 'and I'm worried it's becoming a real issue as she doesn't want to come to school.'

Mr Huxtable and Mrs Hardick exchange loaded glances. 'Make a note of that, Miss Mandy, please.' Miss Mandy, who quite honestly looks as though she is aged about twelve, scribbles down some notes. 'Elise doesn't want to come to school, Miss Mandy,' prompts Mrs Hardick.

'I don't think that's the point,' I add, hurriedly. 'It's not that she doesn't want to come to school, but her behaviour when we were at the school parents' evening.'

'So it's about her behaviour,' parrots Miss Mandy, scribbling on her pad. God, I feel like grabbing it and ripping it into a thousand pieces, she is so annoying.

'No,' I say patiently. 'Prior to this, Elise has been a happy, well-behaved student who liked going to school. But now she doesn't.'

'But, she has only been here a few weeks, she's bound to find it all a little different,' Mrs Hardick comments with an air of long suffering as though I am having difficulty understanding.

'Of course, I know that. I didn't expect it to be easy but she's been okay until the last week or so, when she's been too frightened to go into certain classrooms when certain girls are present.' Oh no, over use of certain but I'm beginning to feel a little frustrated.

'Okay,' Mrs Hardick purses her mouth, not unlike a bottom. 'Can you tell me which girls these are?'

Oh God, this really feels like being back at school. I feel terrible giving these girls' names, but then again, the ones I saw looked as though they could look after themselves. I harden myself, 'Courtney Weaver, Jenna Evans and Myra... I can't remember her surname.'

'Mitchigan...' replies Mrs Hardick.

'Right okay,' I say. 'Do you know these girls then?' Aha! so they are obviously renowned troublemakers.

'Of course,' says Mrs Hardick. 'They are very confident young women, shall I say, but there's no harm in them. Has your daughter ever thought of having some 'how to make friends' sessions?'

'What?' I ask flabbergasted. I've always wondered what it's like to be flabbergasted and now I know because my flabber is most definitely gasted. 'Making friends?' I echo weakly.

'Yes,' interrupts Miss Mandy unexpectedly enthusiastically. 'We offer those to children like Elise who struggle to make friends. They're great.'

'But... Elise has always had loads of friends. I mean, she was really popular at her previous school. It's just that these girls seem to run the year group from what I understand.'

Mrs Hardick's smile becomes fixed. 'I think you'll find, Mrs Greene, that these girls can seem a little intimidating to those who are less confident. I'll put Elise down for some 'making friends sessions' with

Miss Mandy.'

'I do have a waiting list though,' says Miss Mandy cheerfully, 'but at the moment it's about a hundred long so you'll only be waiting six months or so.'

'Six months?' I stutter. Quite honestly I'm now totally confused. 'But surely it would be better if Courtney and Jenna and Mya or whatever her name is, have the lessons on how to make friends, then they wouldn't feel the need to bully other children.'

There's an audible sharp intake of breath around the table, 'No...no...no, we don't have bullying in this school, Mrs Greene,' states Mr Huxtable emphatically. His words make me jump as I actually thought he'd gone to sleep, he'd been so quiet until now. 'And, after all,' he adds, '*bullying* is a very strong word isn't it?'

I'm so grateful to get out of that hot, sweaty, interrogatory room. I storm back to the car and am forced to blast my music out really loudly as the only available form of therapy, as I have no chocolate on my person. Bloody incompetent lot of idiots!

'I'll have a gentle word with the girls,' Mrs Hardick had said. Gentle word? If these girls have been mean enough to sap all Elise's confidence they must be pretty hard. It's going to take more than a gentle word to sort that out.

'In fact, they're so helpful I often use them as guides around the school for new parents,' Miss Mandy had added. 'Keeps them out of trouble if they're busy and it gives them a feeling of power.'

It had been all I could do to control myself. Girls like that don't need more power over the others than they already have. As I had walked out the gate, I'd spotted the evil trio looking as though butter wouldn't melt as I walked past, then breaking into snorts of laughter as I left. I've met so many teenage girls like this; the fake smile can hide all sorts of bitchiness underneath. I know, I went to an all girls' school. I've been there, done that and this little lot are not going to get away with it. I'll just have to think of something.

Thank goodness it's Zumba this evening and I put everything I have into it. 'My gosh, you're on fire tonight,' laughs Debs.

Out loud I blame it on the Double Decker I ate on my way to the class, which it probably is in part, but personally I think most of it is due to pent up frustration. I enjoy the dance moves but not quite as much as usual because to be honest, my thoughts are elsewhere. Elise seems to have taken on board the fact that the school is going to deal with the evil trio of cool kids from school and has promised she'll go in tomorrow. I, on the other hand, am not at all convinced, but I'm fresh out of any other ideas on how to help her. More guilt for having moved here in the first place. This would never have happened if I'd stayed with Dan. I push these negative thoughts from my mind and put my back into Little Mix's Power – fabulous lyrics and a great routine with a lot of air punching which as always starts to help. I punch the air thinking of Mrs Hardick, punch, punch, then imagine Mr Huxtable 'No no'ing' punch, then Dan, punch, punch, punch, then The Coffee Factory possibly closing, punch, punch, punch.

How am I going to help save this factory? It's all very well Tania saying she'd do some fund raising outside Zumba, especially at the school fete – oh how embarrassing, I look forward to Mr Barton's face watching me doing my squats. Of course, Walter's donation is going to help but this place is going to take a lot of money to save it. I think of Walter and my determination grows even more steely. Failure is not an option. Before I realise it, we're on the cool down and we stretch to 'Feeling Good', one of my all-time favourite songs. I hold the last pose in a squat with my fists ready. Yep, I'm ready for this, but the only plan I can think of is to get into the enemy's den – I need insider information and the only way I can do that is to get into Melstock Manor with Mark. The point to point is coming up this Saturday and I'm going in.

Saturday comes around quite quickly as the week is full of work and chores, shopping, cooking, eating, sleeping, distributing flyers and preparing notes for the talks at The Coffee Factory, which are due to start next week. Walter is super nervous about it, but I told him he'll love it when he gets going; he's a born storyteller. Elise, thank goodness, has gone back to school, but from what I can understand although that harridan Hardick had a word with the little lambs, they've simply gone underground with their bullying campaign.

'Everything alright?' I had asked Elise when she came home from school yesterday.

'Yeah,' she had replied and slunk off to her room so I knew it wasn't alright at all. When questioned, it seems that the girls have, in a way that only girls can, fabricated an underground network of not so subtle rejection. Pupils from Elise's other classes had been getting up and moving away from her when she sat down. Her things had been moved so she got in trouble because she couldn't find them. Her locker key went missing and still hasn't turned up and the evil trio keep smirking and asking her if she'd lost anything. Sometimes I think teenage girls can be the meanest in the world. I'm going to have to do something about it, but I can't think what yet. First I have to try to get through this hideous point to point meeting with the even more vile Ma and Pa Whittaker.

I've thought up a plan which will hopefully mean that I avoid them. With Elise and Summer's help, I've straightened my hair and piled it into a low chignon. I'm wearing a long spotty blue dress that I managed to get from the charity shop in Stamforth and a large blue hat which mostly hides my face.

'Do I look like me?' I had asked Summer before I left.

'What do you mean, do you look like you? You always look like you!' Summer had giggled peering under my hat. 'You need a wig or something.'

'No, I'm not going that far,' I replied. 'It would be bound to fall off or something, and anyway Mark will have to recognise me.'

'You look fabulous,' reassures Elise, who for once is in a good mood as it's the weekend and she can sit and watch her iPad without me moaning at her and telling her to go out in the fresh air. 'You don't really look like yourself with that make up. Very glamorous.'

'Thanks,' I say trying to act nonchalant. Elise has kindly painted a lovely black eyeliner over my eyelids, so the effect is rather Audrey Hepburn. In fact I slip on my heels and parade in front of the mirror. 'Hmmm, I think I look rather like Julia Roberts in the race scene in *Pretty Woman*,' I say out loud.

'Oh, Mum, you're so old,' groans Elise.

That put me in my place, but actually as I trip out the door and manage to right myself without falling flat on my face, I think I look pretty darn gorgeous and I feel more than ready for my new career in espionage. Melstock Manor, Ma and Pa Whittaker, Mark 'hot as a fox' Whittaker, bring it all on! This girl can do whatever she puts her mind to!

Chapter 21

My optimistic mood doesn't last quite as far as the magnificent gates to Melstock Manor, and I feel quite queasy as I edge down the sweeping drive. We are ushered to a neighbouring field by smart looking stewards, and I feel relieved that at least I can arrive a little more incognito than I had on previous occasions. There are quite a few vehicles, mostly 4 x 4s, so at least I feel my trusty old Volvo fits in. Well, sort of anyway. The cars are pretty much all Mercs or brand new Range Rovers with gorgeous cream seats and built in TVs, tinted windows and personalised number plates. It's all very country – people in tweeds and caps and expensive looking wellies. I manage to park without disgracing myself and get out ready for action. I must admit however, I'm not feeling as though I fit in too well with the surrounding countryside. My dismount from the car is none too easy. My heels immediately sink into the grass and I wobble along precariously. I'm not sure I'm quite cut out for this country life. A woman in tweed britches, tartan socks and a trilby hat wanders past, raising her eyebrows at me and then stomps off, whistling to her dog, Tilly.

I wait for her to get a little ahead and then gingerly edge my way down the dirt track towards the house. As I get nearer to the imposing forecourt, I notice various waiting staff handing out glasses of something that looks hopefully like Pimms.

'Hello?' My voice has gone all high pitched and uncertain. Why does it always do that?

The waiter is professionally non-reactive to my gauche behaviour. 'Would Madam like a glass of Pimms?' he asks, pleasantly.

'Yes, definitely. Thank you very much.' I take a gratifyingly large sip, which makes me feel a bit better as I survey the scene around me. The stretch of hills around Melstock Manor are simply beautiful; green towering up into vibrant moorland heather. I'd like to just sit here and enjoy the peace but realise I should probably try to mingle. I look around nervously as I'm really not sure where I should be going. Mark had been pretty vague when he'd told me to just turn up to the old family shack at 11am. For goodness' sake, that's totally useless and after all, he's not exactly gagging to meet me at the front gate. I give myself a little shake. The guy is as hot as Rupert Campbell-Black, so he's not going to be waiting around for a middle-aged mum with about as much experience of rolling around in the hay as a nun.

I am woken from my reverie by the approach of a dishevelled looking old chap in a tweed jacket with leather patches over the elbows, long brogues and a natty moustache. He takes a glass of Pimms with a practised air and wallows up to me.

'Are you part of the welcoming party, what?' he mumbles.

'Good morning. No, not really.' I smile, willing him to go away. Sadly this is not a new experience for me, however. If I can pick up a total weirdo, I will. There seems to be an invisible force around me that attracts them in droves. I blame my mother for it, as she has exactly the same problem so it must be hereditary and hitherto I've not been presented with a cure. I've tried talking about it to Jess and she just laughs and rolls her eyes. 'You just attract them, Rom. It must be something about your allure.'

I've given the matter serious thought as it's happened too many times to be a joke anymore. There was that weird guy with a limp at the train station and the man on the first floor of the Eiffel Tower. That was particularly scary because I just couldn't get away from him. If there's a bizarre person around, you can guarantee they'll come and talk to me. My conclusion is that I must just be too nice and they know I'll listen instead of telling them to get lost. That's another thing, people tend to tell me all their problems too. I mean I'll just be standing there having what I think is a perfectly normal conversation with someone I hardly know, or have just met, and the next thing they're telling me their entire life history, why their boyfriend recently left them or how horrible their mother is. It's just one of those things.

'Looking a bit like posh totty, I thought you must work for the press,' he observes glibly.

'No,' I say as pleasantly as I can manage considering his total male chauvinism. 'Are you here for the point to point?' *Or just to make sexist comments* I add mentally.

'Rather! Jolly good show, the Melstock Manor Point to Point and damn fine nosh as well as good ground.'

'Oh,' I reply at a loss. Come on, Mark, where are you?

'Name's Fanshaw, Gregory Fanshawe,' he extends a rather sweaty and hoary hand.

'Romilly Greene,' I say and shake it politely.

'Really? Dear me, you have my sympathy. Such odd names they give people nowadays. You can walk across with me, m'dear, if you don't know where you are going,' and without waiting for a reply he takes my hand, tucks it in his arm and we disappear off at a speed most uncomfortable for my impractical footwear.

'Good God, Fanshawe,' drawls a familiar voice. 'Can't leave a girl within a square mile of you without trouble.'

'Mark, you young whippersnapper. Can't blame a chap, jolly fine filly and good ground after all, what?'

Thank God I manage to withdraw my arm from Fanshawe's damp armpit, but it's all I can do to try to prevent myself from slapping him hard around his florid face.

'Sorry, Romilly darling.' Mark gives me a careless kiss on the lips and takes my arm. I'm sorry to say my traitorous body responds. 'Meant to be here at 11 but had to see a man about a dog. We'll catch you up in a while, Fanshawe. Romilly and I need to pop up to the stables.'

Fanshawe temporarily concedes defeat, tilts his cap and drifts drunkenly off towards the point to point field.

'Thank God you came along when you did,' I say pointedly.

‘Had enough of old Fan, had you? Don't want to take any notice of him. He’s a good sort, Foghorn Fanshawe, was at Harrow with my Pater, you know. Plenty of jolly jackanapes they got up to back in the day.’

‘I can imagine,’ I add drily. I don't know much about public school, never having been to one but I saw the documentary on the subject and they seem to be a breed unto themselves, these upper class privileged males. They chunter and play rugger and clap each other on the back and call each other Stilton and Stinker. It’s practically a foreign language, and one I simply don't speak. ‘Where are we off to then?’ I ask, ‘I thought we were watching the point to point.’

‘In a jiffy, darling. I just need to check over one of the stallions and they won’t be starting for another half an hour or so.’

‘I’m not exactly dressed for the stables though,’ I laugh nervously.

‘Oh, I don't know,’ Mark roves an appreciative eye over my dress and I feel a frisson of excitement somewhere in the lower pit of my stomach. Quite honestly, he is just too good looking. Sometimes I feel annoyed with myself for being so shallow, but I guess a girl’s allowed to be impressed. We approach the spick and span stable yard. It’s not like a normal stable that I’ve ever been to before. It’s immaculate, perfect, there’s not even a blade of hay out of place. One of the grooms nods his head to Mark on our approach, another is hosing down a horse’s legs. ‘I want all that water mopped up when you’ve finished, John’s,’ Mark commands.

'Yes, sir,' the groom touches his cap. I'm not really sure what that's about, why would you need to mop water in a stable yard? Isn't it meant to have a little water spilt on the floor? I mean, isn't it somewhat inevitable? This stable yard really is like a toy town stable; it simply isn't real.

'Morning, Olivia.' Mark gives a stunning longhaired blonde girl one of his devastating grins. Olivia smiles back revealing perfect pearly white teeth. She's quite intimidating with her young curvaceous body, her jodhs fit perfectly along with her polo team top. I turn to comment to Mark in time to catch him wrinkling his nose at her; she catches his look and flushes. Oh yes, this guy is definitely Rupert Campbell- Black although I would admit he's a little less cruel. I really must arm myself against him, all I need right now is more emotional anguish. As his father commented, he's obviously a total player. What he wants with me is a total mystery, as I simply can't compete with models like Olivia.

I follow Mark to a nearby stable where he expertly examines the leg of a gorgeous thoroughbred. 'A poultice once every three hours, Gibson,' he orders the stable hand. He straightens up. 'I'm sorry, Rom, but I'm going to have to stick around here for a while, some unfinished business has turned up.'

I feel a flush of annoyance. I can just imagine what his unfinished business is but then I figure this is a good thing on two counts. Firstly, it means I'm free to go off snooping, and secondly I don't really want to get in any more positions on my own with Mark. I have no intention of being a notch on his bedpost – my self-esteem is still far too fragile.

'That's fine,' I force myself to smile happily as though it's the best suggestion ever. 'I'll just wander across to check out the point to point.'

'Excellent, and I'll be right with you in a moment.' He kisses me on the cheek and murmurs in my ear, 'I think we have some unfinished business of our own.'

Oh, for goodness' sake. I have no intention of sloppy seconds. I, for one, am not up for being one of a list, even if he is good looking and I'm well and truly over the hill. I'd rather be a nun for the rest of my life. Well maybe not a nun, but single, perhaps with a cat. I manage to pull away a little, hopefully not looking too obvious.

'Mandy will take you across to the field,' he motions to a girl with long dyed grey hair and bright pink jodhs. It's a surprisingly good combination actually.

'Oh no, that's not necessary,' Darn it, that's going to foil my plan for sneaking off to the house.

This was not part of the plan, but Mark won't hear of it. 'It's the least we can do and Mandy can show you the best spot. I'll catch you up.'

There's nothing for it but to acquiesce and follow Mandy out of the stable yard and across the sweeping drive, round to the point to point field. Mandy's okay actually. She seems quite chatty and at least she doesn't make me feel judged for what I'm wearing, or my total lack of knowledge about racing. Very efficiently she marches me through the crowds around the fenced off field, and checking I don't need anything else she leaves me. How awkward. I stick out like a sore thumb as everyone's dressed in tweed and jodhs or cords, and here I am in a spotty summer dress looking as though I might be attending Ascot. At least I opted to leave the hat. I decide to pretend to watch a little of the racing, otherwise it's going to look really odd, and then I wander off in the direction of the house on the pretext of needing the loo or something, do some prying and then get the heck out of here.

This plan seems to be working out fine as I observe the horses gallop round the field in a cloud of summer dust, veins bulging, legs flying, their necks outstretched in a desperate attempt to get over the finishing line first. It would be useful if I could blend in with the people around me, but they're all in mid conversation with each other and merely peer at me as though I am a stranger in town – which of course I am – before returning to their discussion. Anyway, I'm not really sure what to say to them as they'll probably think I'm a complete idiot. On my left a superior woman called Lavinia, who obviously rides hard to hounds, is conversing with her daughter Lettice (I mean what sort of name is that) at top volume on the only which way to ride the dressage test. Her youngest son seems hell bent on digging a hole in the turf with a riding crop he appears to have pilfered from somewhere. 'For goodness' sake, Johnny.' She snatches the whip, whops him with it and places it back in her riding boot. He immediately starts a loud wailing which seems to go on forever, but his mother just ignores it. I wonder if she's immune to the noise. On the other side, a group of old men are discussing the ground, the various points of the horse etc.

I'm just thinking I'll casually edge away when a horsey looking woman descends on Lavinia next door. 'Lav, darling!' she blasts. They immediately start an entire conversation which is fine as I think this is a good time to leave, until I suddenly realise the stud they are discussing is Mark Whittaker.

'Apparently he's got a new bit of stuff,' the horsey one says excitedly.

'I've heard, but she's divorced and has two kids,' Lavinia replies as though this is the greatest crime in the world.

'And she's ancient. Well past forty!' retorts her companion. I freeze unable to move from the spot.

'Perhaps he wants to try something different; make a change from all those gorgeous young things he's always shagging,' remarks Lavinia maliciously.

'More like he's using her for some reason,' comments horsey lady. 'He's probably got some scheme or other. Doesn't sound like she's his usual type at all.'

'I heard she went riding and trashed the entire garden because she couldn't control her horse and it ran amok!' chortles Lavinia.

'I know,' remarks her companion wryly. 'Shocking business, nothing worse than bad horsemanship. I'm amazed she had the cheek to show her face here again after that.'

'Well, he's still on to marry Lady Penny, Lord Stanhope's daughter, isn't he?' asks Lavinia. 'I'm sure their engagement was in *Country Life Magazine*.'

'No, not yet, but I'm sure it soon will be,' finishes her companion.

I can't stand there and listen to any more. I turn

and blunder away from the edge of the course. I'm sure I hear Lavinia's high-pitched tones, 'You don't think that was her, do you?' There's a burst of laughter, but I keep going and run for cover.

Chapter 22

'Oh, it's the handsome young filly from the gate, Ron something or other.' Foghorn Fanshawe lives up to his name.

'Hello again, Lord Fanshawe.' I force myself to stop my hurried walk towards the house.

'How nice to shee you again,' he slurs. 'Come and have a dwink with me.' He's obviously had more than a few since I last saw him.

'Erm actually I'm in a bit of a hurry,' I say desperately, trying to shake off his sweaty hand, which he has placed surprisingly firmly on my arm.

'Hurry?' He chortles, 'you must have time for a quick one.'

'No, she doesn't actually,' comes a voice. Oh, my God, it's Mr Barton. I goggle at him, bemusedly. He really does turn up in the most unexpected places. 'Come on, Romilly, we're going to be late for our meeting.'

'Meeting? What meeting?' blasts Foghorn Fanshawe staggering slightly on absolutely nothing at all.

'Goodbye!' I say with relief, as I take Henry Barton's proffered arm and follow him across the lawn.

'Can't you walk properly?' asks Henry.

'No I can't,' I retort. 'These shoes aren't designed

for grass.'

'Why on earth did you wear them then?' he asks, half dragging, half supporting me along.

'What's the flipping hurry?' I ask breathlessly. I mean this is totally surreal. What is he doing here for goodness' sake?

'To get away from that hideous old perv, Fanfan or whatever his name was,' says Henry, doggedly.

'But how did you know I needed to?' I ask puzzled.

'Let's just say you looked like a damsel in distress,' says Henry, who's now smiling.

'I was perfectly able to look after myself,' I say indignantly.

'Really?' Henry stops and looks at me sternly.

'No, not really!' I smile. 'Thank you. It was very kind of you, I was struggling a bit.'

'That's okay,' Henry smiles back and it transforms him. He has a nice smile and his eyes sort of crinkle at the corner and are kind when he's not glaring. 'What on earth are you doing here anyway? I thought you'd be with Mark?'

'Yeah right,' I say sarcastically. 'He's off discussing business, probably with a stunning blonde right as we speak.'

'Oh, I'm sorry,' says Henry.

'I'm not,' I laugh. 'He's not really my type to be honest, too horsey and flirty and,' I look over my shoulder at the point to point crowd, 'this isn't really my scene.'

'No, I didn't think it was.' Henry seems to visibly relax. 'So what are you doing here then if you're not with Mark?'

I peer about in a suspiciously comedy spy way. 'I'm here on a mission.' I say seriously.

'A mission! What sort of mission?' Henry snorts.

'Shhh, don't give it away. I'm trying to find out what's going on with this whole selling The Coffee Factory business,' I say, unsure whether I should be telling Henry this: I mean he still ranks as the enemy after his previous behaviour.

'Really? Most impressive,' says Henry. 'How are you going to do that?'

'I'm going to sneak into the house and do some snooping,' I say matter of factly.

He laughs. 'You're a woman of hidden talents,' he says. 'But how are you going to get in past the staff on the front lawn?'

'I'm sure I'll find a way,' I say confidently. Darn, I hadn't thought of that. I'd been assuming Mark would be with me or I could get in round the back, but perhaps I hadn't thought this whole thing through properly.

'Okay,' says Henry and stands back expectantly, his arms folded as though I am about to do something amazing and James Bond like, which involves running across the lawn, vaulting up a neighbouring tree and par courting my way onto the roof of Melstock Manor.

'Oh,' I say. 'Yes, okay. Well, unless...'

'Unless what?' says Henry, his expression completely serious.

'Unless you could help me?' I ask, putting on my best persuasive and shamelessly manipulative feminine face.

'I'm not getting arrested for breaking and entering,'

he says defiantly, ‘even for you.’ Oh my gosh, I try not to faint from the shock of my fluttery eyelashes working for once. I mean, I thought the guy hated me. ‘But,’ he looks at me again speculatively, ‘I could perhaps cause a distraction amongst the staff so that you can slip in the door unnoticed.’

‘That would be amazing,’ I say. ‘You are a nice man after all.’

‘What do you mean?’ he asks, obviously hurt.

‘I thought you hated me,’ I answer without waiting for his reply, and turn and sashay towards the house. It’s now or never; here starts my life of crime. After all, I’ve trashed the Whittaker’s lawn, so who’s to stop me breaking into their house? I slope nonchalantly down the drive, take a glass of Champagne from a friendly waitress on the way round and take a sip, watching out of the corner of my eye as Henry Barton breaks into a jog across the lawn from the direction of the stable block. ‘Escaped horse!’ he pants, breathlessly. Honestly it’s as though he’s been running miles. He could win an Oscar for this performance. He stops and bends forward as though unable to catch his breath, then he points in the direction of the stables to the goggling waiters. ‘Quick! Mark will have your heads if you don't come and help,’ he shouts. In a trice they all break from their trance, place their trays on the table and run for the stables. Quick as a flash, I dump my glass and slip stealth-like into the house. Well, I say stealth-like, but in reality I stumble on the stupid doorstep, which really does seem to be my nemesis, and crash over the threshold banging headlong into an old gong and foot scraper. There is a terrific crash, which is dramatically echoed round the whole hall, reaching a tremendous crescendo. I slide behind the vast wooden door, waiting for footsteps or worse still that horrible flipping dog. Miraculously there is nothing. Nada. What a relief, they must all be out at the field.

Gingerly I creep out of my hiding place and start my search of the ground floor. I had meant to be methodical, but in practice I find myself darting in and out of rooms, searching randomly for I know not what. But actually it's quite disappointing; there are no papers left anywhere, not even in the library. It is quite depressingly tidy. Not that I know what I was expecting, this is not a mystery story. In real life people just don't leave important documents out on the top for others to read.

I try upstairs next. Might as well have a quick look round as you never know where people are going to hide things. I sneak up the stairs quiet as a mouse and pause at the top. Annoyingly, I need the loo, I wonder momentarily if I can wait, but it's no good, I can't. Since having kids I'm totally hopeless. I bet this never happens to spies. I sneak into the bathroom, mentally lamenting my overactive bladder. At least I know the loo is on the top right of the landing as I used it on that fateful night I visited for dinner. I lock the door for no apparent reason other than habit – I don't want to turn into my mother-in-law. Just as I sit on the seat with relief, I think sneaking around makes me anxious, I hear a noise. It's a kind of funny groaning which appears to be coming from nowhere at all, then it becomes accompanied by a melodic squeaking which seems to co-ordinate exactly in time in a rhythmic manner. Finally there's a loud grunt and all the noise stops. I finish my wee and go to flush the chain.

'I'm going to have to get back to the field,' comes a familiar voice. It echoes uncannily from the other side of the wall. My hand hovers, shaking over the long chain handle, and I stop myself from automatically flushing just in time.

'What a shame, darling.' It's a woman's voice, but not one I recognise.

'There'll be plenty of time later,' drawls Mark. 'Anyway, I have to be back in time for the cup giving and I've left poor little Romilly on her lonesome.' I clench my fist at his mocking tone. Now I really want to punch him.

'I don't know why you bother with that numbskull,' replies the woman. I actually hate her voice; it's harsh and scratchy, just like a cheese-grater. Most unpleasant. 'She's a complete and utter joke. What was she wearing today? Looked like she was going to afternoon tea with the Queen Mother.'

'Penny!' Mark laughs, and there's an interlude during which I don't want to even think what they might be doing. I'm glad I locked the door; I'm safe in here. Then a terrible thought strikes me. What if Penny needs the loo or something? But surely they'd have an ensuite in the bedroom, wouldn't they?

'In any case, darling,' Mark continues. 'You know exactly why I'm with her; we need to keep her onside. She might be a bit of a loose cannon left to her own devices.'

'Scream!' giggles Penny. 'That girl couldn't frighten a blackbird from her nest. She's completely useless.'

I think I'm becoming more and more scarlet by the minute; I seriously need to get out of this bathroom and punch this woman.

'That just goes to show what you know,' says Mark. 'I think there may be more to Romilly Greene than meets the eye. Ciaran says she's come up with some really effective marketing strategies to help the business.'

Ha! Thanks, Mark. At least he believes I might have some brains.

'Bloody woman! That's all we need. She could screw everything up right at the last minute,' says Penny crossly.

Oh, my God! My blood runs cold. Screw what up exactly?

'Yes, she could, but I think we have all that in hand,' says Mark.

What? What do they have in hand? I edge my ear nearer to the wall; I really need one of those ear trumpets or doctor's stethoscope things.

'But if she comes up with a way to make The Coffee Factory profitable, we'll lose our cover story,' moans Penny.

'She won't,' says Mark impatiently. 'I'm off to see Mannerton-Smythe tomorrow afternoon. He just needs to get the documents drawn up and the job will be done.'

'I don't know if I can keep Jenny waiting much longer,' warns Penny. 'Strathcombe Homes have very tight credentials,' she adds in her hoity toity tone.

'I'm sure you can persuade her to wait a little longer, my darling.'

‘Of course! I’m a very persuasive woman,’ purrs Penny.

Yuk, this makes me want to throw up.

‘Then stop worrying about tiny details. I’ll deal with Romilly and keep her off the scent. Until it’s too late anyway and the deal is finished.’

‘Make sure you’re not too persuasive,’ warns Penny. ‘I know how attractive you are to the opposite sex and she’s split up from her husband. She’s probably desperate.’

Okay, that’s it; I’m going to have to go in there.

‘It’s the rest of the village I’m a little worried about,’ continues Mark. ‘They’re a tight knit lot. Don't fancy them turning nasty on us.’

‘Very manly,’ snaps Penny.

I have to say for a moment I agree.

‘I haven’t finished actually. I was going to add, darling, that by the time they find out, their coffee factory will be bulldozed and turned into a nice tidy block of retirement apartments and we’ll be on the next plane out of here to Barbados.’

‘I simply can’t wait,’ smiles Penny. ‘Okay, I’m ready to go down, but I’ll just pop to the loo first.’

Oh my God! Panic galvanises me into action; they can’t find me here. It’s absolutely so not an option. Then I realise the door’s locked. I jump into the bath and lie down, covering myself with a bath towel. Why I don't know, I mean they can’t get in here unless they break the door down and also I’m not exactly well hidden. I hear footsteps on the landing and the door handle starts moving. Oh God, it’s like a horror movie.

‘Darling!’ comes Penny’s sharp voice, horribly near

now, just outside the door, 'I can't open your bathroom door.'

'I'll do it.' More footsteps and the door handle goes again, harder this time, making the whole door shake. I shiver under my bath towel. He's going to break the door down. What am I going to do?

'That's odd. I'll have to get James in to fix it. Sorry, darling, I'm going to have to run.'

'But, Mark, I need the loo,' laments Penny.

'Use the one downstairs!' comes the reply and to my great relief the footsteps move away, creaking down the stairs.

I'm left spread eagled in the bath, quaking under my towel and wondering what on earth I've just heard.

Chapter 23

'Are we all here?' I ask the assembled company. 'Are you ready, Walter?'

'As I'll ever be, my dear,' replies Walter, shuffling his papers. 'So I press this button to change the slide?'

'Yes, it's a simple as that and the computer will change the image.' I move the stand closer to him.

'I wish we could bring back cine cameras,' he says loudly into the microphone. Everyone laughs.

There's a great turn out for Walter's talk; mostly the usual suspects from the village, but also quite a few new faces who I think are tourists. It's certainly a sell-out. Walter clears his throat and begins.

'Today I'm going to tell you a story. Not one that moved mountains or changed the world particularly, but one about a coffee factory that transformed the lives of everyday people both near and dear to me, and also the shape of this whole village. Someone once said it's not the big things in life, but the small things that make the difference, and lots of small things add up to one amazing triumph, and that is what we are standing in here. This factory is where I grew up, man and boy, where I met my wife, where I brought my children, where I bring my grandchildren, where I still come to meet my friends.' He glances across at me and I have a job not to cry. 'Where I meet people old and new. This factory is the whole point of the community of Melstock and without it so very much would be lost,' he pauses for a second, obviously struggling with his emotions.

'But I don't need to tell you all this. The people who live here already know it and those who have visited can already feel it. So for now I'd like to share with you my special memories of this factory and how it's been such an integral part of my very long and mostly happy life.'

Along with the rest of the room, I watch Walter, totally transfixed as he weaves his story, interspersed with pictures and artefacts from the factory floor. He's a born storyteller; momentarily we've all forgotten the outside world and our own petty problems and are lost in a love story which took place in this factory seventy years ago. When Walter finally finishes speaking, the room is totally silent. You could hear a pin drop – if anyone were thinking of dropping a pin, which is, I must admit, a bit random, and then as though waking from a dream, everyone claps like mad. Some of them stand, and Walter, overcome, waves his hand and mops his brow with his hanky.

'Thank you, Walter,' I say when the hubbub has died down. 'Thank you for giving us such an amazing insight into village life, highlighting the importance of this factory in the last century and also for sharing with us such a beautiful personal story. It's made us all most envious and given us hope to believe perhaps that even in this tawdry world, care, romance and love still exist. It has also reinforced for many of us – and informed those new to us – the great importance of The Coffee Factory as part of this village life and how it must,' I peer round the room for emphasis, 'must be saved. As the villagers are aware, it's the hub of our village. So many fascinating talks take place here on ornithology, local wildlife, great literature. Local authors come and discuss their latest works, the food festival is held here every year with local delicacies, the art group, Knit and Natter,' I pause for breath, 'Zumba, just the most amazing fun.'

'I'm even thinking of trying it,' interrupts Walter, who has now recovered and swings his leg high in the air.

I laugh and continue. 'It's a meeting place for the whole village, both young and old. It's where people hold their wedding anniversaries, birthday parties, the school disco and let's not forget as well as all this, we serve an amazing cup of coffee, which we are about to sample now along with some of Mrs Miggins' world renowned pastries and brownies.'

There's a cheer from the floor and everyone claps. 'If you'd like to come into the café there'll be samples of our freshly ground coffee. I recommend trying them all as they're delicious. There'll also be sparkly new boxes ready to take home. Please give any further donations in the buckets at the back of the hall and thank you very much for your wonderful and warm support.'

People mill about and wander off into the café to sample coffee, and Mrs Miggins' delightfully warm melt in the mouth chocolate brownies.

'Well done,' says Phil advancing through the hordes. 'That was very rousing.'

'My dear, you really are one of us now.' Alexandrine comes over and gives me a hug. She looks well, though her head is still covered with a scarf after her latest treatment.

'I feel as though I've lived here all my life,' I say happily, 'but it was Walter who did all the work. He really is a master of the art.'

'He is,' agrees Phil. 'I hope you have him down for plenty more talks like this.'

'He's fully booked for the season,' I say. 'Such as it is, we only have two months.'

'That's okay,' says Alexandrine. 'If we carry on like this, we have a fighting chance, and Phil has an idea.'

'That's great! I try to make myself sound enthused but how am I going to break this to them gently? It's been on my mind ever since yesterday's fiasco at Melstock Manor. 'But we do have a problem, I'm afraid.'

'Why do I think I'm not going to like the sound of this?' asks Phil.

'Sound of what?' Debs storms up and hugs me. 'Well done, Rom, we're going to crack this. Wasn't Walter fabulous?' I look over to where he is still surrounded by a group of fans, all asking questions about the factory and his life. I haven't been able to get near him.

'I went to the point to point at Melstock Manor yesterday,' I say seriously.

'Oh my gosh! I forgot it was yesterday you were going to spy on Mark, how did it go?'

'Well, it was a bit of a nightmare,' I reply.

'Poor you,' sympathises Debs. 'We'll remember you took one for the team.'

'No, not like that.' I peer at Debs. I mean now I

know what he's really like, yuk what a horrible thought, 'but I've found something out and it's a major problem.'

'Well, come on then spill,' begs Debs.

'I can't.' I look around the room surreptitiously; once a spy, always a spy. 'We all need to get together for a meeting and it must be top secret.'

'Ooh, how mysterious!' says Alexandrine.

'We need to keep it just between us,' I say, 'and Walter and maybe Jim, Molly of course, Clive from the pet shop, Mrs Miggins, Ciaran, Skye and probably Henry.'

'Can't we just ask the whole village?' asks Phil. 'And what about Mark, he needs to be there? He's the one with the most power.'

'No,' I blurt in a loud whisper, making everyone jump. 'Mark must not know anything about this. That's why the numbers need to be small, otherwise it will get back to him.'

'I don't understand,' replies Debs. 'What on earth has Mark done? Was he that bad?'

'No. Well yes, but not like that. Anyway, he's up to stuff so we need to get together behind his back.'

'Okay, we'll meet upstairs above the Post Office. It can't be here, or Mark will wonder what we're doing after hours.' Phil takes charge of the situation. 'I'll get a message to the others; Alexandrine can take over at work this afternoon.'

'Can everyone do tonight?' I ask. 'We need to act as quickly as possible.'

'I just can't wait,' Debs says jiggling about. 'Can't you give us a tiny hint?'

'No, someone might overhear. Call me paranoid if

you like, but I'm beginning to wonder who our friends are,' I reply.

'You're paranoid!' says Debs.

'Ha ha!' I say wryly, but in all seriousness it's hard to be optimistic about saving a factory when I know its owner is determined to sell it to the highest bidder. I haven't had much time to mull over things but on the face of it, it's a disaster. There's absolutely nothing we can do if Mark intends to sell the factory for building land. Him and that bloody Penny make a right pair, but I hate Mark the most for his sheer shamefaced lies to the whole village about his love for the factory and how they'd like to keep it. Anyway, the costs aren't adding up. I mean, perhaps they aren't, but I really don't know who to believe anymore?

It was all I could do to stop myself from sitting in a corner and sobbing during Walter's beautiful and heartfelt speech. Losing this factory will be the end of him. How could Mark even think of pulling it down and making it into a block of retirement flats? Stupid man, what's the point of having more older people coming to live in the village when you're removing the very epicentre of their community activities? It doesn't make sense; it's just their own greed talking and the Whittakers have got plenty of that. I mull over the conversation, trying to work out what else I can think of which might help. There was the name of the lady who Penny was talking about at Strathcombe Homes, but I can't remember it at all. In fact I'm generally useless with names. It doesn't say much for my memory as I can be introduced to someone, they tell me their name and five seconds later I've completely forgotten it. Most embarrassing!

Back home over lunch I fire up my laptop and Google 'Strathcombe Homes'. Of course, there's nothing about future acquisitions. I guess they wait until it's all signed and sealed. However, I scroll down through the endless images of supposedly ecstatic and unnaturally cheery looking old people sitting in anonymous magnolia, personality free new rooms which makes me feel more and more depressed. There are hairdressing clubs, poker and knitting clubs and all sorts of facilities. It looks a bit like a bland hotel. In any case, all those things are provided in the café at The Coffee Factory, and there's a little hairdressers in the village. Milly Clarkson from Cute Cuts will happily go to the homes of Melstock's older residents to do a home haircut at a very reasonable cost.

I scroll through the website, looking everywhere for prices. Of course they are nowhere to be found. I finally discover under the contact list: 'Please phone us to discover a personalised package for yourself or your loved ones.' Maybe I should phone and find out what's being offered here. I'm just about to dial on my mobile when it rings out, making me jump. This spying business is definitely not doing my nerves any good, and to be fair they haven't been great in the first place lately.

'Hello?'

'Good morning! It's Janine Hardick here,' Oh great, finally she's returned my call. I had asked her to phone me last week and she hadn't. 'Sorry it took me a while to get back to you, but I've had other important things to deal with.'

‘Well, thanks for getting back anyway.’ I can’t help but be pleasant even though I feel like grumbling at her. It’s just my way, but sometimes I wonder if it would be better if I were more assertive. There’s an awkward silence.

‘I was wanting to talk to you about Elise?’ I say in a rush. Still silence. ‘It’s just that she’s still having difficulties in school with this group of girls.’

‘Impossible,’ snaps Mrs Hardick. ‘We had a chat with the girls in question and they agreed to be much kinder to Elise as our new addition.’

‘But it doesn't seem to be working. Elise tells me they’re still being unpleasant,’ I say indignantly. I sense Mrs Hardick sighing heavily at the other end.

‘In what way?’ she asks tightly.

‘They seem to have gone underground, whispering behind Elise’s back, moving her stuff, throwing her lunch away, getting up and deliberately moving seats from her in class so she has to be on her own.’ I feel emotional saying it, because I know how hurtful girls can be with their bitchy subterfuge.

‘Ms Greene, I seriously cannot imagine these girls behaving in this way. As the Phase team and I mentioned in our meeting the other week, these girls are simply highly spirited, confident young women who know their own minds. I think you’ll find Elise is perhaps a little overwhelmed by them and is therefore struggling somewhat.’ She lowers her voice confidentially, ‘and after all, it must be difficult with her having things going on at home.’

‘What do you mean?’ I ask indignantly.

‘Well, your separation from her father and setting

up in a new village. She's been used to a very different type of school and it's all bound to have an effect, you know.'

'I admit it's difficult for both the girls, but we keep the channels of communication open and I'm doing my best.' I feel emotional now.

'I'm sure you are, Ms Greene.' This woman is sooo patronising, 'but with the best will in the world, your circumstances are bound to affect Elise far more than a group of highly spirited girls at school. Has she had any therapy?'

'Of course this affects her, but it would be somewhat more useful if she had the support of both school and pupils,' I retort. 'Are you able to give her some therapy or counselling?'

'Our list is currently very long as we have many students who need help with their issues,' coos Mrs Hardick. 'But if you think it's necessary, I can add Elise to the list.'

'But it was you who said it was necessary,' I say confused. 'Personally, I think it would help if you could point her in the right direction of a nice little group of friends. There must be some like-minded girls in the school she could hang out with.'

'Of course there are. We have fifteen hundred pupils in the school, but we really can't be nursemaiding them by helping them to make friends, Mrs Greene!'

'No, I understand that, but I just wondered if you could make a suggestion of a nice quiet girl or two who might have the same interests, such as reading or Conservation Club or something.'

‘We have Reading Club every Thursday and ‘Ecoclub’ on Tuesdays after school, so Elise can simply go along.’

‘But she’s too scared to go along since these girls have made her lose all her confidence. Now she’s too anxious to even go to lunch. She’s coming home without having eaten, and certainly won’t want to stay after school. It’s as much as I can do to get her to come in at the moment.’

‘Well, Mrs Greene, all I can say is that if these problems continue, we might have to call in Social Services.’

I gasp, ‘What! Why?’

‘Due to her attendance levels, Mrs Greene. We’ll have to wait and see if these improve, but I’m afraid as a school that will be our next step.’

‘But I’m asking for your help, so that Elise will feel confident and safe coming to school with a nice group of friends,’ I say weakly.

‘As I said at the meeting, we have Elise on our list for making friends so that should help.’

‘What number is she on the list?’ I ask feebly.

‘One hundred and twenty-three,’ replies Mrs Hardick.

At the end of the call, I put my phone down on the table and sit and stare at it. Great, just great! The whole system seems ridiculous. The support simply isn’t there, but worse than that is the way the school doesn't seem to understand the situation. I’ll have to think of something, but right now I’m not sure what.

I’m due back at The Coffee Factory in twenty minutes but have just enough time to dial the number for Strathcombe Homes. Time for some more subterfuge.

A lady answers the phone in a suitably sing song tone, ‘Strathcombe Homes. How may I help you?’

‘Hello. Yes, I wonder if you can,’ I say in a posh voice. (This is quite fun actually.) ‘I am enquiring after a place for my mother in one of your lovely retirement homes.’

‘How wonderful, and may I say, what a wise choice, Madam.’ Is this woman for real? I ask myself. ‘What is your mother’s name?’

‘Valerie,’ I improvise quick as a whizz. I’m really rather good at this. ‘Valerie Singleton.’ Oops maybe not quite so good. Fortunately the lady doesn't comment. She’s far too professional for that.

‘Whereabouts does your mother live?’ she asks.

‘She lives near Melstock in Devon,’ I say casually, ‘but I’m not sure you have a home near there.’

‘If Madam would just allow me to look on the system?’ says the lady. I can hear her tapping away on the computer and imagine her sitting in an office somewhere with her immaculate long nails, perfectly coiffured hair, and wearing a Hermes scarf. ‘Here we are. I’m sorry but the nearest would be our beautiful Harbour Heights in Truro.’

‘Oh, that’s a lovely place, but miles away from us,’ I say disappointed although not really surprised. The office staff are unlikely to know the company’s future plans yet.

‘There are some simply stunning places to stay nearby if you wished to visit,’ says the lady, enticingly. ‘You would be very welcome to come and have a look round.'

'Oh yes, that would be lovely,' I annunciate. 'Please could you give me an indication of your yearly fees? They appear to be omitted from your website.'

'Of course, Madam. I would be happy to send you our very exclusive brochure.' She pronounces brochure, 'broshure' which makes me want to giggle. Very Hyacinth Bucket, pronounced Bouquet.

'That would be lovely, but do you think you could give me a rough idea?' Just so I can start saving up, I add mentally.

'Of course. Our basic package starts at £3,000 a month but my personal favourite is the premium which works out at £8,000 a month.'

I am totally speechless. For goodness' sake, who on earth can afford that? I don't even earn anything like that a month so how is an old person supposed to find that amount of money?

'Hello, are you still there?' asks the woman, sounding alarmed.

'Yes, I'm here,' I squeak, trying to control myself.

'If you give me your address, I'll send you a brochure.'

Of course I can't give her my address so I simply give Vanessa's, which seems the most sensible solution. After all, she is near that age, is jolly wealthy and I can ask her for it when I next see her, or better still she might actually go to their home in Cornwall and with any luck we can all be rid of her forever.

I finish my cup of tea, which has now gone cold and dash towards the door nearly treading on an envelope on the mat, which I hadn't seen. Please not another letter from Dan. On closer examination, it's not his handwriting and I breathe a sigh of relief. The writing is rather ornate and swirly and the envelope is expensively stiff and good quality. I tear it open with difficulty and read the embossed card.

Richard and Jacinta Mannerton-Smythe request the pleasure of Mr & Mrs Daniel Barrington and Girls at their Summer House Party in celebration of the Golden Wedding Anniversary of Vanessa and Anthony Barrington on 14th July. Dress will be smart casual. Carriages at 11pm. RSVP to Smitherton Manor, Bramstock TA21 34B

Oh, just great! That's all I need today. An invitation to the event of the century! I haven't heard from Dan since his letter and to be honest I've been incredibly relieved. I guess I could just not go – I've escaped the clutches of my horrible mother-in-law, well until she next turns up that is, so perhaps I should just ignore the whole thing. I pick up my bag to return to work, placing the invitation in the drawer. I won't show it to the girls until the right moment. I glance at it again. Mannerton-Smythe, what an utterly pretentious name. Wait a minute, it rings a bell, was it because Vanessa mentioned it? No, it was more recently than that I heard it, perhaps it was at Walter's talk? But then it comes to me. Oh my God! Mannerton-Smythe was the name I heard Mark say he was visiting to clinch the deal on The Coffee Factory.

It looks as though I shall be going along to the summer house party at Smitherton Manor after all.

Chapter 24

'Come on then, spill,' says Debs.

I am sitting on the sofa in Phil and Alexandrine's cosy little flat above the Post Office sipping a restorative glass of wine, which they have kindly found me. I think the events of my day must have reflected in my face as Phil had taken one look when I arrived and passed the glass to me pretty rapidly. I look at the expectant faces all seated or perched on various bits of furniture. There're too many of us for the room really and I don't know where to begin.

'It's Mark,' I blurt. 'He's involved.'

'Involved in what?' asks Phil.

'In the sale of the factory,' I reply.

'In what way?' asks Jim, angrily.

'I'm going to go and take him down with my bare arms!' shouts Clive.

'Shh, everyone. One at a time otherwise we're never going to hear what Rom has to say,' points out Henry, obviously used to crowd control as a teacher.

'Right. Thanks, Henry.' I try not to flush saying his name as it's only until recently I saw him as the worst enemy in the world. Apart from Dan, that is, and his mother. Well, you know what I mean anyway. 'I'll start from the beginning.'

'That's as good a place as any,' quips Debs, but is

rewarded by a raised eyebrow from Henry and she subsides into silence. He really is quite masterful actually.

'So anyway, I managed to get into Melstock Manor on Saturday to do some spying as I suspected there was something not quite right about the financial difficulties of The Coffee Factory.'

'Quite right,' shouts Clive. 'Bloody fishy if you ask me; the whole family's loaded!' He ignores Henry's glare.

'Yes, so I couldn't find anything in writing when I was snooping round but...'

'Anyone for a chocolate brownie?' Mrs Miggins walks in from the kitchen with a plate of steaming cakes.

'Yes, but don't interrupt!' says Henry. 'Poor Rom is trying to speak.'

'So I went upstairs and whilst I was in the loo...'

'What were you doing in the loo?' asks Jim.

'I needed to go,' I say, embarrassed.

'When a girl's gotta go, a girl's gotta go,' says Debs, philosophically.

'Anyway, when we've finished discussing my toilet arrangements.' I'm getting frustrated now. Everyone is finally quiet. 'Whilst I was in there, I heard a conversation between Mark and his girlfriend, Penny.'

'Oh, that must be Penny, daughter of Lord Percy. Their engagement was in *Country Life*' chunters Mrs Miggins. (It's funny really because I had no idea what her Christian name was, and I didn't like to ask her.)

I give up to be honest. 'Can I carry on?' I ask.

'Yes, please do,' says Henry. I'm beginning to like

him actually.

'So during their conversation, Mark mentioned that he was planning on selling The Coffee Factory for the land to be built on.'

'What?' asks Walter, weakly.

'Yes, I'm afraid so. He's in talks along with his horrible sidekick Penny to sell the land to a company who build retirement homes.' I feel terrible sharing such awful news.

Everyone sits there completely stunned. 'That's unbelievable,' says Ciaran who is the first able to speak. 'I knew he was involved in various business schemes but I could never have imagined he would sell the place from under our feet, so to speak.'

'I know,' I say, 'and it sounds as though the process is pretty far along so if we are going to act, we need to do it soon.'

'But what are we going to do?' asks Alexandrine, who is close to tears.

'Don't stress yourself, love,' says Phil, squeezing her to him. 'Don't get upset, it's never worth it.'

'But what about all the fundraising?' asks Jim. 'Surely we can find enough money so they can't justify selling?'

'Not really,' says Ciaran. 'Apart from anything else, I've seen some of the figures for the café, the factory etc, and to be fair we're only just making a profit. I don't think Mark's making anything up unless he's been fiddling the books.'

'Bloody scoundrel!' retorts Walter. 'I wouldn't trust him as far as I could throw him. No morals, no care for the small people who actually do the work. Never did like him.'

'Calm yourself, Walter,' says Mrs Miggins, passing him a brownie. 'Have some of this and I'll make you another cup of tea.'

'I have to admit,' I say, 'I don't trust him at all either; he could be changing the figures or anything else. Look at how keen he appeared to be about my marketing ideas, but it was all a front.'

'He's a lying little bastard,' says Debs with feeling. 'How could he pretend he's trying to save the factory when he's secretly selling it?'

'I know! He's down to be guest of honour to open our fund-raising fete – Save The Coffee Factory,' says Henry drily. 'Talk about ironic.'

'On the positive side, if there is one. I've done some research and found out a little bit about the company they're trying to sell to, Strathcombe Homes.'

Everyone looks at me. 'That's not much help though, is it?' asks Phil gloomily.

'No, I just found out that it offers a few of the many things The Coffee Factory does at a huge price and half as well,' I reply.

'Typical,' says Phil. 'So what are we going to do to move forward?'

'We can't just give up,' says Mrs Miggins emphatically.

'Well, I don't know.' I say slowly. 'But the most bizarre coincidence has just happened. Whilst Mark was talking about his and Penny's dastardly plans, he mentioned he was going to meet with somebody called Mannerton-Smythe. Now I didn't know who on earth this was.'

'Never heard of them in my life,' says Walter.

'No, I didn't think I had, but it turns out that bizarrely I have an invitation to their house party next weekend.'

'How did that happen?' asks Henry, bemused.

'Through my mother-in-law actually. Even though Dan and I are separated, she came to visit me recently and insisted we were to go to this party at her posh friend's house she's always on about, swimming pool, room for a pony, you know the sort of thing.'

'How nice she wants you to go,' says Mrs Miggins. 'She must be very fond of you.'

'Er no, don't be fooled. She can't stand me,' I reply, 'but she wants the girls to come.'

'Well, you can't blame her. She's hardly going to be your best friend when you left her son, is she?' Henry has gone rather red, a whole flash of it is spreading right up his neck like wildfire. There's a sudden awkward silence as everyone sits and stares either at me, or the floor.

'No, I'm not surprised at all, although maybe if she'd been as kind to me as I always was to her, her son and I might still be together,' I say tersely. For a moment Henry and I glower at each other. Bloody rude man! I take back what I said. I absolutely hate him.

'Now, now, children,' says Walter, unexpectedly. 'Let's get back to the point in hand. Where do these people live, Romilly? Are they local, and more to the point are you able to get to this party?'

I try to get myself back together after Henry's attack. 'Yes and yes, they live at Smitherton Manor in Bramstock.'

'Never heard of it,' says Walter, 'but if you can get in there, Romilly, we might be able to find out what's going on.'

'Absolutely,' says Ciaran. 'Although it's not going to be easy for you.'

'No,' I say, 'but I don't see what choice we have, although I must admit I was dreading going. I really don't want to talk to Dan as there's nothing more to say and his mother really is the last straw.'

'You're making them out to be the enemy, yet you're the one that bailed on them,' remarks Henry, looking steely.

'Sorry?' I'm so taken aback I don't know how to answer for a moment.

'Look, I've got to go. It's Cubs at 7pm and I need to be down there to set up.' Henry dumps his glass on the table. 'Keep me updated. Of course I'll do anything I can to help.'

I just can't make this guy out. There's an awkward silence when Henry has left and we all stare at each other momentarily. I feel very tearful to be honest as that was really uncomfortable, and also this whole meeting up with Dan and his mum thing as well as the threat to The Coffee Factory, is all a bit much.

'Come on, chuck. Let's go make a cup of tea.' Debs, sympathetic as always, puts her arm around me and we go into the kitchen. Thank goodness the others start talking amongst themselves.

'Well, that was pretty embarrassing,' I say, relieved to get out of the spotlight for a moment.

'Oh, love, don't worry, they've seen worse.' Debs gives me a hug.

‘I just feel so rubbish about it, and I can imagine it might look to other people that I’m being a bitch of a daughter-in-law and a horrible wife.’

‘We don't feel that at all,’ says Debs. ‘Don't be silly. It’s just that Henry has had a bit of a bad time, that’s all.’

‘I had no idea,’ I say in surprise. ‘He didn't say anything, Not that we’ve ever talked that much.’

‘No, but of course at the time it was the talk of the village. You know how everyone loves a scandal, but his wife left him last year, out of the blue, took their little girl and went.’

‘But that’s terrible,’ I say shocked. ‘Was there a reason?’

‘There’s always a reason,’ says Debs, sagely. ‘But to be frank, none of us ever liked her. She was a nasty piece of work right from the start. You know the type, blonde and cute, looked like butter wouldn't melt. Yet behind Henry’s back she flirted with anyone and everyone. Poor old Henry was totally oblivious to it. Then she begged for a baby and I guess he thought it might settle her down. Yet when the little mite was only a year old she upped and left, child and all, with a sales rep.’

‘That’s terrible,’ I say, ‘I bet he was devastated.’

‘Totally and utterly,’ says Debs, adding two generously large spoons of sugar to my teacup.

‘So that’s why he’s hated me since we first met. Although surely he didn't know my circumstances,’ I say confused.

‘Don't you believe it, love,’ says Debs. ‘In this village news gets round practically before it happens.

Now have a big slurp of this sweet tea and a chunk of chocolate and you'll be ready for our action plan.'

I follow Debs back into the lounge and sit down. A sip of tea has already made me feel better; I can feel the sugar coursing its way through my body.

'Okay then,' says Phil. 'So, we've been talking things over and one of the ideas brought to the forefront is for us all to club together and maybe form a co-operative to buy The Coffee Factory as a village.'

'How amazing!' exclaims Debs. 'That's a brilliant idea.'

'Definitely,' I reiterate. 'That would be fab, like on those programmes where the community buy up the village pub.'

'Yes, exactly like that,' says Ciaran.

'We're all going to have a whip round,' says Walter.

'You've already been more than generous,' I say. 'But without wishing to be rude, will it be enough?'

'Yeah, that was my concern,' says Jim. 'We're never going to be able to outbid the amount these ruddy rich care home builders can afford.'

'Aha yes, but all is not yet lost,' says Walter. 'I have faith in young Romilly. Let's wait and see what she manages to dig up at the Mannerton-Smythes' or whatever their name is. The only way to deal with crooks like this is to beat them at their own game.'

'That's true, knowledge is power,' says Debs.

'Okay then, it's this Saturday night, so I'll go along and as soon as I can I'll sneak off and snoop about a bit. The girls can cause a bit of a distraction and I'll use the excuse of needing the loo or something.'

Everyone laughs. 'I don't know,' says Ciaran,

stroking his immaculate little goatee.

'I thought it was a great plan,' says Skye who has hitherto been very quiet.

'Indeed it is,' says Ciaran, 'with if I may make just a few amendments. Mrs Miggins and I think we should come along with you, Romilly.'

I gawp at them open mouthed, rather like a goldfish. 'Come with me? But won't that give the game away as representatives of The Coffee Factory?'

'Not really,' replies Ciaran, 'Mark won't be there, will he, and Richard Mannerton-Smythe will hardly recognise him. In any case we aren't going as Ciaran O'Leary and Mrs Miggins.'

'Who will you be then?' I ask intrigued.

'That night, Matthew, we will be Will Jones, your new bit of hot stuff and his mother, Mrs Margaret Jones,' he says smoothly.

'Wait a minute, I'm confused,' I say, wondering what on earth I am hearing. 'But I don't have a new boyfriend.'

'No, but we both think you need back up to go in and face this nest of vipers.' He gazes at me with that clear decisive look he always has. 'It's no good protesting. We're all agreed on this. You're one of us now and as your surrogate family, Mrs Miggins and I are going to support you through the ordeal. All for one and one for all, and all that!'

I laugh at the sudden image of Ciaran, Mrs Miggins and me all dressed as the Three Muskateers, but equally I'm totally overwhelmed by their kindness. I feel more at home here than anywhere else; these people are my new family, although I still love my old one of course, perhaps at a bit of a distance.

'I don't know what to say,' I reply, overwhelmed.

'You don't need to say anything,' says Mrs Miggins. 'It's all sorted,' and by the sound of it, it is.

Chapter 25

'Oh my God, I can't believe you!' laughs Jess, as I explain my action plan for Saturday.

'No wonder you moved to Melstock,' she says. 'You never had this much fun at home looking after Dan and the girls.'

'No I didn't,' I say, 'quite the opposite.'

'And you'll get to see Dan.'

There's a silence.

'Yes I know,' I say quietly.

'He still loves you, you know.'

'I haven't even heard from him.'

'No, but that doesn't mean he's not thinking about you,' she replies.

'I don't see what difference that makes,' I say. 'It's not enough for me anymore.'

'What isn't?' asks Jess.

'Loving me, but not contacting me,' I say awkwardly. It is after all a bit of a mouthful.

'I don't understand what you mean?' she says.

'Well, since I've been here, I've escaped all the pettiness, the snipes from his family, the put downs, his constant comments on my neediness. And better than that, I really feel I belong, you know. Look at these guys coming along with me on Saturday. For the first time in my life – other than you of course, someone's got my back.'

'I'm only trying to help with Dan, you know,' says Jess. I've obviously hit a nerve.

'I know, Jess, and I think the world of you but I'm just not sure there's any room in my life left for Dan.'

'Why don't you wait until after Saturday. You never know, you might change your mind,' says Jess, mysteriously.

'I don't think I will,' I say resolutely, but underneath I must admit to being in a bit of a quandary. What if Dan has changed? I mean, we do have a lot of history together. This new me feels a little wobbly, rather like a new butterfly freshly emerged from the chrysalis, still fragile and hesitant. If I get back with Dan, I may lose my new rediscovered sense of self. I'd thought it was having children that made me lose it, but instead it was marriage. Yet at the heart of it there's an uneasy feeling; a bit like an indigestion stomach ache, that maybe I do still love him.

Either way, my plans for Saturday evening are meticulous. After extensive consultation with Debs, I have picked out a long strappy dress in a beautiful shimmery light grey, with large flowers subtly etched on it. I am amazed I fit back into it as I haven't worn it since having the girls, but the combination of stress, healthier eating and a great deal of Zumba has all combined to give me definition, and miraculously it fits.

Skye has kindly curled my extremely straight hair into long ringlets and pinned it to my head, so I feel quite grown up and different from my usual self, which is a good thing as inside I'm totally bricking it. A subtle touch of makeup and even a long swipe of Audrey Hepburn style liquid mascara makes my eyes look more almond shaped than they really are, and I'm quite pleased with the result.

'Oh my gosh, Mum, you look like a different person.'

'Thanks, Elise, but I hope you mean that in a good way,' I say smiling.

'Definitely, you look really sassy. Are you trying to impress Dad?'

'No,' I say probably unconvincingly. 'Definitely not.'

'Methinks she protests too much,' says Elise. For goodness' sake, this child never misses a trick. 'You totally are.' Will she ever stop hoping Dan and I will get back together? My phone rings out loudly.

'Hello?' I answer it, trying not to touch or smudge my foundation.

'Romilly?' It's my mother. Oh for goodness' sake, who else does she think will answer my phone? 'I'm glad I caught you.'

'Hi, Mum, I'm just on my way out.'

'Yes I know, dear, to the posh party with Dan.'

'Well, I'm not going with Dan, but he's going to be there.'

'It's the same thing,' snaps my mother irritably.

'Not really, Mum. The girls have been asked by his mother and I have to go along too.'

'Well, it's a lovely idea, brings you all together as a family again.'

'Mum...' I protest.

'Romilly, it's all very well you playing these games,

running off and gallivanting about with the local horsey hero, but you're middle-aged now and it's time to settle down. You've had your taste of freedom and now you need to go back to your responsibilities.'

'I didn't think I'd left them behind,' I say tersely.

'Of course not all of them, but look at Elise. Jess tells me she's having trouble at school,' Oh great. Thanks so much, Jess, that was supposed to be confidential.

'Just a few teething problems, Mum, that's all. It's bound to happen at a new school.'

'It's bound to happen when you remove her from a school like Riversmeet Seniors and put her in a local free for all,' retorts Mum.

'I know it's not ideal, but it's about building resilience,' I say.

'Hmm. You wouldn't have liked it, so we went without and sent you to Riversmeet Seniors,' says my mum. 'And the sacrifices it cost, I couldn't go gallivanting off leaving your father, much as I would have liked to.'

Oh God, here we go. 'How is Dad?' I ask, desperately trying to change the subject.

'He has a new project on the go,' says Mum. 'He's bought himself a shredder from Ebay and I've hardly seen him since. Been out in the garden two days running, totally obsessed with it he is.'

'Oh, well at least that gives you a bit of peace for some of your hobbies.' My mum loves her bridge club and has constant groups she likes to get involved in.

'Huh! Chance would be a fine thing, I've had a problem with Uncle Clarence again,' she says.

‘Oh dear. What’s wrong this time?’ I ask. Elise is peering at me from the bottom of the stairs, tapping her watch. ‘Okay,’ I mouth back to her, ‘just coming.’

‘What?’ asks Mum confused.

‘Nothing. What’s wrong with Uncle Clarence?’

‘It’s those wretched bagpipes again,’ laments Mum.

‘Not the neighbour, Jock?’ I ask.

‘Yes, the situation got worse yesterday morning when Clarence rang your dad and told him he was going to break into the store cupboard at the end of his corridor, remove a load of the heavy stuff and use it to blockade his neighbour, Jock, in his room.’

‘Why would he do that?’ I ask totally confused.

‘Well, apparently Jock goes out by taxi every night, gets totally drunk at the local pub, then comes back and plays the bagpipes. So he thought...’

‘If he stopped him going out, it would solve the problem,’ I finish for her; after all I do need to get out this evening.

‘Your dad told him not to attempt it because he would get into terrible trouble and be thrown out of his flat.’

‘He would too. They’d never put up with behaviour like that, and in any case it would be a fire hazard.’

‘Quite,’ says Mum. ‘So I thought he’d listened to your dad but he rang up yesterday evening and said he’d done as he threatened and blocked Jock in.’

I struggle not to laugh. I mean, that is kind of funny, a vision of corridor wars going on in an old people’s block of flats. ‘What on earth happened?’

‘Well, I got so uptight and stressed that your father kindly rang Jess and asked her to have a word with

Clarence.' My sister Jess is one of the only people my Uncle Clarence takes any notice of, it's a shame her son Bradley doesn't follow suit. My mum continues, 'So she phoned him and it turned out although he really had barricaded the door, he said he let Jock out anyway.'

'Like a sulky little boy,' I say.

'Yes, I think Jess made him realise that he would lose his flat and he needed to behave himself.'

'Good for Jess,' I say, then realise with a start it's nearly 7pm. 'Look, Mum I've got to go. We need to get to this party.'

'Of course. Off you go, and don't be late. You always are, you know. And Romilly?'

'Yes,' I reply.

'Give it your best shot, love. You belong with your husband.'

For goodness' sake. This conversation is just what I don't need before the evening I'm about to face and now the doorbell is ringing.

'Who on earth is that?' asks Elise.

'Ciaran and Mrs Miggins,' I say casually.

'For crying out loud, they're going to make us late,' exclaims Elise.

'Yeah, I hate being late,' grumbles Summer descending the stairs in full party regalia and the obligatory sparkly pink hair band. She does love her bling! 'I'm always at school after the bell's rung.'

'Look, girls, we have a slight change of plan.'

They both look at me suspiciously. 'You are coming, aren't you?' says Elise who knows me well and probably thinks I'm backing out at the last minute.

'Yes, of course, I'm coming. I wouldn't miss it for

the world!' Ha bloody ha! 'Anyway we need to carry out our spy mission. It's just that Ciaran and Mrs Miggins have offered to come and help with searching.'

'Oh,' says Summer unabashed and carries on buckling her new sparkly shoes.

'Okay,' says Elise. 'I guess.'

'And there's just one other thing,' I say as we start to head out the door. 'Ciaran is pretending to be my new boyfriend and Mrs Miggins is his mother.'

'What the...' retorts Elise, her head snapping round at me so fast it's almost comical.

'I needed backup and they are it,' I say losing all track of comprehensible grammar.

'What about Dad though?'

'It will keep him at bay as well. A girl's got her pride, you know,' I say glibly.

'Mum!'

I stalk my way to the car where Ciaran and Mrs Miggins are waiting. I knew the only way to get away with this part of the plan was to throw it in at the last minute so there could be no argument.

'And you'd better not give the game away to your dad,' I retort.

'I won't flipping need to, it's bloomin' obvious,' Elise laughs. 'No one would ever believe you two are a couple.'

Sometimes I really hate teenagers. They always think they know everything.

Chapter 26

The Mannerton-Smythes' house is suitably impressive, nestled at the end of a long winding drive with a landscaped pool and a fountain in the front of the property, which is all floodlit with pale blue atmospheric lighting. The house itself is imposing dark brick with shiny new windows and clean looking paint work; the slate roof is a mass of solar energy. Everything screams wealth and the latest in technology.

'Pretty impressive, huh?' says Ciaran, admiring the sweeping gravel area where there are already parked an array of expensive car models I don't know the names of.

'Yes, I guess it is,' I reply, taking it all in.

'Look, Mum! There's a beautiful new stable block!' shouts Summer.

Elise would normally comment on this but she's still sulking with me over my little charade. I can tell she is quietly impressed though.

'It's not a patch on Melstock Manor,' says Mrs Miggins.

'No, I agree, that's much more homely, except for the presence of smelly dogs and the toxic Whittakers,' I add.

Richard Mannerton-Smythe is a seriously good-looking older guy, swarthy but clean cut, smelling of a delicious expensive aftershave and has very nice chinos and a Burberry jumper. I like his style. He's also pleasant enough and welcomes us in an apparently friendly manner, although I can't help feeling the warmth doesn't quite reach his eyes.

'This is my wife, Jacinta,' he says, putting his arm round a blonde woman with a dreamily soft looking, pale blue off the shoulder jumper. She has tiny hips and waist and skinny jeans, designer of course. Looking at her she seems much younger than her husband.

'Hello,' she smiles, revealing beautifully bleach white veneers. We make the necessary introductions and expected noises. The kitchen is huge with stunning oak beams, immaculate gleaming granite tops and wooden floor. There are several people standing around sipping drinks. Oh God, I hate parties like this. Lots of small talk and chat about absolutely nothing with people you don't like; have nothing in common with and don't care if you never see again.

I plaster a suitably sincere smile over my face and nod and greet everyone. To my delight there's a sudden flash of brown, and a gorgeous cocker spaniel plants her paws firmly on my legs.

'Hello, you're sweet,' I say, bending down precariously to stroke her soft ears. At least I think she's female, you never like to look when it's someone else's dog and it seems a bit rude to ask, a little like when you're not sure if a baby is a boy or a girl. She jumps up and puts her paws on my knee, which is wreaking havoc with my satin dress but I forgive her because her eyes are kind and soulful.

'What a lovely dog,' I say to Jacinta.

'Thank you,' she answers. 'I've had her since she was a pup.'

I feel a surge of unusual envy for this woman; I mean her life is bloody perfect. She has a dream house, substantial grounds chock full of stables, horses (yes I have stalked her on Facebook and seen pictures of them, all Arabs of course), a swimming pool, a rich and very cute husband. I can cope with all that, but now on top of all this she has the most amazing dog. I suddenly notice someone skulking in the background, a rather awkward looking girl dawdling against the wall. She's not unattractive, with long curly hair caught back in a plait, braces and a spattering of freckles.

'Is this your daughter?' I ask politely, trying to make conversation. Always a mistake I find because, like now, I invariably put my foot in it.

'God no!' Jacinta gives a little tinkly laugh, which automatically puts my teeth on edge and makes me kind of want to slap her. To be fair, the girl looks equally as horrified by the suggestion.

'She's my stepdaughter, Anna,' she says. 'Say hello, Anna!' She speaks to her as though she's about five, and my heart immediately goes out to this gawky kid who, like me, obviously wants to be anywhere but here.

'Excuse me. I must go and check on my other guests,' tinkles Jacinta as she sashays off.

Both Anna and I visibly heave a sigh of relief. I hope that Elise or Summer might say something, but they seem to be overcome by shyness. Mrs Miggins has wandered off because she was 'parched, absolutely parched' and has struck up conversation with a rather flamboyantly dressed lady who is standing next to a table of drinks, and Ciaran has disappeared to find the cloakroom. So much for backup!

'So,' I say, desperately searching for something to say to Anna who is still standing next to us, seemingly unable to move. 'What's the dog called?' Oh great, really interesting question that is!

But Anna seems happy with it. 'Daisy,' she says, 'and she's the sweetest dog, I love her to bits.' She appears momentarily quite animated but immediately resides back into her shell.

'I bet she loves cuddles,' I say taking refuge in stroking Daisy's long silky ears. Elise and Summer abandon ceremony, bend down next to me and stroke her too. There's nothing like a dog to break down barriers.

'She does and she's having puppies soon,' says Anna.

'Oh wow, that's so exciting.' Elise forgets her shyness.

'Don't you have a dog?' asks Anna.

'No, but Mum said we might be able to get one now we've moved down here,' says Elise looking at me wistfully.

'I would if I could have one like this,' I say. 'I love Spaniels.'

'Well my step-mum may be selling some of the pups,' says Anna. 'You can ask her to phone you when they're born.'

'Please, Mum!' exclaims Summer. 'Please can we have one?'

'Maybe, we'll have to see,' I say, trying to be a responsible parent, but inwardly wanting to jump up and down with excitement like a kid.

'We've got horses too, if you'd like to see them,' says Anna shyly.

'Can we?' asks Summer. She has less inhibitions than Elise, but I can tell Elise is desperate to go along too.

'Of course, if Anna doesn't mind.'

The girls disappear off out the front door and I watch them go, pleased at their distraction from the earlier argument.

'Romilly, isn't it?' Richard is back but fortunately he's offering me a glass of fizz. He doesn't wait for me to answer. 'All alone? Come through and meet everyone, although I believe there are some familiar faces.'

There's no escaping now. Ciaran doesn't seem to have reappeared and Mrs Miggins is well into her second glass of punch, which judging by the glow on her cheeks, is going straight to her head. I follow Richard into a huge lounge area with a frighteningly immaculate cream carpet. I wonder aimlessly how they cope keeping it clean with a dog, and wish Daisy were here instead of at the stables with the girls. She would be a welcome distraction. When I spot my mother- and father-in-law in the group, I wish I were at the stables or pretty much anywhere rather than here.

'Hello, Vanessa, Anthony.' I kiss them both on the cheeks in the obligatory greeting and try to act pleased to see them.

'Where are the girls? Did you bring them?' asks Vanessa snappily as she peers past me. No hello, pleased to see you or anything vaguely polite. I mean she could at least pretend.

'Yes they're here,' I reply smoothly, hiding my resentment under as pleasant a smile as I can muster. 'They're out at the stables with Anna.'

'Oh Anna! What a charming child, so polite. She was taking round all the canapés earlier, proper little waitress she is. It's a pity your girls aren't a little more outgoing, rather than skulking off with the animals.'

'I'm sure they'll come back in a moment. It's just all rather exciting as they don't get to see horses very often. It's a shame as Elise loves them.'

'She would have seen a lot more if she'd stayed at Riversmeet Senior, plenty of rich horsey people there. Might have found herself a nice young man too. She's got a pretty enough face when she's not sulking. A pretty face is all a young woman needs, I think.'

Give me strength! I'm just wondering whether it's socially acceptable for me to tip my glass of topped up bubbly over her head, but satisfy myself instead with taking a large swig of it for strength. It doesn't do a lot actually except make me feel a bit swimmy. I decide not to have any more until I've completed my mission; I need a clear head for this espionage lark.

'How's work?' asks Anthony.

'Good thanks,' I say, grateful for the change of topic. 'I really enjoy it and have lots of ideas for improving sales.'

'Oh,' says Anthony, 'working full time, eh?'

'No, just part time. It fits round the girls,' I answer.

'Don't believe in women working for that very reason,' grunts Anthony. 'Better for them to be at home, clearing up. In any case they clog up the work place with their maternity leave and part time nonsense round the kids. Bloody ridiculous namby pamby idea. The great British Empire wasn't built on this sort of thing, you know.'

I would like to say I'm about to make a really impressive and suitably squashing feminist retort to this man who I've had to put up with for far too many years as a father-in-law, when I am distracted by the appearance of his son.

'Hello, Rom,' he bends in to kiss me before I can react and I inhale the familiar scent of Armani. I struggle to fight against the pheromones; I always loved that smell. He looks much the same as always, though he now has a little stubble, which actually in the light looks a tiny bit ginger. That's a shock; the hair on his head is so dark. I battle against the urge to randomly shout, 'See ginger does happen in your family,' at Vanessa. I'll never forget when I was pregnant with Elise and wondered aloud if the baby would be ginger when she had announced with outrage, 'The Barringtons have never had a child with ginger hair,' as though it were one of the worst possible outcomes ever. What I have had to put up with from this lot, no wonder I ran away.

'Hi, Dan,' I squeak, totally unsure how to behave. I mean, I did leave him and have since totally ignored him so it's pretty awkward really. I needn't have worried though. In a manner in keeping with his emotionally repressed family, he simply acts as though nothing has happened. This is always his way. I remember telling him it was over during a huge row when we'd been going out for a short while. His way of dealing with it was to ignore it and pretend it never happened. Obviously in his eyes denial is everything.

'So how's tricks? You're looking lovely, by the way,' he says.

'Good thanks. The girls are well, looking forward to seeing you,' I say politely.

'I had a chat with Elise on Wednesday,' he says. 'She seems happy enough, I suppose.'

'She's enjoying this evening,' I say, deftly changing the subject. 'She's out with Anna looking at the horses.'

'Lovely girl,' says Vanessa again. 'Jacinta isn't her real mother of course, but she's kind enough to have her here. Don't you just love her shawl, Romilly? I'm sure it's L'acroix?'

'Oh yes, maybe,' I say vaguely. 'She looks lovely in it.' I thought it was a jumper actually, but what do I know?

'And she's three months pregnant, looks simply marvellous as always,' adds Vanessa supposedly sotto voce, but as loud and embarrassing as ever.

'Oh,' I say trying to appear interested, but secretly feeling sorry for Anna, poor kid, not only to have a wicked stepmother but one who's pregnant and about to have a dear little baby with her father who will take all their attention in the way cute new babies do.

'Rom, do you think...' Dan leans in to whisper in my ear, putting a presumptive arm around me, but I never find out what he was going to say because Ciaran swoops in fighter pilot style and slips his arm through mine.

'Sorry, darling, I got waylaid. Met an old business associate.' He gives me a kiss on the cheek as though to stake his claim, which practically makes me jump twenty feet in the air because a) I just wasn't ready for it and b) I just can't get over the awkwardness of the whole working with him thing. I mean the idea was fine in theory, but I really can't take Ciaran seriously as a potential partner.

Briefly I give myself a good talking to, *for goodness' sake, Rom,* as my Mother says, *think actress. I can do this.*

'That's okay, sweetie,' I say smiling rather in the style of Princess Kate, charming and stylish. Well, that's what I'm aiming for. The reality is probably rather more Cheshire Cat. I take a peek at Dan from under my eyelashes. To be fair he momentarily looks a little taken aback but instantly in the true manner of the charmer he can be, he quickly recovers himself.

'I don't think we're acquainted?' he says, extending his hand and shaking Ciaran's firmly. 'Nice to meet you.'

'And you,' Ciaran smiles. I imagine he's thinking, 'Well, he seems okay.'

'So what do you do?' asks Dan, tilting his head slightly on one side and taking a sip of his beer in a manner which I know only too well means trouble.

'I'm a Sales Manager,' says Ciaran tightly. We've already had this little conflab where we worked out he wouldn't admit he works at the factory.

'How fascinating! What's your speciality?' Dan observes him through narrowed eyes.

'Various things, mostly product placement; working out what's going to sell in the next couple of years. It's about predicting trends really.'

'I suppose it is,' says Dan. 'Are you in fashion then?'

'Erm no,' Ciaran pauses momentarily. 'More the gift market really.'

I heave a sigh of relief. I guess that's similar enough to coffee to be fairly truthful but not close enough to give anything away. 'Yes, very handy to have around, Ciaran,' I say in a jolly tone. Oh God, how embarrassing! This is proving more awkward than I thought.

'How's the car world?' I ask Dan, hoping to change the subject rapidly.

'Booming,' he says, glibly. 'Whereabouts are you based?' Typical Dan, he never lets anything drop.

Ciaran's about to open his mouth and come out with some kind of answer or other, but I can't cope with the suspense and hurriedly interrupt with, 'Ah, here are the girls!'

Summer, Elise and Anna all traipse into the room in their fluffy socks, looking happy and flushed from running about outside.

'Here they are,' coos Vanessa. 'Come and say hello, we haven't seen you for so long.'

It's only been a couple of weeks, I think to myself drily and quite honestly that was too recent. Dutifully the girls go and kiss Anthony and Vanessa whilst Anna hangs back awkwardly.

'So lovely you're making friends with our lovely Anna,' coos Vanessa. She appears to start suddenly. 'What are those in your ears, Summer?'

'I had my ears pierced for my birthday,' Summer answers happily. She's so proud of her new earrings.

'Oh,' says Vanessa, 'what a shame, and it must have

been awfully painful.'

'No, it was fine,' says Summer. I can tell she's a little crestfallen.

'Well, you have got quite big ear lobes, haven't you? Must make it rather easier. Mine are so tiny, I was always too frightened to have them done,' she simpers.

'There you are, my love,' interrupts Mrs Miggins who meanders across and puts her arm around Ciaran. It makes me want to giggle as he looks as though he is about to burst.

'Oh, this is Will's mother, Margaret,' I say politely, 'and this is,' Oh God, how on earth do you introduce your new boyfriend and his mother to your not yet divorced husband and his parents? I dither momentarily. Especially when it's all a lie and they aren't even your new boyfriend and his mother. Everyone is looking at me expectantly, 'and this is Will.' Okay, so I don't have to explain any more than that.

Everyone murmurs their hellos and I can see Vanessa looking disdainfully at Margaret aka Mrs Miggins' homely clothes.

Mrs Miggins smiles round happily. 'So what a lovely party, isn't it?'

'And such a beautiful house,' adds Vanessa.

'Yes, Richard's donc a good job with it,' says Anthony. 'Everything you need in this place is simply designed for a comfortable existence, every mod con going.'

'Hmmm I suppose it has,' says Mrs Miggins. Ciaran and Dan have started their own conversation and I wonder uneasily what they are talking about. 'Although personally I prefer old properties like Melstock Manor.'

'Oh?' responds Vanessa, 'I've never heard of it. Terrible to clean old places, dust traps I think. Much better to have modern, clean, hygienic (oh here she goes again).'

'But rather less character don't you think?' says Mrs Miggins with a charming smile. Oh, she's good at this game. The only thing is she needs to watch how much information she's giving away. I'll just have to hope for the best though. The girls have sloped off again. Not that I blame them, so there seems like no time like the present to slip off and try to find out some info.

'Just off to the ladies,' I say casually, but I needn't have worried as Mrs Miggins and Vanessa are in full battle about the only which way to clean windows, and Ciaran and Dan are totally immersed in sales forecasts. Anthony seems to be more interested in whatever is in the bottom of his glass of scotch.

I walk to the door and slip out into the hallway banked on one side by an imposing row of beautiful wooden doors. Which one is the loo for goodness' sake? The first turns out to be a kind of gym/fitness room; I shut the door hurriedly. The next one leads off down a corridor but I decide to leave that until later. The final door is the loo. I lock myself in and start to peer around the room for the note Ciaran is supposed to be leaving me. Oh great, there's no bathroom cupboard. This minimalism business has an awful lot to answer for. The plan was Ciaran would hide a rough map of the house (which he hopefully checked out for me whilst he was sneaking off) in the bathroom cupboard.

'Everyone has a bathroom cupboard,' Ciaran had

said.

'Not necessarily,' I replied. Well great, it looks like I was right as I often am, but that isn't much help right now.

I look behind the loo roll holder but that's too obvious, someone might have discovered it. Behind the mirror proves to be empty – we had discussed this in advance and Ciaran had thought that some have a space at the side and others haven't. This one hasn't. I stand puzzled – there's nowhere else in this bathroom where you could possibly hide a note. No pictures, nothing. Just bare walls.

I turn and face the door. The wood stares back at me blankly. Maybe Ciaran didn't leave a note. Then I notice, just a tiny, inconspicuous irregularity at the bottom left of the door, right by the corner. Could it be? I squat down and prod at it with my finger; I'm not sure. I thank goodness for my long nails as I manage to get a grip under the corner and sure enough, a wadge of paper comes out towards me. Phew – Ciaran is a genius.

I unfold it and study the rough drawing. Crikey, this place is bigger than I imagined. The corridor I just passed by leads on down to the swimming pool and sauna room. There's also an orangerie on the side of this and some kind of pantry before the garden. No point in going round there then. On the other side there's another turning off the same corridor, leading to a sort of snug and then another door, which looks like the study. Rather comically Ciaran has drawn an emphatic arrow, scrubbed over several times in angry blue biro with an exclamation mark in bubble writing.

Subtle.

Okay, so here goes. I fold up the paper, shove it in my shoulder bag, gingerly open the toilet door and creep down the silent corridor. At first I hesitate, which door was it? Fortunately I remember and manage to open the correct one and travel on round to where the corridor splits right, goes down to the pool according to Ciaran's diagram and left to the study. I take the left, hoping I've remembered correctly and come to a large oak door. Surreptitiously I listen outside. It would be terrible if I opened it to find Richard sitting in there. How on earth would I explain that? I guess I would just say, 'Oops sorry, I was just looking for the loo and got lost'. I mean, he wouldn't believe me of course, but it would get me out of an awkward situation. I grasp the door handle and slowly open it, holding my breath. Thank goodness there's no-one in there. The room is in darkness, but I can just make out a large curved desk in the corner, filing cabinets, drawers. At first glance this feels rather daunting; the documents could be anywhere in here.

Taking a deep breath, in a stealth like manner I creep into the room using the torch light on my mobile phone. First stop, the desk; it's got to be the most obvious place surely. I carefully open each drawer, rifle through the contents looking for anything which could have something to do with a contract. Actually the drawers are neat and tidy and there are no papers at all, just post it notes and paper clips. I move on to more drawers, but although there are folders and papers, they seem to be more to do with household accounts. Suddenly there's a noise, and quick as a flash I huddle into the gap under the desk and stay as still as I can. For a while there's nothing, then over the top of my loudly thumping heart which makes my ears feel as though they are going to explode, I hear light footsteps on the floor out in the hall. I am so not cut out for this espionage business. I'm sure it's not good for my health. I'd almost rather be back in the main house talking to Dan and his parents. Almost.

Chapter 27

The door swings open and whoever it is comes padding in. I hold my breath. A warm furry head with a startlingly wet nose appears. Thank you, God; it's Daisy who has happily greeted me with a waggy tail. I love this dog.

'Hello, Daisy! You're a sweetie pie, but you startled me!' I stroke her silky ears for a second; waiting a couple of moments to make sure no-one has followed her. They haven't, so I crawl out carefully and move on to the filing cabinet; this looks the most likely place. I return to the job in hand. Great it's locked; I guess that's not surprising really. Richard probably keeps the key on his person if he has any sense. I glance around the room wondering where anyone might keep a key to their filing cabinet.

I decide on the most obvious place and feel about under the desk; perhaps it might be stuck under there. I even get on the floor and peer about, the process is definitely not helped by Daisy, who seems to think this is a fun game and keeps trying to lick my face. After scrubbing about like a beetle stuck on its back for a while (I really am getting too old for such things), I sit back on my heels; I can't go back to the others with nothing. Then it comes to me. I pull open the top drawer and slide my fingers about under the top of the desk, a small hidden shelf pops out and in my hands are the keys. Let's hope they fit.

With shaking hands I slide the keys in the lock and after a bit of jiggling manage to open the top drawer of the filing cabinet. I run my eye over the subheadings, Investments, Stocks, Shares, there's so much here and I haven't got time to go through all of them. What on earth am I going to do? The others are going to be sending out a search party soon. Desperately I open the second drawer and scan the titles, they are fairly similar. Suddenly I spot a divider at the back marked Pending. I wonder...

I pull out the folder and a sheaf of papers. There right on the top is an official looking letter with embossed heading, Mannerton-Smythe Land Management Solutions, with Richard's address and in bold, outlined letters 'Regarding the Sale of land comprising The Coffee Factory, Melstock.' I scan through super quickly. Thank goodness for the skill of skim reading I still have left over from uni days. The letter is signed by Richard Mannerton-Smythe and pertains to the offer from Strathcombe Homes. I flick through the papers underneath until I discover the legal contract. Bullseye! It's typically long and tedious, but the bottom line is, this is the contract for the sale of The Coffee Factory right here in my hand. I utter up a silent prayer of thanks for all the temping jobs I did in my student days. Working as a legal secretary was one of them, so I understand quite a bit of legal jargon. Underneath the contract is a professionally outlined map of the plot and the building plans are on a separate sheet. For goodness' sake, they're trying to build two hundred flats in there. How ridiculous. Before I can finish skimming the text, I hear a sudden noise, this time of a door opening down the corridor. Crap, I am totally in it now.

I grab the top documents, carefully making sure I have left the header sheet and a couple of bits underneath which I don't think are anything to do with it. I don't want Richard thinking someone has stolen the contract. I fold the papers carefully once across and place in my handbag. They just fit. Just in time. The door opens and in walks Dan.

'Rom? What are you doing?' he demands.

'I got lost looking for the loo,' I say as convincingly as possible, 'and then the dog went wondering off so I followed her.' I bend down and stroke Daisy who is obligingly waiting at my feet.

'How very convenient,' says Dan with a smile and starts advancing towards me. I feel a bit like a cornered rat; surely he can't possibly know what I was up to. 'You must have sensed I wanted to get a bit of time with you alone.'

Oh great! I do not want to have some kind of weird marriage reconciliation in Richard Mannerton-Smythe's office. This is beyond surreal; I just want to get the heck out of here and check out the terms of this contract. I wonder if there's another copy elsewhere, I didn't have time to check.

Dan's still talking to me. 'Rom, I've really missed you.' He tries to take me in his arms and kiss me, which is awkward as I step away at the last minute and he misses. He stares at me, puzzled, 'Haven't you missed me too?'

'Not really,' I say, just wanting to get out of here. Then I realise I must sound a bit harsh. 'I mean I did a bit at first but then...'

Dan gives me that hurt puppy dog look he's so good at. He only saves it for major occasions, or when he's done something he knows has upset me big time. I find it hard to resist and even now after all this time, something deep down still responds. Darn it, I was trying to be the cool woman who's moved on.

'I know I was wrong, too busy, too hard at work but I've changed that now. I've realised I need you in my life; you're good for me. Without you, I've been a mess, not able to sleep; the house has been so quiet; I miss the girls. I miss you, Rom.'

'You mean you miss the warmth, the cooking and the cleaning,' (okay, maybe I'm exaggerating a bit here. I don't exactly do that much cleaning but it's time to go big or go home now).

'Not just that, Rom. I had to go round to Mum's the other day and everyone was there and I didn't know what to say as everyone was asking after you.'

'I'm sure they were,' I reply tightly. Dan's extended family have never been very kind to me. His brother is pretty much downright rude and his sister spends most of her time sniping at me beneath a very thinly veiled veneer. 'Come on, Dan, I don't exactly think they miss me.'

'They do,' says Dan with his best sales face on. I stare at him.

'Okay, so only a bit, but I miss you and that has to count.'

'Yes, it does,' I say slowly, 'it's just...'

'You've found someone else,' says Dan angrily. 'I knew it! What would you want with me? I bet you've found someone sporty with a six pack who's better in bed, though I'm not sure that Will fits that description. You could do much better than him.'

Oh God, he's got to the self-pitying stage. He always used to try that one, 'I expect one day you'll find yourself a fit man and you'll leave,' he used to say. That was my cue to reassure him, 'Oh no, I'd never do that. I love you just as you are.'

'Do you really think I'm that shallow?' I ask. 'I don't give a monkey's about someone with a six pack or how fit they are (though Mark was nice to look at) but I've grown up now. I've realised I need a man who is emotionally there, who wants to just be with me.'

'But I want to be with you,' says Dan, edging closer.

'I don't just mean like that. I mean be there for me,' I say simply.

'Oh, I see we're back to that. You want me to be there twenty-four seven. I guess I could give up my job and stay home all day, although I think we'd all starve,' he remarks.

It's as though nothing has changed at all. He always used to say these things. If I were upset about him being away overnight for work, especially if one of the girls were ill, his response would be 'Sorry, I have to go out to work to earn money.' 'But this is a drinks and party evening,' I would respond, but he'd never understand. I know it was work, but it wasn't the point and now this argument doesn't wash any more. Not that it ever did with me.

‘As always, you’re being ridiculous. Of course I don't want you home all day, we’d drive each other nuts,’ I laugh, ‘but I would like you to be back in the evenings sometimes early enough to have dinner together or to arrange a spontaneous date night. When did you ever arrange an evening out for us? I always had to suggest it to you, organise it myself, sort the babysitter, book the restaurant.’

‘I’ll do that, I really will if you come back, Rom,’ says Dan, putting his arm round my shoulders and I must admit it feels kind of familiar and nice. There’s a spot on his chest where my head just rests nicely, it always has. ‘Of course, it all costs, you know, that sort of thing, so of course I’ll have to put extra hours in at the office. Money doesn't grow on trees, does it now?’ Oh for goodness’ sake! He’s putting on that patronising tone again.

‘That doesn't matter anymore,’ I say proudly, shrugging his arm away, ‘I’ve got my own job now, so I have my own money.’

‘Yes, but for how long?’ replies Dan sharply. ‘It may not last.’

I stare at him, shocked. ‘What do you mean?’

‘Well,’ he says, rather red faced as though he realises he shouldn't have said anything. ‘I did hear the factory might be closing.’

‘It’s not going to happen,’ I say firmly. ‘Anyway, how do you know about that?’

‘Oh, it’s common knowledge,’ says Dan, glibly brushing it aside, his sales face firmly back on again. ‘Anyway, you’re changing the subject. Will you come back to me? Come on, Rom, the house is too big without you.’

‘I have a new life here,’ I say slowly, ‘friends, hobbies, good people, the girls are settled in school.’

‘Huh! That’s not what I’ve heard,’ snaps Dan. Honestly, he’s just like a little boy.

‘There’s a whole host of reasons why I don't want to leave Melstock,’ I say roundly.

Dan stares at me a moment. ‘Okay, so what if I move here?’ he suggests.

Oh my God, no. I feel sick to the stomach. Not here, no. Dan can’t come to Melstock, it’s my safe space. ‘But what about your work?’ I ask trying not to panic; the old helpless feeling coming over me again. ‘You can’t commute that far.’

‘I won’t need to,’ he says triumphantly, and for a second I think perhaps it could work. Maybe he could work locally; he could set up a business. My stupid optimistic mind jumps at this possibility, but then he adds, ‘Work has an office in Gloucester. I could commute it.’

‘But that’s miles away,’ I stammer. My voice now has a crack in it. For God’s sake, Rom, get a grip. You’re stronger than this now.

‘Not really,’ he replies. ‘I could stay up a couple of days a week and commute the rest, or there might be a bit of working from home, although we have a new financial year coming up so I’d have to prove myself.’

Here we go again. I stare at Dan incredulously; it’s the same old crap, the same nonsense but in a different location. I know I’d have my hobbies, and hopefully if we can save The Coffee Factory I’d have work, but Dan would be here squashing everything. My friends would all become his friends too and he was so clever at only showing them his kind and caring side. I can't face it; this is a total disaster.

In any case, I have to get back to the others. If we're found in here, Richard will wonder what on earth is going on.

'Look, Dan, I just don't know,' I say and brush past him firmly. 'We need to get back to the party.'

I leg it back along the corridor, Daisy at my heels. I wish I could take this dog home with me; she's so loyal. I don't look back to see where Dan is, I just can't cope with any more of him this evening. I make it back to the main lounge, heaving a sigh of relief as I seem to have managed to get away with my mission. As long as Dan doesn't say anything, but I hope he won't before we can get home and sort out what, if anything, we can do to stop the whole charade. Mrs Miggins is beginning to look a bit the worse for wear. I wonder how I am going to extricate her without further embarrassment, but Ciaran appears to have it vaguely under control as he seems to be bringing her some water. He glances at me questioningly, and I give him a slight nod as I enter the room.

'Oh, there you are, Romilly,' says Vanessa blandly. 'Have you seen Dan? I thought he was with you?' she adds this last section with meaning as though that is my rightful place.

'He was,' I say cheerfully, 'but I think he got caught up.'

'I was wondering if it might be time to take Mother home, darling,' says Ciaran approaching and putting his arm around me.

'But you haven't had any food yet,' tinkles Jacinta, 'and the girls are having such a lovely time.'

'Yes, I've hardly seen them,' says Vanessa in a complaining tone.

Hardly surprising. They'd far rather go and hang out round the horses than stand here and make aimless small talk about nothing. What odd children. How strange.

I'm about to attempt to make some kind of response when I feel my phone buzzing through my bag. Of course, I put it on silent before my assignment. I pick it up and check the screen just in case one of my parents are ill or something. It's Debs, 'Excuse me a mo,' I say to the assembled company and back off a little.

'Hi, Debs, are you okay?' I say casually. I hope she doesn't mention our mission, as although she isn't on speakerphone, we are close enough to be overheard.

'Oh, thank goodness I've got you,' she says breathlessly. 'It's Walter.'

Chapter 28

'Is he okay?' I ask instantly stressed. 'What's happened?'

'He's had a bit of an accident,' Debs explains. 'The paramedics are just checking him over now. He seems to have hurt his leg, so I guess it might be broken.'

'Oh, poor Walter. How on earth did he do that?'

'Apparently he was moving rocks in the stream early teatime and slipped climbing back up the bank. It sounds like he caught his leg underneath him and was trapped down at the bottom of the bank.'

'Did you find him?' I ask.

'Yes eventually, but I think he'd been there a while. Because it was quite late, people weren't walking up and down the lane as they usually are.'

'Thank goodness you went past when you did,' I say. 'Is he okay in himself, if you know what I mean?'

'I think he's pretty shaken up,' she says, 'but they've given him some morphine so he's quite sleepy now.'

'Are you okay to go with Walter, Debs?' I ask. 'Which hospital are they taking him to?'

'Exeter,' Debs replies. 'I'll go with him, but I might need to be brought back as Josh is at home.'

'That's fine,' I say decisively. 'We'll come and find you.'

I am amazed at how quickly we manage to get out of the Mannerton-Smythes'. You'd think they were all glad to see the back of us or something. Vanessa can't believe her luck as I have left Elise and Summer to spend the night with Anna, but for once I'm not too worried about them as I know both Anna and Daisy dog are lovely. They'll have a wonderful time. The only person who seems sorry for me to leave is Dan; he was obviously hoping for another little chat. I'm actually incredibly grateful to escape, but sorry it's in such horrible circumstances.

'Did you find anything?' asks Ciaran as he pulls out of the Mannerton-Smythes' drive.

I look over my shoulder surreptitiously and have to fight the urge not to whisper. This spying thing is making me a bit paranoid. 'Yes, I managed to get hold of the contract.' I open my bag and carefully pull out the documents.

'Well done, that's a girl!' exclaims Mrs Miggins loudly, making me jump nervously and bang my head on the roof of the car.

'Yep, I reckon this is the original too,' I say proudly examining the document. 'I can't be certain, but it's on good quality headed paper so I wouldn't think it's a copy.'

'Hmm. Looks like the real deal to me,' says Mrs Miggins peering at the paper. 'Good grief! They don't half go on something terrible though.'

'What's the plan then, Rom?' asks Ciaran.

'Sounds like a complete knock down of the factory and then two hundred old people's flats will be built. Should be complete by the end of next summer.'

'The callous lot,' says Mrs Miggins, indignantly.

'Any mention of Mark Whittaker?' asks Ciaran.

‘He’s referred to here as the vendor of the land, but thank goodness he hasn't yet signed. I guess that was what he was talking about when I was ear-wigging the other day.’

‘Thank goodness for that,’ remarks Mrs Miggins.

‘Yes, but they’ll have it all on computer,’ Ciaran points out. ‘It’ll only take them a few minutes to print out another copy and all will be sorted.’

We all sit in gloomy silence for a moment.

‘I guess it doesn't really matter as long as Walter’s alright,’ I say philosophically.

‘Not on your nelly. It’ll finish him off if this bloody fiendish scheme goes through,’ remarks Mrs Miggins. I look at her shocked, she never swears.

‘Then we have to come up with a strategy,’ I say more optimistically than I feel. I seem to be fresh out of plans right now.

By the time we arrive at the hospital, Walter is back from his X-ray and in the urgent care ward.

‘What did I tell you about digging about in that stream?’ I scold as I rush up and kiss him on the cheek.

‘Done it all me life,’ he says stubbornly. ‘And I’m blowed if I’m going to stop now.’

‘Looks like you’ll have to for a while,’ says Mrs Miggins pragmatically.

Debs appears with some chocolate bars and a motherly looking nurse. ‘Well done, Debs,’ I say. ‘Chocolate’s the best medicine.’

‘Hmmm, that and rest,’ says the nurse. ‘Looks as though you’re not going to be gallivanting for a little while, young man. That leg’s broken.’

‘For goodness’ sake,’ moans Walter. ‘How long

have I got, Sister?'

'Plenty longer I reckon by the look of you,' she says cheerily, 'but we'll be off to the plaster room now to get it sorted and you'll need someone at home to look after you.'

There's a silence. 'My daughter is bound to come down and visit,' says Walter, 'but she's got a farm to run.'

'I can come and stay for a bit,' I say, 'though I'm not sure about the girls.'

'Plenty of room for them,' says Walter perking up quite noticeably. 'There're three bedrooms upstairs and I suppose I'll have to sleep in the dining room til this silly old leg of mine recovers.'

We're a far more cheerful party on the way home. Walter is spending a couple of nights in hospital as I think the whole accident has shaken him up more than he's admitting. Also, as the nurse points out, he's no longer a spring chicken and they need to keep an eye on him. I'm a bit worried, as I know falls at this age can really weaken a person, but to my relief the nurse seems quite optimistic. Tomorrow the girls and I will move our stuff in. I actually feel quite pleased to be leaving the cottage, albeit temporarily. Much as I love it, I'm worried that soon it's all going to hit the fan when this whole Coffee Factory malarkey comes to light and I don't want to be in Mark's cottage when it does. Somehow I feel rather beholden to him as I've found myself mixed up in it all.

The next day is filled with trips to and from Walter's little cottage with sheets and bedding, and bits and bobs. The girls help, as they are full of excitement.

Of course, Winston the tabby cat is thrilled to see us, insisting he hasn't been fed or had any love or attention for at least a month. 'Can he sleep on my bed, Mum?' asks Summer.

'If he wants to. Cats tend to choose their own space themselves,' I comment over my armfuls of bedding. Whilst I'm scrabbling about on the floor after a sock that seems to have got stuck under the bed (don't ask me how it fell under there), there's a halloo from the doorway. 'See who that is, will you, Summer?' I ask.

She runs to the window and peers out. 'It's Mr Barton!'

For goodness' sake, what is he doing here? I look a complete mess as well, hair all over the place, holes in my trousers. Not that I care what he thinks but it's probably best not to go to the door looking like the wild woman of Helsinki. Desperately I peer at myself in front of the mirror. Nope it's no good; this will have to do. I mooch down the stairs trying to act casual. Hold your head high, Rom. I'm totally above how rude this guy was to me the last time I saw him. Though to be fair, I guess it's not surprising – he has had a tough time of it with his horrible first wife. Easy for him to mistake me for another one I suppose, although I would hope he might have realised I'm not a complete and utter witch like her.

As I walk down the stairs, my foot slips. I knew I shouldn't wear socks on wooden stairs and I lose my footing. For a second I'm in freefall, poised to crash on down but by some miracle I manage to catch hold of the banister and land on my other foot, not very glamorously either. I catch my breath; just grateful I haven't hurt myself when I catch sight of Mr Barton waiting in the hallway. Just great; how embarrassing!

'Are you okay?' he asks in a concerned voice.

'Yep, fine thanks,' I say nonchalantly sauntering down the last few steps, trying not to limp as my foot does hurt. Nothing to see here; I can style this out.

I arrive safely at the bottom of the stairs and we both stand there awkwardly. Summer wanders in stuffing a biscuit. 'Summer, it would be nice if you offered one to Mr Barton,' I say politely.

'No, no I'm fine,' he declines hastily. 'I just popped in to see if there's anything I can do to help.' I must be staring at him blankly as he continues. 'It's very kind of you to look after Walter. His daughter must be super grateful.'

'Yes, I spoke to her on the phone last night after Debs had phoned her to tell her about her dad. She's coming down as soon as she can get cover. I'm just holding the fort really. She's lovely. I think we'll get on as she seemed really down to earth.'

'They're a great family, very close,' remarks Henry. 'Shall I give you a hand with some more stuff?' He looks rather obviously at my things thrown everywhere.

'Please do,' complains Elise who's just wandered in with a small handful consisting of her makeup bag and a couple of pairs of shoes. She throws herself down on the sofa exhausted.

'Don't strain yourself!' laughs Henry. I have a job not to laugh out loud.

'It's very tiring work,' protests Elise.

'Well, I'm free all afternoon,' says Henry amicably, 'so tell me what to do.'

'Well if you're sure.' I peer at him uncertainly; I mean he's acting so differently from last time. 'Come on then, girls. We'll go and get some more bits. To be honest, Mr Barton, it's been a case of just wandering backwards and forwards with this and that, so I'm not surprised it's taking us forever.'

'I'm not going to the cottage again,' says Elise. 'My back hurts. I'll stay here and make sure no one gets in and moves anything.'

'I'll come,' says Summer. 'I've got some string at home and feathers that I'm making into a toy for Winston.'

'Lucky Winston!' says Henry. 'I presume he's either a child or an animal.'

'He's a cat,' laughs Summer. 'I think he's upstairs checking out my bed, he's always snoozing.'

'Yes, I think cats have pretty much got it right,' I say wistfully thinking back to my short night's sleep after all the excitement yesterday. 'Do you have any cats, Mr Barton?'

'No, but I'd love one,' Henry replies. 'In fact I'd love a dog too, but I'm back living with my parents at the moment so don't feel I can have one in their house.'

'Aren't you too old to live at home with your mum and dad?' asks Summer skipping along next to us as we walk back down the lane into Melstock and across to Larkin Cottage.

'Summer, that's a bit rude!' I say embarrassed.

'Not at all,' smiles Henry, 'I had to move back with my parents for a while but I'm hoping to get my own place probably in the village sometime soon.'

I open my mouth, tempted to say something and

then close it again. It just doesn't seem the right time. We reach the cottage and I feel embarrassed inviting Henry in, but I don't know why.

‘Excuse the mess,’ I say hurriedly sweeping bits out of the way and hoping he won’t notice the clutter.

‘You should see my room,’ he says. ‘My mum still tells me off and I’m thirty-nine.’

‘Are you?’ I shriek a bit too loudly for comfort. I mean, oh thirty-nine. Right. I mean who would have known? I thought he was about twenty-two. He has such a baby face. Not that it matters anyway, but still. ‘Right, if you could carry this?’ I give him a suitcase, which in my usual style is far too full for a stay of a couple of days. He swings it up easily and we start the return journey. Summer has brought her scooter and speeds on ahead.

Henry looks at me as though he wants to say something but doesn't. ‘Erm,’ I stumble. I just hate awkward silences.

‘I just wanted to say,’ he says. (Thank goodness, just spit it out.) ‘I wanted to say sorry for the other evening, for how I spoke to you. It must have seemed – well, it was really rude.’

‘Oh,’ I stutter, not sure what else to say.

‘It’s just I heard that maybe things weren’t very easy for you and that’s why you came here, and I think I was hurt and angry about my own situation and placed the same meaning on yours.’

‘Pardon?’ I say politely. I’m so confused.

‘What I mean is, well ...’ he flounders.

‘I think what you’re trying to say is that you took a violent, and might I add unfounded, dislike to me because you thought I'd abandoned my lovely husband and taken his kids away from him because I am a heartless bitch.'

Henry flinches slightly at my strong words and goes a deep red. Yep, I think I've pretty much hit the nail on the head. 'Well, that's a little harsh, but I guess you've heard that my wife left me last year and took our little girl, so...' I can tell it's difficult for him to talk about it still.

'Look it's okay, Mr Barton. Shall we just agree to draw a line under it? I'm not really offended that you mistook me for a mean and nasty person, as long as you're not really offended that I thought you were a miserable, rude, arrogant...'

'Okay, okay,' he laughs. 'I get your gist. Shall we start again and forget this whole misunderstanding? And can you please call me Henry?'

'Yes, I guess, it's less formal but I'm still confused, what made you change your mind?' I ask puzzled.

'Well, to start with, I wanted to really dislike you because I thought you'd...'

'Abandoned my family...yes,'

'Okay, moving on, but then I began to admire the way you've fitted into the community, how you're prepared to stand up for your principals, how kind you are to Walter, so yeah... I think you're pretty cool.' He goes a bit pink again and shuts up.

'Thanks,' I say, pretty embarrassed myself. 'I love this place,' I gaze up at the sloping hillsides spreading up above us towards the moorland, which are now beginning to show tufts of flame pink heather ready for the summer. 'To be honest it now feels like home more than home does... so it makes it difficult...'

'Makes what difficult?' asks Henry.

'Oh nothing really,' I say. For goodness' sake I'd been forgetting who I was talking to.

'Oh okay,' says Henry, but I can tell he's kind of offended, and to be fair I don't blame him. I hate it when people say it's nothing when it's very obviously something. Because that basically means it's something they just don't want to tell you.

'I mean, it's just I love it here and want to stay, but I still question myself sometimes. It's the old guilt thing, too much oestrogen. Makes me doubt myself and worry if I'm doing the right thing for the girls.'

'Well, they seem pretty happy,' Henry replies. 'They're young. They'll have their ups and downs with all this. I know I might have been rude about it before, but honestly Summer has been settling in really well lately.'

'She has. It's just the senior school isn't really suiting Elise and...' I look at Henry, 'and well bottom line is Dan has asked me to go back to him.'

'Oh,' says Henry, looking at me seriously. 'Well, I guess that does make a difference.'

'I don't know whether it does or not,' I say. 'I mean, I still care about him, but I'm just not convinced he's changed.'

'No, I guess it's difficult to trust someone again when they've behaved in a certain way,' says Henry, 'I know that myself.'

'Do you get to see your little girl much?' I ask.

'I have access every other weekend in theory, but the reality is actually very different. Her mother always rings up at the last minute, saying sorry but she's ill or she's unable to come.'

'I'm sorry. That's tough,' I look at him sympathetically. 'I think she should let you see her, she's your child,' I say simply.

He looks away and I can see the tears threatening at the edge of his eyes and feel sorry to have pushed it, an abrupt change of subject is necessary. We are just approaching Walter's cottage anyway. 'Erm, thanks for your help by the way,' I say as he lifts my heavy bag over the much trodden doorstep.

'Where do you want it?' he asks.

'Upstairs, in the front bedroom, please.' I watch Henry lug my heavy bag up the stairs as though it's far lighter than it actually is. He's really quite sweet and to be honest it's so unfair that a man can be left without his children. It makes me feel kind of bad actually; bad for how many times Dan has seen the girls in the last few weeks. He is their dad after all, even though he hasn't really asked to see them. Perhaps he's hurting inside or something deep and meaningful like that, but they are his children.

Elise appears from the kitchen scoffing biscuits. 'Elise, get a plate. This is Walter's house and he keeps it beautifully.'

She rolls her eyes at me and stuffs the rest of the biscuit in her mouth. 'I've eaten it now,' she comments. 'What's for tea anyway?'

'I haven't even thought about it,' I say impatiently. What is it with teenagers? They always seem to be hungry even though they haven't necessarily seemed to do very much?

‘Can we have pizza and salad please?’ Elise loves that takeaway from the little shop in the village – they do an amazing nut and seed noodle salad which I love too.

‘Yes pizza, pizza!’ chants Summer.

Henry comes back down the stairs. ‘Are you staying for dinner, Mr Barton?’ asks Summer in the way young children do without checking with you first and making it really embarrassing,

‘Oh, I don't know,’ says Henry and looks rather awkwardly at me.

‘You’re very welcome to,’ I say. ‘It’s the least I can do to say thank you for your help.’

‘No, no, you don't need to,’ he replies. I feel a bit disappointed actually, although I don't know why. ‘But I’d love to stay if I’m being asked as long as you promise I can pay.’

‘We’ll argue about that later,’ I say amused and secretly pleased, ‘but yes I’ll carry on sorting stuff here, then we’ll go and organise some dinner.’

As it happens, sorting everything out and cleaning the house up as well as borrowing a bed from Debs all takes longer than I expected. I don't know what we’d have done without Henry.

‘I see you have a helper,’ comments Debs innocently as her husband, Mick, helps Henry wrestle with the foldable bed for Walter.

‘Debs,’ I say in a warning tone. ‘It’s very kind of him.’

‘I know,’ she says. ‘He’s a very sweet man and he’s available, in need of cheering up. You could do worse, you know.’

‘Shh, he’ll hear you. I don't think he feels like that and quite honestly I’ve made enough of a mess with men.’

‘I think he rather likes you. Trust Aunty Debs.’

‘Yeah right.’ I blush and busy myself checking my texts, which are all old. ‘I think my life is too complicated as it is.’

‘You could be friends with benefits,’ says Debs with a cheeky wink.

Before I can respond, to my complete embarrassment Henry walks in and I could swear he heard the end of our conversation. Quite honestly, I feel like curling up and hiding behind a cushion somewhere, but Debs just carries on chatting away totally oblivious.

With wonderful timing my phone really does ping the arrival of a text. It’s from Elise. ‘Anna just messaged me. Please could she come over for tea?’

‘Oh that’s nice,’ I remark randomly, pleased to remove that attention from Henry. ‘Anna, you know the nice girl I was telling you about at the party on Saturday, she wants to come over for tea tonight.’

‘Great,’ says Debs. ‘Does she go to the secondary?’

‘Yes, so Elise might finally have a friend to hang out with,’ I say, ‘but do you think Walter will mind – I seem to be entertaining at his cottage without his permission.’

‘Give him a ring,’ says Henry. ‘I don't mind not staying though if it’s awkward.’

‘I’m absolutely certain he won’t mind,’ says Debs with heavy intonation.

I give her a murderous look. ‘No I’m sure he won’t

too,' I say, 'but it's probably polite to ask.'

Dinner is a surprisingly cheerful and riotous affair. Henry is really quite comical actually and keeps us all in fits with tales about his crazy aunt who used to breed cats and was quite randomly also a ballroom dancer. Of course, the conversation has to move on to my Uncle Clarence and the bagpipes, so there is much hilarity all round. Anna is a totally different child away from the awkwardness with her stepmother at the Mannerton-Smythes' and to be honest I know how she feels. She chats away with Elise and after dinner they wander off upstairs and I'm pleased to hear fits of laughter and messing around. Summer is happy playing with Winston with her new toy and a cheery conversation with Walter reassures us that he's doing okay. He's fractious to be back in his cottage and is looking forward to seeing us tomorrow.

'Thanks for a lovely evening,' says Henry as I turn on the porch light so he can see his way down the winding path across the stream.

'That's okay; it was really fun. And thanks for your help today.'

'It was nothing, the least I could do after being so rude and misjudging you completely.'

'It's all forgotten now,' I say, shyly.

'Oh, before I go, Debs said you might like me to come with you to pick Walter up tomorrow – just to help bring his stuff.'

'Thanks, but I'm sure I can manage,' I say awkwardly. For goodness' sake Debs, she's making me out to be desperate.

'I'm sure you've got better things to do tomorrow,' I

say.

'No, not at all. It would be a pleasure,' he replies. And thinking about it, I'm looking forward to seeing him again too.

Chapter 29

I'm feeling pretty okay with the world this morning; I've managed to make sure Walter's cottage is looking warm and welcoming ready for his return. Miraculously, Elise has got up early and walked into the village to buy some of Debs' home-made scones ready for our afternoon tea later, and Summer is happily cutting holes out of a cardboard box for Winston to jump in and out of. I'm not sure he's going to want to do that but it's keeping her occupied and after all, it's a kind thought.

At the back of my mind, I'm still worrying about The Coffee Factory and what we're going to do about it, but I'm sure we can get together and think of a plan in the next couple of days. The main thing is Walter is okay; the thought of anything happening to him was unthinkable. I also feel uncannily as though today is going a bit too well, if you know what I mean? Some days you feel that everything is going brilliantly and something's bound to go wrong. It's that whole Sod's Law thing. I think a group of scientists once did an experiment to prove whether it existed or not. To do this they buttered pieces of white bread and dropped them on the floor. Sounds strange I grant you, but they counted how many times the slices fell butter side down or not. Sure enough it turned out more pieces fell butter side down, which the scientists said showed that this Sod's Law or Murphy's Law that if anything can possibly go wrong it will, does exist. I do think they're probably right and after all, they were terribly scientific and professional looking, dressed in goggles and white suits so they must know what they are talking about.

Just as I'm moving a couple of pots outside the door further apart in readiness for Walter's wheelchair, my mobile blasts out – I've changed it to 'I need a miracle,' which I think is quite relevant actually. It's Dan – oh for goodness' sake what on earth can he want now?

'Rom?' he says.

'Hi, Dan,' I reply trying to sound enthusiastic.

'How's it going?' he asks.

'Fine thanks.'

'Just fine thanks,' he mimics. 'Pleased to speak to you too.'

'I'm just a bit distracted,' I reply.

'Well, I'm glad I can still distract you. It was lovely to see you the other evening tho' it was cut short.'

'Yes, poor Walter had an accident.'

'Oh that's right, I forgot his name. I'm phoning to see if you want to catch up again soon, have a bit more of a chat about my coming to Melstock. I could drive up and see you.'

'I'm a bit busy at the moment. Walter's about to come home from hospital and I've agreed to look after him for a bit.'

'Can't his own family do that?' Dan asks, sounding irritated.

'They can, but it will take a couple of days for his daughter to get down here as she has a farm and stuff to deal with.'

'That's okay then. Next weekend would be fine.'

'Erm maybe.' I try to think desperately of an excuse. I really don't want Dan here.

'Mum and Dad enjoyed seeing you the other day. Wasn't the Mannerton-Smythes' place amazing?'

'Yes it was, very impressive.' I don't believe for a minute Vanessa was pleased to see me.

'Also it's Melissa and Jeremy's wedding anniversary evening coming up in a couple of weeks. I hoped you might come?'

'Why would I do that?' I ask, horrified. 'I think it'd be better if you went without me.'

'Well, I don't really want to. You know what it's like when everyone gets together, I'd much rather you were there.'

'You mean to deflect any difficult questions, to make social chit chat because you don't want to?' I ask.

'Maybe there's a bit of that.'

'I don't want to go to Melissa's anyway – she's constantly sniping.'

'You always say she is, but if you can't say anything nice.'

'But you never notice,' I say. 'You never notice with your mum either.'

'Oh, Mum doesn't mean it. She's just a bit ditzy, doesn't always know what she's saying. She would never be unkind.'

Yeah, right, and Donald Trump is a humanitarian who cares about the future of the planet. Somewhere inside me something totally snaps. I'm sick of this crap. That's one of the main reasons why I left Dan in the first place and he hasn't changed at all. It's all the same old rubbish excuses for everyone around him. He always knocked my confidence and I just don't want to go back there again.

'Actually, Dan, I've just realised something,' I say abruptly.

'Sorry?' he asks.

'I've just realised I've got to go.'

'Okay,' he sounds a bit surprised. 'I'll speak to you later about the party and stuff.'

'No, you won't actually,' I respond very firmly.

'Another day?' he asks, and it's almost pitiful, but I don't care, I'm so over this.

'Do you know what, Dan? I just don't think this is going to work. I'll send you some stuff to sort out access for the girls. I know you need to see them.'

'The girls?' he asks, dazed. 'But what about you?'

'I've found a better alternative.'

'I knew it. It's another man. You could have told me the truth, Rom,' he blasts angrily.

'It's not actually. It's about being part of a village community where both I and my opinions matter; they don't put me down or try to squash me, they accept me as I am. It's about a whole load of small things that have given me back not only my identity but also my life,' I say firmly.

'But I don't get it,' Dan replies.

'No, you never did. Bye, Dan,' I say, putting down the phone.

'Was that Dad?' asks Summer who has just come back in the room.

'Yes,' I sit down shakily.

‘Chocolate?’ asks Summer. She doesn't wait to hear the reply, just wanders off to the kitchen and returns shortly with a Double Decker, my current chocolate bar of choice.

‘Thanks,’ I pause and scoff a couple of mouthfuls gratefully.

‘You’re not getting back together, are you?’ asks Summer sadly.

‘No, I’m afraid we’re not. It just wouldn't work here, Summer. I’m happy in this village and Dad’s happy with his family and his job. But you can go and stay when we’ve sorted out visiting.’

‘I’d like that,’ says Summer, ‘though Granny Vanessa is a bit weird. Can’t you and Dad get along anymore?’

‘No, I’m afraid not, love. Sometimes if you’re not good for each other, it’s best to live separately. If you’ve done your very best to try and sort out a compromise of course,’ I add. After all it would be nice for her to at least aim to have a happy marriage.

‘A bit like Mia and me?’ she asks.

‘Exactly like you and Mia.’ Mia had been Summer’s best friend at her last school but she had been quite toxic, controlling who Summer was friends with and knocking her confidence. Thank goodness that in the end Summer found other friends to help support her against this manipulative girl.

Somehow I feel happier in a weird way. I mean that’s it; no more Dan. Henry’s talk had made me realise that the girls are the most important casualties of our relationship breakdown, and whatever I feel about Dan and his horrible mother, they’re still related to the girls and it's important for them to be able to go round. As long as they're kind to them of course, and aren't rude about me. After all, there are limits.

Henry drives Elise, Summer and me to go to get Walter, who though a bit frail seems able to get himself into the wheelchair with surprisingly little assistance. He is thrilled to be back home, but it becomes immediately apparent he's going to need a lot of care, as his cottage isn't really designed for an invalid. Fortunately, the hospital is sending the community nurse in every day to check on him from a medical point of view, and Elise and Summer are happy to help fetch and carry for him.

We manage to get him sitting comfortably in his chair with his leg up on an extra padded stool. 'What's all this then?' he asks holding up a thick package.

'Just a little something to keep you busy,' I say, bringing him a cushion for his back.

'You're a dear,' he says opening the parcel. 'My goodness! That's the biggest book of crosswords I've ever seen.'

'I thought we might be able to have a go at a few of them later,' I say.

'Definitely,' he chuckles, 'although I do warn you, I've been practising in hospital.'

After an afternoon snooze for Walter, and strict instructions from the bossy but kindly Sister at the hospital, Elise and Summer lay the lounge table for afternoon tea, with beautiful napkins, the best flower tea set and large fluffy scones from Debs. Other than a fervent argument about whether cream or jam should be applied first, tea goes well. Even Winston deigns to join us for some cream, lapping it up daintily from a saucer with his little tongue.

'Room for a couple of small ones?' calls a voice and in walk Debs and Mike, laden with a lemon drizzle cake and some chocolate brownies. 'Mrs Miggins sends these with her apologies, but she's calling in later in the week,' says Debs.

Soon the room is full of laughter and happy contented munching. There's another knock and Henry puts his head round the stable door. 'Just thought I'd pop by to see how Walter's doing?' He had gone home for lunch after dropping Walter and us off from hospital but I hadn't expected him to return for tea although I had extended the invitation. Soon he's tucking in with the rest of us.

'Any more people coming round?' asks Walter with a smile.

'Well, I may have mentioned it to Jim, Phil and Alexandrine, but other than that, no not really,' I add casually. I had checked with the hospital that a few visitors would be alright for Walter, as I was unsure if it might tire him out. The Ward Sister had assured me it would do him good to have everyone round as long as we weren't too rowdy. Sure enough, Phil and Alexandrine turn up with a plate full of delicious looking tuna and cucumber sandwiches and crispy sausage rolls.

'Well, we sure aren't going to starve,' laughs Walter, obviously thrilled to bits with all the fuss. Summer carefully places all the get well cards and notes around the fireplace.

'Isn't anyone a bit cold?' asks Elise.

'Not really,' says Alexandrine.

'I don't think so,' I reiterate, then catch sight of Elise's face. 'Oh, erm yes, it is a little chilly.'

'I thought it was,' says Elise and hops up to the fireplace where she has carefully placed all the sticks and kindling ready for a fire, Walter style. I'm a bit worried she might crack under the pressure but soon enough she has a crackling blaze roaring away in the hearth.

'Now that's what I call a jolly good blaze,' says Walter, obviously chuffed she's remembered how to do it. 'Well done, child.'

I peer at Elise, wondering how she's going to respond to being called a child, but she takes it in her stride, looking pleased as punch. 'Can I toast marshmallows?' she asks.

'I thought you'd never ask,' says Walter.

A little later we're all sitting dozily, stuffed full of yummy cake and sandwiches when Phil sits forward in his chair. 'I don't mean to cast a shadow on proceedings, and can I say, Walter, how happy we all are to have you back.'

Walter smiles and does a small mock bow.

'I just wondered how we're doing with The Coffee Factory? How did you get on the other evening, Romilly?'

I glance at Walter. 'I don't want to wear our patient out by talking about stressful things, maybe we should wait another day or so.'

'Nonsense,' protests Walter. 'Total tommyrot! We need to get on with this otherwise there won't even be a factory to talk about.'

'Okay. Well, as long as you're sure,' says Alexandrine soothingly, 'but you mustn't get het up about anything.'

'I shall get het up sat here all day, I can tell you. I might as well have something to think about. Spill the beans, Rom. What did you find out?'

'Well, I've got the contract,' I say shyly. 'I'll go and get it if you like so you can all have a look. But basically, once that document is signed, the factory will belong to Strathcombe Homes and it's all over.'

'But if you've got the document, surely it will take them a while to get another one typed,' says Walter hopefully.

'Not really,' says Phil. 'If it's on the computer, it can just be printed out again.'

'Oh fiddlesticks,' says Walter, which makes me want to laugh in spite of the serious subject matter. I don't think I've ever heard anyone say that before.

'At least I hope it will delay things a little,' I say, 'but we do need to have a concrete plan in place.'

Phil scans through the document. 'This looks pretty standard,' he says. 'We could get a solicitor to look through it though.'

'Huh! at great cost,' adds Walter. 'Earn a flipping fortune those guys.'

'We could all club together,' I say desperately. 'Not that I've got very much.'

'That's exactly what I was going to suggest,' agrees Phil.

'Put me down for whatever I can give,' says Walter heartily, 'though it won't be enough to match those rotters at the housing company, Stroppy Homes or whatever it's called.'

'I was thinking of something along those lines but on a bigger scale,' says Phil thoughtfully.

'You mean like crowdfunding?' asks Henry scratching at his stubble.

'Yes exactly,' says Alexandrine. 'Phil and I were talking about it because it worked at a local village. They managed to save the Brewer's Arms like that.'

'But isn't that different?' asks Henry, 'because no one wanted to build on the land there.'

'Yes, I guess we'd have to raise a lot of money,' I say. 'Strathcombe Homes will be offering a huge sum of money I'm sure.'

'Do it on the Internet,' says Elise simply. 'That's what Megan Michaels does and she's made millions.'

'Yes, but she's got three million followers,' says Summer. 'And she sells stuff.'

'Exactly my point,' says Elise animatedly, but blushing a little as everyone's staring at her as though she's speaking a different language, which from our perspective she actually is! 'We can set up a Coffee Factory website and get followers, Instagram, then we ask for donations.'

'I guess I could do a blog and updates, even merchandise, that sort of thing,' I say excitedly.

'I think I've just slipped into the space age,' says Walter completely lost.

'What about your ideas on exporting Melstock coffee further afield, Rom?' asks Henry.

The fact he used my nickname floors me a bit to be honest. 'Absolutely, that was one of my ideas. If we set up a company website, we can easily start giving details out to present customers, holidaymakers etc, so they can still drink Melstock coffee when they've gone home. I also thought of an online gift shop, selling cafetieres etc.'

'Steady, hold your horses,' says Phil. 'This is all going to cost money to set up, that's the problem.'

'I know,' I say wistfully. 'We need a lottery win.'

After more chat and getting Walter comfortably settled in bed with his radio story on, I return to the lounge to find everyone has gone apart from Henry. We've already agreed to talk about it more over the next week. Phil thinks he might have a friendly solicitor who can pass his eye over the contract, but I'm not sure they're going to find anything useful. We seriously need a miracle.

'Do you fancy some air?' asks Henry. 'I've got a bit warm in here with the fire on, lovely though it was.'

'Phew, yes,' I say laughing. 'Elise did a great job but I'm not sure we really need a log fire in May.'

'The marshmallows were tasty though,' says Henry grabbing another one from the packet.

We step out into the cool night air and stroll up the hill alongside the stream.

'You don't think we can do this, do you?' I ask Henry.

'Do what?'

'Save The Coffee Factory,' I say.

'I reckon we can, but it's going to take a heck of a lot more money than we have and I'm not convinced crowdfunding alone is going to be enough.'

'So we just give up and go home?' I ask frustratedly.

'Not at all,' he replies. 'I might just have an idea,

although as it might not work I don't really want to mention it until after I've done some more digging around.'

'Oh come on! You can't leave me hanging like that,' I joke.

'You're a very persuasive woman, Rom,' he stops and smiles at me. It makes my heart leap a little actually, he is very sweet and there's something about the warmth of his eyes.

'I wish,' I say laughing. 'I don't normally manage to persuade people on anything much.'

'You fibber face,' laughs Henry. 'Look what you've already achieved in this village.'

'Yeah right,' I say disbelievingly. 'Anyway, you're just trying to change the subject. What is this master plan?'

'I might have an investor,' says Henry mysteriously.

'Who might back The Coffee Factory?' I ask.

'That's what I'm hoping but you're going to have to leave it with me. I'm due to take a trip to London next weekend and I'll see what I can dig up.'

'Who is it?'

'Just an old uni friend who's involved in property in the City and has done well for himself. He might know something.'

'That's brilliant,' I say clapping my hands like a young child.

'Don't get too excited yet, it might not happen. But if it does we're going to be needing all your figures, marketing ideas and everything else up together.'

'Okay, I'll have a chat with Ciaran about it,' I say. 'And to think I thought you were just a kid out of teaching college.'

'How very dare you!' retorts Henry. 'I'm nearly as old as you are!'

'Thanks a lot. I'm not that old, and anyway you're as young as you feel,' I retort.

'Yeah right, race you to the top of the park,' he laughs and starts jogging off.

'Cheat!' I shout, as I race after him across the grass, past the tennis courts and towards the dusky hills and moor beyond. Of course I beat him. I think he might have let me win, but that's kind of cute anyway.

Chapter 30

'I wish it was the weekend again,' moans Elise as we pull round the bend to the school.

'At least you're hopefully meeting up with Anna?' I say, consolingly.

'Yeah I guess, as long as we can find each other, the school's so flipping huge.'

We pull into the drop off area. 'Oh there's Anna!' Elise calls excitedly and with that she's gone, rushing out the car and to the gate where I can see Anna hovering awkwardly swamped by her huge rucksack, but she smiles when she sees Elise. Phew what a relief, I feel so much better about today already. Back in Melstock, Summer and I powerwalk to the Junior School and drop her to the playground. I spot Henry by the doorway and he smiles and waves.

It's amazing the difference it makes when your children are happy. It almost feels as though everything might actually be okay. I meander back through the village towards The Coffee Factory. I'm worried about this sales business however; it makes me uneasy. There's a quietly confident power about people like Mark which scares me, probably because I've been traumatised by my in-laws. These wealthy people have such influence that it may be totally impossible for us to do anything about their plans, they always know people in high places. Yet there must be some way of managing it, if only we can think of it.

The morning at work speeds past as I spend much of it getting my plans together into a presentation ready for a potential investor. Ciaran has kindly produced all the sales figures for the past few years, which to my inexperienced eye look reasonable but I can't be sure. Mrs Miggins bustles about preparing delicious food ready for customers and I help her look after the toddler group with refreshments in between tweaking my presentation.

'Any news on the fund raising?' asks Steph, one of the mums. 'I can't face the thought of losing Rhyme Time, it's mine and Zac's favourite time of the week.'

'No, but we'll keep you posted,' I say. 'We're hoping to do a crowdfunding site, so as soon as it's up and running we'll let you know.'

I've had so many people asking me what's happening to the factory and it's making me feel sick with apprehension. It matters so much to everyone; we really can't fail. On the other hand, I'm unable to see how we can stop Mark from selling. I'd love to know how much he's getting but the contract doesn't specify and I guess it won't make much difference anyway.

'Want anything from the village?' asks Ciaran poking his head round the door.

'Just some chocolate, thanks,' I say. 'I need something to help me finish this document.'

I manage to get most of my work done and Ciaran hasn't returned when my phone rings.

'Mum? It's me,' says Elise. 'Can you talk?'

'Er yeah, just for a couple of minutes, I'm trying to

finish this presentation,' I say, distractedly.

'Oh okay, sorry. It's just that Anna and I had a problem today.' Elise sounds teary.

'What sort of problem?' She's instantly got my attention.

'Just some kids came and shoved us off the bench where we were eating our lunch.'

'Not the same group of girls?'

'Yeah, Shayanne, Courtney and that lot. Then they threw my lunch away and most of Anna's.'

'Oh, sweetheart, that's terrible. Didn't you tell the teacher?'

'I don't like to,' Elise answers. 'They made it worse last time.'

'Well, I'm bloody well coming in,' I say angrily. 'This is going to stop.'

'Please don't, Mum.' Elise sounds pitiful.

'Okay, I'll wait a mo, but I'm not promising,' I say. 'I'm not going to stand by and let this keep happening to you. Have you eaten anything at all?'

'Yeah, I managed to eat my snack at break and Anna shared the crisps she had left in her bag.'

'Oh well, that's something then.' For some reason I have every mother's worst fear that my child might actually starve during the school day. 'I'll make sure we have your fav spag bol for tea. And keep your chin up, we'll sort this.'

'Okay, thanks, Mum.' Elise hangs up. For God's sake, I hate this. I hate having a child at a school where other girls are deliberately picking on her and I'm powerless, especially as the school's refusing to do anything about it. I just want to go in and shout at those bloody girls. I'm still moodily musing on this and what I'm going to do about it, when Ciaran bursts in like a human tornado.

'Oh my gosh, Romilly! You're so never going to guess what just happened?' I must look bemused as he thrusts a Double Decker at me. 'Come on, eat this and you might be able to focus on what I'm saying.'

'Thanks,' I peel open the chocolate and start munching for a few moments. 'Okay, I feel a tad better. Come on, spill.'

'I was just walking down the main high street near the Post Office when I bumped, and when I say bumped, I mean totally bumped straight headlong into Gerry Bramshaw.'

'Gerry Bramshaw?' I repeat wondering if I have fallen into a parallel universe. 'Am I supposed to know who that is?'

'Yes. Gerry. You know, Gerry Bramshaw, the one I used to work with at John Lewis – he was a buyer too.'

'Oh wow! What a coincidence. I bet you had a lot to talk about.'

'Yes, I did, and we grabbed a bite of lunch together because it's been simply forever since I last had a good old chinwag with him. But that's not the point. There might just be hope for The Coffee Factory after all.'

'Oh my gosh! How come?' I immediately snap to attention.

'Well, good old Gerry has come up trumps – you'll never guess where he's a buyer now?'

'I can't imagine, Next, M&S?'

'No. Think higher, bigger, more major!'

'Erm,' I really don't feel very bright, 'TK Max?'

'No, you'll never guess so I'll tell you. Gerry Bramshaw works for none other than Harrods.'

'Oh my gosh, that's amazing! And he's interested in Melstock Coffee?' I mean, I know it's good, but...

'That's the thing! He might be. He's on his way round in half an hour or so.'

'Half an hour? You're kidding me. Why are we just sitting here? We need to get into the kitchen, prepare some samples. Does Mrs Miggins know?'

'Alright, alright, calm down, kid. No, she doesn't. I guess we'd better get some coffee on the brew.'

'Ready? It's all got to be totally perfect.' We hasten into action. Ciaran and I frantically pick out the most important bits of paper and Mrs Miggins excels herself with a couple of cafetieres of our finest coffees.

A ring on the bell at the front desk stops us abruptly from our frenzied preparations.

'Here he is,' says Ciaran, rushing round the room straightening things and spraying napkins everywhere. 'Stay calm, nobody panic.'

'I'm sure he's just a regular guy,' I say, trying to convince myself while popping the last couple of papers in the pile. Just a regular guy who happens to buy for Harrods. Yeah right!

'Good afternoon!' Gerry has a quirky little smile, is dapper in a neat way and built on a larger scale than Ciaran, but other than that, rather amusingly he could be his older brother. 'Now, if your coffee's half as good as it smells then I'm not going home empty handed.'

'You must be Gerry,' I say, cheerfully extending my hand. I've taken an instant liking to him actually.

'Aha' he says, 'You must be Romilly with the

fabulous ideas.'

I'm totally bowled by this and I'm sure I've flushed bright red. 'Well, I have some ideas anyway,' I say modestly.

'We'll have a look at them after the coffee tasting,' adds Ciaran.

'Rather,' says Gerry. He's so easy going, on the surface at least. I guess you can never tell with these buyers, underneath they probably have a core of steel.

'Here we are,' says Mrs Miggins bustling into the café with a beautifully laid tray of different tiny cups and a plate of her legendary pastries.

'First we have our Melstock finest ground coffee,' Ciaran announces, proudly passing the first small cup across to Gerry.

Gerry takes the cup and sniffs with the air of a seasoned connoisseur, 'Mmm, smells delicious,' he says. He tips the cup this way and that, peering at it carefully. I'm not quite sure what he's hoping to see, to be honest. Whatever it is, he appears satisfied and takes a tiny sip. He then rolls it on his tongue, gargles several times and swills the liquid round in his mouth. It's as though he's tasting fine wine. To be fair however, Melstock coffee does warrant this level of appreciation.

Ciaran and I anxiously await his judgement.

'Jolly fine cup of coffee,' he says with a contented sigh. 'I wish they served this in more restaurants. The number of times I've been disappointed in the wishy washy stuff they provide at the end of a Michelin Star Award winning meal.'

Ciaran and I breathe a large sigh of relief.

'Would you like to try the Indonesian Brew?' I ask.

'Rather,' he says. 'Very unusual, isn't it?'

'Absolutely,' I reply, enthusiastically. 'Old man Wetherby travelled all the way to Indonesia himself back in the nineteenth century to procure these beans and worked with local people to learn the process. And then a few years ago an initiative was set up called Little Beans, an international non-profit organisation working to improve the quality of life of children and their families in coffee growing communities in Indonesia.'

'That sounds a brilliant scheme, how does it operate?' Gerry takes another sip of steaming coffee.

'Well, we work in partnership with other local organisations to help with the communities' basic needs such as food, health care, security, education, growth and expansion. It's kind of like a fair-trade agreement but offers so much more support to the locals.'

'We're due to take a trip out there again shortly,' says Ciaran.

Gerry repeats the same procedure as with the other cup, but this time he stops. 'My goodness!' he exclaims. 'What's this? It's a really unusual aroma.'

'Take a guess,' Ciaran replies quietly.

'Hmm. It's a hint of grape, almost fruity amongst a lovely bitter tang,' says Gerry thoughtfully.

'That'll be the lychees,' says Ciaran.

'Really? How very unusual,' Gerry replies, taking a sip.

We wait in tense silence.

'Wow, now that is ... well, it's just incredible,' says Gerry enthusiastically. 'I've never tasted coffee anything like this.'

'In a good way, I hope,' I say cautiously.

'Definitely! It's amazing! Can I have another cup? And I'd like to discuss numbers, production costs etc.'

'Absobluminlutely,' says Ciaran and gives me a smile. We're in with a chance.

Several hours later, I dash off to Zumba having given the girls their spag bol. Elise has kindly agreed to help her sister with her homework, which is kind of her. But she's quiet; too quiet. This wretched business with the gang of bullies at school. Just as I'm about to leg it into the car park, my mobile rings. I'm tempted not to answer it, I don't recognise the number and I hate being late for Zumba. But for some stupid reason I swipe right instead of left and a lady says 'Hello?'

'Oh, err hi?' I answer, questioningly.

'Is that Romilly Greene?' asks a faintly familiar voice, which I can't quite place.

'Yes. Can I help?'

'I don't know. Let's hope so. It's Jacinta Mannerton-Smythe here.'

'Oh hi,' I say awkwardly, feeling instantly guilty. What does she want? Has she found out about the contract? This life of crime does not suit me; my conscience is triggered far too easily.

'I want to talk to you about Anna.' Oh thank goodness, what a relief! She obviously hasn't found out after all.

'Oh?' Perhaps she wants to ask Elise round for a sleepover, how nice.

'Yes, I'm very unhappy about her friendship with Elise.' Oh okay, perhaps not.

‘What?’ I exclaim loudly making a passing caretaker jump out of his skin.

‘I understand since being with Elise, Anna’s having problems with a group of girls at school,’ she continues oblivious to my response.

‘Well, yes, Elise does have some girls who have been picking on her. I’ve spoken to the school about it,’ I say.

‘I’m not at all happy about it,’ retorts Jacinta. ‘I’ve had her mother on the phone in tears, and Richard and I really don't need this level of stress right now. Richard has some very big deals on at work and I’m in the process of setting up my own hair and beauty business. This is totally inconvenient.’

I try to keep calm. ‘Obviously it’s very upsetting for all of us if our girls are being bullied, but I can assure you I’m not prepared to let it continue,’ I say tersely. ‘Perhaps if we demonstrate a united front to the school.’

‘Oh, I don't have time for all that,’ snaps Jacinta. ‘I have no quarrel with the school; it’s your daughter these girls seem to have the problem with so I suggest you sort it out. Until then I will ensure Anna stays away from Elise as I have no intention of her being picked on as well.’

‘But, Jacinta,’ I protest. To be honest, I’m too shocked to know what to say. I can’t believe her rudeness and arrogance. But even if I had something sensible to add, I couldn't because she’s hung up.

‘Bloody bitch,’ I snarl furiously as I march into Zumba and throw my jumper and water on the chair.

‘Thanks,’ says Debs, a bit shocked.

'I don't mean you,' I smirk, as we get in line for the warm up.

I really think Zumba should be prescribed on the NHS. It just changes everything. By the time we've done Power I'm totally infused with Little Mix's sassy outlook, a load of air punching and some loud singing and I feel vaguely human. It only needs some rock and 'I like the way I feel' and I defy anyone to feel crap during this song.

'You okay now?' asks Debs, eyeing me warily.

'I reckon,' I pant, slugging down a load of water.

'What was the problem?'

'Oh, just Jacinta being a complete cow,' I say.

'Jacinta? The one from the other day?'

'Yes, the very same. Ranting at me that her stepdaughter's being bullied because she's hanging out with Elise. It's been the only thing that's made Elise want to go in to school and now she's not allowed to be with her.'

'What a total cow,' comments Debs. 'Do you know who this group of girls are?'

'Yes. Shayanne, Shannon, Courtney,' I reel off the list of names.

'Oh my God, Josh knows them,' says Debs.

'They're not his friends, are they?' I ask horrified.

'No, of course not. They're in the year below and nothing but trouble. They're from the Millhurst Estate, so shouldn't even be in that school as they're not in catchment.'

'Typical,' I say though I'm relieved to hear that Josh isn't friends with them.

'Yes, but that's not the point. There's no problem,

Josh'll deal with them.'

'Can he?' I ask, doubtfully.

'Of course he can. Those girls are terrified of him and his mates. He'll go and give them a bloody good talking to.'

'But what if they go to the teacher?' I ask. 'They seem to be real favourites up there.'

'They wouldn't dare, not with some of Josh's mates. A couple of them are well over six foot, wouldn't hurt a fly, but look and sound intimidating. Consider it done, my love.'

'Debs, you're an angel.' I give her a huge hug.

'Steady,' she quips. 'You'll dislodge my halo.'

Chapter 31

I don't know why, but for some reason my life seems to lurch from one crisis to the next. Perhaps reading this book you may just have noticed that. I'm so relieved to have potentially sorted out Elise's problems in school, although admittedly there's still the issue of The Coffee Factory but there could be a lifeline there and I momentarily think I might be able to heave a sigh of relief. But no, I can't because once again life poos on me from a great height.

It was all going so well. I'd done the school drop offs and was on my way to work when I got a phone call from Dan. Yep, I know, I told him to go away in no uncertain terms but as usual he really hasn't taken any notice at all. I tut in exasperation and leave him to go to voicemail. I have nothing more to say to him at all. Nothing, nada, rien de tout!

Maybe I'll just listen to his voicemail though. It's probably nothing but... I dial 121.

'Hi, Rom, it's Dan. I need to speak to you urgently. It's very important so please can you ring me back.'

Whilst I'm listening to the message, the phone rings. It's Dan again. I'm so not going to pick this up. He leaves another mail.

'It's no good ignoring me; we need to talk. Now. It's about your strange and not so coincidental presence in the office at Richard's house the other night. Call me.'

For goodness sake! This is a total disaster. How on earth has Dan got hold of this information? Though I guess it's not that surprising really, is it? Of course it will have been noticed that the document has gone missing and I suppose Richard might have mentioned it in passing to Dan. Or would he? Unless Dan's in on the whole scheme? I didn't know he had much to do with property, but his mum is thick with the Mannerton-Smythes. They probably all have fingers in the pie.

'It's a disaster,' I pant at Ciaran as I lurch into The Coffee Factory pantry.

'No it isn't,' crows Ciaran happily. 'Guess what? Gerry wants to place quite a large order for our Indonesian blend and also for the original Melstock Coffee to be stocked in ding dong, no less than Harrods.'

'That's amazing,' I say, as excitedly as I can muster.

Ciaran draws himself up to his full height, which isn't very tall to be fair. 'Amazing? It's fabulous! My dear girl, you do realise it might become the favourite drink of His Majesty the King himself.'

'Oooh. I've always fancied a trip to the Palace,' coos Mrs Miggins, bringing in some clean cups. In spite of my stressed state, I have to push away a comical image of Mrs Miggins meeting the King, bobbing a curtsey, and announcing in a motherly tone, 'I'm Mrs Miggins, Your Majesty.'

I push the rather amusing thought from my mind. 'That's simply amazing news, guys, but I'm afraid I do have a rather pressing problem.'

‘What?’ they both ask, I finally have their attention.

‘Dan knows about the document.’

‘Oh my goodness me,’ murmurs Mrs Miggins and sinks herself down onto a nearby seat.

‘Oh shit,’ mutters Ciaran. ‘How on earth can he know?’

‘Er maybe because he found me in Richard Mannerton-Smythe’s study and then soon after he must have heard from Richard that the document had gone missing?’ I say sarcastically.

Ciaran is oblivious, ’What did you say? Did you deny it?’

‘I haven’t said anything yet,’ I reply. ‘He left a voicemail but I’m going to have to get back to him.’

‘Deny everything,’ says Mrs Miggins, shrilly. ‘That’s always the best way. Least said, soonest mended, I always think.’

‘I don't think it will be as simple as that,’ says Ciaran, thoughtfully stroking his stubble.

‘No neither do I,’ I say anxiously. ‘Dan’s the kind of guy who likes to be in control and he may try to use this to blackmail me.’

‘Oh good heavens,’ says Mrs Miggins. ‘It’s like one of them stories.’

‘There’s only one thing for it,’ announces Ciaran. ‘You’ll just have to deny everything.’

‘I’m good at doing that at least,’ I retort.

‘After all he hasn't got any proof,’ says Ciaran.

‘That’s what we hope anyway.’

After a brief conflab we decide it’s safest for me to make the call to Dan well outside the vicinity of The Coffee Factory, in a field where I can be sure I won’t be overheard. Not that I'm getting paranoid or anything. He answers immediately.

'Hello, Rom, nice to hear from you,' he says as though it's a pleasant afternoon call.

'Hi, Dan,' I say tersely.

'Kind of you to call me back so quickly so we can have a little chat.'

'Yeah right,' I say.

'Sounds as though someone has been pretty naughty. To tell you the truth, I'm surprised at you, Rom.'

'I don't know what you mean,' I say casually.

'Well, it's a funny thing but you know I met you in Richard's office the other day.'

'Yes.'

'Not long after that evening Richard informed me that a certain document had gone missing from his office.'

'Well, I don't see what his or his secretary's inefficiencies has to do with me? I was in there trying to get the dog out,' I say nonchalantly – oh, I'm good at this.

'The strange thing is the missing document is a contract regarding the sale of The Coffee Factory.'

'So?'

'So you work there and stand to lose your beloved job if this sale goes through and I think you stole it.'

'That's a very rude accusation,' I say, struggling to keep calm. 'I am, as you know, a very law-abiding person, I would never do such a thing.'

'Come on, Rom. You don't expect me to believe that, do you? You and your mates from the factory were there.’

Oh darn, that little deception didn't work quite so well. Perhaps I won’t turn into an international spy after all.

‘They just came along as my friends,’ I say firmly, ‘and for once, Dan, you can’t mess things up for me.’

‘Oh here we go. I’m always the bad guy, and here you are Miss Goody Two Shoes stealing documents from private studies.’

‘Look, Dan, I’m not prepared to stick around for any more of these nonsensical arguments, so if that’s all...’

‘No it’s not. My good friend Richard currently knows nothing about your presence in his office. I felt it was not worth mentioning. However, my conscience may soon get the better of me and I may feel as though I have to let him know.’

‘Your conscience! Don't make me laugh!’

‘You can laugh all you like, but I mean it. You’d better have your bags packed and get right back here where you belong pronto, along with the girls, or you’ll leave me no option but to tell Richard about the whereabouts of his document.’

I’m completely shocked. I knew Dan was a rat, but this is beyond anything. I don't think for long before saying, ‘Dan, you’ve done nothing but make me bloody well glad I don't have to live with you anymore.’

‘I’m warning you,’ replies Dan. ‘Richard is going to be very interested...’

I interrupt before he can say any more. ‘I have one thing to say to you, Dan.’

‘What?’ he asks moodily.

'You have no proof.' And I slam the phone down. I'm shaking like a leaf. What a moron. How on earth did I stay with him so long? And to think now he holds the trump card. Although does he? Surely these are just empty threats? He has no proof and to be honest Richard can easily get another copy together. This is just Dan's usual sick manipulation.

Blindly I start walking across the rest of the field and down towards the beach. I can't face going back to the factory feeling like this. What if through my rubbish past I mess up the whole future of The Coffee Factory and this village which has been so welcoming to me? I rummage in my bag and pull out the Rescue Remedy. It's so good actually. My dad always says it's psychological in its effect, but does it really matter whether it is or not, if it works? Perhaps I'm getting in a stress about nothing – so Dan is throwing his toys out of the pram again. We're all tougher than this at Melstock, we'll think of an answer won't, we? I'm so lost in thought I don't notice a man walking towards me until it's too late.

'Romilly?'

'Henry, I'm so sorry I was lost in thought, I totally didn't see you,' I stutter.

'Are you okay? You look...'

'Crap?' I finish his sentence for him. I'm aware I've been crying so my mascara has probably run everywhere.

'No, let's just say romantically tragic,' he says with a straight face. 'Like a heroine in an Austen movie.'

'Oh my God, do you watch Austen movies?' I ask, completely forgetting the point.

'Yes, but not through my own choice,' he confesses. 'My sister makes me watch them with her.'

'She sounds a fabulous person,' I say.

'She is as a matter of fact. I'd love you to meet her.'

I stare at him taken aback. 'Do you manage to stay awake til the end of the movie though?'

'Of course, I loved the end of *Sense and Sensibility* or was it *Pride and Prejudice*? I can't remember, anyway it was really good.' He coughs awkwardly. 'Anyway, we digress. What's the problem? Can I do anything to help?'

Trying not to sniff all over him, and stepping high above the long grass, I walk alongside Henry towards the beach, explaining as I go.

'You poor girl,' he says shocked.' I thought my ex was a right one but Dan beats all. There's nothing he can really do though. It's just idle threats.'

'Do you think so?' I ask.

'Of course, he has no proof. Unless Richard had a camera in his office, he's had it. Did you see one in there?'

'No, not that I'd noticed. I don't think I really looked. Perhaps I wouldn't make such a good spy after all!'

'You're hilarious! I think you did a jolly good job. You've got pluck and that's what counts,' says Henry.

'Thanks, I think,' I say embarrassed.

'Mind you, he must be desperate to have you back.'

'I guess, he aways was very controlling.'

'Some people are like that but in his case, I'm not really surprised,' he says stopping and looking at me.

'What do you mean?' I ask, puzzled.

‘Well, I can imagine losing the love of someone like you must be pretty devastating.’

Oh my God! I feel so awkward. I’m no good at this liking people thing, I mean does he really like me or is he just being friendly? I peer at him shyly as we seem to be by the water’s edge. ‘Aww stop it, you’re embarrassing me,’ I say flushing red. I’m totally rubbish at taking a compliment.

‘I mean it, what you’re doing for this village, I don't think you’re generally the sort of person who breaks into offices and steals documents, are you?’

‘Oh, I was quite the rebel at school,’ I say nonchalantly.

‘Yeah right! I bet you were a prefect,’ Henry laughs.

‘Okay, so maybe I was,’ I reply.

‘Look, Rom, I’m sure things at The Coffee Factory will sort themselves out, but I think...’ he stops.

‘Yes?’ I ask.

‘I think you’re wonderful,’ he says. He takes me in his arms and kisses me on the mouth as I put my hands in his windswept hair. To be honest, it feels pretty darned amazing and right now I don't care about much else. As the waves lap, the sun sets, and life and the tide go by, and for the first time in forever nothing really matters.

Chapter 32

'I've had an idea,' I say to the girls later that evening, although to be honest I'm still tingling all over from the kiss with Henry. We had walked slowly back along the shore hand in hand, it was perfect.

'We can buy a horse?' asks Elise, ever hopeful.

'What about a dog?' chirps Summer.

'No, silly billies. It's about The Coffee Factory,' I say. Although to be fair, I don't know how I can be thinking of anything so mundane, I'm still buzzing.

'Oh right,' says Elise going back to her phone.

'Well, you could take an interest. It's part of the whole fabric of this village.' He's asked me out actually, we're going on Saturday night and I can't wait to see him again. I feel about fifteen.

'Sorry, Mum. I'm listening really, what were you going to say?' Elise actually puts her phone down momentarily on her lap. Wonders will never cease.

I grin at her. 'I was wondering if I should go and tackle this thing head on?' I mean the factory, not Henry, although I really can't get him out of my mind.

'Please don't tell me you're going into school again, Mum. Anyway I didn't hear a peep from those girls yesterday. Not a thing, even though I was in two classes with Shayanne and one with Courtney.'

'Elise, that's wonderful.' I stop and give her a hug.

'It's early days yet, so they may be building up to something, but I wonder if whatever Josh said, worked.'

'I reckon,' I say cheerfully. 'Anyway, back to the next problem. I'm thinking of tackling the Whittakers about The Coffee Factory myself.'

'Not the hideous old perv and the woman with the smelly dog?' laughs Elise. 'You're joking me.'

'No, I'm deadly serious,' I say. 'Something needs to be done.'

'But I thought this Gerry guy was coming up trumps with an order for Harrods?'

'Yes, he is but I've looked at the books and even by my basic maths, things are looking tight compared with the amount likely to be offered for the land by the property development company.'

'Oh, that's pants, but you can't go annoying the Whittakers. They already hate you.'

'Thanks, say it how it is!' I laugh. Maybe I'll wait a bit longer, or I could speak to Mark and find out the lie of the land. After dropping the girls to school the next day, I pluck up courage and dial his number.

'Hello, Romilly darling!' He sounds as suave and plausible as ever and I suppose I have to give him points for trying.

'Hi, Mark. Just wondered how things are going with the factory fund raising? Ciaran says you haven't had a chance to catch up for a while,' I say getting straight to the nub of the matter.

'Oh no, busy, busy, you know, darling. The point to point fund raiser went quite well but we're a little concerned that in spite of all the wonderful efforts of the village, we may not be able to afford to turn the builders down, you know.'

'But that's terrible, Mark,' I say outraged.

'These things happen, sweetie, but that's my father for you. Can't change his mind, the old duffer's totally set in his ways.'

'But surely you could persuade him?' I ask, not trusting him as far as I can throw him.

'Pah, old Pater, not on your nelly, darling. Now then, are you free for a quick snifter at the Purple Painter tonight? Got to catch up with the Hunt Brigade and haven't seen you for ages. You'd like them, friendly bunch really. Just wear something scrummy and I'll shout you dinner.'

'Not on your nelly, darling,' I reply sweetly and switch my phone off. Bloody arrogant, annoying man. But at least I know he's out this evening and maybe, just maybe, I should put my plan into place. After all, what do I have to lose? At this rate the factory's going to be pulled down and there's absolutely nothing we can do about it.

It's Zumba again, thank goodness! And for once my mind isn't on the moves as much as it should be. 'Oops sorry, I'm freestyling tonight,' I laugh to Debs as I cannon into her.

'Nice one,' she replies, doing some crazy ad lib arm movements of her own. Tania whoops from up the front and we all laugh. I just love this. We have a short break to grab a drink of water.

'By the way, I need to thank you,' I say, slugging water and hiccupping.

'For what?' asks Debs.

‘For getting Josh to sort out those mean girls at the school,’ I reply.

‘Oh yes, he said he’d have a little word. I told you it would work.’

‘It’s worked like a charm,’ I say. ‘It’s early days, but I think they’ve backed right off, thank God. What a wonderful lad Josh is. You should be really proud of him, and as for you, you’re the best friend ever.’

‘Awww, Rom, thanks. He’s a good lad. Think of what you’ve brought to the village though, a breath of fresh air.’

‘Yeah right,’ I laugh, but she doesn't know the half of it, because tonight I’m going in to Melstock Manor to beard the lair of the Whittakers.

I have to be honest, but my positivity doesn't quite last driving the length of the long winding driveway in my trusty Volvo. It’s funny, when I was dancing I felt as though I could rule the world with the girls, but now I’m totally alone. This place gives me the heebie-jeebies after all the hideous times here, but I pull up to one side with purpose. Come on, Rom, you can do this! It’s for the village. If the worst comes to the worst, I can run away and go home to Mum and Dad or Jess. Okay maybe not, but still, I can change my name, wear a different wig or something, there are always options.

I stalk to the front door and ring the bell, hoping against hope the smelly Labrador is not at home, but that his owners minus Mark are. ‘Good evening, Madam,’ It’s the rather doddery and ponderous butler. He raises his eyebrows so high they disappear into his hairline. ‘Are you expected this evening?’

‘Er no,’ I say, but add quickly, ‘I’m sure the

Whittakers will wish to see me, however. I'm happy to wait in the hall.'

'Certainly, Madam. If you will wait here momentarily.' He shimmies off down the hallway. I can hear muted voices, in the other room. To my embarrassment I can hear a certain amount of disagreement. Then again I wasn't really expecting a warm welcome.

'Please come this way.' The butler has reappeared, and his visage expressionless, waves me into the drawing room where Pa Whittaker is sat, florid faced as ever in his high-backed chair, a smoking cigar resting on the arm alongside a perilously balanced glass of scotch. In fact, I'm fascinated by it. How does he manage not to knock it on the floor with his elbow, especially whilst reading the paper? Whoever said men can't multitask? Perhaps they can in spite of all evidence to the contrary.

'Good evening, young lady. Excuse me if I don't get up.' Okay, so maybe they really can't multitask after all! 'Are we acquainted?' His bleary roving eye ranges over my legs as usual and I figure that he's certainly acquainted with those, that's for sure.

'Good evening, Lord Whittaker. I'm sorry to bother you and wander in unannounced like this, but I do need to speak to you on a very urgent matter,' I say, sitting myself down on the edge of the sofa with my legs arranged neatly sideways, very Princess Kate style. Studying all those Hello Magazines obviously wasn't a waste of time after all. I've put careful consideration into my outfit, opting to whizz home, shower and change after Zumba into something more country set, so that hustle-like I could find some subliminal way to appeal to Pa Whittaker's conscience, or at least reduce his feeling of being threatened. Thus here I am in a long sleeved shirt over a reasonable length pencil skirt, tights opaque of course to add extra protection from perving, and high heeled long boots. The outfit is completed by a countryish Burberry style scarf, which I managed to find at the local charity shop.

'Ahem,' coughs Pa Whittaker, taking a slug of whisky and replacing it to teeter precariously once more on the arm of the chair. 'And what, my dear, is your name?'

'Romilly. Romilly Greene,' I say quickly in the hope he won't really recognise it. 'I wanted to talk to you about The Coffee Factory.'

'What about it?' Pa Whittaker's tone notches up a level from merely disinterested to frosty and cantankerous, if that's possible. 'What's that to do with you?'

'Well, for a start I work there,' I say matter of factly.

'That's a shame to be sure. but I'm sure you'll find another job especially if you work hard. What do you do there anyway?'

'All sorts of things,' I say calmly, 'but especially marketing and publicity. That's what I want to talk to you about.'

'Eh? I leave all that to m'son Mark, not really my scene quite honestly, m'dear.'

'Ah but Mark's going to sell the factory for building, isn't he?' I stand back and wait for this bombshell to explode and sink in, but it doesn't.

'Of course he is. There's not much profit being

made as it is and the building company are offering a tidy sum.' Oh great, that's my plan totally scuppered. I thought Pa Whittaker was unaware of this dastardly scheme.

'But you can't want to lose such an iconic part of local history,' I say passionately, recovering my fight. 'It's irreplaceable.'

'It's a pain in the backside,' he retorts, sharply raising his voice.

I desperately try a new tack and attempt to be tactful. 'I can understand it's a nuisance and it would be easier to take the building money, but we have new schemes, ways of making it more profitable. Ciaran has found a chap who wants to buy Melstock Coffee for Harrods.'

'Harrods huh! Can't be bothered with the place. Used to be really something, a sign of British quality but these days it's gone to the dogs, except the dogs would do a better job with it.'

I goggle at him, speechless.

'Look, Rebecca, or whatever your name is, in fact I'm sure I recognise you as that petulant woman Mark was parading the countryside with. Whoever you are, this is none of your business. And either way a few quid in extra sales from Harrods is hardly going to sort out the financial issues we have with that factory.'

'But what about the community? As Lord of the Manor (I'm desperately hoping to appeal to his feudal roots) you have a responsibility to keep the community going. Old people rely on that centre to meet up, for clubs, drinks and so do the young, dance classes, toddler groups, it's the centre of the village. We're even setting up a crowdfunding scheme so we can support the factory ourselves.'

'Sentimental claptrap! Not your business, when you've only lived here a few months, nor that of the village. If the old people knew what was good for them, they'd be jolly pleased to have a nice tidy block of retirement housing popped in there for them. All self-contained. you know, all the mod cons.' Pa Whittaker is getting redder and redder in the face until I think he might explode.

'But people like Walter would hate being trapped in a flat. Besides they'll be far too expensive for the old people who live here. It would be new rich people coming in from London who have no link with the village.'

'Someone's been doing their homework then,' says Pa Whittaker, sharply. 'Look, m'dear, I'm sure you mean perfectly well, but it's all done. You're too late, it's all fixed and the factory is sold. You, my dear, will have to crawl back under whatever rock you came out from and accept the inevitable.'

I stare aghast at his florid and hoary face and I'm unable to believe my ears. I'm too late, it's all been for nothing. It's so easy for him in his ivory tower like a Greek God moving people around and ruining their lives at a whim. It's all so unfair.

I'm about to open my mouth and start castigating this man because quite honestly who the heck gives him the right to tell everyone else what to do? Well, apart from the fact he owns The Coffee Factory of course. Suddenly the door opens abruptly and in walks Ma Whittaker larger than life. Oh great, that's all I need, both of them berating me.

'Oh hello, erm,' she flounders awkwardly obviously completely at a loss for my name.

'Romilly, but it doesn't matter anyway,' I say dispiritedly. 'I'm leaving you to enjoy the rest of your evening.'

'Yes quite,' says Pa Whittaker jumping to his feet, miraculously managing to avoid knocking the whisky tumbler off the arm of his chair. 'I'll call Bentley to show you out.'

'No, no it's fine; I can take myself. But I'll tell you this, Lord Whittaker,' I turn and give him a steely glare, interrupting his hurried ushering of me out of the door. 'If you get rid of this factory and replace it with an anonymous block of old people's flats, it will be remembered for all time that you, Lord whatever your name is Whittaker, finished the legacy of Lord Montmorency who started that factory in the early 1800s. No one's going to look at that block of flats and think happy thoughts of you.'

'What?' screeches Ma Whittaker, so loudly I jump nervously and lurch towards the door.

'Nothing, m'dear; Mrs Greene is just leaving.' Pa Whittaker opens the door and practically shoves me through it.

'Mrs Romilly Greene is going nowhere,' retorts Ma Whittaker. 'Sit down immediately!' She glares at her husband who plumps himself obediently but sulkily on the scruffy sofa. 'Right, Romilly, come and sit down – I want to hear what you have to say.'

'But, darling,' whimpers Pa Whittaker.

'Silence!' she shouts and he resigns himself to

huddling deep within the old cushions like a recalcitrant schoolboy.

I take a breath, 'Lady Whittaker, I came here to talk about the situation with The Coffee Factory. The whole village is trying to raise money to save it and I was just explaining to your husband that we even have a potential buyer from Harrods.'

'Harrods – how wonderful!' Mrs Whittaker completely changes persona and becomes almost simpering. 'I can just imagine telling Lady Mucknell about our coffee factory selling to Harrods. The look on her face!'

'Well, you won't be telling anyone if the factory closes, will you?' I say resignedly.

'It won't close will it, Cyril, if we start getting some decent stockists? If Harrods starts to sell our coffee, who knows what might happen. Even the King might be drinking it next.'

'Exactly my thoughts,' I say amused, 'but that's not going to happen if it goes for building land.'

'Building land? That was only a last resort if we couldn't save it,' says Lady Whittaker, 'but with deals like this coming in, everything will be tickety boo.'

'But it's too late if you've already signed the deal with the builders,' I say, blatantly ignoring Pa Whittaker's desperate signals behind his wife's back.

'What builders? Who says we've sold to builders?' demands Ma Whittaker shrilly.

'Your husband,' I say quietly.

Chapter 33

I thought I'd heard some disputes in my time, but nothing, simply nothing, has ever come vaguely near competing with the one I'm hearing now.

'What deal is this, Cyril?' shouts Ma Whittaker. 'Why do I know absolutely nothing about it?'

'I don't know what Rebecca here is talking about, dear. She must be unhinged,' snivels Pa Whittaker.

'Well, you appeared to know just a moment ago,' I say blandly. I turn bravely to Ma Whittaker. 'It seems that your son and your husband have sold The Coffee Factory and the accompanying land to Strathcombe Homes.'

'What!' I put my hands over my ears as Mrs Whittaker shrieks at a thousand decibels. Monty the Labrador comes running into the room at the noise but seeing Ma Whittaker branding a fire poker at his master, whimpers and promptly vacates the room. I wish I'd known pokers were so effective with him; I'd have used one earlier in our acquaintance.

'Put that down, dear,' pleads Pa Whittaker. It would be rather comical actually if it weren't for the seriousness of the loss of The Coffee Factory. 'I don't know what she's talking about.'

'She!' bawls Ma Whittaker. 'Who are you talking about? The cat's mother? She has a name and it's

Romilly, you doddering old fool. Now, you'd better start explaining yourself.'

Way to go, Ma Whittaker! Women's lib has finally entered this house, a hundred years late but better late than never I guess.

'Calm yourself, woman,' says Pa Whittaker, but not very convincingly, 'Romilly is obviously quite mad.'

'No, I'm not. You've just informed me yourself that you've signed the contract with Strathcombe Homes.'

'No, I didn't. What contract? There is no contract.'

'This contract here in my hand.' I whip out the copy I took from the Mannerton-Smythes' and pass it to Ma Whittaker. She takes it from me and quickly scans the document in a business-like manner.

Finally she removes her glasses and points her finger ominously at Pa Whittaker. '*You* have a hell of a lot of explaining to do, sonny Jim.' I have to stifle a giggle, I thought people only said that in books?

'Well, I might have known something about it, but we have no choice. Dash it all, woman, we need the money.'

Ma Whittaker glares at him.

'Okay, we could do with the money. This place costs a fortune to run and that factory is nothing but bloody trouble,' he adds quietly.

'That factory was created by my great great grandfather, and you and my son have the temerity to think you can just sell it from under me! For goodness' sake, man, this isn't the eighteenth century. My property is my property and not yours or Mark's to do as you wish with.'

'Bravo, Lady Whittaker!' I applaud in a supportive

manner.

Monty comes trotting in having peered round the door rather sheepishly and I almost feel sorry for him glancing at his soulful brown eyes, that is until he marches straight up and sniffs my crotch.

'Monty, stop that!' blasts Ma Whittaker. Monty looks at her out of the corner of his eye and slopes off into a corner, slumping in his bed with a sigh.

'Thanks,' I say with a smile. Gosh! The woman is actually human after all.

'Now then,' she whips round at her husband, 'what's all this about the contract is already signed and who are these Mannerton-Smythes?'

'Well, I think the contract's signed,' prevaricates Pa Whittaker. 'I don't really know as Mark's mainly dealing with this.'

'And the Mannerton-Smythes?'

'Erm, business associates of Mark and Penny.'

'Penny? Is she in on this?'

'I'm afraid so,' I reply, as Pa Whittaker is too busy hiding behind a cushion to answer.

'The scheming, manipulative hussy! And how do you know all this, young lady?' asks Ma Whittaker advancing ominously towards me.

'I'm afraid I overheard a conversation between Mark and Penny whilst unwittingly hiding in your upstairs toilet some weeks ago,' I confess. I have no pride left with these people.

'Why on earth didn't you come and tell me, girl?' she retorts.

'I thought you and Pa Whittaker, I mean Lord Whittaker, were in on it. I thought you were all in on this scheme.'

'We certainly were not!' exclaims Ma Whittaker. 'That factory belonged to my family. It's part of my heritage, and I wouldn't sell it for millions of pounds.'

'Bravo,' I say. Finally someone in this house is speaking some sense. 'But what if it's too late?'

'It can't be too late, m'dear,' she says roundly, 'because the factory is still mostly in my name so the contract can't be legal. Can it, Cyril?' She stares at him.

He looks shamefacedly at the floor as though he was a little schoolboy. 'Cyril?'

'No,' he mutters, 'it's not signed. We were finalising the contract this week. I was going to ask for your agreement of course,' he adds.

'Can I just say something?' I ask delicately. 'If you're requiring more funding for the factory, we do have future crowdfunding activities planned. and with this guy from Harrods stocking the product, I believe we can really make Melstock Coffee into a nationwide brand.'

'I reckon you are a rather remarkable young woman,' comments Ma Whittaker, 'and in future I shall be having a lot more personal contact with the factory. Mark shall no longer be involved, and Romilly, I would like to promote you to Marketing Manager.'

'I'd be simply delighted,' I say shocked, but enthusiastic.

'Let's shake on it then,' says Ma Whittaker. 'Cyril, for goodness' sake get up off that sofa and pour us both a wee dram. I'm gasping and I'm sure Romilly would appreciate a drop after all this stress and trouble she's been put to.'

I leave Melstock Manor some time later with a spring in my step and a feeling of being happier than I have for a long time. Although it's late by now, I know there's somewhere I must visit immediately on my way home.

'Romilly, how nice to see you,' says Walter's daughter, Beth who has managed to escape from the farm for a week or two to help nurse her father. She's a lovely person and I liked her immediately when she turned up a few days ago to take over from me. 'Come in, we've just made a cup of hot chocolate.'

'I'm sorry, but I didn't want to disturb you. I won't stop, I just had some rather wonderful news which I thought Walter would like to hear.'

'What's all this then?' Walter calls from the lounge. He looks considerably better, and despite his plastered leg he at least has some colour in his cheeks. 'You been causing trouble again?'

'Yes, I have,' I say, gratefully plonking in a chair next to him. 'I've been to Melstock Manor and sorted it all out.'

'You haven't? You're having me on! What did you do? Make them come to their senses?'

'Something like that. It turns out Lady Whittaker knew nothing of the sale of the factory at all.'

'Good grief, and did you work that out for yourself, my girl?'

'No I'm not that clever. I just went along to berate them for selling the factory in the hope I could shame them into pulling out. Instead I alerted Ma Whittaker to the connivances of Pa and Mark Whittaker.'

'Golly, not just a pretty face, are you?' Walter

laughs. ‘So have they pulled the scheme altogether?’

‘Absolutely, but we’ll still be continuing our crowdfunding activities. Ma Whittaker is going to be more closely involved in the day to day running of the business and I’m to be promoted to Marketing Manager.’

‘All pretty good news apart from Ma Whittaker’s interference.’

‘Do you know, I actually think she may do a pretty good job, better than Mark at any rate. And we’ll be needing you too, Walter, so you’d better hurry up and get out of that cast. There are talks to be organised, coffee to be sold and crosswords to be solved.’

‘I’ll drink to that,’ says Walter and we all do.

Chapter 34

'Come on, Mum, we're going to be late.' For once Elise is up and out of bed on time, hair freshly washed and ready to rumble, her costume immaculate. Quite honestly, it's a miracle.

'Okay, okay, I'm done.' I put the finishing touches to my lipstick, moving with care. Corsets might do wonders for your waist, but nothing at all for practical movement and I leg it down the stairs, nearly tripping over Summer who is trying to do up her ankle straps on the bottom step.

'Flipping child!' exclaims Elise angrily. 'You're always in the way.'

'You're such a b,' grumbles Summer.

'Summer! That's not language we use, and especially not today. Being a child from the Edwardian Era, you should probably be seen and not heard,' I say crossly.

'I am a person, therefore I have words,' she retorts. For goodness' sake, I suppose I can't argue with that. 'Milly at school says far worse than that all the time,' she adds for good measure.

'That doesn't make it right,' I say and chivvy them all out the door. 'Come on, you lot, we haven't time to argue.'

We run down the road as fast as our costumes will

allow, towards The Coffee Factory and already my senses are awaft with the deliciously familiar scent of rich roasting coffee beans. The streets are full of people dressed in bizarre costumes for their various floats. To be honest, it's rather like the cast of Fraggle Rock.

'Hi, Debs,' I call as she bustles out of the shop with armfuls of goodies, looking the part in her long dress. 'Can I give you a hand?'

'Yes please, love. Take these.' She shoves a load at me and returns into the shop for more. 'Sam and Anna are already down there, Elise,' she calls.

'Thanks, Debs, I'll go on then, if that's okay with you, Mum?'

'Course it is, but take some pain au chocolate with you, there's a love.'

Summer, Debs and I struggle to the factory entrance where half the village are already here to help before the main event. Henry is hovering near the door looking extremely fit actually in his Edwardian top hat and tails. In true gentlemanly fashion he takes my armfuls of stuff from me, then gives me a quick peck on the cheek.

Flushed red, I thank him and continue our route in the front door. 'Mum, why did Mr Barton kiss you?' asks Summer plaintively.

'Oh, just being friendly I expect,' I say, amused.

'Yeah right,' says Debs. 'Thank goodness you two have finally got it together, after all this 'will they, won't they' business. It's as obvious as the nose on your face you two are made for each other.'

'Debs! We're merely friends,' I protest but Summer just grins and says, 'Oh, wait till I tell everyone at school. I like Mr Barton. Do you think he'll let me join his tennis club?'

Before I can answer, I am hallooed by Ma Whittaker, resplendent in a long dress with a rather prominent bustle at the back. 'Romilly, there you are! Do come and look at some of the final arrangements. I'm all at sixes and sevens. Rather deal with a pack of dogs to be frank with you, than this lot.'

Trying not to snort with laughter at the surprised and slightly annoyed faces around her, I hurry to intervene as she has upset most of the village, especially Barbara Asquith, who is not only Head of the WI but manages the flower arranging club on Tuesdays and is very used to having her own way with planning village events.

'Okay, Lady Whittaker,' I start.

'You must call me Mary,' she says brusquely so I guess I'd better, although it really doesn't feel right.

We hustle through to the back room, which smells divine because Mrs Miggins has baked enough chocolate brownies to feed a small army. 'Morning,' she says, smacking Ciaran on his hand as he's just stolen one.

'Merely quality control testing,' laughs Ciaran, who is looking even more immaculate than ever.

'Yes, but have you checked the float?' I ask anxiously.

'Of course. Come and see.' He steps aside with a flourish and there out in the car park behind the factory is the finished display.

'That looks amazing,' I say excitedly. 'I've never seen anything quite like it.'

For today as well as the grand celebration of The Coffee Factory, the village is holding its annual carnival and for a couple of weeks now we have been working on our entry – a magnificent float, part Coffee Factory cleverly created by huge pieces of card painted and decorated, part elaborate coffee shop, in Edwardian dress. I have to admit I haven't been around to help over the last couple of days and the team organised by Ciaran have surpassed themselves.

'Huge well done to all of you, Tania and her daughter, who turned out to be a brilliant painter, Jim, Sam – it's so professional.'

'We've loved it,' says Jim.

'Hear hear,' chips in Alexandrine. 'Given us all something to do in our spare time.'

I smile as I know running the Post Office there is no such thing as spare time.

'Goodness me, someone's been hard at work,' admires Lady Mary Whittaker and for once I agree with her. We've all rehearsed like mad, but we've never had a chance to put everyone on the float in their costumes.

'Up you get, everyone,' instructs Mary Whittaker. 'The man from the local paper is here to take a photo of us all and I believe *Country Life* will be along later.'

I hide a smile; trust Mary to know the right people to get maximum publicity.

'Come on then, Walter. Easy does it.' Henry, Debs and I propel Walter from either side as he climbs the steps of the float and sits in the Edwardian Café. He looks so suave. Thank goodness his leg has mostly healed, although he has ongoing physio and walks with a bit of a limp. So far we've managed to dissuade him from rooting about down in the stream again, but I don't know how long it will last. We all climb aboard the float, which, to my relief, Jim has obligingly attached to his tractor. I had visions of us all tipping off as it does look a bit rickety.

We pose for several pictures. Even I think we look incredible. The effect is amazing, and I'm hoping we can even use the idea for advertising to take to Harrods, Harvey Nicks and other high-end stores. We're going to use some sepia print pictures to add to the effect.

The atmosphere is so much fun. Everyone from the village is talking and laughing. Jim tows us round to the lower car park where we wait our turn to parade through the village. After weeks of secrecy there are oohs and ahhs as everyone discovers what the other businesses have created. Phil and Alexandrine have set up a 'Where's Wally Float' and to the girls' great amusement, Phil as Wally, keeps popping up from different very well camouflaged parts of the float and throwing sweets to the kids. Tania and the Zumba girls have created a colourful Spanish style float with all the girls dancing, I'm joining them for a display after a quick change of course on the playing field by the park. The pet shop has done a safari theme with Clive in an old-fashioned explorer's outfit, with deer antlers appearing from bushes and there are stilt walkers dressed in elegant sea god outfits cleverly created by Skye from the craft shop. The town cryer, Barbara Asquith of course, after all she has the perfect voice for it, dressed from top to toe in resplendent red, heads our procession along the high street, which is packed full either side with waving and cheering crowds, throwing pennies in the collecting buckets which are going to a homeless shelter charity for street children in Indonesia.

I smile and wave, as do Elise and Summer. Walter is in his element, tipping his top hat vigorously at the crowds and sipping his favourite coffee with the other.

Suddenly I notice some very familiar faces in the crowd. Summer and Elise spot them at the same time, 'Granny, Gramps, Aunty Jess and Bradley!' I peer at them unable to believe my eyes, then wave and grin at their surprised faces. Bradley is jumping up and down with excitement and throwing pennies in the bucket.

'Did you know they were coming?' I ask Elise surprised, wondering if she has been doing an impression of the girl on Mamma Mia – arranging for her three dads to appear, except in this case it's my parents and sister. I have a sudden thought, 'You haven't invited your dad, have you?' I ask anxiously.

'No, of course not, though I'm going to stay with him soon – is that okay?' asks Elise.

'Yes.' I look at her anxious face and give her a hug, 'You must of course, go for a weekend. I'll miss you but it will give me a chance to clean up your room!'

'Well I'll soon be back as Anna and I are planning a sleepover.'

'Sounds fab,' I say enthusiastically. I used to love sleepovers. 'We can toast marshmallows and you can tell ghost stories and no doubt be too scared to sleep.'

She grins and I look at her happy and contented face. This move seems to be the right decision after all. The carnival goes by in a flash and we pull into the field for the presentations.

Barbara Asquith and Phil welcome everyone and chat about the village fundraising and the scheme to save the factory, then hand the microphones over to us.

Ciaran, Mary Whittaker and I are ready with our presentation on the factory, an introduction to the intricacies of Indonesian coffee making and our fund-raising efforts as well as future plans.

'Thank you so much for all your support,' says Ciaran. 'We'd like to inform you all that thanks to some major new investors sourced by an old acquaintance of mine from John Lewis days and also by Mr Henry Barton's fantastic networking, and the help of Lady Mary Whittaker, the venerable descendent of our original founder, The Coffee Factory is going to be saved.'

He is forced to pause for a moment due to the deafening cheers and whistling from the crowd. I spot Doris from Knit and Natter waving her knitting in the air in triumph and the little tots from the toddler group dancing with their mums. This is major and I'm so happy it's all going to be okay.

'My latest piece of news – which I haven't even told my colleagues, especially Romilly who is soon to be my superior,' he gives me a cheeky wink, 'is that none other than Tesco, that is Tesco, have agreed to stock Melstock Coffee in their stores in the south.'

Everyone including me whoops and cheers. Walter gets up and does a little lop-sided dance with Doris and I notice my family somewhere in the crowd. Mum and Dad are actually clapping and Jess is whooping loudly.

'I want to say a huge thank you in particular to

Romilly who is new to all of us, but now feels like part of the furniture in this village.' He breaks off as to my great embarrassment Mary Whittaker hands me a massive bouquet of flowers and kisses me on the cheek. 'Thank you, my dear. This means more to me than you'll ever know,' she whispers loudly.

'Is Lord Whittaker not coming along?' I ask mischievously.

'No,' she whispers, 'but if he knows what's good for him, he'll put in an appearance later.'

I brush aside a smile and take the microphone, feeling like I'm giving the thank you speech for winning an Oscar. 'I just want to thank everyone for making me feel so at home in this village and for all the wonderful support. When I arrived here several months ago, dishevelled and rather an emotional wreck, you were all amazing. You picked me up and plonked me firmly back on my feet. And as for the incredible, magical Coffee Factory, this has become the centre of everything for me as it has for all of you. It's where I've made lifelong friends, found a rewarding and fulfilling career and rediscovered myself and my identity, which I'd kind of lost somewhere along the way.

'This village has worked together as an invincible team, and on behalf of everyone here I want to thank Phil, Alexandrine, Debs, Tania, Ciaran, Mrs Miggins,' – I break off as all of them come up on stage and take a bow and receive boxes of handmade chocolates from The Coffee Shop. Mrs Miggins doesn't seem to mind the fact she made them herself. Summer and Elise also hand her a bouquet of flowers and she blushes and dips a curtsey to the crowd.

'Can I just take the microphone back for a moment?' asks Phil, grabbing it from my hand. 'I just want to make a very important announcement, hot off the press, that Alexandrine has finally been given the all clear.'

Now the audience really does go crazy, shouting and cheering, Alexandrine is being vigorously clapped on the back by us all and is laughing and crying all at once. I'm so pleased for her and Phil, they're such a wonderful couple. I glance round at this village full of people who have all come to mean so much to me. I can't believe I only arrived here a few months ago and now I feel as though I have known them all my life.

The prizes are given out by Barbara Asquith and Mary Whittaker and the best float award goes to Tania and the Zumba Brigade, which I'm over the moon about as Zumba is just the most amazing thing ever and is now such a huge part of my lif. Tania flashes me a smile as she collects the prize. 'Don't forget we're performing later this afternoon!' she calls.

'Looking forward to it,' I call back, although to be honest I'm pretty nervous as although I now know every move like the back of my hand, it's nerve wracking performing in front of everyone. Once the applause and speeches end, my mum and dad appear, having managed to fight their way through the throng.

'Hello, stranger! Can't believe the change in you,' comments Dad, giving me a hug. 'Up in front of all those people as well.'

'Did you really save the factory?' asks Mum, giving me a perfunctory kiss on each cheek. 'Who is this Lady Whittaker? You must introduce me. Is she a friend of

Dan's mother?'

'No, she isn't,' I retort trying to stay calm.

'Rom!' Jess storms in to save the day, enveloping me in a huge hug. Bradley seems to be attached to my leg.

'It's so good to see you guys.' I really mean it; it seems like forever.

'Can I have some candy floss, Aunty Romy?' asks Bradley leaping up and down as though he's eaten a load already.

'If your mum says it's okay,' I say, looking at Jess affectionately.

'Dan not here?' interrupts Mum. Honestly does she never give up?

'Mum and Dad aren't together anymore,' says Summer matter of factly, hoiking Bradley up onto her back for a piggyback ride. 'Which is a good thing because they don't get along and Mum is now going out with Mr Barton who is my form teacher.'

Oh for goodness' sake. How on earth am I going to get out of this one?

'Romilly Greene, I'm surprised at you!' Quite honestly my mother still treats me as though I'm about six.

'Sorry to interrupt,' says a voice. Fortunately it's Ciaran, who is closely followed by Walter. I could simply hug him for his timing. 'I just wanted a quick chat about something important.'

'Business calls,' laughs my dad.

'I know! That's what it's like being a high-powered executive, you know,' I say, 'all work, work, work and no play.'

‘Well. I hope you’ll all make time to come round for tea and crumpets later,’ says Walter.

Even my mum simpers slightly and says in her posh telephone voice, ‘That is a kind invitation, and this whole factory business is rather impressive. Romilly dear, when will you introduce me to Lady Whittaker?’

‘Later of course, and if you play your cards right she might invite you to join us all at her garden party at the Manor tomorrow.’

‘Oh, that’s nice.’ Mum really perks up and for once seems to have momentarily forgotten about Dan and Henry which is a great relief. She’s such a social snob. I think she might even forget Dan after a while, although he is a favourite because his parents are rich, but Lady Mary Whittaker is at least a distraction. Speaking of which, Henry comes along, his hair ruffled in the slight breeze and I introduce him to everyone. Dad shakes his hand and looks him up and down. I reckon he likes him as he doesn't say a lot, but I can tell.

Mum is rather cold and formal but then she always is unless someone has a peerage, a Range Rover, or a double-barrelled surname and unfortunately for her Henry has none of the above.

‘I’m going to pony gallop over with Bradley to get some candy floss,’ says Summer looking exhausted as I think he’s got rather heavy.

‘I’ll take you all over there,’ says Jess, looking at Henry and me speculatively. She leans in close and says, ‘I envy you this place, Rom. I almost think I might come and join you. It’s quite magical the transformation it’s had over you.’

I look at Walter and all my close acquaintances, the factory chimney extolling waves of exquisite coffee and agree. This is magic this place, my magic.

'Will you bring your other half?' I ask naughtily.

'Maybe, if he plays his cards right,' she replies. 'Mum, Dad, I think there's a beehive over here and they're selling real honey,' and she herds the whole group off towards the candy floss.

'Just before you go,' says Ciaran, 'I wanted to talk to you about some news.'

'Sounds exciting,' I say, glancing at Henry.

'I can come back in a mo,' Henry says shyly.

'No you can hear it as it may involve the school as well,' says Ciaran.

'Intriguing,' I say.

'There's a possibility of a visit to Bali to the Kintamani Highlands to meet our growers out there and set up an exchange programme whereby they can visit the factory. I just wondered, Romilly, whether you'd like to go as our new Marketing Manager?'

'Me, go to Indonesia?' I ask incredulously.

'Yes, it would be a good opportunity for you, wouldn't it?'

'I don't... I just don't know really, I mean wouldn't you go?'

'I'd rather not,' Ciaran says. 'It's not part of my role and I do have some commitments here I'd prefer not to leave right now.'

I look at him questioningly but don't like to pry. Maybe he'll talk to me about it sometime over a coffee.

'I'd love to go to Indonesia, but what about the girls?' I ask, 'I mean it's a wonderful dream but impossible for a mum in my position.'

'Not necessarily,' Ciaran replies. 'It's only a three week trip and surely their dad could have them, or your parents or sister?'

'Yes. I guess they could,' I say. But inside I'm quaking, I don't even remember the last time I got on a plane. I think it was on honeymoon with Dan over a decade ago and even then I had to have a Bacardi and Coke to settle my nerves.

'Furthermore,' says Ciaran, 'there's an opening for a visit to the Little Beans site to organise a fund raising trip for Indonesian kids, so I felt it might be an opportunity for a member of the school to go out at the same time. Maybe the school could create a partnership with the Little Beans Educational Community. In addition, the Kintamani Highlands are located between two volcanoes, that's what makes the soil so fertile. Would be very educational.' He looks at Henry seriously, his head on one side. 'Do you think a member of staff might be interested?'

Henry smiles and says, 'I think I know someone who would simply love to go with Rom to Bali.'

I smile at him and he wrinkles his nose at me, which makes my heart flip.

'I'll leave you guys to think it over,' says Ciaran.

'Wow!' I exclaim. I mean, I'm not sure what to say.

'How about a stroll? It's a while till you need to do your Zumba isn't it?' asks Henry.

'I'd love to,' I reply and we walk hand in hand out of the playing fields, up the hill towards the shadowy trees and high up above them to the sun drenched vivid heather strewn moors where eventually I feel the heat of the sun on my bare back and we kiss and make love amongst the skylarks and mass of blue sky. Later we sit and stare down at the rocks, which meet the sea and the cove in which Melstock and its factory and tiny toytown houses sit comfortably as they always have in a picturesque curved pattern.

'Do you know something?' I ask Henry as he absentmindedly tickles my face with a long grass seed.

'What?' he asks and drops another kiss on my mouth.

'Walter's right. This place is magical .... It really is.'

'I know, and so are you,' he says with a smile and for a long time we don't speak as the whirling skylarks squeal overhead, the buzzards soar high over the heather and far, far away there is a faintly delicious, but nevertheless unmistakeable whiff of coffee.

The End

Acknowledgements

I am so excited to finally be able to release this book into the wild. *For the Love of Coffee* was actually the second novel I wrote, back in 2019, having completed *The Jane Austen Dating Agency*, which some of you may have read. Then for various reasons, this little offering has been hiding away shyly on a back shelf, hidden amidst many scribblings on my computer for a rainy day. This year I decided the time was right for its debut, so here it is. I really hope you enjoy.

For the Love of Coffee is a story of community, overcoming obstacles and the importance of holding on to hope blended with a love of delicious, freshly ground, decadently rich coffee. Although a lighthearted novel, Romilly and Dan's failing marriage highlights that abusive relationships can take many forms. Gaslighting is particularly hard to identify and escape from especially when others simply can't see it. Elise's difficulties with the school bullies too, are sadly not uncommon. This is something I hope in time may change for many young people who currently struggle to deal with bullying in school. I wanted to celebrate the importance of community and how if we all work together we can achieve the impossible. The novel was originally titled *It's the Small Things*, as it concentrates on the importance of the small shiny things in life which can often mean the most. As our dear late Queen Elizabeth once said, 'It's worth remembering that it is often the small steps, not the giant leaps, that bring about the most lasting change.'

For the rest, well it's a love letter to Devon, a place of many childhood holidays and idyllic walks on the high moors which do in fact stretch down from the heights, through deeply wooded valleys, to the rippling blue sea. At the time of writing I hadn't been able to visit for a few years, due to family illness and of course then the pandemic, so for me this book has a sense of nostalgia and longing about it.

As always there are many people to thank for their help along the way. My editor, Nancy Callegari for her sterling work, also my copy editor Maureen Vincent-Northam for making sure everything is perfect. Thanks to my formatter, Rebecca Emin for putting it all together and advising me on how things work in the self publishing journey. Many thanks to my super talented cover designer, Cathy Helms who worked her wonderful creative magic to produce the beautiful cover, recommended the rest of my wonderful team and tirelessly gave advice and without whom I could never have produced this book.

I would also like to thank the phenomenal group of lovely and super talented fellow writers online who are an incredible support network as well as the Romantic Novelists' Association who helped me on the way to my writing career when I started out as part of The New Writers' Scheme. In fact, *For the Love of Coffee* was part of this scheme in my second year of taking part and

I still remember the constructive, warm and lovely feedback I received from the reader. Whoever you are, thank you so much.

I would like to express my gratitude to the super energetic, lovely Sharon, for the most amazing Zumba classes. Her routines are so much fun and really good exercise. Along with Romilly in the book, I find Zumba, a wonderful stress relief and I'm grateful to my eldest daughter Marianne for finding the classes and dragging me along even when I'm feeling sluggish.

As always thanks go to my wonderful long-suffering family. My mother to whom I dedicate this book, thank you for listening to the ins and outs of all of it so patiently and for all your support and help since childhood, inspiring my love of writing and books. To my late Dad as well, who we sadly lost last year, I know you're looking down and I will always thank you for your love and encouragement with my writing.

A particularly big thank you to my nineteen-year-old daughter, Grace, my sounding board and editor extraordinaire, who read this manuscript at ridiculously short notice. Also thank you to Marianne for your cheerleading for my writing, to Madeleine for being an earpiece on secondary schools and to Francesca for listening to my writing dilemmas and for being chief baby bottle washer. To my husband Keith as always thank you for your unerring support and patience with my determination to write novels.

Finally a huge thank you to you all my lovely readers for your support. I have had some very kind requests for another book, so hope this hits the spot.

Printed in Great Britain
by Amazon

28422815R00219